ACROSS THE SWEET GRASS HILLS

ACROSS THE SWEET GRASS HILLS

Gail L Jenner

FIC
85.

CREATIVE ARTS BOOK COMPANY
Berkeley • California

For information contact:
Creative Arts Book Company
833 Bancroft Way
Berkeley, California 94710
(800) 848-7789

ISBN 0-88739-302-0
Library of Congress Catalog Number 99-64934

Printed in the United States of America

This book is dedicated to my husband and children, my parents, and my sisters and their families. Their encouragement and confidence in me never wavered. Indeed, they often saw into the future when I could not. Thank you.

AUTHOR'S NOTE

*A*CCORDING TO MANY HISTORIANS, THE BLACK-
foot were among the most aggressive of the Plains Indian tribes.
They actually encompassed three major bands: Bloods,
Blackfoot, and Piegans (the native word is actually Pikuni,
hence that is the name I use here).

The Blackfoot occupied the country surrounding the
Missouri River tributaries east of the Rocky Mountains. The
Bloods, the most northern band, occupied territory into what is
now Canada. Like the Crow, however, Blackfoot bands roamed
freely, even into the Rocky Mountains, warring against other
tribes frequently. An early estimate placed the total number of
Blackfoot at 40-50,000.

Early in the nineteenth century, the Blackfoot accepted
missionaries into their tribes and many adopted Christianity.
Around 1837, smallpox epidemics ravaged various Plains groups
and it is believed that as many as 6-8,000 Blackfoot perished.

When the Civil War ended, Major General William T.
Sherman, hero of Atlanta and the Great March, was given command of the Military Division of the Mississippi (later to be
changed to the Division of the Missouri). He administered the
army's affairs over the entire Plains area and his overriding goal
was to rid the West entirely of Indians.

In a letter to his brother he wrote, "The more we can kill
this year, the less will have to be killed the next war, for the
more I see of these Indians the more convinced I am that all
have to be killed or maintained as a species of pauper..."
(ANDRIST 1964, 154).

After the inauguration of Ulysses S. Grant in 1869,
Sherman succeeded to the post of commanding general of the

army. Though President Grant intiated a "pro-Indian" policy and a series of reforms within the Indian Service—even appointing the first Native American to be commissioner of Indian Affairs-Westerners were not in agreement with Grant's approach or sympathies.

In 1869, a fight broke out between the Blackfoot and whites at a Montana trading post. Several warriors were killed, and, to display their contempt for egalitarian treatment of the Indian, the whites cut off the heads of the slain warriors, pickled the ears in whiskey, and boiled the flesh from the skulls. The bleached skulls were then inscribed with reminders of what many endorsed: "I am on the Reservation at last" **(Andrist 1964, 170)**.

Ironically, there were still some Blackfoot leaders pursuing policies of peaceful negotiation. However, with the constant movement of trappers, miners, and settlers into Blackfoot territory and, as treaties were signed and broken, there were an increasing number of attacks made on whites. The skirmishes continued until one small campaign, now called "Baker's Massacre" or the "Marias Massacre," occurred in January 1870. General Sheridan, who replaced Sherman as commander of the entire Missouri Division, decided that a winter campaign was the best way to subdue the Blackfoot.

In pursuit of a small group of hostile Pikuni led by Mountain Chief and his son, Peter Owl-Child, Colonel Baker and his cavalry struck the winter camps of Heavy Runner, Standing Wolf, and other Pikuni along the upper Marias River (known as Bear River to the Pikuni). More than 170 Pikuni were killed, 41 lodges burned, and many were captured, only to be turned loose because of a smallpox epidemic raging through the camps.

Although there were discrepancies in the tallies, the Blackfoot Indian agent reported that 140 of the dead were women and children, 18 were old men and 15 were warriors. Sherman, in defense of Baker, stated, "Did we cease to throw shells into Vicksburg or Atlanta because women or children were there?" **(Andrist 1964, 171)**

Tragically, the army learned later that these camps had

not been those harboring the notorious Mountain Chief. These camps had indeed been those of friendly bands of Pikuni. After this campaign, the Blackfoot never retaliated, knowing only too well what the results might be.

✠ ✠ ✠

It is against this historical backdrop that *ACROSS THE SWEET GRASS HILLS* takes place. Red Eagle and Liza Ralston are fictitious characters, as are several other lesser characters, but the historical figures, places, and major incidents are based upon historical research. Every care has been taken to represent the events and details accurately.

ACROSS THE SWEET GRASS HILLS

PROLOGUE

*T*HE OLD WOMAN CAME TO HIM IN SLEEP, HER DARK EYES round and large, white eyebrows a stripe across her forehead. From the yawning black hole of her mouth came a haunting cry that curled up through the darkness like a thin thread of smoke. Another cry answered it.

The man shivered as the sounds whirled around him, rising higher and higher. He wanted to cover his ears, but couldn't move his hands. Instead he closed his eyes, trying to stop the pain in his head, but there was no way to shut it out. He wanted to shout at the old woman, but his throat was dry and his words transparent.

The woman's black turtle eyes closed suddenly and her mouth snapped shut. Then she glided away, strands of long gray hair billowing about her like a cloud, the ends twirling like ribbons around her beaded white buckskin dress. Beyond, blue shadows weaved back and forth.

He reached out, hoping to capture the old woman and draw her back. What secret did she hide? What warning did she bring? But as quickly as she had appeared, the old woman vanished. A strange, chilling emptiness descended upon him.

✠   ✠   ✠

Red Eagle sat up slowly, his heart thumping, his hands damp. He looked around, but saw only the dying embers of the cooking fire and the shadowy darkness of a night when the moon is hiding.

"Tomorrow," he said out loud, addressing his restless spirit, "I must find Crying Wind."

Surely his uncle would know why the old woman wept.

CHAPTER 1

Montana Territory, September 1869

*L*IZA STIRRED RESTLESSLY, TRYING TO MAKE HERSELF more comfortable. Was she home in her own bed? She opened her eyes, then closed them, remembering where she was. She drew the wool blanket up to her chin, frowning. Her dreams had deceived again. St. Louis was a lifetime away.

She crawled out from under the blankets and took a deep breath, pushing aside the tears that threatened to weaken her spirit. She had to remain strong, or the fear that followed like a shadow might overwhelm her.

Stepping carefully over the rocky soil, Liza felt her way to the fire, spreading her hands out over the glowing coals. Glancing up at the moonless sky, handfuls of stars glittered like fool's gold, and she found herself wondering if this journey wasn't just a fool's dream.

If only she'd remained in St. Louis. Perhaps, if she'd said no to Father, he would have reconsidered. He might have changed his mind altogether, and then, Mother—

Mother would be alive, even now...

That instant Liza felt, rather than heard, a faint rustle. It tickled her spine like the brush of a feather. Was that the distant pounding of hooves?

She drew herself up and peered into the night, but it was impossible to see past the sleeping figures of her father and Giles. The scout, a giant of a man, turned and mumbled something unintelligible.

Liza relaxed. It had probably been nothing. Just the ghosts that seemed to haunt prairie nights. She chided herself: what had happened to her nerves, anyway? Father had once declared that his daughter, Elizabeth Ralston, had more grit than her two brothers combined.

There was a second strange rustle, and it seemed to be moving closer. Liza clasped a hand to her mouth. She would not scream.

Falling to her knees, the darkness covered her like a black cloud; hopefully it would shield her from being spotted. Pulling up her petticoats, she crawled toward her father, shins scraping against spiny brambles and rough sod.

Before she could rouse him, however, a flurry of howls split the night.

Liza flattened herself against the ground. "Papa!"

His dark eyes opened and he pressed a finger to his lips. She nodded and waited, her heart pounding like a hammer. This was no time to weep or grow faint.

Her father reached for a rifle.

An arm's distance away, Giles had clambered to his feet and reached for a pistol. Leaning forward to get a second look, his voice was strangely hoarse, his marble eyes bright as he turned and cried, "Run, girl, run! It's savages, sure! Go!"

Liza hesitated, choking back fear as the big man's warning was instantly swallowed up by gunfire. Stunned, she watched Giles drop to the earth like a felled tree, dark red blood spilling where his face had been.

"Dear God," she cried, and her stomach roiled up against her ribs.

"Move, Liza!" her father yelled, his own voice sickly.

She glanced down at the dark drops splattered across her hands in astonishment. *You've seen blood before*, she scolded herself. She forced herself to crawl along on her belly until she felt Giles's long-barrelled pistol at her fingertips.

The weapon was so big, Liza's hand shook as it wrapped around the barrel and dragged the pistol towards her. She righted it by grasping the butt firmly in both hands, then peered into the darkness as if she could see beyond it. Her hands trembled even more as another round of gunfire exploded.

Perspiration burned her eyes. "Where are they?" she whispered.

Her father wheeled on one knee. "Hush!" He leaned forward and brushed at the monstrous weapon in her hands. "Save your shot, Elizabeth, and get out of here!" Another bullet whizzed past them. "Go, Daughter, go!"

"No!" Resolved to stay and fight, she drew the hammer back and this time released it, jerking as the pistol leaped in her hands. She would fight. She had to fight.

Her father's dark eyes pleaded with her. "Hide yourself, Elizabeth. Do it for me. For your mother."

Tears clouded her vision. She had not often stood up to her father. "No, I won't leave you."

And then it was over. Another bullet sung past her and, as if in a dream, she saw her father collapse, his face to the ground, body winding in the dirt like a snake's. She cried out in disbelief. "Papa!"

"Liza-"

Throwing down the pistol, she scrambled over to grab her father's arm. "Oh, dear God, please."

His body sagged as she buried her face against his shoulder, and she tasted the slimy thickness of blood as it soaked his shirt. She drew him near to cover the wound. "Papa! No!"

Hot tears trailed down her cheeks. *He couldn't die! He couldn't leave her like this. Not now, after losing Mother. How could God allow her father's life to come to such an end, when he had chosen to sacrifice so much for his faith? Why had they even come here, if their lives were to be swallowed up beside a nameless stream in the middle of the Montana Territory?*

No, she would not allow God to take her father from her.

Swallowing her cry, she hesitated when there was no response. "Please, Father," she whispered, bitterness dissolving into grief.

But there was only a haunting echo in her brain as she recalled his hushed command. "Go, Daughter, go!"

In the distance, she heard the muffled voices of men nearing the camp. Their laughter filled her with a burning desire for revenge, but there was only one choice now. Looking into the vacant face of her father, she inhaled deeply.

She had to obey.

Jumping to her feet, heart pounding in her ears, hands wet with sweat and her father's blood, she glanced around for a safe hiding place. Except for the few trees lining the stream, nothing offered shelter. She would have to make a run for it.

She took up Giles's pistol and her father's rifle and headed away from the camp, into the blackness of the Montana prairie, her heartbeats resounding in her head like more gunshots. She hurried over patches of nettles and pebbles littering the ground, but willed herself to ignore the rough earth as it tore at the soles of her bare feet. Her life was all that was left now; St. Louis, her grandparents and brothers, her friends— they were as dead to her as Giles and Father.

She pushed on, not knowing where she was or where she could run. *Had they seen her? Would they follow?* She slowed her pace, long enough to listen. There was only silence. Mercifully, they'd be satisfied with the animals. There was certainly little else of value stored in the wagon.

Liza passed through a patch of trees, their thin, spidery branches slapping at her arms and face. She tripped and fell over a stump, and the rifle landed in a tangle of thorny brush. Sobbing, she rocked back and forth before getting up. *How could she could go on? Maybe if she left the rifle; it was so heavy.*

She struggled for a breath and started off again, her chest heaving, ears ringing. Ahead, a ridge blocked out the stars. Without hesitation, she scurried up and over the lower ledges of it, groaning as her knees banged against the rough, hard rock. Her shins scraped the narrow granite slabs, and she felt, rather than saw, a small, black cavity before her. It was hardly bigger than a rabbit's den, but large enough.

Easing into the cold hollow, she curled up in a tight ball. Waves of fear and grief washed over her, but to calm her trembling body, Liza closed her eyes and tried to think of something else.

Oh, Father. Oh, God.

✠ ✠ ✠

How long she remained huddled inside the pit, Liza couldn't tell. The darkness seemed to last forever, and the cold Montana night quickly penetrated the layers of petticoat. Her lips were so dry, and throat so parched that her tongue scraped against her teeth.

Not until the rays of dawn pierced the black night, stretching across the gray stone that rose like a wall around her, did Liza press her cheek to the cold granite. Perhaps now she could rest.

The sun was high when Liza felt something move lightly against her shoulder. She jumped and Giles's pistol clattered to the stone floor of her hiding place.

"Do not fear." The male voice was low and soft.

Finding it difficult to move more than her head, a flash of pain ran up her spine. She held her breath and tried to focus, but could see only a silhouette. All she could feel was the warmth of the stranger's presence and the pressure of his fingers. Then, as he leaned closer, the heat of his breath warmed the chilled air around her.

"Do not be afraid," came the deep voice again.

Struggling to move forward, Liza whispered, "Please. My father! Giles! We were attacked. They were shot—dead."

"Ssshh." Hard fingers had wrapped themselves around her wrist and were guiding her out of the rock cavity. Her legs were stiff and numb, her mind hazy. She stumbled forward.

Immediately the man's arms went around her. His body comforted hers in an embrace that absorbed the fear. For an instant, she was tempted to stay there, huddled against his muscled chest. Perhaps last night had only been a nightmare.

At last, flushed and panting, Liza pulled back, her eyes widening. The woodsy smell of the stranger had awakened her dulled senses, and she saw that the man was dressed in a leather-fringed tunic trimmed in long, flat, black beads. Near-black hair flowed past broad shoulders. Intelligent eyes flashed as they moved over her carefully.

7

Liza swallowed. Dear God, the stranger was an *Indian*.

Fear swept her forward and she jerked free of his warm grasp to scramble over the rocky ledge. Jumping the last distance to the ground, she collapsed as she hit the hard earth. Too late she thought of Giles's pistol.

"Stop!"

Terror caught in her throat as the Indian rapidly overtook her. "You're one of them!" she cried as he grabbed her wrist and spun her around. Making a fist, she tried to swing, but he pulled her roughly to him. She snarled, all the while, her heart pounding.

"Stop," he ordered again, his voice almost inaudible. "I am not one of them! They stole my horses as well. I've been tracking them. That is how I tracked you."

Ignoring his words, Liza kicked him squarely in the shin. He lost his balance, but instead of releasing her, he held on. Together they fell to the ground. He grunted as he landed on his back, and she fell across him, her face buried in the breadth of his chest.

She pulled back and stared down at him.

He pushed her over and rolled on top of her. The heady smell of leather and sweat, and the weight of his body, enraged her all the more. She twisted in his grasp.

"I will not hurt you," he said. "Listen."

Liza closed her eyes and shook her head.

She heard him inhale as he slid off her, but he continued to hold her by one wrist.

She hesitated. Only the sounds of their breathing could be heard. Biting her lip, she tried hard to remain calm.

"Open your eyes." The words were so soft Liza barely heard them.

Frowning, she raised her eyes to his. His face was inches from hers, his eyes as deep as a Montana twilight.

"Good." He took a quick breath. "I will not harm you."

She searched his face. "Who are you? How did you find me?" She couldn't let him see the fear that burned in the pit of her stomach.

"I am Mekotsepetan. Red Eagle. I am not an outlaw. I am traveling to my mother's people. I saw your tracks, the tracks of a woman's small bare feet." He seemed to be waiting for a response. "I lost four good horses and supplies to the thieves," he said at last.

Red Eagle's grip was firm, his touch burning her flesh. She pinned her gaze to his tunic as an inner voice warned her that no red man could be trusted. Even one that spoke English as well as this one. *A half-breed, no doubt, but still, an Indian. How was it her father had dreamed of coming west to live among them?*

"When Lieutenant Cole and General DeTrobriand hear of this —" she began, hoping to intimidate him.

Red Eagle's dark eyes narrowed as his voice deepened. "The army cannot rescue either of us," he replied. "We are twelve days' walk from the fort, and the thieves left very little. What foolishness brought you this far from the fort anyway?"

Liza felt her spine stiffen. How could she explain her father's dream to travel where others dared not, when she had not understood it herself.

Red Eagle pulled her upright. He released her wrist and stepped back. His voice had a somber tone. "We need to go back. Perhaps we can save something. And your father—"

She shook her head. "They killed my father!" Her voice trailed off as she turned and stared into the distance. "Dead. He and Giles. Their bodies. Yes, we must go back!" And then she was running again, skirting the rocks and clumps of coarse grass as she raced back to camp.

The campsite was further away than she remembered, but winding past the familiar grove of trees, she spotted the stream where she had collected water and Father had caught fish. Its peaceful sounds tore at her heart. How could the sun be shining when her whole world had collapsed around her?

The wagon was on its side, its contents scattered.

Giles's enormous body, only a few yards to the east, lay half-hidden in the yellow grass. Flies circled it, buzzing hungrily. Liza staggered on.

Her father lay where he had fallen, his large frame slumped against the ground. Liza ran to him, dropped to her knees, and wrapped her arms around him.

Unexpectedly, he seemed to relax and Liza pulled back. Tiny droplets of sweat clung to his forehead, shimmering against the dark strands of his hair. Blood covered his shirt.

But he was alive.

Liza cradled him. "Papa!"

At her words, his eyelids fluttered open, but the glassy brown circles beneath seemed to float in their sockets.

"Can you hear me?" Liza said, placing her lips against his ear. "Father?"

Having forgotten Red Eagle, Liza jumped when she realized he was standing behind her. Bracing herself, she turned and scrutinized the features of his face through her tears: dark eyes, set apart by a strong nose; full lips, drawn in a tight frown, a small scar cut into the lower lip. Was this someone she could trust?

"He can't die!" she whispered and tore off a piece of her petticoat to press against her father's wound. Blood oozed through the heavy cotton.

Red Eagle pulled off his own tunic and, dropping to one knee, wrapped it around the white man's broad chest and left shoulder. "He has lost much blood."

"We have to stop it!"

"The bullet must come out."

"But you're not a doctor! He needs a surgeon." Liza pulled her father closer in protest. What could a heathen, even a half-breed, know of medicine and surgery? "He needs a real doctor," she blurted.

Eyebrows raised, Red Eagle shrugged and stood up. "Then find a real doctor. But he will die before many days."

"Wait! What if we take him to a settlement? There

must be a trading post or settlement somewhere nearby. We can keep the wound closed, then..."

Red Eagle shook his head, his jaw tensing visibly. "Your army fort is almost two weeks away on foot. The closest white settlement is seven days' ride. Your father won't last half that long."

CHAPTER 2

*R*ED EAGLE BENT OVER THE BIG MAN AND PULLED AWAY the blood-soaked tunic. "I do not know how deep the bullet has gone."

Liza followed the movement of Red Eagle's hands. Half in anticipation, half in dread, she turned from the bloody scene. What other choice did she have? The Indian was Father's best chance for survival. If only his calm assurance could ease her fear: would this prove a deadly mistake?

As Red Eagle probed for the bullet, blood flowed again; Liza raised her skirt and tore off more strips of petticoat. Red Eagle took some and dabbed at the oozing blood. She watched him, but his expression revealed nothing of his thoughts or character.

Red Eagle seemed to have found the spot. Fingering the fringed sheath that hung from his rawhide belt, he drew a long, heavy knife.

Liza leaned forward. "Wait." Pushing to her feet, she rushed to the overturned wagon and returned with a thin, shining blade. "Use Father's boning knife. He keeps it impeccably sharp."

Red Eagle raised an eyebrow as he took the knife and ran a finger along the edge, then turned back to his patient.

He cut quickly, his furrowed brows drawn together in a dark line. In seconds, his hands were drenched and the blade dripped red.

Liza panicked. The color in her father's face was fading. Immediately she regretted letting Red Eagle cut. "He's going to die," she protested. "Look!"

"This is his only chance," returned Red Eagle through clenched teeth.

"But he's going to die. You're killing him!"

For a moment, Red Eagle flashed his dark and unfathomable eyes on her. She straightened her shoulders, thinking to protest, but seeing his determination, forced herself to sit back. It was too late, anyway, and she knew it. They had to go on.

"Bandages," said Red Eagle.

Liza fumbled with the folds of her skirt, again tearing off several pieces. She flushed at the blood covering Red Eagle's fingers and tried to swallow the knot in her throat.

Don't faint, she told herself. Instead she focused on each dip and stroke of the boning knife. It seemed Red Eagle might never reach the bullet.

"I feel it," he finally whispered, leaning closer.

She pressed the last bandage against the outer edges of the wound. There was not a clean piece of fabric that was not soaked now, but she didn't dare move her hands away even to tear off more petticoat.

It was with a groan that Red Eagle managed to reach the lead ball. "There!" he said. Carefully he picked the bullet out and placed it in Liza's lap. They immediately covered the gaping wound with their hands. Red Eagle grabbed his tunic and slid it under her fingers. "Do you have thread?"

"Yes, of course." He replaced her hands with his as she ran to the wagon to rummage through the scattered remains of her trunk. Finding a small cloth purse, she removed a needle and a few strands of embroidery floss. She wiped her bloody hands on the front of her skirt before threading the needle. She'd wash later.

Taking quick, short strokes, Red Eagle stitched the wound tightly closed. But Liza had to turn away as he pierced the bloody ends of flesh.

Finishing, Red Eagle sank back on his heels and sighed. "He will sleep now."

Liza shivered as she reached out to touch her father. "But is he all right? Will he live?"

"He is alive now," Red Eagle said carefully, but did not say more. Perspiration clung to the fine lines around his eyes.

With trembling fingers, Liza touched her father's lips, waiting for his almost indiscernible breath to warm her skin. Tears came to her eyes when she realized that he was, indeed, breathing. Wiping them away with the back of her hand, she stood up, anxious to avoid this man's scrutiny. His entire manner was so different, so austere, that it was almost frightening.

She glanced down at Red Eagle.

"It was very near his heart," he said. In the palm of his extended hand he held the bullet. It must have fallen when she had gotten up to find the thread.

She took the slug and rolled it between her fingers.

"I will make a poultice," said Red Eagle, standing and stretching.

"What sort of poultice?"

"From special plants my mother taught me to use."

Examining the lead ball once more, Liza nodded her response. Red Eagle's eyes were bright in the glow of the noonday sun, and beyond him the pale sky melted into the rugged mountain peaks. The prairie shimmered in the yellow sunshine. It seemed strangely peaceful, inviting, possessing a tranquility that contrasted sharply with the confusion, fear, and exhaustion she had struggled against all morning.

She smiled tentatively, resisting the pull to relax; this wild land had already claimed her mother and nearly her father. She couldn't forget who and what was the enemy.

Like as not, she had been a fool to trust this stranger, a half-breed. But what other choice did she have? She had been too frightened to think beyond the moment.

Her lower lip trembled as she caught Red Eagle's querying glance. Was it compassion or curiosity reflected there?

"The poultice and the bandage will ease the bleeding," repeated Red Eagle. "In a day, perhaps two, he will be strong enough to travel."

She nodded, but said nothing, letting the melodic quality of his voice soothe her. She couldn't think anymore about the disturbing feelings swirling inside her. They weren't feelings she recognized.

15

"He needs sleep now," suggested Red Eagle.

"Yes, sleep."

"And you need rest. Food and rest."

She tried to shrug. "Food? I think there are some beans, maybe coffee, left from last evening." Liza ran her fingers through her tousled hair and frowned. "I must do some wash," she stammered, then rubbed the palms of her hands together as if to emphasize her intention. "Everything is so soiled."

Wandering over to the wagon, she found the last of a bucket of water. She quickly washed her hands and dried them on her skirt. "Look at this," she said, more to herself than anyone else. "I'll have to wash it, too."

Red Eagle frowned. "Not today. Tomorrow will be soon enough."

Liza didn't argue. She felt so exhausted, she was relieved to do nothing.

"You should sleep," he said, pointing to the overturned wagon. "It's more protected there. I will stay with him."

"No," she said. "No, I must be near Father."

Red Eagle nodded as if he understood. "Then I will see to the scout—"

"Giles?" Liza bit her lip. She had forgotten that the poor man still lay in the ankle-high grass, his body a blackening carcass on the sunlit landscape. "There's a shovel in the wagon. Perhaps a tarp, to wrap him in?" She started for the wagon, but Red Eagle stopped her.

"I do not need your help. Take care of your father and yourself."

She drew a slow breath. She had dreaded moving too near Giles's distended, wretched body.

Watching Red Eagle dig Giles' grave, Liza couldn't help but be touched by his manner. He possessed such calmness and fortitude. He hadn't recoiled at the sight or smell of the swollen, putrid body, even while rolling it into the shallow hole. She noted that he had worked on her father with the same compassion.

When Red Eagle was finished, he sauntered down to the stream that flowed through the tall, gray-green trees and berry-laden brush. He dropped his stained tunic into the water and removed his moccasins. Captivated by his movements, Liza moved back to her father's side to sit down, keeping her casual glances hidden behind the loose curtain of her long hair.

Squatting along the muddy bank, Red Eagle rinsed his long, dark arms in the clear water. It ran off his shoulders and down his back like penny ribbons of tinsel. Liza watched the muscles of his shoulders and arms contract and relax.

She had not often seen a man bare-chested. Once, when she was a girl, she had walked in on her father, not knowing he was half-dressed, and once, when she was thirteen, she stumbled across two boys, perhaps fifteen, as they swam, stark naked, in the river. Amazed by their muscled bodies and male parts, she had watched them from the bushes until she feared discovery. She never told anyone what she'd seen that day.

Turning back to her father, Liza wound a lap quilt into a pillow to slip under his head and tried to make him as comfortable as possible.

She stole another glance at Red Eagle, strangely fascinated by his ruggedness. Biting her lip, she blushed, quickly turning back to wipe the dark hair from her father's forehead.

She was still blushing when Red Eagle returned, his damp shirt in place, hair neatly tied back with a thong. Liza noticed the beaded design outlining the yoke of his tunic and the tiny shells attached to the shoulder seams. Had someone lovingly stitched the shirt for him? Some woman, with flashing almond eyes and a willing heart?

Once more, she reproached herself.

Red Eagle dropped to the ground, grunting softly. Liza tried not to be too curious, but found herself repeatedly stealing glances. Red Eagle had stretched his long legs out in front of him and was peering out across the vast eastern plain. What did he see, scanning the emptiness?

He frowned.

Instantly, she wanted to wipe away his frown. Was he already regretting helping them?

17

✠ ✠ ✠

It was only later, as the camp's fire sent sparks glittering into the ebony dome of night, that Liza remembered she had neither thanked Red Eagle nor introduced herself. She pulled her blankets up around her shoulders. Well, tomorrow, she would.

✠ ✠ ✠

In the morning, Liza checked on her father, sighing when she saw he was still breathing. Excited, she jumped to her feet to tell Red Eagle, but he was nowhere in sight. She looked toward the stream, but the banks were empty. Taking a small, quick breath, she moved to the wagon to retrieve her personal articles. Perhaps he had gone to take care of his own needs.

She tried not to think beyond what needed to be done: dress and wash; build a fire; prepare food; change Father's bandages.

But when all those things were done, she still found herself alone. And suddenly, like a summer thunder shower, the horror of the last two days washed over her. *Had Red Eagle left for good? Was she truly all alone? What would she do now?*

✠ ✠ ✠

Red Eagle sat down near a stand of buffalo brush. Like a hedge, it followed the steep edge of the rocky bluff. He had thought it would be easy hunting here on the ridge, but it was taking longer than expected. Unfortunately, he had passed up a young antelope earlier. Now he would be satisfied with a blacktail.

He should have wakened the girl, he thought, *told her he would be back.* She'd been sleeping so peacefully, curled up beside her father that he was afraid to disturb her. In fact, he had been transfixed, feeling inexplicably drawn to her.

She needed him, that much was clear. But he didn't need the burden. He was headed to his uncle's village and before much longer, would have to resume his journey. Only last night the haunting image of the old woman had returned to his dreams, filling him with dread. He had to warn Crying Wind; the old man would know if real trouble was coming.

Absent-mindedly, Red Eagle reached out to the buffalo brush and gathered several clusters of fruit, but after two bites, tossed the rest away. Not until they had been touched by frost would the berries be palatable.

He spotted a small grove of cottonwoods and aspens lining the winding shoreline of the gray-green river beyond. He could see several places where animals had grazed or slept. Resting the white man's rifle, which he'd discovered in the brush, he slid down the dry, gravelly embankment, catching himself as he lost his balance on the loose shale. Near the water, he came across a fresh pile of pellets. He waited, inhaling the fresh morning air.

Red Eagle held his breath as he spied a young antelope grazing. It raised its round head, honey-colored ears twitching. Running his hands down the stock of the Henry, Red Eagle raised the gun carefully, taking slow, sure aim. He fired and the animal, stunned, fell to its knees. In several strides Red Eagle reached the floundering antelope and slit its throat.

It did not take long to skin and quarter the animal. With a horse, he could have salvaged more, but Red Eagle would not complain. The girl would have meat to eat tonight; *he* would have meat to eat tonight. Then he would talk to her about leaving.

✠ ✠ ✠

Liza watched her father closely as the hours passed. She washed him down. She sang to him, melodies her mother had sung to her when she had been ill.

She stayed busy all morning collecting whatever twigs and limbs she could find, even dried buffalo pies. She stacked

19

them on either side of the tiny campfire, then made a pot of coffee and a pan of fried bread. Once she thought she heard the distant sound of gunfire, and ran to grab Giles's pistol and ammunition, discovering that her father's Henry rifle was nowhere in sight. Seated beside her father with the loaded weapon, she remained determined not to run if someone should come.

But no one came and time seemed to stop as the summer sun beat down. She constructed a lean-to for shade, but it was only wide enough to shelter her father's face and shoulders. She wondered if Red Eagle would return and then cursed out loud. No different than any other renegade or scoundrel wandering the territory, no doubt the half-breed was gone for good. With her father's Henry to boot.

Oh, but she had been a fool for trusting him.

It was well past mid-afternoon and her stomach growled loudly, yet Liza couldn't eat more than a few bites of bread. The coffee in her tin cup grew cold. Surely someone would have to come along.

Then she frowned. This was not a well-travelled trail. It was a short cut Giles had suggested when her father pressed him to find the shortest trail north. Biting her broken fingernails, she scanned the horizon. Anger once more knotted inside her.

Oh, her naive father. And the foolishness of dreams. How could anyone think the West was a place of new beginnings and great opportunities? What right-thinking man wandered into the wilderness to minister to wild Indians?

Too restless to sit, Liza got up and wandered down to the water's edge. She climbed onto a large rock that stretched out over a pool of shimmering water. Dragging her fingers through it, she pressed a handful to her lips. It burned her parched lips.

She took a second drink, then wiped her wet fingers across her cheeks. She yanked off her boots and stockings and slipped her toes into the water. The bitter tingle brought feeling back into her feet. She gasped. Steeling herself, she pulled her skirt up and slipped deeper into the cold swirling pool. The water lapped at her knees and she shrieked as she moved deeper and deeper into the stream.

"They say women often go mad in the wilderness," she announced to herself. Looking across the sweeping plain that disappeared into the blue-gray horizon, she wondered, *will that happen to me?* She laughed. *Well, it would be a fitting end to the bizarre nightmare life had become.*

She unbuttoned the tattered dress and let it slide off her shoulders. It billowed out around her as it sank. She scooped up a handful of sand and rubbed the stains on her dress, scrubbing the dark places where her father's blood had dried.

When the water became unbearable, Liza climbed out, skin icy, feet heavy and numb. Water ran down her legs, staining the sandy shore as she scurried up the bank. In her hands were the dripping dress, muddy shoes, and stockings.

She hadn't gone very far when she felt a strange chill.

Someone was watching.

Taking a deep breath, Liza pressed the cold folds of the dress to her belly and turned.

It was him. The half-breed, Red Eagle. He stood not more than thirty yards away.

She blinked in confusion. Was it an animal carcass draped over his shoulders? Father's rifle was in his left hand.

Why hadn't he told her where he was going? Her cheeks burned as she swallowed her frustration. "How dare you leave without saying a word!" she screamed, then stopped, chest heaving, as the cooling breeze blew across her bare arms and shoulders.

Hadn't he guessed how frightened she'd been?

Staring at each other across the flat stretch of dry yellowed grass, the silence grew heavy. Neither moved and nothing more was said. Finally, Red Eagle's gaze travelled up and down Liza's scantily-clothed body; he shifted his bloody load as he raised his eyebrows and smiled.

Liza colored fiercely, feeling his scrutiny. Though clad

in only undergarments, she ignored her discomfort and decided she couldn't allow another outburst. She grit her teeth and flashed a hard stare, daring him to make a move.

Red Eagle seemed to enjoy her struggle. He stood for another long moment before nodding and turning away.

She tossed her unkempt hair back across her shoulders. Tongue-tied, she watched him. Then, not wanting to face his sardonic smile again, she stepped into the wet and wrinkled dress. The material clung to her clammy skin. She pulled the wet stockings on, but they would not roll up. She jerked her boots on and impatiently folded the stockings over the tops. Finally, weighed down by the clinging skirt, she marched up to camp. She ignored Red Eagle's bemused expression as she lumbered over to the campfire.

"It's good that you kept the fire burning," he said, his dark eyes taunting her. "You will need to hang yourself above the flames to dry."

"If you would kindly leave, I could change my clothes," she snapped.

"I have already seen you without clothes," he reminded her. Light smoldered in his dark eyes.

Liza glared, trying to calm her tumultuous emotions. Red Eagle's smile, as much as his unexpected return, had unnerved her more than she cared to admit.

"I will go and fill the bucket with fresh water. Then we will eat." Still smiling, he picked up a small wooden bucket and turned back toward the stream.

Liza waited for him to move out of sight before pulling off the cold, wet dress. Eyeing him, she stumbled into her brown calico, but her trembling fingers made it difficult to fasten the double row of loops and buttons. Red-faced, she started over, managing to fasten all but two tiny pearl buttons at the base of her throat.

Stepping out from behind the wagon, Liza's attention returned immediately to Red Eagle. He was kneeling by the fire, his golden skin made more so by the red-orange flames dancing only a foot from his face. In his right hand he held a knife.

Without a word, he pointed to the haunch of fresh meat. "Supper," he said. "Are you hungry?"

"Uh, yes," she stammered, awed by the sight of a man preparing food for her.

"There is enough to keep us for many days if we care for it properly."

Liza nodded, warmed by his concern. He gave her another smile and she moved awkwardly toward the fire, afraid to admit she knew little about carving meat. Giles rarely hunted anything but rabbits, and one day, he captured a snake, which she refused to clean or eat. Her father had little luck with hunting, either; instead, he fished, so she had learned to clean brook trout. Back home in St. Louis, there had always been a house servant to attend to the meat.

Red Eagle extended the butt end of his long knife, teasing her with flashing eyes. Liza took the knife, turning it slowly in her hands. It was made of horn, perhaps elk or deer. The blade was broad, sharp, and deadly. For a moment, she wondered if Red Eagle had ever used it on a man.

Stifling the thought, she knelt beside him, eyes averted. She didn't want to look into this man's eyes; they seemed to look through her, and she feared Red Eagle would see the apprehension and anxiety in her face. Liza timidly reached for a slab of red meat, grimacing at the blood that ran down her fingers.

Red Eagle grunted. "You have not told me your name," he said.

She flushed, realizing he was right. "My name is Elizabeth Ralston, but only my father calls me that. Everyone else calls me Liza."

"Then that is what I will call you. Li-za," he said carefully, nodding. Red Eagle's teasing smile scorched like a brand. "Do what I do, Liza," he instructed quietly, attention diverted by the way she'd begun cutting the meat.

Liza frowned, seeing that her slices of meat were thick, rather than thin. But she would learn all that this half-breed could teach her. Having always relied on her father and her brothers, she now had to rely on herself.

At the same time, she would have to remember where she was, who she was, and, most of all, what *he* was.

She could never forget that.

CHAPTER 3

ON THE THIRD MORNING RED EAGLE APPROACHED Liza. He walked toward her with long, purposeful strides, head bent, black hair flowing past his shoulders. When he spoke, his voice was soft but firm.

"We must go."

Taking a quick breath, she stepped back. "Go where? Surely, someone will come along if we wait."

Red Eagle's dark brows slanted in a frown. "This is not a trail that many follow. If the men who attacked return, we are too few to stand against them." He looked across to where Liza's father lay. Liza followed his glance. "You were lucky your father was left alive and that you were not discovered. These men would not let you escape a second time."

The color rose in her cheeks. Liza knew only too well the truth of Red Eagle's words. But to leave?

"How would we move him? We have no horses and the wagon is no good."

"We will build a travois. My mother's people, the Pikuni, carry their belongings and old people on such travois. Sometimes dogs, even people, pull them."

"I've never heard of such a thing," said Liza, biting her lip. "Besides, you already said the fort is two weeks away, and we never came across a single trading post."

Red Eagle turned and pointed. "We will go into the South Fork Basin and wait. The Pikuni stay there during Leaves Falling Moon and they will be arriving from the Sweet Grass Hills any day. That is where I was headed when I crossed your path."

"The South Fork Basin?"

"Yes. The Pikuni travel there to gather Mississa,

Okkunokin, Kachatan, and Omuckaiixixi. There is not much time left before winter, but those who can treat your father's wound better than I will be there."

Liza tried to imagine herself in the company of an Indian tribe. She shook her head.

Red Eagle continued, "It will take three days to travel there, and it will be safe. My mother's people will help you."

"But they're Indians!" sputtered Liza. *What could they know about medicine? Ok-kun-okin and O-muck-ai-! He needs a real doctor, not some heathen medicine man.* She felt short of breath as she considered Red Eagle's suggestion. "What if they decide to remove his scalp? Or mine?" she said, shaking her head. "No, it's out of the question."

Red Eagle drew a deep breath. Standing solemnly, he clenched his jaw and frowned.

"I'm not your captive," she said. "And I know what is best for my father. Not that I'm ungrateful," she added quickly. "You helped my father, but I won't move him yet. At least not without knowing where we're going. Someone will come along soon."

Red Eagle's dark eyebrows knitted together as he slipped his fingers under the rawhide belt encircling his waist. His voice was hard. "And who has come so far?" He looked down at Liza's father, then back at her. "I will build a travois out of the wagon. You will prepare the meat and blankets and supplies. Pack only what you need. We will leave tomorrow, when everything is ready. I cannot leave you and we cannot stay here any longer."

Liza stared wordlessly. Had he not heard her? Or did he think he could just bully her? She swallowed and met his gaze. "No, we will *not* be leaving this place—not my father, not me. We have water here and our things." She waved a hand in the direction of the wagon. "There isn't much left, but it's all we've got. And I'm not going to let some heathen doctor dance around my father, shaking bones and rattles in his face. Besides," she added, taking a deep, unsteady breath as she turned back to her father. "There have to be people passing this way in a day or two. Perhaps a trader or soldiers. So if you must leave, do so. We will make our way back to the

26

fort when he is well enough." She took another breath. "Who asked you to stay, anyhow?"

Red Eagle's eyes flashed and his lips dipped in a frown. "I will return you and your father to the fort when he is strong enough to travel that far. Until then, we go to the Pikuni. It is safer that way. Better for you—and him." His voice faded, losing its steely edge. "There is another reason I must go to my mother's people. But I promise I will take you and your father back to Fort Shaw or even Fort Benton."

Liza said nothing. After all, the man had helped her. But he was still a stranger, very much a stranger, and she must not let anything imperil her father's chances for survival. So far he had not regained consciousness, except to moan or move in deep sleep as if he were in great pain.

Abruptly, Red Eagle turned in silence. Liza watched him stride away, shoulders tense against the lines of his tunic.

Well, she thought, *if he must go, she would not stop him. Hadn't Lieutenant Cole warned her of mixed bloods, declaring they were ofttimes more conniving and unpredictable than full-blooded Indians? No doubt the lieutenant knew more than she about Indians.*

She pulled at her waistcoat impatiently. She couldn't afford to be swayed by fear or confused by conflicting emotions. Even still, a quiet voice reminded her of what Red Eagle had done for her father. *Why would he lead her to harm? Hadn't he proven himself a friend?*

Liza admitted she'd never been more helpless in her life. Yet, how could she agree to travelling deeper into the wilderness?

✠ ✠ ✠

Liza did not move from her father's side, bathing him, watching him, aware that he was already a shadow of the robust, striking man he had been. She brushed aside the tears that tickled her cheek. She had to make the right decision; her father's life depended on it.

27

✠ ✠ ✠

Red Eagle avoided Liza that morning. He did not approach the fire nor did he speak. She wondered if he was punishing her. Perhaps he would walk away and leave when she wasn't watching.

At noon, Liza wandered out to where Red Eagle sat, perched on the large rock where Liza always sat. Sharpening his knife along the edge of a long flat stone, he did not look up, even when she offered a plate of braised meat.

Finally, he raised his eyes. "We will leave tomorrow," he said in a somber voice. "At sunrise. We must find my mother's people. Then I will escort you and your father to Fort Shaw."

Liza stiffened, the harsh scraping sound of Red Eagle's knife sending a chill down her spine. "We'll see," was all she said.

Red Eagle returned to his task, his frown as forbidding as his glowering glance.

Pretending not to understand his look, Liza returned to camp.

CHAPTER 4

*L*ATE IN THE AFTERNOON, AFTER BATHING HER father's wound and rewrapping it carefully, Liza shook out a blanket and lay down. The sunshine was warm against her skin, so she slipped a bonnet over her head and face. Before closing her eyes, she cast a glance at Red Eagle. He had not moved in more than two hours; evidently he had expected her to acquiesce without argument. But why couldn't he just remain with them here, at least until her father improved?

Exhausted by her emotions, she escaped by letting her thoughts drift back to those last days in St. Louis. The St. Louis of her dreams. To the dances and the strolls along the river, arm and arm with her best friend Mary. To her bedroom upstairs in their stately brick house on McKinney Road. She loved that tiny room, with its white lace curtains and pale yellow walls. She recalled the coverlet Mother helped her to make when she turned twelve. Mother took pride in the perfect stitches adorning everything she made. Liza wished she had kept the curtains...

Just then she heard a shout.

Liza stumbled to her feet, sure that it was Red Eagle who hailed her. *Was he ready to concede, or would this be their showdown?* She turned, cheeks hot, pulse quickening.

But there was no one. The rock platform where Red Eagle had been sitting was empty. The shoreline was abandoned, too. Only a hawk circled high above the yellow-green landscape.

The shout came again, and immediately, Liza spotted not Red Eagle, but a rider, coming at a trot across the hazy, rolling grassland. The sun, already slipping behind the Rockies, sent a burst of pink rays north and south, highlighting the approaching man and horse. Liza felt her heart take a sudden

29

leap. *She had been right! There was someone coming. But where was Red Eagle?*

"Here! Here we are!" She ran to greet him. "Hello!" she laughed, her hands raised above her head. "Over here!" *How could she help but smile. Someone had come. They would be rescued.*

And the man was in uniform. *A soldier? Perhaps he was a scout or a messenger, and more were following.*

"Thank God," she said out loud as the rider waved his cap through the air. He wore a broad, toothy grin. Liza waved again. He was just a boy, she realized, noting the trooper's pimpled cheeks and fair skin.

"Well, if this don't beat all," he said brightly, drawing up his reins and leaning over the neck of his prancing horse. "What are yuh doin' way out here? Pickin' wild flowers?"

Liza blushed, then put her hands out to touch the soft muzzle of the horse. It snickered gently, and Liza sighed. The animal felt good, reassuring and comforting. She pointed to where her father lay. "We were attacked," she whispered. "My father..."

The soldier swung down and stood before her. His eyes were bright blue, but his teeth, yellowed and crooked, gave his round face a jaunty appearance. He looked her up and down. "An' if yuh ain't as handsome as an ace-full of queens," he said. He reached out as if to touch her.

Liza took a step back. "My father is hurt," she stammered, wishing the soldier would take his eyes off her. "He's over there. We—I—am doing the best I can, but he hasn't stirred since getting shot. That was four days ago."

"Renegades, eh? Dirty heathens'll leave you with nothin', not even yer hide, mosttimes. Too bad we cain't jest clean 'em all out. Well, now, let's take a look," drawled the blonde-haired trooper. He followed to where her father lay. Pulling down the blanket, he peered at the neatly bound wound. "Yuh did this? Guess yuh must know somethin' 'bout tendin'," he said approvingly. "Most pilgrims come out here useless as warts on a purty girl's bottom! 'Scuse me," he added, dropping his head.

"Please, can you help us? I mean, are you headed to a fort? Are you a scout?"

The soldier mumbled an unintelligible reply. "In a manner of speakin', I am," he added quickly, cocking his head. "But I sure could eat and drink somethin'. I feel like a post hole 'as ain't been filled up." He grinned again and Liza felt the rush of blood to her face. "Lost my pack horse," he added, shrugging his shoulders.

"Of course. I—I have a small stew, antelope is all." She refrained from telling him about Red Eagle, to protect him, although she didn't know why. Perhaps because the soldier so clearly hated Indians, and he would despise Red Eagle for abandoning her now.

"Snake stew would taste good right now," interrupted the soldier.

Liza made a wry face. "Please, what about my father?" She stepped over to the fire and lifted the kettle of meat prepared earlier for Red Eagle. She placed it on the tripod Red Eagle had built the day he killed the antelope.

"Who dug the bullet out? You?"

She shrugged, still not wanting to reveal anything about Red Eagle. "Well, it had to come out..."

"Ain't yuh as gritty as aigs rolled in sand!"

Liza looked away. The soldier's flattery was more than disconcerting. She stirred the meat carefully, stealing an occasional glance as he flopped down beside the fire. He had light brown hair, curly and unkempt, and his face was as round as a pie, though he was not fat or particularly big. The soldier's uniform was ragged and soiled and looked as though it needed stitching in a dozen places.

Perhaps he had been on the trail a good while, she thought, suddenly sympathetic.

She ignored her next thought: *why would a soldier be travelling alone for so long?*

She picked up a plate and spooned up some meat.

"Sure don't know what to tell yuh about your pa, miss," the trooper said consolingly. "He looks like he's asleep, for sure."

31

He took the plate, but as he did so, let his gaze linger on her face. "By the by, my name is Willy Scott, Private."

Liza nodded. "I'm Elizabeth Ralston."

"Well, it is a pleasure, Miss Ralston," smiled Private Scott.

Feeling like a tongue-tied school girl, Liza did not know what to say next. She lowered her eyes.

"Uh, sit down, won't you, Private Scott?" She pointed to the ground, not far from the fire. "Shall I tie up your horse? It's a fine animal."

"Nah," returned Scott quickly. "He's so genteel yuh could stake him on a hairpin. Can't survive very long in this country without a good hoss."

Liza nodded. "I know. The rustlers who attacked us took ours."

"Rustlers, not a chance. They was Injuns, most likely. Not a one of 'em you can trust. Yuh was lucky yuh wasn't scalped. There's heathens runnin' all over the Territory, lookin' for folks to terrorize. The Blackfeet. They's the worst. Scalpin' and raisin' hell ev'rywhere." He took an enormous spoonful of meat and chewed noisily, smacking his lips as he ate. "Oughta take 'em all out and hang 'em up to dry."

Liza looked away. She did not suggest that there was at least one Indian she hoped to trust.

She sat down across from the trooper, keeping the fire between them. For some reason, her nerves tingled when he looked at her. *Was she safe with this man?* Red Eagle had never made her feel this way.

She chided herself. A soldier was certainly the only sort of man she should trust in this wilderness. Hadn't the troops been sent west to keep peace and protect settlers? At Fort Shaw, the soldiers had been coarse but kind, anxious to answer her every need. Lieutenant Cole had ushered her around quite gallantly, even bringing flowers one morning.

She took a deep breath. "I wish I had some biscuits or bread to go with the meat."

Will Scott took another enormous spoonful. "Yuh don't know how good this grub tastes. The last meat I et was so ripe it didn't need cookin'. They don't serve up much in the way of grub out here," he added. "Coffee tastes more like water scalded to death."

Liza shook her head. "I'd have thought the army feeds its men better than that."

"Half the time you'd athought they was dishin' up soup made outa dirty socks."

"Well, it's not much, just stew. Not even much salt on it," she said.

She felt his blue eyes moving over her once again, and wished she were not sitting here alone with this young soldier of the crooked smile and sly looks. She got to her feet and returned to her father's side.

If only Red Eagle hadn't disappeared. He hadn't even said good-bye. Perhaps there was a reason he'd hidden from the soldier. If so, she couldn't betray him. If not, she had to accept the fact that he was gone.

The soldier's voice broke into her thoughts. "Where you from, anyways?"

Liza turned around. "St. Louis."

"Never ben there," said Scott slowly, scraping his spoon across the plate. "I bet it's quite a city, eh?" His blue eyes surveyed her, admiration clearly reflected in them.

"It's a wonderful place," she said. "Only, my father always dreamed of coming west."

"Is he a miner?" asked Scott. He held out his empty plate. "Don't suppose there's any more?"

"Of course," said Liza quickly. She dished up another hearty serving of meat. "My father's a minister," she added.

Will Scott coughed. "Oh." After a brief silence, he held up his spoon and said, "Ain't never ben to no church. Seems like a body oughta before they dies, but I never ben in one place long 'nough, I guess."

Liza handed him his plate. "Sometimes I think I've spent my life inside too many."

The trooper took a mouthful of steaming meat, wiping his chin with his tattered sleeve.

"Tell me," Liza said, changing the subject, "where are you headed? I mean, are you on patrol or something?"

"Guess yuh could say I'm on er—uh—special duty. Headed north," he added.

"That's where we were headed, only we got detained at Fort Shaw when my mother took sick. She died, but by then, the rest of our companions had left. They took our scout and all but our wagon with them. I had hoped we would return to St. Louis after Mother's death, but my father is a very stubborn man."

"He'd hafta be if he was movin' north. There ain't nothin' but mountains and Injuns and wild animals."

"Not even a trading post or settlement? Oh, don't you see, Private Scott, I've got to get my father to someone who can help him. Some kind of settlement, hopefully where there's a doctor," she whispered, fighting back her tears. "I was thinking you might be headed back to Fort Shaw, but anyplace would do. Perhaps a town?"

Will Scott raised his eyes, his smile gone. "I kin see yuh need help. I guess I gotta do somethin', that's for sure." He set his plate and spoon on the ground beside him. "Out here it's fittin' to help people when they're hurtin', cuz anywhere's a trek to nothin' much—if yuh don't know the way—"

Liza felt warm tears at the corners of her eyes. "I would be forever in your debt."

"Don't thank me yet," he drawled, almost angrily, then settled back against the ground, drawing his cap over his eyes.

※　※　※

Red Eagle sat down. Pulling out a piece of jerked meat, he looked about him. As he noted familiar landmarks, his thoughts returned to Liza.

She was never far from his mind.

Was it because she was beautiful, with her dark, snapping eyes and long, chestnut-colored hair? Or because she had the spirit of a fine horse, sometimes skittish, sometimes arrogant, sometimes downright foolish, but always alert? Of course, he hadn't known many white women, only a few at the forts and settlements he and his father visited over the years. Most of these, however, made their living doing laundry for the soldiers, or by satisfying their needs. Liza was in no way like them.

He sighed, angry for running off, but knowing she would quickly choose the trooper's help over his. He had seen her eyes light up upon seeing the blue boy's tattered uniform. Liza had not looked at him with any of the same excitement or relief.

A flash of feeling settled in his gut. No, lower, in his loins. Red Eagle spit out a hunk of sinew and frowned. The yearning he felt was different than anything he'd ever experienced.

He wondered what it would be like to lay with Liza. To touch and feel her skin beneath his. He had only known a woman once, an old, wrinkled woman whose soft, flabby layers of flesh repulsed him, even then.

He had been perhaps thirteen summers old. He'd been to the fort frequently with his father and the soldiers liked to tease him and sometimes gave him small, hard candies. This particular day, he wandered off, a piece of licorice in his mouth, while his father traded with the man at the mercantile.

His face flushed with shame even now as he remembered. An older woman, with flaming red hair and freckles across her dusted face, approached him, calling him by name. Curious, he entered her small cabin. She closed the door behind him, dropped her robe, and exposed her naked, pale flesh. He nearly fell backing away. But she caught him and drew him to her, pulling him into another room. At that point, a pulsing desire overwhelmed him and he didn't struggle.

Even now he heard her bitter laughter, for after he was done, his shame was greater than his satisfaction. He rushed to get away. Since then he had avoided all white women.

But Liza had stirred the same desire deep within his loins, evident the moment he spotted her standing by the water. Her skin had shimmered with water. Her eyes had shimmered, too, in the bright afternoon light.

And in their depths he had glimpsed a certain curiosity.

There was something else, however, that she'd kindled. It was a feeling he had never experienced. Something which made little sense.

But it didn't matter. Liza had made it clear she did not want his help. She couldn't trust him and preferred the dirty, dog-faced soldier who had arrived out of the emptiness. That was why, without a backward glance, he left.

Red Eagle shook off his disappointment. After all, he needed to find his uncle. Crying Wind would know about the haunting dream that still disturbed Red Eagle's nights. His mother's brother was a wise man, a holy man, and surely would know what the dream meant.

So why was he angry? Liza and her father would be taken back to the fort and her father would get help. She would return to her world and he would find his place in the Pikuni world.

But Red Eagle had not visited Crying Wind's village in many summers, not since before his mother's death. His father had stayed away, too, because of the resentment growing between the whites and many Pikuni bands; he had known that marriage to a Pikuni woman would not protect him forever, that relationships could easily deteriorate.

And would the bitterness lodged in the hearts of his mother's people extend to him? Perhaps they would not welcome him after all the years. People spoke of the Pikuni who had taken up the war trail, following Mountain Chief and Owl Child, two renegade warriors bent on vengeance. Would there be the same hardness in Crying Wind's heart toward Red Eagle?

Red Eagle stood, retying his parfleche to his belt. He still remembered the summers spent crossing the beautiful Sweet Grass Hills with his uncle and the people. Like the other boys who waited impatiently to become warriors, he spent those days trapping and hunting small game or riding a pony across the golden prairie at a dead run. There were other days spent feasting and dancing with bands who had come from all over. The food had been plentiful, the laughter warm and friendly.

He recalled the faces of the slender girls, too, who had watched the warriors dance, their glances hidden, smiles shy. With their bright, dark eyes, he now realized they had been hungry and curious.

But they would not be Liza.

CHAPTER 5

*A*S DARK CLOUDS MOVED ACROSS THE STARS, LIZA sighed. She had not been able to sleep, though a soldier of the United States Army lay but fifteen feet away.

Rolling over, she reached out and touched her father's shoulder. Even though he could not feel or hear her, his presence gave great comfort.

But it was Red Eagle's disappearance that filled her with confusion. True, she had told him they would not go with him, that she didn't want his help; her position had been clear and he had heeded her words.

So why was she annoyed? Why was she angry? *Good heavens, he was a half-breed, a heathen, certainly not someone she could ever trust—really.*

Oddly enough, her disappointment lingered. He could have at least said goodbye.

Liza glanced towards Private Scott, who lay near the fire, cap pulled down over his face. She had covered him with a blanket after he fell asleep, and he had curled up in it like a child. Only a few feet away, his horse, just as Will Scott had boasted, stood watch. In the gathering darkness, the animal's familiar smell and occasional snorts were comforting. Liza rolled over. She should feel relieved; after all, Mr. Scott had agreed to get them to a white settlement.

And the nightmare would be over. Or would it?

Resolved to forget Red Eagle and the feelings he had kindled, Liza closed her eyes and returned to memories of St. Louis. To that time before this journey into hell and her mother's death, even before her two brothers' sudden departure and her father's irreversible decision to move west. She imagined

39

herself in new dresses, at afternoon tea, with school friends, listening to music, and beside a roaring fire in the study of her grandfather's grand home.

Just as she fell asleep, she saw a man with black, flowing hair and dark, flashing eyes. He smiled and moved away; she followed him into the hazy distance.

✠ ✠ ✠

Liza awoke with a shudder. The air was cold and the morning damp. Feeling for the blankets, she pulled them up. Autumn was indeed coming to the northern plains.

She reached out and felt for her father, adjusting his blankets, worried that a chill would settle over him. His breathing was shallow but steady. She turned over and stroked his black hair and touched his sunken cheek. He was such a different man than just one week ago. So dependent on her now, even to the point of attending to his most personal needs. Never had she dreamed she would tend a man in such a way, especially her father. But she was grateful she could. She only wished to do more. Perhaps she'd try to feed him again today. Red Eagle had made some broth, but her father hadn't rallied enough to be able to swallow; all they dare was press wet clothes to his lips to keep his mouth damp.

The thought of Red Eagle made her feel empty inside. She glanced around the campsite as if he should be standing nearby. Silly, she scolded herself, he was gone, *gone forever*.

She got to her feet. Today would be a great day. Private Scott would help them get to a doctor, or, at least, to a trading post or settlement. Perhaps the travois, as Red Eagle had suggested, could be rigged with the horse. Or, better yet, perhaps they could repair the wagon enough to make a cart to carry Father.

Yes, today would be a great day. A day to turn her back on the terrible past.

Shaking out her skirt, Liza looked over to where Private Scott had been sleeping. His bed was empty.

"Probably washing up," she thought. Perhaps he was more modest than appearances. She cast a casual glance around the campsite. Where was his horse? A sudden fear gripped her, and she wrapped her arms about her waist to steel herself against the weakness overtaking her.

She started for the wagon, then stopped and frowned. The few boxes and barrels she had rescued from the attack and stacked carefully nearby had been ransacked and scattered.

Liza swallowed a cry of alarm, but as she raced to the wagon, mind reeling, her glance took in everything at once. The little bit of coffee and flour she'd scraped together now dusted the ground like fine, dirty snow, the bags that held them tossed aside. Even the small barrel that contained her winter clothing, and had been overlooked in the first attack, lay on its side, empty. Her heart seemed to settle in throat.

Private Will Scott had done this.

She picked up the sack where Red Eagle had stored their fresh meat. Nothing!

They'd been left with nothing.

How could he? How could a soldier in the United States Army do this to people dependent on him? *And how would her father survive if she couldn't feed him?*

How would she survive?

She screamed, "I'll kill him!" Yes, if she could only find him, she would shoot him. She looked around for her father's rifle, the one Red Eagle had used to take down the antelope. It was nowhere in sight, and Giles's gun was gone, too, even Father's boning knife—all gone. Extra blankets, dried fruit, anything that could be carried off.

Gone.

Liza stood, transfixed; reality was like a slow thaw after a hard freeze. She had foolishly trusted one man because he was white and mistrusted another because he was not. Even the savages, if indeed the attackers had been Indians, had left their provisions; this man had left nothing, save the clothes on her back and her mother's dainty pistol, which had been hidden under her pillow.

41

There it was. The terrible truth.

Liza dropped to her knees, balled fists pressed against her thighs. How could he do this?

Then she spied a man on horseback, moving into the western skyline, the great purple and white Rocky Mountains rising like the painted backdrop of some stage play. He moved easily, as if his horse were nothing more than a wooden rocking horse. In another few minutes, he would be a black mark on the horizon.

Jumping to her feet, Liza stumbled forward, trying to yell. She ran, feet pounding the earth like muffled drum beats. Suddenly, he turned in the saddle, his cap moving across the blue sky like a flat disc. *Was he waving at her? Mocking her?*

Oh, what a fool she'd been.

"Damn you!" she screamed after him. "Damn you to hell!"

The figure continued on, sending out brown dust. In a moment, even that little bit of him would be gone.

"Please!" she shrieked then, dashing over the hard earth. "Come back! You can't leave us here to die!"

She followed the rider's trail, leaping stones and ignoring the knife-like stubble of the bunch grass. A flock of birds, yellow and black, fluttered up as she ran straight through a patch of taller grass, their shrill twitters filling the air around her. A coyote, on his way from here to there, stopped to watch her, eyes keen, ears twitching.

Liza splashed through a rivulet that twisted around the contour of a ravine. The water was cold and burned her tender feet.

She continued until she could run no more, her legs too feeble to hold her up. She pushed herself forward. Like the night of the attack, she moved as if in a dream, unable to think or feel. As on that terrible night, her life was disappearing before her, even as Will Scott disappeared into the landscape.

At last she had to stop. Panting, her heart pounding, she stared into the skyline. There was nothing, no one, only the phantom shadows that haunted the prairie.

Terrified, Liza began running again, mumbling, telling

herself to hang on. But the world was turning upside down. The sky was at her feet, the rolling landscape was floating past her. A tree, stripped by lightning, stood up out of the emptiness like a scarecrow. She screamed. A band of geese flew past overhead, honking, and she screamed again. Looking up, Liza realized that they, too, were leaving her in their wake.

"Dear God," she sobbed, dropping to the ground, stomach rising to her throat. Tears overtook her as she pressed her face to the dirt. What would she do now?

✠   ✠   ✠

Willard Lee Scott rode on, his faded blue cap pulled over his brow. The morning sun was bright, but the air was still brisk.

He knew he ought to feel some sort of remorse after abandoning the dying preacher and his daughter, but he didn't. He patted the Henry, now strapped to his saddle, and thought of the unexpected bounty stuffed into saddlebags and tied onto his horse. Even the Bibles and clothing ought to be useful in trade, particularly the overcoats.

The girl had been pleasing enough, with her flashing brown eyes and shapely body. But a minister's daughter? Whoa, the thought gave him the heebie-jeebies. Not that he was a religious man.

Besides, the posse would be on his tail soon enough, especially when they discovered he'd killed the fat squaw that brought his meals. *Course, it was an accident*, he reminded himself; *if she'd akept her mouth shut, she'd be alive today. The old toothless fool had tried to stop him.*

"Ain't no one gonna string me up," he said out loud, passing a hand over his parched lips. "Wish I had a drink," he sighed. He hadn't had as much as a jigger of whiskey in over two weeks. Too bad the preacher hadn't any. An empty bottle and a dry jug was all he found stashed in the wagon. He had found some coffee and flour, beans, and of course, the best haul was the hind quarter of meat rolled in the sack cloth and the bag full of jerked meat.

"A body's gotta plow with the horses he's got," mused Scott. That included taking when the taking was good. "No sense in getting winded about a foolhardy preacher and his purty daughter," he said to his horse. Besides, the preacher was as good as dead and even if the girl got found by Blackfeet, she had to know it was her own damn fault. She'd either live or die.

"Cause there ain't nothin' worth tamin' in this wilderness," laughed Scott, "only outlaws, Injuns, and fools!"

☒ ☒ ☒

Liza struggled to her feet, confused by the landscape. She had run a great distance, but in what direction? The looming mountains were her only landmark, while the rolling plain was deceptive—and dangerous.

What a fool she'd been to trust a perfect stranger—yes, the *perfect* stranger. He'd been what she had hoped for: a soldier, a white man.

Oh, if only she'd not doubted Red Eagle. Red Eagle! His name was like vinegar to a swollen tongue. What a fool she had been.

By afternoon, Liza knew she had travelled the same paths over and over. One ravine had rolled into another, and she had wandered from stream to rivulet, hoping to spot the familiar line of trees that signalled the campsite. But if she didn't find camp soon, her father would not survive. He needed water, he needed tending, and perhaps he had even stirred to discover himself alone! Turning her face to the sun which had long passed its zenith, she spun around and considered her choices once more. She swore camp had been east and south of here.

With nothing else to trust, she had to rely on that instinct.

She set off at a good pace, keeping the Rockies behind her right shoulder. Liza sang as she walked, refusing to weaken and give in to her fear. Father needed her.

Without stumbling, she followed the raised contours of

44

the grasslands; it was as if her feet directed her steps. Finally, she recognized the pretzel-shaped ribbon of water and she ran to the cold water, letting it eddy around her toes. She sat down on a flat wide rock and let the water soak her hot, dry legs while she scooped up water to drink. It didn't matter that the water ran down her face or her dress was wet to the hips—it was as if she could breathe again.

As she scooped up another handful of water, she spotted a small bush. There were several patches of dark berries and she decided to grab some. The first handful was sour and she spit the pulp out after trying to suck the berries' juice. Four smaller bunches were sweet and juicy.

Revived, Liza resumed her march across the open land, growing more anxious about her father. Several times she startled birds and prairie dogs, but they skittered away each time she approached them. She wondered what else might be under the ground waiting or watching. If only she had paid more attention to the things Giles had said, details she had considered irrelevant a week ago.

The afternoon shadows stretched across the yellow horizon as Liza approached a ridge. Rising up out of the grassland, she thought it might give her a bird's eye view of the area. Hopefully she hadn't travelled in another circle.

She climbed slowly to the top, her bare feet toughened by all the walking. She peered across the distance and quickly spotted the copse of cottonwoods hugging the tiny stream and there, not much farther, was the abandoned wagon.

She dashed down the embankment; grabbing the folds of her skirt, she slipped in the loose silt, lost balance, and tumbled to the bottom of the ravine. As she caught her breath and stumbled to her feet, she slapped her grimy hands against her dress.

"Papa!" she cried as she ran to him, dropping to her knees. "Thank God you are still alive." Her words were lost in the ragged breathing she fought to control, and as the tears came, Liza did not stop them.

Efficiently she tended him, changing bandages and

cleaning him as best she could. Then she moistened a small towel and applied it to his lips, letting water run into his mouth. She bathed him, too, talking to him, all the while, about her foolishness. It didn't matter that Will Scott had abandoned them, at least for the moment. It was enough that she had found her father and that they were together. She would not leave him again, and if it was the last thing she managed to do on this earth, she would keep him alive.

She would keep them both alive!

Finally, as the sun cast its amber spray across the western horizon, Liza crawled alongside her father and curled up next to his ribs. She closed her eyes and let her mind drift. If only she knew what tomorrow would bring. If only...

Reminding herself that regret was wasted, she pushed aside the image of Red Eagle, his dark eyes studying her carefully, his mouth turned down in a frown. She had ignored the goodness there, the kindness—

Well, like this fleeting image, he was a phantom now, his goodness an illusion. It was time to forget.

CHAPTER 6

*T*HE CLIP-CLOP OF AN APPROACHING HORSE STAR-
tled Red Eagle. He had run for nearly two days, covering many
miles and had just now stopped to rest on a ledge overlooking
the ravine below. He hadn't realized anyone was following him.
Picking up his leather pouch, he quietly slipped behind a thick
wall of brush and waited.

The horse came up the ridge slowly. Had the rider
already spotted him? Red Eagle pressed his body closer to the
rock, letting the brush shield him. The animal finally came into
view and he recognized the dirty blue uniform and the long
Henry immediately.

Red Eagle felt the stab of anger and fought to keep his
hands steady and mind clear. Where was Liza? Where was her
father?

The heat of his blood filled his face. What a fool he'd been
to leave Liza to the mercy of this man. *Why hadn't he waited to
be sure she was all right?*

Lacing his fingers around the butt of his long knife, Red
Eagle knew what he had to do. He stepped forward boldly, but
as he did, several dry twigs cracked under his feet. He hesitated,
but it was too late.

Blue eyes flashed wickedly as Private Will Scott slipped
off his horse and drew a pistol. "Come on out," he ordered, his
cold glance darting left to right. "Hands above yer head!"

Red Eagle held his breath trying to remain calm. There
was enough cover to shield him, but his curled fingers shook
as he resisted the desire to plunge through the dense brush.
He had never killed a man before, but he'd hunted enough
panthers and bear to know the heat of passion that rose in a

man moving against his prey. He felt like a mountain lion, waiting—

Private Scott moved so close that every line of his face was visible, his crooked teeth, pocked cheeks and stubble chin. The soldier's blue eyes were narrowed and cold with hate. Time stood still as Red Eagle watched and weighed the soldier's every movement. When he turned, Red Eagle sprang.

Instinctively, his hands closed around the startled man's throat. The two men tumbled over and over, crashing through the brush, then down the ragged slope of a rocky ledge. The soldier was stronger than Red Eagle had thought and, still holding the pistol in his right hand, he had the advantage.

When the two duelers crashed into a wall of rock, Red Eagle grabbed for the gun. It flipped end over end into a narrow crevice below them. Red Eagle scrambled to retrieve it, but Scott drove his boot into Red Eagle's groin, sending him against the granite surface. He then leaped over Red Eagle and reached for the gun.

But Red Eagle regained his foothold and kicked Scott between the legs. It was a well-placed kick and the soldier doubled over, dropping the gun again. Red Eagle knew he had the advantage now and so did Scott. Enraged, teeth bared and nostrils flaring, the trooper howled and cursed, but Red Eagle had already seized the gun and jumped clear of the escarpment.

The soldier climbed after him, his fists flailing wildly as he tried to cover the distance between them. Red Eagle spun around and faced him, gun level and cocked, his eyes never leaving the blue-eyed man's wild face. Simultaneously, Scott lunged at Red Eagle, wrapping both hands around the butt of the gun. They tumbled over another ledge and Red Eagle felt the barrel against his ribs. He grimaced as he wriggled out of Scott's grasp, but before he could get away the blast sent him spiraling backwards.

The flash of pain was like a branding iron, hot and searing. Red Eagle erupted, ignoring the blood that seeped down his side and leg. With the gun still in his hands, he flew at the soldier, sending him crashing against the hard earth.

Panting, he rushed again before Scott could even scramble to his feet. This time the gun flew out of his hands and he pounced on top of the bewildered soldier. Every nerve in his body quivered as his fists pounded Scott's face.

Scott tried to fight back but Red Eagle would not let up. Blood ran from the soldier's nose and mouth and he growled, like a she-wolf, but could not free himself from Red Eagle's blows.

In a final motion, Red Eagle drew his long knife. "Liza?" he growled, pressing the blade's tip into the soft flesh of the man's throat. "Where is Liza? And her father?"

"What'da you care?" returned the soldier, gritting his teeth. Red Eagle drove the point in further. The man's racing heart throbbed against the blade but he never took his swollen eyes off Red Eagle.

"Liza?" growled Red Eagle again.

"The girl?" said Will Scott, a snicker passing over his blood-smeared face.

"What did you do to her?"

"You filthy breed!" snarled Scott. "I'll see you in hell!"

"Not before you tell me what you did with Liza—"

"Well, now," grinned Scott suddenly, running his bloody tongue over his battered, bloody mouth. "I give her a poke. An' she liked it. She liked it so much, I poked her agin n' agin!"

Red Eagle plunged the knife through Will Scott's throat. He closed his eyes to the man's hideous expression, startled by the bulging eyes and sputtering sounds. He loosened his grip for a moment, watching as the knife wallowed in the blood bubbling up around it. Pulling the knife free, he rolled away, weak from the pain in his side and the oppressive smell of death. Even the soldier's horse had wandered away, sniffing at the heavy air.

For several minutes, Red Eagle sat and watched the man, his bloody hands still wrapped around the knife.

Finally, as blood encircled the soldier's moon face, Red Eagle stiffened and turned aside. He struggled to his feet, then wandered down to a shallow stream that cut across a narrow coulee. He hesitated as he peered down into the clear water. It was like handfuls of crystals, sparkling, clean and fresh.

Dropping to his knees, he leaned over and dunked his sweat-soaked face. The water ran down his neck and across his buckskin shirt. He rinsed off his hands as he dragged the bloody blade through the water, his attention fixed on the pink-tinged water rushing downstream.

Relaxing, Red Eagle looked down at his side. The pain was intense and as he studied it, he was surprised by the upturned skin and bloody flesh. He fingered it, remembering how he had dug for Liza's father's bullet, then grimaced as his fingers probed deeper into the wound.

He could feel the bullet.

It didn't take long to cut it out, but as he did his heart pounded in his brain like a slow drum and sweat beaded up in his fingers. The knife was difficult to grip.

He cried out only once, just as the tip of the blade pried the lead out. And, just before fainting, he wrapped the palm of his hand over the wound.

✠ ✠ ✠

The sound shattered the stillness of the night. Terrified, Liza's eyes flew open and she pulled herself to a sitting position.

A minute later, it came again, only louder. Liza caught the edge of her blankets with her fingers. This time she would not run. She would die here, next to her father. Trembling, she reached for his limp hand.

The low rumbling moved closer. Liza squinted, breathing rapidly, searching the night for signs of storms. There were none. Only a strange, oblong moon and a sky sprinkled with silver stars.

The sound stirred closer, and the rumbling became a growl. She dug under her pillow for her mother's small pistol. *Was it loaded?* She scrambled to her feet as she tried to remember where Father had hidden the boxes of ammunition. God forbid that Will Scott or the thieves had returned.

"Who's out there?" Liza hollered, her voice shattering the night as she fumbled with a round of bullets. There were no more than a handful of extra cartridges. "Come out where I can see you!"

The only reply was the rustle of prairie grass stirred by wind or foot. Only there was no wind. *Was it Red Eagle? Or Will Scott?*

"Who is it? Why are you trying to scare me?" Liza's hands shook and her right forearm began to ache from squeezing the pistol grip so tightly.

"Is it you, Private Scott? Is it? If so, you better move 'cause I'm going to fill you with lead!" But her hands continued to shake and her knees grew weak. "Dear God," she whispered, "if there was ever a time to work a miracle, it's now. Please!"

Just then she recognized the sound. It was a cough. A cough and a growl.

A bear.

Liza bit her lip to keep from screaming.

The beast was moving clumsily now across the stream and she knew the bear was moving towards them, though nothing more than its small, glittering eyes and pale silhouette were visible.

She had no time to think. Rather, without aiming at all Liza raised the pistol and jerked the hammer back. Her finger shook against the trigger.

"Wh-wham!" The whistle pierced the ebony cloud of night. Stumbling backwards, she steadied herself. Her ears hummed from the bullet's explosion but carefully, evenly, she pulled the hammer back again. This time she did not waver.

A second wh-wham, more ear-splitting than the first, cracked like lightning and there was a horrible cry. She had hit the bear squarely this time, for it wailed and began to crash through the grass.

Immediately Liza fired a third and fourth time aiming high and as straight as she could, and her heart pounded as the screeching animal seemed to stumble and fall. Acrid gunpowder filled her mouth and her eyes burned from the hot smoke.

51

With one more pull, she fired a fifth time and the 'kaboom!' was followed by a shriek of pain and a heavy thud. She fired again but the gun just clicked. There were no more bullets.

The bear's terrible cries continued for several minutes, then turned to groans and finally ceased. Liza remained frozen, unable to move or release her hold on the gun. She listened for any sounds of rustling grass.

There were none.

But Liza continued to tremble, waiting for the howls to begin again. Was the bear really dead? *What if there was another one out there, waiting?*

A long, heavy silence passed before Liza dropped to her knees with the empty gun. She looked at it, wondering if she had indeed managed to do the impossible. The unthinkable. She, Elizabeth Ralston had killed a bear!

Taking a deliberate breath, she got to her feet and returned to camp and her father. Her wobbly legs could hardly hold her, and her head still pounded from the deafening roar of the bullets. But she was safe and so was her father. She pressed her lips to his cheek and whispered, "We'll be all right."

At least for now.

He seemed to stir at her touch and she waited, breathlessly. "Oh, Papa! Can you hear me?" She leaned closer again, left hand against his chest, eyes on his face. *It had to be*, she thought, *it just had to be!*

"Listen to me, Papa. I'm here. And we're going to be all right. Don't you worry, not about me, not about you! You always said Robert Ralston didn't raise his children to be weaklings! And you'd have been proud of me tonight. But rest now, Papa."

Touching his face once more to reassure herself that he was actually breathing easier, she reloaded the pistol and slipped it between their beds. Exhaling, she stretched out beside him still trembling from the bear encounter.

How long she lay there staring up at the night sky, she did not know. A hint of lavender and gold stretched across the eastern horizon when she finally closed her eyes.

✠ ✠ ✠

Red Eagle stirred. Looking up, he realized night had overtaken him. Even now his side burned and his body, stiff from laying in one spot for so long, tingled as he tried to move. He ignored the body that lay not far away and looked for the man's horse. It was nowhere in sight.

He frowned. A horse would have made all the difference. He glanced back at the dead soldier. *Let the crows and the coyotes find him,* he thought.

But his own wound was more painful than he wanted to admit, even though it was a simple one. Slipping off his medicine pouch, he set to work pulling out an assortment of smaller parfleches, each holding his mother's special plants. As he made a poultice, his heart was heavy with worry and his mind reeled with fear.

Was Liza still alive? He had to know. He had to go back—

Suddenly lightheaded, he hesitated before standing up. He had such a long way to go.

He placed one foot in front of the other, moving carefully and ignoring the spells of dizziness that washed over him. *Would he find Liza before it was too late?*

CHAPTER 7

*L*IZA OPENED HER EYES SLOWLY. HER HEAD ACHED AS if she had suffered a blow. She rose carefully, trying not to move hastily. She reached out for her father and pulled back when she realized his body was cool and clammy in spite of the layers of bedding.

Ignoring her head, she pushed him onto his back. She pressed her ear to his chest and groaned. What had happened between last night and this morning? "Oh, Papa, what can I do? I'm no surgeon. I'm not even a good nurse." She touched her fingers to his sweaty brow, then stroked his cheek and forehead. "If only Mother were here! She would know what to do." Mother had helped many of Father's parishioners who fell ill and could not afford a doctor.

In frustration, Liza took up her rags and dipped them into the bucket of yesterday's water. She washed her father down gently, whispering all the while. "Perhaps you've sweat out the fever. I remember Mother used to say a body had to sweat before a fever broke. Maybe that means you're healing."

She dribbled water carefully over his chapped lips. "Drink this, if you can," she said. "Your body needs water, even if it's not much."

Finishing, she stood up and looked around. Her head still throbbed and ears rang. But she was grateful; they had both survived another night. They had even survived a possible bear attack.

She looked for the bear eagerly. Had she really killed it? She couldn't remember—exactly. There had been smoke. Powder burns. Terrifying cries. Ringing ears and burning throat. Throbbing arms and fingers.

She glanced down at her fingers. Smudges of black still

stained the thumbs and right forefinger. Amazed, Liza shook her head. She had only fired a gun a few times back in St. Louis, a long time ago; she recalled that the first time, her brothers tried to convince her that a rifle wouldn't kick. Of course she landed in the dirt and, furious with Evan and Lawrence, ran into the house crying. But the Reverend Ralston had believed in teaching his children not to be so easily frightened and thus made her go back out and fire the Henry over and over until she was no longer afraid.

Liza wandered out past the campfire, stepping carefully over the rocky ground until she spotted it. The black hump, which lay less than sixty feet away, was smaller than she had feared. A crow stood atop its head, as if claiming it for his own, while another crow hopped around on the ground angrily cawing at his companion. Liza frowned. She didn't want to get any closer, but reckoned she should cut off a hunk of meat. She and her father needed food, no matter how objectionable.

※　※　※

Red Eagle could no longer keep his eyes on the trail. Growing weak from the loss of blood, he was dizzy and needed rest. He stopped and leaned his hands against his thighs as he tried to peer ahead.

Just beyond the trees, was that the stream where he'd stood and watched Liza, half-clothed, bathe in the water? He remembered the pale softness of her breasts, how they swelled up against her undergarment. He remembered the sheen of her hair in the bright sunlight and how he longed to reach out and run his hands over her silken skin. Was she there still, standing beside the water watching him?

It was only a mirage. Disgusted, he stumbled to the water's edge, fell to his knees and cupped his hands, letting the cool water run over his fingers. His stomach was empty and the water seemed to roll around inside him. He needed food. He needed rest.

In a few minutes he'd push on.

✠ ✠ ✠

Robert Ralston blinked, his eyes unable to focus on anything except the bowl of blue sky above. *Where was he? What had happened? Where was Liza?*

He tried to raise his head, but it was like a lead pipe. He rolled it from side to side. His mouth was dry, his lips were cracked. His tongue was so swollen it felt like a block of wood. He wanted something to drink.

"Liza?" he whispered. "Liza?"

He moaned, closing his eyes to the bright sunshine. He was more exhausted than he'd ever been in his life. What had he been doing to be so tired? Had he died and gone to Hell?

It was a long time before he opened his eyes again. "Liza?" he whispered. "Where are you?"

He blinked and suddenly her face filled the space above him. Tears were running down her cheeks and a smile crossed her tanned face. Her brown eyes twinkled from the tears filling them.

"Liza," he tried again, "what happened?"

"Oh, Papa." She touched his cheek. "I can't believe you're awake. But I knew you'd survive!" She swallowed before going on. "You were shot—by Indians or rustlers, I don't know. Do you remember?"

He shook his head, but his lips wouldn't respond. No, he didn't remember anything.

"Giles was killed. I ran away and hid, and they didn't follow. It was a miracle they didn't scalp you. Then Red Eagle found me. He was the one—"

Her father shook his head. Red Eagle? Who was Red Eagle?

"Yes, yes, but we'll talk later. Oh, so much has happened. I thought I might lose you—forever."

He tried to raise his right hand, but it was sodden and ached deeply. Liza quickly clasped his fingers and brought them to her lips. "Please, Father, rest now. It's enough that you're alive."

He let his eyelids drop and quickly found himself in the

darkness again, but this time he could hear and smell and think. Only, he didn't want to think right now. It hurt to think, as it hurt to move. There would be a better time to think—

When he stirred the second time, Liza was already seated beside him. With a damp cloth, and a cup of cool water, she waited. She would have something else to offer him once the bear meat had boiled. She had managed to dig up several roots and was able to catch a fish trapped in a small pool of water. She had roasted and eaten it, even the fins and tail.

Her father seemed to be more coherent as Liza washed him down. "Your wound has healed nicely, I think, but you still have a bit of a fever," she said. "Last night you were sweating, so I knew it was going to break soon. Now, if you can manage some water, and then later, some broth—"

She stopped, realizing she had prattled on. Father would not have the strength for more than a few words yet. She smiled as she pressed a damp cloth of water against his lips.

Then, suddenly, he broke into a fit of coughing and rolled his head to one side so the spittle dribbled out.

"It will be all right," she whispered, wiping his lips. "I promise." She tried to smile. "You'd be surprised how much your daughter has learned in the last five days. You always wanted me to be tough. It only took twenty-one years."

Her father's eyes narrowed. She continued. "Father, I'm sorry. Sometimes it's better to laugh than to cry."

At that, her father's expression softened. He smiled a weak, lopsided smile. "I'm tough, too," he whispered.

Tears stung her eyes. "Tougher than you can imagine."

He smiled again, but immediately broke into a second fit of coughing.

"Oh, Father, what can I do?"

"Water," he said, almost silently.

"Of course!" She dipped the rag into a cup of water and wet his lips again. He began to suck like a newborn on the bit of cloth. When he nodded, Liza removed the rag.

His voice was barely audible. "Giles had some— whiskey," he said.

She frowned. "It's gone. Everything is gone."

Her father sighed. He didn't have the energy to say more. There would be time later. When he was stronger; when she was stronger.

His mind reeled with a new urgency. There was so much to tell his daughter, so much he'd kept hidden. Later. He would have to tell her everything.

Liza let him rest but didn't leave his side. She wiped his forehead and cheeks, hoping to bring down his fluctuating temperature. He slept fitfully, but it was a different kind than the strange sleep he'd been in for almost a week.

When he rallied the third time, Liza checked the wound. It had been so difficult when she could hardly move him or reach around him. He tried to help by dragging himself up on one arm while Liza peeled back the layers of fabric until she reached the raw flesh.

"See, how well it's done," she said to her father. "I tore up an entire petticoat treating this wound," she added, with a smile.

If only Red Eagle could see it; he had been a better doctor than she could have hoped for. He had been a better doctor than she had deserved.

"I'm going down to the stream. Maybe I can catch another fish. I trapped one earlier and it was pretty good eating. Then I'll give you a little of the broth I've cooked up—"

She didn't add that it was bear broth.

Her father, weak but alert, smiled. "My daughter, the fisherman. I thought I would be the one to fish—"

"For souls, Father," she quipped, smiling. "But I'm after food for our empty bellies. I'm afraid my desires in life are not as noble as yours."

"Hush, girl," he grimaced. "You have been braver than I could ever be."

"No, you hush," she said gravely. "I'm barely keeping my wits. I've not done anything courageous."

She left him then to catch their meager supper. Tying her skirt up around her waist, she entered the icy stream cautiously, inhaling sharply as it circled her calves. The afternoon had cooled considerably and several dark clouds blanketed the sun. A breeze rustled the leaves of nearby trees and as the sunlight waned Liza knew autumn was coming.

She hiked her skirt higher and moved deeper into the stream. Several large fish slipped right through her fingers as she tried to grab at them. This was harder than she thought or perhaps her luck had run out.

It took several more attempts, but at last, as her legs grew numb from the cold, Liza cornered a small fish near the shore. In the shadows it was hard to see, but she waited until it stopped moving before reaching in and flipping it onto the shore. It wiggled furiously and almost leapt back into the water but she scrambled out and caught it, laughing in triumph.

Ralston slept as the fish cooked. Liza did not disturb him. The broth was still simmering and she sprinkled in a little of the salt she had rescued.

At least there was food for tonight.

But what would she do if no one came along? Could she leave her father long enough to find her way back to Fort Shaw? And even if she could, how could she return in time to save him?

Liza bit her lip. She would have to wait for someone to find them, that was all there was to it.

If only she hadn't refused Red Eagle's offer of help.

✠　✠　✠

Red Eagle rolled over. He groaned, the pain in his side taking his breath away. He opened his eyes slowly. Had his mind been playing tricks on him again or had he actually made his way to Liza's camp? He smelled the campfire.

Glancing around, he saw a fire burning brightly, the flames leaping up to lick the limb wood. Stretching his right hand out in front of him he let the warmth of the fire tickle his palm. He needed the comfort and warmth.

He also needed food.

Red Eagle sat up, still confused. "Liza?"

"Ah! So the varmint is alive!"

Red Eagle jumped, startled by the booming voice.

"Hells bells, there ain't no reason to look like you seen a ghost!"

Swallowing, Red Eagle tried to speak. "I thought I was—some place else," he said, sorely disappointed that his dream had been an illusion. He strained to make out the face of the man who had spoken, but could only see the back end of a gray mule and two arms stretched over a pack saddle.

"Well, I found you over there," came the gruff voice again.

"I must have passed out—"

"Passed out? Nah, you was near dead as far as I could tell. Didn't think you'd ever wake up. Had sorta thought about skinnin' you and addin' your hide to these others!"

Red Eagle's eyes narrowed as the man stepped out from behind the gray mule. He was a big man with shoulders as wide as two men and a belly that hung down over his twisted rawhide belt. Except for his yellow-white hair and long yellow beard, the man looked almost Indian, with his fringed leather tunic and leggings. His clothes were well-worn but ornately decorated. Red Eagle noted the variety of beads and quills stitched down his knee-high moccasins.

"Like 'em, eh, breed?" laughed the burly man. "I got me a good squaw woman," he added briskly. "But bead work is not why I keep her around." He smiled slowly as he covered the distance between them.

"I—I must be on my way," said Red Eagle, getting to his feet. He swayed as he tried to take a step forward.

"You're just wiser than a sheet house rat, ain't you? But I figure I caught you, so's I'll let you go when I'm good and ready. Now sit. I don't like to eat alone."

✠ ✠ ✠

"I want to sit up—"

Liza jumped up and rushed to her father. "Don't move. You're not strong enough."

"Sitting up will not hurt me," he grumbled.

Liza frowned. "Oh, I suppose not, if you're careful." She slipped her arms under his shoulders and helped him slide forward. He grunted as his weight shifted, but relaxed visibly as he sat up. She fashioned a backrest out of a small barrel and her pillow, then shoved her small hand trunk behind it to keep it from rolling.

"How about some broth?" She had to get some food into him soon.

Her father shook his head. "Don't think I can swallow it."

"But you must. Please, for me?"

He smiled weakly and nodded. "Only for you."

She returned with a cup full of broth.

"Smells pretty good," he said. "Didn't know you could cook."

"I don't," she said, raising an eyebrow. "That is, not well. But it's amazing what you can do in a pinch."

"True," whispered her father. He took a sip, pulling back as his lips touched the broth. "Hot!" he said.

"I'm sorry," said Liza. She blew on the soup, then offered it again. He swallowed six spoonfuls.

"Enough," he said and closed his eyes. She watched him closely. If only there was more she could do. If only she could get real help.

His eyes opened again. "I'm sorry you had to face this— all alone, Elizabeth," he whispered, dark brows pinched, mouth turned down at the corners.

"I didn't—exactly—face it alone. I told you, there was Red Eagle."

"Red Eagle? I don't remember anyone—"

"No, of course not. He found me. He was the one who removed the bullet from near your heart. He killed an antelope, too. He—"

"Where is he now?" Her father's eyes widened and he scanned the campsite.

"You won't find him," whispered Liza. "I told him I wouldn't let him move you, and then, there was Private Scott—"

"Scott?" He shook his head.

Liza frowned, looking down at her hands. She pulled at a thread that hung from the frazzled cuff of her shirtwaist. "I can't explain everything," she said. "Too much has happened."

Her father nodded and closed his eyes. She watched him, knowing how hard he was fighting to get well. Always a man to take control, his not pressing her for answers showed just how little strength he possessed.

"Tell me about Red Eagle," he said after a long silence. "He sounds more interesting than Scott. And he spoke English?"

Liza yanked again at the thread on her sleeve. "Yes, very well."

"Where was he from? What tribe?"

"I don't know, really," said Liza. "Only that he was traveling to his mother's people."

"Blackfeet," said her father carefully. "Perhaps he's a half-breed." He reached out for Liza's hair. She had braided it and it hung in two long plaits past her breasts. He fingered one braid, then let it drop. "I have so much to tell you, Liza. I should have done it long ago." He coughed then and Liza frowned.

She pressed her hand to his forehead. "Not now, Father. Later."

✠ ✠ ✠

The next day, Liza's father seemed stronger and spent most of the morning sitting up. Liza managed to gather several plump roots along the shoreline and added them to the chunk of bear meat still cooking in its broth. She wondered how long it would feed them.

He watched her in silence and several times looked as if he might cry. Unaccustomed to seeing her father emotional, except in anger or behind the pulpit as he preached, she found it disconcerting. He had always been a strong man, determined and demanding.

She filled a tin cup with hot broth and sat beside him.

63

He smiled. "You finally have the upper hand, eh? How does it feel?"

"Hush. You're stronger already. You'll be back to yourself in a few days."

She guided a spoon to his mouth but his gaze remained fixed on her. He swallowed slowly, licking his lips. "I will never be the same," he said suddenly. "I never want to be the same," he added.

Liza was startled, not understanding why he would say such things. "Hush," she said brightly, hoping to divert his thoughts. "Eat this."

He studied her, then said, "All right." He took two more spoonfuls. "It's good."

"No, it's not. It's horrible, but it's all there is—" She grew quiet, not wanting to bring up their lack of provisions and Private Scott's deception.

"You're wrong," quipped her father. "It's manna from heaven. You've done very well."

"Father, you don't understand. I trusted a white man, Private Will Scott, because I was afraid to trust Red Eagle. Yet Red Eagle had already proven his friendship and honesty. This no-account scoundrel left us with nothing. How could a soldier be so untrustworthy? How could I be so stupid?"

Her father said nothing but turned his strained, pale face to her.

"Red Eagle would not have done such a thing, Father! But I refused to trust him—"

"Daughter, your mother and I did not raise fools. You were being cautious. That's not stupid."

"Papa! Listen to me. I was sure you were going to die and then I would die, too. I've been afraid, of everything! Even shooting the bear. I was so frightened, I simply held the gun— and fired. I fired until there were no bullets left. That's all."

Ralston closed his eyes and leaned against the back rest. "Courage is never something we choose," he whispered, almost to himself. "We merely do the best we can with the challenges God gives us."

"Well, I don't understand why God has done this to you," she stammered, setting the cup and spoon on the ground. "I don't understand why God would bring such misery to some-one who trusts him. You were doing what he wanted!"

He took a long, slow breath. His eyes were still closed and his hands trembled as he folded them in his lap. Liza bit her lip, wishing she hadn't spoken so harshly.

"This world is not where I place my faith," he said at last. "Situations come along in each of our lives that confound us, discourage us, even destroy us. But the heart and spirit," he placed his hand against his chest, "don't have to be touched. My heart belongs to God and someday I will return to Him. Until then, I will do the best I can. Just like you."

"I still don't understand," said Liza.

"In time we each come to understand what God has in store for us."

She sighed and squeezed her father's hand, not wanting to upset him any further.

He turned his face to hers. "Elizabeth, there is something else that we must talk about."

"No, Father, nothing more need be said. You need rest."

"Listen to me. I have a confession—"

"You? Don't be ridiculous!"

"Oh, Elizabeth, let me speak." He leaned over and coughed, a cough that seemed to come from deep within.

"May I get you some water?"

"No."

Liza bit her lip.

"There," he said at last. "I'm going to tell you something I should have long, long ago. I'm going to be honest and I don't want you to say anything until I'm done."

"All right, Father," she whispered.

"You will be furious," he said calmly, "but I can't prevent that."

"No, I won't," she broke in.

"Yes, you will," he said, "so I won't hold you to your promise."

"Go on."

"Have you never wondered why I longed to come west? Have you never wondered about me? Why I was so different than other men?" He turned away. "I have never shared much with you, have I? I've been a difficult father. But I thought I was doing the right thing at the time. Can you understand that?"

Liza nodded, but her stomach rolled over just the same.

"I tried to tell your brothers once—just before they ran away—but they wouldn't listen. They left, disgusted and angry, and swore they could never forgive me."

"Oh, Father," she said, remembering the day Evan and Lawrence left. It had been a bitter parting. Mother had cried for days and Father retreated further into himself and his work.

He held up his hand. "You see, Elizabeth, my mother— your grandmother—was Kootenai. An Indian woman—"

Liza pulled away, eyes widening, heart racing, even as he continued.

"My father was a trapper. He came west early on. And he met a young woman. I don't even know her name. They met somewhere in the Bitterroot Valley and lived there for several years."

He was panting now and Liza held her breath as she wrapped the thread of her ragged sleeve around and around her fingers. How could this be true?

"She died after giving birth to me, their only child. My father was heartsick and couldn't care for an infant. He sent me back to his family in Pennsylvania. I was raised there but didn't learn my true parentage for several years."

Liza couldn't stop her tears. They were sweet, even as her throat burned bitter.

He raised his hand again. "My father continued trapping, living with one tribe after another. Then he met a man who was a missionary to the Salish and a few Blackfeet. He became a Christian out here in this wilderness."

"You're lying, or else you're mad with fever!" Liza burst out, unable to sit still any longer.

Her father ignored her. He spoke haltingly now, but

rushed on. "I knew nothing of my father because the family was so ashamed of his Indian wife and my blood. It would never do to admit such a thing to the respectable people of Pennsylvania. Then, one day, my father came home to die."

He collapsed against the back rest, face drained, breath coming in sporadic puffs. Several times he coughed. Finally he closed his eyes. "After I got to know him I decided to come west. To learn about my mother. To learn more about my father. To know these things before I die."

Liza was stunned. Unable to speak, she watched her father laboring to finish the story but her heart betrayed her. She wanted to scream and yell and fight. She wanted to kick and run away. *How could she have been lied to all these years?*

How could such a bizarre thing even be true? Her father, the son of a Kootenai woman?

"Liza," he whispered, but she was already on her feet, her hands brushing his away. She had to get away from him before she said something regrettable.

The cup of broth spilled across the rocky ground tinkling in the ensuing silence.

CHAPTER 8

*L*IZA PACED BACK AND FORTH ALONG THE STREAM-bank. Her mind whirled with a thousand disconnected thoughts. *How could such gibberish be true? Wouldn't she have known somehow, suspected something over the years? Dark skin and dark hair were not unique to Indians, but Indians were different, a different breed.*

She pressed her memory, but there was nothing, no clue that her father had such a secret. Yet, how could it be true? She would have to deny it. She could never let anyone back in St. Louis know the truth.

But she would know.

Her father, *part Indian.* She said it over again; it seemed to stick to her lips. She rubbed her hands across the back of her neck. The idea was so preposterous. Kootenai? Who had ever heard of such a tribe? They might as well have come from the bowels of the earth.

Well, it was simply impossible she decided, picking up a pebble. She watched it skip across the water and thought of every reason why she couldn't believe her father's story.

Her father, Robert Andrew Ralston, was a minister, a well-respected, successful minister. Her mother, the only daughter of Herbert Poole, was heir to one of the most admired family fortunes in St. Louis, a family that had come from the deep South only a few years before the war. Grandfather Poole had been known for his conservative politics and supported Missouri's position on slavery, in spite of his son-in-law's abolitionist views. No, Grandfather would have been horrified, would have forbidden a union between his genteel daughter and a half-breed!

Most likely, the story had been conjured by Father's fevered brain. No telling what one might dream after being unconscious for five days.

She took a deep breath and glanced back at the camp-fire. Her father was resting now. His hands were folded and eyes closed, giving him a death-like appearance. She tried not to study the dark, straight hair falling across charcoal-colored brows and tawny cheeks.

She shook herself. He had come so close to death, she just couldn't be angry with him for creating a fantasy. He would come to his senses soon. He might not even remember the story he had concocted.

Liza sat down on the flat rock, the same rock where Red Eagle had sat the last time she saw him. Passing her hand over the rough surface, she wondered where he'd gone. What did it matter?

She marched back to camp, a cluster of blackbirds swooping past her as they flew to a stand of reeds along the bank. She watched them land, their bodies rocking on the long, broad blades of grass.

She approached her father, then stepped back. He looked so pale, so weak. She swallowed the lump in her throat; she had promised not to be angry. She would leave things as they were, at least for now.

✠ ✠ ✠

Liza dropped to the ground beside the wagon. She had recalled something from the past she had not remembered earlier, something her father had triggered. About her brothers, Evan and Lawrence.

What was it he'd said? That he had tried to tell them about his past but they refused to listen. Instead, they left home forever?

Tears began to fall as that terrible day returned to her mind. Certainly that part of her father's tale was true. The boys had argued with him. Liza remembered clearly the shouting

70

and cursing. Her brothers, red-faced, their voices shrill with anger, stomped out of Father's library and though Father yelled after them, they didn't return.

They left that day and never came back. Both refused to tell Liza what happened and Mother locked herself in her room for two days.

Liza's pulse raced as she relived that last encounter over and over. If her brothers had known the truth, why hadn't they warned her? Surely, she had had a right to know. Yet, what would she have done, or said, or thought? Her life as Grandfather Poole's beloved granddaughter would have been destroyed forever. His deep hatred for anyone not white was well-known and much appreciated by St. Louis society.

She ran a hand through her hair and yanked the ribbon out viciously. Her hair tumbled down as the ribbon dropped to her lap. Dragging her knees to her chest, she wrapped both arms about her legs.

"Papa, how could you have done this to me?" she whispered. "How can I ever go back to St. Louis and act as if nothing has changed?"

Pressing her forehead to her knees, she took a slow, deep breath. *Who else had known the whole truth?*

Liza bit her lip. Mother?

Of course Mother knew. That's why she never spoke of Liza's brothers' leaving, never explained what happened that day.

Mother had burned with the shame of it and the fear of exposure, understanding its power to destroy their lives.

✠　✠　✠

She slid a spoon of steaming broth into his mouth. Her father watched her carefully, but she refused to look into his dark, questioning eyes. Liza knew he saw the tears which stained her face. Even now her eyes burned from crying.

"Liza," he whispered, "I don't know how to apologize. It was wrong to keep the truth from you or your brothers. But

71

your mother feared it would ruin your life, put you at a disadvantage—"

"It has," interrupted Liza, wanting to hurt him as badly as he had hurt her. "I can never hope to return to St. Louis."

"Nonsense." Pain glittered in his dark eyes.

"You don't understand, Father. I could never preserve the lie that has followed you all these years, no matter how ashamed I might feel about a person like your mother."

Her father's eyes narrowed. "Ashamed of my mother? I raised you to be stronger-minded than that, to weigh worth by the quality of a person. I am not, nor have I ever been, ashamed of who I am. Because your mother begged me to, I kept it secret. She was terrified of her father. I only wanted to please her. Now I know it was a mistake."

Liza held the spoon out as she spoke. "Tell me, did she know the truth before you married her, or did you trap her first?"

His eyes flashed. "No, I did not trap her. In fact, I told her everything in the beginning, but she still wouldn't let me tell her family. She knew her father would never condone our marriage and she couldn't live with his rejection. Remember, that was before the war."

"Of course," she returned, her voice rising abruptly. "Grandfather would not have allowed it. He'd have sent you packing—"

"Is that what you think should have happened?" her father asked. "Do you believe a man's skin denotes his worth? Did I raise you to believe that?"

"I don't know," said Liza. "But it changes everything— everything!"

The spoon in her hand shook as she dipped it into the broth. If only feelings were like layers of clothing one could shed or even throw away. If only she could discard the bitterness she now felt about her father and his secret past.

He held his hand up. "No more."

Liza dropped the spoon into the cup. "So why didn't you tell me after we left St. Louis? Or at least after Mother died? Did

72

she insist you keep it a secret forever?"

Straining to sit up, her father raised his eyes to hers. "I was afraid I would lose you. And your mother was so convinced that I shouldn't that I couldn't take a chance, even after we buried her. We had lost our sons and she'd given her life to our dream."

"Your wilderness killed her," Liza sputtered, feeling the blood rush to her face. "You and your crazy notions killed her! Had we stayed in St. Louis, she would be alive today. Alive! Instead, cholera killed her and she died in a hovel on the banks of the Missouri." Shaking uncontrollably, she stood and threw the remains of broth across the fire, causing it to spark and crackle. She tossed the cup down and stomped away, her hands drawn into fists at her sides.

"Liza!" Her father's voice was hardly more than a whisper. She kept walking.

She had never felt so angry and suddenly she realized how bitter she had become about coming west. Bitter that Mother had been consumed by disease and now lay under the ground in some remote, forgotten place.

All this because of Father's secret desire to return to some strange, unknown past. A past that included an Indian grandmother.

She didn't know if she could forgive her father for hiding the truth. He'd always said that telling the truth took courage, yet he'd taken the coward's way.

So how and why should she forgive him?

CHAPTER 9

"GIT UP! IT'S DAYLIGHT IN THE SWAMP!"

Red Eagle rolled his eyes open and studied the face peering down at him.

"I said, git up! You sleep more 'n the devil hisself," added the big man as he prodded Red Eagle's wound with his foot.

Crying out from the pain, Red Eagle grabbed the moccasin, nearly toppling its owner.

"Don't make me mad, Injun," growled the mountain man. "I ain't et yet, and I just might take a bite outa you. Now git up and make us a fire. An if you try anything, I'll blow your head clean off."

Red Eagle stood slowly. As he did, his hand slid automatically to his knife. The big man grinned as he noted the surprise on Red Eagle's face.

"It's a dandy," he tittered, his pearl eyes glinting with amusement. "I ain't seen one like it in quite a spell. You know, a body ought to take better care of hisself than to let something as purty as that get lost. You slept so long an' hard, guess you didn't notice you dropped it. Right over there."

Red Eagle burned with anger, realizing the man had had his hands all over him. *What else had he taken?*

"You lookin' for your poke?" quipped the trapper, pulling up the familiar medicine bag. "Is that how you dressed your wound? My woman'll be mighty pleased when I give her this little thing." He patted the bag as it hung from his belt, nearly hidden by his enormous belly. "Now, enough small talk. I ain't got no plans for you that cain't be altered, if you know what I mean. Now, fetch us some wood and git us a nice big fire. Then we'll eat. Then I'll decide what I'm gonna do with you."

Red Eagle clenched his fists as he considered his choices. This man was no fool and perhaps meant him no real harm, but he would tread carefully until he could catch him offguard. Moving cautiously, he collected an armful of wood and headed to the firepit. Noting the coals, Red Eagle stirred them before adding more fuel.

"Now that's more like it," hummed the burly man, hands on his belly, head cocked to one side. "I ain't had me no company for such a spell, I rather like havin' you around. We'll see if we cain't improve the situation here. You like pork, Injun? I reckon you've eaten most everything at one time or another. You're certainly no full blood. I see a white man in there somewheres. Who was your pap, anyway?"

Red Eagle turned toward the man, but his pale eyes were as flat and unreadable as two stones. He wondered if the man was a friend or enemy?

"Caine McCullough."

"You tellin' the truth?" came the reply. "I knowed him! A good man. Didn't know he died til just last spring. A cryin' shame, that. Heard he had hisself an accident. Ain't much older than me, I don't think," he mumbled. "So your mammy was that little thing, Pikuni she was. I seen her ridin' with your pap up in the mountains. She was as good with horses as she was with medicines. No wonder you carry them medicinals with you." He scratched his belly then, his eyes still following every move Red Eagle made.

The fire crackled, sending small sparks up into the pale morning sky. Blue-gray, the pre-dawn dome of space grew lighter. It wouldn't be long before the sun would rise and cast its golden light.

Red Eagle waited, his eyes on the flames, but every sense alert to the man standing less than five feet away.

"I guess I should interduce myself," he chuckled, wiping one hand over the length of his yellow beard. He squinted as he cleared his throat. "I'm Bull. Bull Lassly, but mostly Bull. That she-wolf I lives with ain't never been able to say Bill, which was my before name," he added. "I'm a bull when it comes to the squaws, though, eh, eh. They parley up to me cause they know I can give 'em what they like!" He laughed, revealing several empty places where teeth had been.

Red Eagle said nothing, letting the man enjoy his own joke. But he watched him carefully, eagerly.

He had to make his move soon or it would be too late. Perhaps it already was. Perhaps Liza was beyond needing his help.

✠　✠　✠

The morning was still, the air cold against Liza's cheeks and hands. She had managed to catch a fish the evening before, which she wrapped in sack cloth.

If only she knew how to figure a better way of trapping fish.

Her father had raised himself up to his elbows and watched her intently. Liza had refused to say more than good morning to him; otherwise she might say something terrible. Even now she burned with anger, thinking of the lie he had perpetrated all her life.

She built the fire up and stirred the last of the bear broth. It smelled horrible and she held her breath as it bubbled over the heat of her small fire. But it was the only thing she had for her father. If only they had some fresh meat or beans. Or fruit! Her mouth watered at the thought of real food.

Just then she heard her father moving. Turning, she gasped. He was on his knees.

"Don't!" she cried, running to him. She caught him as he rocked forward and together they fell to the ground.

"Ugh!" he moaned, trying to right himself.

She wriggled out of his way, pulling her skirt out from under him, then helped him lay down. "What were you doing?" she sobbed, tears filling her eyes.

"I'm sorry," he said, teeth locked together, dark eyes blazing. "I'm sorry!"

"You haven't the strength of a baby! You can't move around. You have to get well, don't you understand?" She pant-ed as she helped him lean up against the barrel back rest. "Oh, Papa, I don't mean to yell at you. But I don't know what to do! We need help. And I don't know where to go for it—"

She broke off then, her tears renewed. The fear she held at bay was overwhelming her. If she gave in to it, they would never survive.

Her father nodded, brows knitted together, mouth drawn into a frown. "Yes, yes, I know. I was trying to get up to help you. Elizabeth, don't you see I'm a worthless old fool? I can't even stand! I can't do anything but lay here, watching you. And I brought you to this, just like your mother! How could I have been so selfish, so arrogant? I had no business dragging you across this wilderness when I didn't even have the guts to tell you the truth. Dear God, what have I done? Daughter, what have I done to you?"

Liza wiped her eyes.

"I've got to get you out of here," he said, half aloud. "If it's the last thing I do, I swear I'll get you out of here." He reached out with his trembling hands, touching her cheeks. "You are all I have left. All that I have of your mother, all that I have in the world."

It was almost more than she could bear. She closed her own fingers around his. "Yes, we will get out of here, Father. We'll go back to St. Louis—or somewhere," she added quickly. "Anywhere—"

He didn't answer. Exhausted, he fell back and closed his eyes. Liza studied him, noting the lines that creased his cheeks and eyes and the ghostly pallor that clung to his features.

If they didn't get help soon, it would be too late.

CHAPTER 10

CRYING WIND STOOD AT THE DOOR OF HIS LODGE shouting his invitations. One by one the men came. Each sat around the host according to his standing in the tribe; first, Red Quiver, the sun priest, then warriors of higher rank and others.

After all were seated, Crying Wind's wives placed dishes of food before them while he cut up tobacco. The guests ate slowly. There was boiled meat, berry pemmican and stewed berries, as well as berry soup.

Finally, Crying Wind spoke. Others spoke, too, each in his turn sharing past victories in battle or thrilling escapes while riding for buffalo. After awhile the talk turned to visions, quests, and dreams; Red Quiver shared the dream he'd had during the night.

"We were moving along the edge of Big River when it grew dark. As the sun set, a raven, black against the dim sky, flew toward us from the east. He circled three times, then flew back to the eastern foothills. When he returned, he circled three more times. We watched him closely. This time he flew north. We waited and watched until the night was black but the raven did not return."

The men seated nearest the sun priest looked around the circle. Closing his eyes, Red Quiver continued. "My vision is a good sign. The Above Ones have favored us. The raven came to give us their message."

"Yes!" cried Running Antelope, a younger warrior seated across from Red Quiver. His eyes shimmered in the halo of light encircling them. "The raven is the wisest of birds, a true friend of Pikuni warriors."

Others nodded in agreement. Then Red Quiver spoke

again. "It does not free us from being cautious now that we have left the Sweet Grass Hills. But our journey will be a good one and if Earth Maker gives us plenty of buffalo, we will have a good winter in the valley along Bear River. Our women and children will grow fat."

Several men grunted and smiled, turning to one another.

Crying Wind spoke last. "Your vision is a powerful one, Red Quiver."

Red Quiver nodded sagely, his gray-black hair falling around his wrinkled face. "The signs are good."

The men returned to their food, their voices soft and pleasant. When all his guests had finished eating, Crying Wind picked up a stone bowl and dropped the chopped leaves of tobacco into it. He handed the bowl with its long stem to Red Quiver.

Because he was the sun priest, Red Quiver touched a burning stick to the tobacco mixture, blew a whiff of smoke to the sky, and spoke several words of prayer. He blew another puff of smoke to the ground, repeating the prayer. He inhaled deeply and handed the pipe to the man seated next to him in the circle. The pipe was smoked by all present, travelling east to west in accordance with the daily course of the sun.

The pipe circled three times. Then, knocking the empty bowl, Crying Wind said loudly, "Kyi! Itsinitsi!"

Immediately the men rose and left the tipi.

Crying Wind followed them out into the brisk evening air and stretched. He had always hated being closed up for long periods. His world was wide, limited only by the rugged mountains that were the backbone of the Pikuni world. His peace he found when the wind brushed his face.

At last, Crying Wind slipped back into his lodge and stretched out on his pallet. It was good that the tribe's departure this morning was blessed. As a holy man, he believed in the power of prayers and signs. He would add another prayer, too, one to the God Who Hung on the Cross, the god he had learned about while living with the whites. This god had something to offer the people, though he was unsure about those who had brought word of him.

He touched the crucifix hanging from his neck and remembered the question the old black robe had asked him, his blue eyes filled with wonder. *"Who knows the final truth?"*

Crying Wind had never forgotten that question and often considered it as he examined the tiny figure engraved on the cross. It seemed logical that the one with the most to give would give himself over to death. Any great warrior understood that sacrifice. Any great warrior was willing to die for his people and for truth.

But Crying Wind had not shared his questions or this god with others in the band. Even as a respected leader, he was not sure the people would listen. There had been too much heartache as the whites settled across the Pikuni lands, taking what did not belong to them.

Indeed, apart from matches, guns, beads, and blankets, Crying Wind believed this god was the only thing of value the white man possessed.

Now, as the Early Fall Moon approached, Crying Wind prayed that this god would also listen to the prayers of his people. They needed a good hunt, since the tribes competed, not only with each other but with the white buffalo runners, for meat and hides. Bitter feuding had erupted between neighboring tribes as they invaded each others' territories in search of the migrating buffalo herds.

But according to Red Quiver this winter would be better than last.

✠ ✠ ✠

Red Eagle and Bull ate their breakfast in silence. Careful to avoid any confrontation, Red Eagle kept his eyes on his food.

"So, where you headed to, breed?" grumbled Bull, wiping his mouth with his sleeve. Oil from the bacon slid down the long strands of his yellow beard, making it shine.

"To join my mother's people," said Red Eagle. He had no

intention of telling him about Liza and her father.

Bull's voice hardened and his small, pale eyes narrowed. "That be ole Crying Wind's band?"

Red Eagle hesitated before responding. "Yes."

Bull nodded. "Hell of a buffalo hunter," he said approvingly. "I once saw him drive his lance plum through the eye of a big, fat cow. At a dead run," he added. "I hafta admit, I ain't never been that capable."

Red Eagle glanced at the trapper without raising his eyes.

The big man continued. "Crying Wind never did me no harm. No sir, guess I gotta say that as a Injun, he's about as white as they come. He ain't like Mountain Chief. That one's as full of venom as a rattlesnake in August. When they catch him, they oughta hang him after they skin 'im. Leastwise, that's what I'll do if I cross his path."

Red Eagle kept eating, but his attention was on Bull. He wondered if the man carried more than the two knives and pistol hanging from his belt. No doubt he had taken his share of scalps over the years, for both his enormous square hands boasted one missing finger and several deep scars.

This man was no fool, even though he enjoyed playing the part. That made him dangerous.

As the trapper continued ranting about Mountain Chief, Red Eagle's thoughts returned to Liza. He had to get to her. If she was still alive she needed his help.

If only he hadn't left in the first place.

"You ain't listenin' to me, breed!" bellowed Bull. "I expect you to listen to me."

Red Eagle turned his attention back to the trapper.

"That's better," grinned Bull. "I know you talk plain enough and you understand plain enough, too."

Red Eagle concealed his growing anger. He had to get away.

Suddenly, the big man jumped to his feet. "You know, breed, I ain't had no kind of fun in a hell of a spell. I tell you what! We gonna have us a contest. See that spindle tree over there, by the water, ten yards from them others? If'n you can take the single branch off its left side, there, then I'll let you walk outa here. How's that? If'n you cain't and I do, well then, you're mine."

Red Eagle had already gotten up, his eyes searching for the limb Bull indicated. It was a small one, twisted and broken.

Bull shouted, "Speak up! Is it a contest?"

Red Eagle nodded. "Yes."

"Well, bully for you!" he chuckled. "Your pa woulda been game, too. Indeed, that's the reason I'm even considerin' such a deal. Had in mind to haul you into the fort and demand a ransom. Figured you was one of Mountain Chief's renegades. Maybe on the run."

Red Eagle let the big man finish. "I am not an outlaw and I do not follow Mountain Chief."

"That's good, cause if I had reason to doubt you, I'd just plug you with a bullet—and end the matter. But I do believe you an' I always did admire Cryin' Wind. I ought to give you a chance for his sake. His and your pappy's."

Bull Lassly ambled over to his mule and slipped his long rifle out of the scabbard. Cradling the carbine carefully in his arms, he took a wide stance and slowly raised the gun. Red Eagle followed the direction of his aim. Suddenly the trapper turned to Red Eagle. "Mebbe I'll let you fire the first shot."

Red Eagle stepped up and took the gun. Bull's voice hardened. "I'll have a bullet for you if'n you think you can wheedle your way outa this."

Ignoring his threat, Red Eagle raised the rifle slowly. It was heavy and awkward, but Red Eagle had learned to shoot all manner of guns. As a boy at the forts, the soldiers often challenged him to shooting and knife-throwing contests. He had rarely missed.

And he couldn't miss this time.

He took slow and steady aim, even as he held his breath. He drew back and fired.

The 'kaboom' shook the air around them. Bull hollered and laughed. Red Eagle let the rifle drop to his waist, narrowing his eyes as he studied the target.

83

"Hells bells," chuckled Bull. "I knowed you could do it! Well, a deal's a deal an' I ain't ever been known to renege on no deal. Not even with a Injun!"

Red Eagle moved uneasily toward the big man. *Was this a ploy or did the trapper mean what he said?* A warning voice whispered in his ear and he heeded the warning.

Bull smiled. "I tell you, I'm lettin' you go! Hell, I growl bigger than I bite, boy, don't you see that?" He laughed heartily and stretched out his hand. "Take your blade and git on outa here, afore I change my mind. You got a hell of a scalp and a fine hide but I don't relish takin' no hide off'n Caine McCullough's pup. So, foot it!"

Red Eagle hesitated for only a moment, then slipped his knife into its scabbard and glanced up at the big man. Then he was gone, moving down the foot path that wound away from the stream and trees, into the emptiness that rolled eastward.

If he was lucky, maybe he'd reach Liza by tomorrow.

✠　✠　✠

"I must build some kind of shelter," Liza announced. Their situation was growing more desperate by the day. They had few supplies and the weather was changing quickly. No one had come along since Private Scott and it was unlikely anyone would come now. Autumn was brief in the Montana territory and winter came quickly. Settlers travelled in the spring and summer not the late fall.

"We will use the wagon," she continued. "I think we can get you under it today. In the meantime, I'll gather some branches and mud."

"Splendid," her father said, trying hard to smile. Liza knew only too well he still struggled with guilt over hiding his past and shame that he couldn't move more than a few inches by himself. He had never been helpless in his life.

"I bet you never thought I could manage on my own," she said briskly, hoping to cheer him. "I was pretty useless."

He shook his head. "Never," he said. "I have dreamed all

my life of living off the land, of teaching you and your brothers how to hunt and fish. I never doubted your ability to survive," he added. "If I had, I wouldn't have brought you west. Only I didn't bargain on you having to teach me—"

Liza bit her lip. She had only meant to tease him.

Her father's next words startled her. "Elizabeth! Over there!"

Dropping a load of branches, Liza gasped. She tried to keep her heart still as she choked back a cry of fright.

A hundred yards away on the far side of the stream, sat an Indian warrior on horseback. Only it wasn't Red Eagle.

He was magnificent. The ends of his long hair waved softly in the breeze, even as the mane of his dappled horse moved.

Liza hesitated, taking another look at the stern-faced brave, then ran to her grab her mother's pistol. Trembling, she faced the enemy holding the weapon out in front of her. There were only three bullets in the gun, but perhaps he'd move on if she stood her ground and she wouldn't have to shoot. She'd often heard that an Indian, like any beast, respected strength.

She tried to conceal her fear. Holding the gun as steady as she could, she stood with her legs apart and head up, unblinking, her breath coming in short, shallow puffs.

Silence loomed like a heavy mist as the man on horseback stepped carefully through the stream bed. The horse seemed to sense the currents and sniffed at the water, keeping to the shallower depths.

Liza cautiously moved to her father's side as the Indian warrior approached, still keeping the pistol pointed on the man's chest as she crouched on one knee. Unexpectedly, her father reached up and pulled the gun out of her hands.

"Don't be a fool," he said, his face paling from the effort. "He's probably not alone. Besides, I didn't come out here to kill innocent men."

"Innocent? How do we know that?" returned Liza. "He could be part of a war party. He looks nothing like Red Eagle. Maybe he's after scalps. Ours!"

"He may be peaceful. At any rate, I came west to *live* among the Indians."

"*I* don't want to live among them! You've heard the stories. You can't want us to be taken captive. How could you?" Holding her emotions in check, she glared at her father. *Dear God, how crazy could he be?*

She eyed the gun but Ralston had already slipped it under his blanket. "Elizabeth, what has come over you?"

"I can't believe you'd sacrifice us like this. I can't believe you'd turn your daughter over to a heathen!" She glanced over at the warrior; his eyes were bright and his expression hard. But her father had raised his right arm and was waving to him. "Father, no! What are you doing?"

"What else is there, Elizabeth? We have nothing left, and I do not expect the United States Cavalry to come for us; there is no one to report our absence. Lieutenant Cole made it clear he could not ensure our safety if we travelled without escort. And your friend Red Eagle is gone."

Liza crossed her arms and glared at the Indian brave swinging down from his horse. She pursed her lips to stifle her fear.

✠ ✠ ✠

Running Antelope approached the girl cautiously. His horse whinnied as if he, too, sensed a snare.

He could see the man was weak and disabled, though the girl was healthy. She was also angry and, therefore, dangerous.

Two long, dark braids hung down to her breasts, which swelled with each intake of air. Taller than most women in his tribe, he could see her form even under the layers of garments. From this distance he could also see that she fought to control her emotions. Her slender face and her wide, round, dark eyes were steeled against him. He liked her eyes, the color of brown leaves in autumn. Sparks seemed to fly from them.

This would be one to tame, he thought idly, noting the stubborn chin and stony expression. He liked her courage.

He stopped and hesitated, pointing to the man and his blanket. Under it he knew there was a pistol. He had seen the man take it from the girl and he had seen her protest.

Running Antelope pointed again. This time the man tossed the gun aside. The girl looked as if she might go after it but the man stopped her, his voice hard and demanding.

Running Antelope pointed to his horse. He told the man he must go with him, that he would ride the horse and the girl would walk. He could not speak English, so his words were sparse and he signalled with his hands.

The man understood. So did the girl, but she was not happy. She frowned before bending over the man. Then she ran to the wagon, and Running Antelope, afraid she meant to get another weapon, drew his own rifle. He pointed it at the girl.

Immediately the man on the ground protested, but Running Antelope waited, watching the girl carefully. A woman could be as cunning as any man. Many Pikuni women were even more so.

As the girl returned, however, Running Antelope could see the tears falling from her eyes. She carried a bundle and had wrapped something around her shoulders. He pointed to the bundle with his gun and, gritting her teeth, the girl opened it carefully. He studied the contents; there was a brush, pieces of fabric and a small blanket.

He nodded his approval then directed the man to get up. The man tried to move but it was soon apparent that he couldn't. Running Antelope led his horse closer and, handing the leather reins to the girl, leaned over and helped him to his feet. He was surprised by how little the man weighed. He had seemed bigger. No doubt, the man had grown weaker and thinner because of his injury.

It was easy to swing the man onto the back of his horse. In pain, he fell to one side and the girl quickly rushed forward, placing her hands on his leg, her voice tremulous and shrill. It would be good to get the man to camp. There Red Quiver could help him.

Leading the horse, Running Antelope pressed the girl to

walk ahead of him. He did not trust her and was anxious to get back to the people. They had already broken camp earlier in the day and were headed north. If he hurried, he could rejoin them by nightfall, providing this man did not die before then.

Urging the girl to step up her pace, Running Antelope pointed to the rising foothills ahead. All the while, he kept his eyes on the sway of her hips. *Yes, she would make a good Pikuni wife*, he thought, and he wondered what her white flesh would feel like under his hands.

✠ ✠ ✠

Liza walked along, suppressing a desire to run. Only for her father's sake had she not struggled. If given the choice yet, she'd shoot the warrior and take his horse.

She kept her eyes on her father, anxious that he might fall from the horse. If he did, would the Indian simply kill him and leave him? Liza bit her lip, her mind a crazy mixture of fear and anger. She had to keep her emotions under control or it might cost them her father's life, even her own.

Occasionally, out of the corners of her eyes, she stole a glance at their captor. The man was not big but gave the impression of being large with his confident and muscular demeanor. His black hair was long, longer than hers and blacker than Red Eagle's, and it hung to his hips. She wondered if he had ever cut it. He was lean and dark and his eyes, again much darker than Red Eagle's, glinted like pieces of flint. He was dressed in breechclout, leggings, and a breastplate that rattled as he walked. There was nothing about him that didn't frighten her.

After two hours, he held up his left hand. Removing a skin flask hanging from a thin belt about his waist, he offered her father a drink.

He was too weak to respond so the warrior poured some into his palm and held it to her father's lips; he took only a sip then shook his head.

Liza rushed to his side. "Please, Papa, you need water."

"No," he whispered. "It's enough. Keep moving—"

The warrior said something then and his eyes swept over Liza, but the words seemed to come from the back of his throat for his lips hardly moved.

She colored fiercely. "All right," she mumbled, wishing she had the strength of a man. She moved forward, pulling her shawl more closely about her shoulders, but was startled by a strange, intense regard reflected in the Indian's eyes as she passed by. A new fear took hold of her.

A dozen or so painted tipis were nestled in a small draw, and as the trio crested the ridge just after nightfall, Liza looked around in desperation. Smoke trails drifted from the tops of the tipis. Women and children were busy moving about. Several people stopped to point in their direction.

Instinctively, an intense sickness swept over Liza and she wondered if she would be ill.

The warrior nudged her with the barrel of his rifle, his words, but not their meaning, impossible to understand.

She closed her eyes and stepped forward, wishing this was just a terrible dream. Perhaps she would wake up, home in her own bed, laughing at herself for having spun such a tale.

Again the warrior poked her.

"I'm moving," she said, then turned her attention to the steep bank, sliding sideways and holding her bundle up to keep from falling head first.

Reaching the bottom, she heard a shrill cry erupt in the distance and a handful of children ran towards them. The children splashed across the stream that criss-crossed in front of the tipis. One child, a girl, ran ahead of the others, her words like the trilling of a bird. But the others stopped and stared, their eyes round and dark.

Two thin, brown-haired dogs ran out next, barking and bearing their teeth. Liza pulled back, afraid they might bite, but the warrior spoke firmly and the dogs retreated. They looked hungry and she wondered if they were more coyote than dog. Liza's fingers reached for her father's.

"The Lord is with us," he whispered.

"He has abandoned us," snapped Liza hoarsely. She

squeezed his hand, her own palm sweaty as she looked from the faces of the children to those of the approaching men and women.

The blunt end of the gun once more jabbed her and Liza turned, her temper flaring. "Don't do that again!"

The warrior smiled for the first time, a wicked smile, a taunting smile. His words came in a garbled rush.

"I detest you," she snapped back, releasing her father's hand. She wished more than ever she'd shot the Indian first, then asked questions.

"Move, for God's sake," croaked her father.

Choking back another retort, she obeyed.

Within minutes, the entire tribe had encircled them. The women and children crowded in trying to get a closer look. A group of older men, sober-faced and scrawny, stood aloof, some wearing little more than a scrap of fabric and an array of necklaces and strange jewelry. The younger men wore little, too, hardly more than leggings and colorful loin cloths or buckskin shirts. Laughing, they called out to the warrior. They seemed to admire him for bringing home captives.

"They don't look to hurt us," said her father, leaning over the blanketed horn of the warrior's simple saddle.

"I don't trust any of them," she snapped.

A hush fell over the small throng as an elderly man stepped forward. He wore a fringed buckskin shirt that hung several inches past his waist. It was painted and intricately beaded; several tufts of hair hung from the seams. His own hair was drawn up, brass bangles hanging from the knot. He wore earrings and several bone and bead necklaces.

"Welcome," he said.

Liza jumped. She had not expected him to speak such perfect English. Tightening her hold on her bundle, she nodded.

"Your father?" he asked, pointing.

"Yes," said Liza. "And he's in serious need of help," she added, biting her lip.

His broad-carved face twisted in deep concern. He

spoke quietly to two men on either side of him. They rushed forward and helped her father down. Liza stepped back, still frightened but relieved the old Indian had responded.

Her father's eyes opened slowly as the men eased him to his feet. "We come in peace," he whispered, "in the name of God the Father."

The older man reached out with one hand. "We welcome you in peace, in the name of your god." Then he carefully slid his fingers under the V of his beaded shirt and held up a crucifix tied to a leather thong. "Is this the god of which you speak?"

Liza stared at the silver crucifix, unable to breathe. *Had this heathen stolen it from some settler? Had he pulled it off a poor man's body after torturing him?*

She glared at him, but he had turned to her father.

"Indeed," whispered her father, a smile across his pale face.

"Perhaps The God Who Hangs on the Cross has sent you to us for a purpose then," returned the old man, sliding his own hand under his elbow. "I have offered up a prayer to him just this morning."

"The Lord hears all our prayers."

Her father slumped forward then and the three men quickly slid their arms under and around him, half-carrying, half-escorting him to one of the lodges. Liza followed nervously behind, taking in their surroundings, her fingers clutching the edges of her shawl. She tried not to look into the curious faces of the men and women still crowded around them but followed her father into the dark, animal-scented tipi.

The warrior that had found them trailed behind, his own gaze never leaving the girl and her father. Frowning, he surveyed the situation. He would have to make his own desires known before many days had passed, for he had seen the admiring glances of more than one man in the crowd.

CHAPTER 11

*B*Y MORNING, THE TRIBE HAD LEARNED THAT IT WAS Red Eagle who first befriended Robert Ralston and his daughter. With Crying Wind's assistance, Liza's father explained that he was a holy man and had come in peace. He also shared how they had survived because of Liza's courage.

Crying Wind listened intently. After a time, the old warrior began to speak of the problems facing the Pikuni and the other Blackfoot tribes. He told of the army's attempts to deceive his people. A man of deep emotion, tears streamed down Crying Wind's face while he spoke.

Then Crying Wind offered to share his lodge with Ralston and Liza. Since he had no children and only two wives there was plenty of room inside the spacious tipi.

At first Liza sat apart, reluctant to speak or move outside the lodge, especially while her father slept, wrapped in a buffalo robe Running Antelope had brought the first evening.

The stern warrior came again several times, bringing food and provisions for Liza and her father. Crying Wind accepted the gifts and encouraged Liza to acknowledge them, too, but she was still afraid of the warrior and refused to speak to him. Confused by her response, Crying Wind's wives shook their heads. It was clear that Running Antelope was admired by these women, a handsome man in their eyes.

Liza's consternation grew as two days melded into four. Still her father slept, waking only for brief periods. One of Crying Wind's wives, Crow Woman, was middle-aged and had long black braids and a bright smile. Crying Wind treated her with great respect and kindness.

Crying Wind's second wife was Come Running. Liza did

not meet her until the third day as she had been confined to another, smaller lodge for reasons Liza had not yet learned. She was as timid as Crow Woman was gregarious and refused to say more than a few words. Strangely, Crying Wind seemed to disregard her most of the time, though she rushed to and fro serving him. Of course, neither woman spoke English.

On the fourth day, Liza's father was able to sit up. Crying Wind, anxious to visit with the holy man, prepared a place for him in the sunshine just outside the lodge. Liza, fearful that her father might not be strong enough to carry on a conversation, sat nearby. The women brought food and water and waited on the two men. It was plain they adored their elderly husband.

Liza had to agree the old Indian was kind and gentle. She was surprised to learn that he was Red Eagle's uncle, but it pleased her just the same. She sensed the man and his nephew were much alike, at least in temperament.

The frequent talk of Red Eagle stirred Liza more than she cared to admit. Crying Wind spoke of him with fondness and related tales of his childhood when he stayed with the people, explaining that the boy's father had, indeed, been a white man, but a well-respected one. Anxious to please and quick to learn, the boy became a favorite with everyone.

Liza tried to imagine the curious and lively young Red Eagle.

Crying Wind expressed hope that his nephew would join the tribe soon. Surely he had been on his way when he stumbled across the holy man and his daughter. The old man did not ask, however, why Red Eagle had not remained with them.

Restless on the morning of the fifth day, Liza took a walk. Crow Woman was busy preparing food, while Come Running was stitching a tunic.

Liza moved through the village cautiously but no one seemed concerned by her presence. She studied the settlement more closely, noting the individual faces of women and children. The Pikuni were a handsome and seemingly carefree people. The women laughed easily with each other, calling to each other between lodges, teasing the children and younger women as they passed by their open fires. Children ran freely, wearing little or nothing in the warm autumn sunshine. Their laughter filled the village and their running kept everyone jumping out of the way.

One group of boys and girls were playing together under the trees with miniature replicas of everyday things such as tipis, cradleboards, and horses. Liza had already noticed the children had dolls, many made of sticks with cut-off branches for arms and legs. Others were much fancier, with fully-beaded clothes and what appeared to be real hair.

Two boys looked up at her as she passed but were not concerned. One small girl smiled timidly. Liza returned the smile. *Had other white women ever come into their village? If so, were they captives or friends?*

Liza glanced back at Crying Wind and her father, still seated outside his lodge. *Was it wise for her father to trust this man? Was he what he seemed to be, or would he betray them some night as they lay sleeping?* She had heard too many stories not to be fearful.

Picking up a handful of dry leaves, she rubbed them between her fingers until there was nothing left but flakes. Studying them, Liza couldn't help but think their lives had become just as fragile and tentative.

She returned to where the children played.

Silently a small boy approached her, his hands wrapped around something. Not more than six or seven and naked from head to toe except for a thong belt wrapped around his stomach, Liza watched him, keeping her eyes averted.

The boy spoke, then opened his hands slowly. She stepped back, anticipating something dead or perhaps ugly. Instead, she took a deep breath and smiled. In his hands cowered a baby rabbit.

"How beautiful," she whispered and he grinned, nodding eagerly.

He held up the bunny. Liza reached out and stroked its satin-like fur. Its whiskers quivered as it wiggled its delicate nose.

"I've never seen anything so small," she continued, giggling softly. Then, looking into the boy's dark eyes she said, "Thank you."

Instantly the boy was gone, the rabbit with him. Liza watched him disappear into the trees, but his kindness had unnerved her. She had once thought Indians incapable of gentleness.

She turned back to the village. In the early morning light, it appeared almost like a mirage. Smoke rose from the tipis, dissipating into the pale blue sky, and the muted sound of the women and children was like a melody. Liza closed her eyes, feeling moved. This was not what she had imagined Indian life to be like.

Unexpectedly, she heard the rapid steps of someone approaching. Opening her eyes, she spotted Running Antelope. Dressed in a new tunic and leggings, he nodded as he stopped in front of her. His sharp features were made sharper by his determined stare.

Instantly she drew herself up, regarding him coldly. She saw the desire in his hard glance and trembling, she attempted to step past him, but he extended one hand as if to grab her.

"I will scream if you touch me," she said, under her breath. She could feel her cheeks grow hot.

Running Antelope spoke, his hands sweeping past her in movements she did not understand. His voice was hard and demanding, his eyes clear and dark. Whatever it was he hoped to say meant nothing to her but his gestures left no doubt that he wanted her to listen.

She spoke again. "I do not know what you are saying, but I want you to stop."

His eyes narrowed and his lips turned down into a scowl as if he'd finally understood. Frightened, she stepped back, then broke into a run.

She didn't stop until she reached Crying Wind's lodge.

"And I want you to stay away from me, too!" she screamed at her father. Without explaining herself, she dove through the tipi opening and threw herself onto her pallet.

Later her father looked in on her. "Elizabeth?"

She rolled over, her eyes swollen and red.

"Daughter, do not despair! Crying Wind intends to help us, not harm us—"

"Oh, Father, how could you bring me here?"

"Elizabeth, take courage. You have been so strong."

"Strong! I'm terrified."

"Of what? Crying Wind? The Pikuni people? Running Antelope? Has he hurt you?"

"Haven't you seen the way he watches me? He stopped me today and said something. I don't know what. But his eyes told me all I needed to know—"

"I will speak to Crying Wind. Running Antelope is a nephew to Crying Wind, just like Red Eagle."

Red Eagle.

His name was a torment to Liza which didn't make any sense. No sense whatsoever.

She turned away from her father, anxious to be alone.

If only she hadn't sent Red Eagle away. If only she'd not judged him so unfairly. But was that what really bothered her?

☩ ☩ ☩

The next day, early dawn broke through the stillness of the night. The camp crier, Lone Person, announced that the camp was to move. Women immediately dismantled their tipis and had them loaded on horse and dog-travois before Liza realized what was happening. Nothing was left unattended and nothing was discarded.

The tribe was on the move in twenty minutes.

Liza stood beside Two Dogs, the small boy who had brought her the rabbit. Undaunted by her silence, he had found several occasions to come and visit her. Once he helped her carry the paunches used for water and another time he brought her a handful of freshly-picked berries. She couldn't help but like him.

But Liza watched the procession anxiously. She did not

want to leave and move deeper into Indian territory, only her father refused to listen. He had grown intensely fond of Crying Wind and trusted him. He ignored Liza's pleading, reminding her sternly, "Why would I choose to leave when we've only just arrived, Elizabeth? Besides, we are safe with these people. Crying Wind will help us. So trust me."

Trust him, she mused. Hadn't she spent her life trusting him, while he had spent his deceiving her?

As the people fell into line, each according to rank, Liza followed Crow Woman and Come Running, who carried a small puppy Crying Wind had given her the day before. Quiet and timid, she had said little more than good morning to Liza, but cuddled the pup protectively.

Liza's father rode on a travois pulled by a bay pony whose tail was so long it brushed the ground. Liza kept her eyes on him, frequently asking how he felt. At one point, he laughed, "Daughter, I've never felt happier in my life!"

With that, she grew quiet and fell back in line.

At the head of their small group, Crying Wind rode a spotted white horse while Running Antelope was on the same dappled mare he'd ridden when he found Liza and her father. Dressed in his finest costume, several girls blushed as he rode past. One young woman watched after him longingly, her heart in her eyes.

Liza frowned at the man's obvious delight. She'd learned that he possessed one wife already, a spindly young thing as wan as a sickly child. Poor girl, thought Liza, avoiding the warrior's fleeting but frequent glances.

She marched on, her attention diverted by Two Dogs and his bunny. He had hidden it inside a leather pouch dangling from his tiny waist. She smiled at him and he smiled in return.

The procession proceeded slowly but steadily. Liza was amazed by the people's stamina, for while some women rode their husbands' finest horses, carrying their decorated shields, most walked, even the children and old people. They carried bundles in their arms and on their backs, but moved as if they carried nothing at all.

It all reminded her of a Fourth of July parade.

The only problem was that she didn't feel like celebrating.

CHAPTER 12

JUST AS THE YELLOW SUN MELTED BEHIND THE western peaks, Crying Wind signalled a halt.

He had brought them to a level, wooded area cradled by several bluffs. It was well-protected and Liza had learned that location, even for a night, was important. The Blackfoot had other enemies besides the army and it was impossible to predict when they might strike.

The women set up their lodges as quickly as they'd taken them down. Each tipi had a designated location and in less than an hour the women were tending fires in front of their decorated lodges while laughing children gathered wood or set off to explore and play. Several young men rode off, bows slung across their shoulders. Hopefully they would return with fresh meat before nightfall.

Liza assisted Crow Woman as she loosened the thongs that bound her father to his travois. Together they helped him to the willow backrest Crow Woman had made for him. He dropped his head against the frame, exhausted, face pale.

Liza brought him fresh water. He drank greedily, then closed his eyes and sighed. "Do not fret, Daughter," he said through half-closed eyes. "It is tiredness, not sickness, that makes me feel faint."

Liza straightened her shoulders and clenched her hands until her nails dug into the flesh of her palms. Caught between concern and love for her father and great, unspoken anger, she felt like a child's top, ready to spin out of control.

Indeed, her life was out of control. She had no power over the choices being made for her. As in their former life, Father had returned to making decisions for her without asking for an opinion. Accountable to no one, he did as he pleased.

But for once in her life, Liza wasn't sure she could obey him, at least not without a fight.

She squatted nearby, her attention on Crow Woman. The older woman was showing her father how to use an awl.

"The Pikuni are incredible, aren't they?" he remarked.

"Yes, they are," she said. "I can't believe how quickly they move and how far they travel in a day. Even the children. I'm exhausted. My feet hurt." She glanced down at her narrow boots and sighed. "Of course, these boots were not made for walking twenty miles a day."

"Didn't I tell you that back in St. Louis?"

"Yes, you did," she said. "But then again, when did you do anything besides 'tell me' what to do?" she snapped.

Her father fell silent. The muscles of his forearms hardened and Liza turned away. Would there be a confrontation?

What difference did it make anyway, she wondered. Even if she could leave, where would she go? It was too late to bring Mother back. It was too late to bring life back as she once knew it. It was simply too late.

Without another word, Liza jumped to her feet. "Sleep well, Father."

She wandered away from the village. No one seemed to notice and Liza was glad. She needed to be alone. To think. To rage. To cry.

Sliding her hands over the folds of her dress, she glanced down and frowned. It had long since grown ragged. No longer a rose-brown, it was simply a dirty brown. Smudges of soot and spots of blood gave it the appearance of a speckled brown egg and the sleeves, once white, were soiled and threadbare. One sleeve boasted a tear along its seam.

What a pitiful excuse of a dress, she sighed, remembering the calicos and velvets she had left behind in St. Louis. What a pitiful excuse of a woman, she added, holding up her hands in the fading light. Broken and split, her nails looked like those of a scrub woman.

✠ ✠ ✠

That night, Liza dreamed of a dark-eyed man. Restless, she rolled over and blinked back the darkness. Haunting drums and eerie voices of men floated towards her.

She glanced around the ring of sleeping figures. Crying Wind was not in the lodge. Her heart pounded as she sat up, and she lifted the edge of the tipi wall carefully. There was nothing to see, no feathered warriors or blood-red arrows, only a hazy line of clouds dancing across the silver-gray moon.

But the strange songs continued and Liza grew curious. She slipped past her father and Crow Woman into the incandescent night.

Draping a buffalo robe across her shoulders, Liza looked up at the full moon—old Night Light Crying Wind had called it. It was high, pale, and partially shrouded by clouds. Many stars were also hidden behind a stream of long, thin clouds. It was a bewitching sight and, for the first time, Liza warmed to its marvelous, wild beauty.

Moving carefully through the camp, she followed the sounds. Coming around a single row of lodges, she discovered one lodge, smaller than the others, sitting alone at a distance. Lit like a candle on the high plains, she could discern figures moving about inside. Some danced, others merely rocked, as voices rose in a strange melody accented by the somber beat of a single drum.

Liza watched, entranced. Without realizing it, the melody touched her, soothed her, and soon she was tapping her bare feet against the earth. Suddenly a second drum joined in and then another. A chorus of drums filled the night air. Liza closed her eyes and swayed. The buffalo robe slid to the ground and her hair fell across her face.

Finally, the drumming subsided and Liza flinched as if waking from a dream. She nervously searched the area. *What if the warriors spotted her?* Perhaps they would be angry if they found her here, a witness to their mystic rites. She picked up her heavy robe and wrapped it around her shoulders, still disquieted by her response to the music. She had never been one to act without thinking.

Turning quickly, she stumbled and found herself face to face with Running Antelope. Angry and surprised, he stood with his legs apart, bare chest and legs shimmering with pearls of sweat, his face painted in circles of blue and yellow. His eyes wore black rings of paint that made him look demonic.

Should she run or stand her ground? He was only inches from her and the black pools of his eyes travelled the open neckline of her unbuttoned dress. Not soon enough, Liza covered herself with the robe and tried to move away. He reached out, one long, strong hand encircling her bare wrist. She jerked back but he grabbed her other wrist, his fingers closing like a vise.

He spoke harshly. The words meant nothing, but the tone of his voice was frightening as his eyes raked her face.

"Please, let me go," she whispered, her heart still beating like a muffled drum. "You're hurting me."

His words came again, a string of harsh notes, punctuated by his stern and angry face.

Liza twisted in his hands but Running Antelope only frowned.

"I shall scream," warned Liza. "Let me go!"

She jerked again, this time bringing one knee forcefully up between Running Antelope's legs. He gasped, releasing her. She sprung away, running as fast as she could and did not stop until she dipped into Crying Wind's lodge. Burying her face in the soft fur of sleeping robes, Liza's heart continued to pound, echoing through her brain.

✠ ✠ ✠

Gray clouds were building along the northern skyline. Red Eagle studied them as he pushed himself into a trot. A covey of quail, startled by his presence, scattered across the path like marbles. Behind them scampered a rabbit. It bounded off in another direction. If he had more time, Red Eagle would devise a trap for the rabbit so that he could offer Liza and her father fresh meat.

He hurried on. In spite of his wound, he had made good

time. If only the rain did not come too soon. The clouds hovered close to the ground now, their bellies black and distended. They reminded Red Eagle of a herd of buffalo cows, ready to drop their calves.

He climbed a rise where a patch of heavy brush grew higher than his head and wondered if he should camp here for the night. The shrub would provide a shelter from the storm.

He looked at the sky and shook his head. No, he would go as far as he could. Perhaps he'd even make Liza's camp before it rained.

As he circled a wide patch of sandy soil, Red Eagle noted tracks. Left by a horse and two people on foot, they crossed the trail ahead of him.

Hunching down, he ran his index finger along the heel marks left in the dry earth. There was no doubt as to the first set of prints. Not the mark of a moccasin nor the tread of a soldier or settler, this was the unmistakable impression of a woman's tailored boot. He spread his hand over the narrow, neat print, as if some hint might have been left there, some indication as to Liza's state of mind and destination.

The second track was clearly that left by a Blackfoot warrior. Whether he was one who might hurt Liza, Red Eagle could not guess. He frowned, his gaze now turned down the long trail that led northeast. Was Red Eagle once more too late to rescue Liza from imminent danger?

And what of Liza's father? Perhaps he had also been taken captive. Or had he been left for dead?

Hesitating only a moment, Red Eagle turned his eyes toward the distant horizon. Ignoring the oncoming rain, he broke into a trot. He would find her soon, he promised himself.

If it took days or weeks, he would find Liza.

✠ ✠ ✠

Early the next morning, as the storm passed on, Crying Wind's band moved again. The wind blew in gusts and the air was wet and cold so Crying Wind called a halt midday.

Camp was set up not far from a narrow stream and as the women unpacked their lodges, the children ran off to play. After them ran several dogs, some yapping at the heels of the boys as they dashed along the water's edge. Their laughter and wild howls were carried away on the wind.

Liza sighed and turned back to her work. Crow Woman had given her a basketful of nuts to crack and grind. She would use them in fried cakes.

Crying Wind stepped up to Liza as she knelt beside her grinding stone. Nodding in the direction of the children, he said, "You go. Watch. Learn. They can teach you."

Liza glanced over at her father who had been propped up just outside the lodge opening. A large robe had been draped around him to keep away chill. He held his small, pocket bible.

He smiled. "Go, Elizabeth," he encouraged her. "Follow them. And if you take a notion, you might find some berries or wild onions to bring back to Crow Woman."

Liza set her pestle down, glancing once more at Crying Wind. "All right," she said. She gathered up the pecans into Crow Woman's nut-gathering basket and set them inside the lodge. Then, taking her own robe, she wandered down to the streambank where the grasses grew knee high or higher.

Around her, a group of young boys had found their way into the water, while some younger boys waded in and out, giggling and splashing each other. Their naked bodies glistened in the pale afternoon sun and Liza shivered, wondering how the children could bear the cooling autumn air.

She passed two girls who huddled together, their toes not far from the edge of the water. They whispered, almond eyes flashing as they watched several of the oldest boys. It seemed years ago that Liza and her friends had sat spying on boys older and devilishly daring.

Liza turned downstream, stopping long enough to break off a cattail spike. Just then she spotted Running Antelope standing on the far side of the stream. With him was another young warrior, Little Otter.

Little Otter called to her haltingly in English. "My friend wishes to speak with you!"

Liza straightened her shoulders and frowned.

Little Otter repeated his words, adding, "My friend is a brave and strong warrior. He has battled many enemies and is respected by the elders."

Again Liza frowned, this time shaking her head. She purposefully avoided Running Antelope's arrogant gaze.

The two girls, curious, watched the stern warrior, their eyes wide, mouths turned up at the corners. They clearly found him appealing.

Little Otter coninued. "My friend will speak to Crying Wind and the one called Many Words. He will speak to them before the next full moon crosses the night sky."

Liza flashed Running Antelope a searing glance. Angry now, she pivoted and ran all the way back to camp. Several women watched her stumble past their lodges, witnesses to the encounter.

Liza turned on her father. "How dare you subject me to these savages! How dare you!"

Her father opened his mouth to speak but Liza pulled the door flap aside and disappeared into Crying Wind's tipi. From inside she yelled, "You can grind the nuts! I hate them anyway!"

CHAPTER 13

RED EAGLE FINALLY REACHED CRYING WIND'S settlement three days after discovering Liza's tracks. Approaching the village, he was surprised and delighted by the familiar banners and tipis of his mother's tribe.

The camp was nestled in a coulee not far from a small creek, but under the protection of several high, jagged rocks. A tangle of brush and scrub provided a hedge-like boundary on the west side.

Red Eagle was not surprised to see a party of braves ride out to meet him carrying rifles. Seeing that it was Red Eagle, they whooped loudly, circling him and calling out his name. One brave rushed back to camp with the news.

Running Antelope was not one on horseback, but when word reached him of Red Eagle's arrival, he stepped out of his lodge to wait. Behind him stood Black Quail. Liza wondered if Running Antelope's sits-by-him-wife was as miserable as she appeared.

The entire village turned out. Children returning from the creek jumped up and down, awaiting the newcomer's arrival. Liza stood with her father, a wave of apprehension sweeping over her. Would Red Eagle be surprised to see her? Certainly, he couldn't have known she'd be here.

She saw him across the open meadow. He rode behind Little Otter but he loomed over the young brave. As the pair crossed into the camp, Red Eagle slid quickly to the ground, a smile across his face. Liza felt her pulse quicken and turned away, embarrassed. Running Antelope stared at her. He wore a hard and brittle frown.

Liza glared back.

She dismissed Running Antelope and his arrogance the moment Red Eagle came closer. She had forgotten how well-proportioned he was, how strong and commanding his presence, how handsome his face, and how deep and melodic his voice.

He did not see her right away and seemed to be looking for someone in the crowd. Liza held her breath, afraid her pounding heart could be heard by others.

Finally his eyes found hers.

✠   ✠   ✠

He had not forgotten how beautiful she was. He had not forgotten the proud way she held her head or the way she tossed her chestnut hair off her shoulders. He had not forgotten her pouting lips, full and sensual, or the swell of her breasts, the shape of her body.

He was anxious to speak to her. Was she all right? He saw her father and, thankfully, he seemed all right.

Taking a step forward, he shouldered past the people calling his name but then Crying Wind was at his side, one hand wrapped around his arm. "Come! We have been waiting for you."

Acknowledging his uncle, Red Eagle followed, relinquishing the desire to seek out Liza. He would find her later.

That instant, however, he caught sight of Running Antelope, his cousin and childhood adversary. Seeing the older warrior's hard, forbidding expression, Red Eagle sighed. *Did they have some kind of score to settle?*

Liza stepped back, trying to calm her erratic pulse. She hadn't expected such an intense or immediate reaction to Red Eagle's arrival. After all, he meant little to her. True, he had helped her father, but he had left them, gone his own way.

Baffled by her emotions, Liza crossed her arms and moved away from her father. Before she could escape, he stopped her. He was smiling and his eyes twinkled. "So, that is our Red Eagle. You didn't tell me he was handsome!"

"I hadn't noticed," returned Liza.

"No, I thought as much," her father chuckled. He hobbled over to the lodge. "Surely the young women in the tribe noticed. I suspect he will have his choice of brides before long."

Liza shrugged, as if she didn't care, but her mind fluttered in anxiety. How many of the young Pikuni women had already taken a fancy to Red Eagle? She hadn't noticed, perhaps because her own eyes had been riveted as he entered the village riding double on the back of Little Otter's horse, slipping off into the throng of cousins and friends.

"Good," she said abruptly. Let the girls fight over him.

"Yes, it would please Crying Wind if Red Eagle found a bride within the circle of his tribe. With no sons left, Red Eagle will be as a son to him. He certainly looks to be a fine man. Crying Wind has told me much about him."

Liza feigned indifference as she mumbled, "Such as?"

"Oh, stories of his mother and father and younger brother, who died of fever when he was a baby. His mother's name was White Weasel Woman. A beautiful name, don't you think? Of course, Crying Wind preferred not to speak of her, but I'm afraid I pressed him. She was his only sister and she possessed an incredible ability to heal people. No doubt Red Eagle learned something of her special gifts."

Liza took a deep breath. "No doubt," she repeated. "I'm going to take a walk," she announced suddenly.

"Take Crow Woman's gathering basket. It's always good to make yourself useful."

Nodding, Liza picked up the berry basket. She liked Crow Woman.

Winding her way down to the creek, she found a place where the rocks were flat and easy to step across. Her shoes were in desperate need of repair, so she dreaded getting them wet. A cool breeze had blown all morning and the air was crisp.

There were several older women picking berries when Liza arrived at the brambly stretch of bushes. Concealing her inner turmoil, she greeted the women in the one or two Pikuni words she had learned, then set to work. She kept her distance, not wanting to suffer the stares the women cast. It was no secret Red Eagle had befriended her and that Running Antelope found her attractive.

Suddenly Liza had to smile. Gossip was gossip, even in a Pikuni village.

It didn't take long to fill the berry basket. Finished, she sat down beside the creek, wrapping her legs under the folds of her skirt. She could still hear the women chatting and laughing behind her. It was a comforting and reassuring sound, bringing back childhood days when she would listen to her mother and her friends as they talked in the parlor and she lay on her cot beside the kitchen stove.

✠ ✠ ✠

Not until after supper that night did Liza see Red Eagle. Accompanied by another young warrior, he approached Crying Wind's lodge smiling.

Before she could greet him, however, Running Antelope arrived on horseback, dressed in his finest array of jewelry and beads, his hair wound up in a top knot. Behind him trotted a dappled mare. A cloud of dust enveloped them as he slid off his horse.

Liza was outside the lodge helping Come Running, shake out the sleeping mats. She froze when she saw Running Antelope. Crying Wind, who was sitting with her father on the far side of the tipi, stood up slowly and spoke quietly to Running Antelope, but it was the warrior's look that startled Liza. Pointing to her, his voice was stern, demanding.

Sensing the conversation was about her, Liza ran to her father. "This is all because of you!" she screamed.

Without waiting for his reply, she picked up her skirts and ran down to the creek. Splashing through the water, her dress caught on the rocks. She yanked at the fabric until it tore free, her mind all the while reeling with anger.

She clambered up onto the far bank, dragging her sodden skirts. Water poured from her shoes, but she didn't care.

She dropped to the ground and let the well-spring of fury erupt. *How humiliating! How wretched! How-*

She hadn't heard anyone approach. "Liza?"

Recognizing the voice, she dabbed at her eyes with her sleeve and sat upright. "What do you want?" She tried to swallow the tightness in her throat.

"To speak to you. I was so glad to see you here, with Crying Wind."

She turned away and took a deep breath. She had begun to shiver. From the water or her own emotions? She drew her knees to her chest and dropped her head.

It was the familiar scent of him that triggered her tears. He was on one knee, his face inches from her shoulder. "Liza?" He spoke in an odd but gentle tone.

She felt the blood rush to her face and stifled a cry. "Obviously, I'm fine," she whispered into the damp fabric of her skirt. "Willy-nilly fine. But no thanks to my father! No thanks to anyone." She sniffed as she turned her head to stare out at the stream. "I almost wish I had died back there. Then it would be over." She wiped her nose on her sleeve, keeping her eyes averted.

Red Eagle said nothing, but she heard him stand up. "I am very glad you did not die, Liza. And I am glad you are here with my mother's people. I only wish—" But Red Eagle did not finish. "I will leave you alone."

"Yes, please. I need a little time."

Without a word, Red Eagle walked away. Liza raised her eyes and watched him move with long, purposeful strides back across the stream, back to camp.

CHAPTER 14

*T*HE NEXT DAY LIZA DID NOT SEE RED EAGLE, AND ALL day she fretted. She had been undeniably rude—not her intention at all. If only he hadn't come just at that moment.

Perhaps she should explain.

"Explain what?" asked her father, hobbling over to where she sat on a reed mat, grinding more nuts for Crow Woman.

"What?" She raised her head.

"You said, 'perhaps I should explain.' Elizabeth, I know you're angry." He dropped to the ground and relaxed against his willow rest. His voice was strained; talking was still an effort.

She bit her lip. Her father knew so little about her and he couldn't seem to understand anything of the way she felt. As if he was blind. Wanting to avoid any confrontation, she turned and studied him closely. "Are you all right?"

"Yes, of course. Only tired."

"Shall I get you something?"

"No. Let me finish. You didn't give me a chance last night. After you ran off, I explained to Running Antelope and Crying Wind that you didn't mean to insult anyone, that we do things differently. Rudeness is unthinkable behavior to the Pikuni. And for some reason, Running Antelope has decided he wants to marry you. I suppose by virtue of having rescued us."

"He didn't rescue us," she snapped. "*He took us.* I didn't need rescuing."

"No, but I daresay, I did."

Liza dropped her eyes. "I know," she whispered, ashamed at her outburst. "But how could anyone think that just because he rescued a body, it gives him license to marry?"

"Apparently, for the Pikuni, it's not unusual. At any rate,

Running Antelope wants to marry you. Actually, you should consider it flattering. He could have just taken you if he'd wanted."

Her temper flared. "How could you suggest—"

"I'm not suggesting anything, Elizabeth. Just relating facts."

Liza picked up a handful of nuts and rolled them around in the palm of her hand.

"But I understand. So does Crying Wind. That's why he has offered to send you back to Fort Benton. If we can get you back there before the snow falls, you can return to St. Louis within the fortnight. Perhaps be there by Christmas. You'd like that, I'm sure."

Liza dropped the nuts, letting them fall on the flat stone at her feet. "What about you, Father? Shall I wait for you at Fort Benton?"

She dreaded his response, knowing full well what he would say.

"Elizabeth, I have no intention of returning to St. Louis. I've told you why I came here. I should have told you a long time ago. I realize that now, though it's nothing I can change. But Crying Wind has given you a chance to go back, to return to your own life. I'm sure your grandfather would be delighted to have you, and then you can begin life all over again."

Liza blinked back the grief that had been with her for so long. It was impossible to speak.

"Don't worry, Daughter. Crying Wind has said that when you are ready, that will be soon enough. He senses how miserable you are, as well. I suppose I never wanted to see it before. If only I could have been a different kind of father."

Mixed feelings surged through her. For so long, St. Louis was all she had dreamed of, returning home to her grandparents, her friends, and her life. Yet now that the offer stood, she wasn't sure she could leave.

✠ ✠ ✠

For the rest of the day, Liza moved without thinking. She helped Crow Woman gather as much wood as she could. Crying Wind had decided the people would camp here another night, there to feast and dance in celebration of Red Eagle's return.

The women worked feverishly, preparing every sort of dish they could. There were fried cakes, berry soups, tender roots, haunches of meat roasted over open fires. The younger women helped, but when everything was ready, they rushed to the creek to wash. Liza listened to their effervescent laughter, wondering how many had already cast their eyes on Red Eagle.

She refused to attend the celebration.

She also ignored her father's request to change for the evening. Crow Woman had offered one of her own deerskin dresses, but Liza mumbled something about her head hurting. Frowning, Crow Woman smacked her lips as she left Liza resting on her pallet.

In fact, she did have a headache.

As dusk settled over the village, an enormous fire was built in an open area and it snapped and crackled as the sticks and bits of driftwood children had dragged back from the shoreline were piled higher. Liza could hear the children laughing and running while the men's and women's voices rose and fell in waves.

Crow Woman came back to the tipi several times, motioning to her, but each time, Liza shook her head. Finally Crow Woman left her and didn't return. Only after she was gone did Liza slip out of the tipi to steal a glance.

It was not long before stars, like glitter, coated the black night and the singers and drummers took their places around the village fire. Liza knew the dancers would join in, too, for the Pikuni loved to sing and dance. She sat down to watch.

She listened, reminded of how the men's music had called to her, but this time, the sound drifted away. Her heart did not beat in synchrony with the drums. It seemed to skip and stop instead, and the ache that started earlier in the day seemed to swell.

She rolled onto her back, one arm across her face, trying

to imagine herself back in St. Louis. She tried to envision the dances and celebrations where she had once laughed, sung, even danced. But it was a blur and quickly vanished. Finally, dozing, she dreamed of a handsome stranger dressed in a new suit. He approached her slowly, his head bent. But when he paused to stretch out his hand her heart skidded to a halt.

It was Red Eagle.

Liza stirred.

Sitting up, she felt chilled and so slipped back into the lodge where a small fire kept the inside warm. Picking up one of Crow Woman's robes, she realized that the animal-smell was no longer offensive to her, but she still found the odd assortment of things hanging from the lodge poles strange and intimidating.

After a while, Liza's curiosity bested her, so she raised one edge of the tipi wall to watch the dancers and singers. Her father, sitting beside Crying Wind, was smiling and talking, his face more animated than it had been in ages. The amber fire-light danced across his lean face and Liza noticed he had changed clothes. Wearing a fringed tunic much like Crying Wind's, with his dark hair combed back, he almost seemed to have changed character, as well.

Red Eagle sat to her father's left. Leaning over, he, too, laughed and chatted. Liza felt her stomach roll as her father nodded enthusiastically in response to something he said.

Her eyes returned to Red Eagle's face. Though his brows were drawn over his dark eyes, a smile tipped the corners of his mouth and the mystery behind it beckoned to her irresistibly. His expression was altogether too compelling.

As she turned away, Red Eagle glanced over his shoulder. But his mouth was tight and grim now, the line of his lips drawn down as he searched her face.

She took a steadying breath. *What was he thinking?* Did he despise her after her outburst?

Just then, she saw him get to his feet. A young woman, Little Snake, approached him. She stood, waiting, a shy smile illuminating her almond eyes. In her white buckskin dress and beaded, feathered necklaces and earrings she looked beautiful.

She led Red Eagle to the ring where other dancers were moving in time to the slow beat of the drums.

Angry, Liza dropped the tipi wall.

"Let her have him!" she stammered. "He means nothing to me. Nothing."

But as she lay in the somber darkness, the fire ebbing, her mind flashed images of Red Eagle tending her father, his eyes dark and worried; cutting meat, intent on teaching her; standing in the shadows, his enigmatic smile hiding deeper feelings.

Once more, she reached for the tipi wall, lifting it slowly. Searching the ring of dancers, she didn't see him. As she looked over to where her father and Crying Wind sat, talking and eating, she realized he was not there, either.

Her heart sank.

☩　☩　☩

It was late when her father and Crying Wind returned to their tipi. As Crow Woman and Come Running removed their dresses, her father wrapped himself in his buffalo robe and turned toward the tipi wall. Liza stirred from her agonized sleep.

"Are you awake?"

"Almost," she said.

"It was a wonderful feast. I'm sorry you chose to miss it."

She bit her lip. She didn't want to admit that she was sorry she'd missed it, too.

"I'm worried about you," her father added.

"Oh, Father, there's nothing to worry about. I guess it's time to leave."

"I'm sorry to hear that. I was hoping you might change your mind."

"I was hoping you might change your mind," she returned. "St. Louis won't be the same—"

"Elizabeth—"

"I wasn't asking," she snapped, raising herself up on one

elbow. "I was only hoping! But can't you see this has been a terrible mistake? Mother is dead, buried in a strange land, away from her family. Lawrence and Evan are gone, perhaps forever. And you—" She lifted her chin and met his dark eyes. "You just expect me to go on. Leave and go on. Without you. Without a family."

A glazed look of despair crossed her father's face. "I know," he said. "I know what I've left you with is very little. I had hoped for so much more. I thought you would come to love this land like I do. Because you're as stubborn and as passionate as I. But I was wrong."

Suddenly Liza felt a wretchedness she'd never known before. Guilt pierced her stubborn pride, but she shook her head and whispered, "I guess I'm not strong enough."

"You are stronger than I," her father interrupted.

Tears spilled over her cheeks as Liza slipped back under the heavy robes that smelled of sage and herbs. She didn't dare think about anything more.

✠ ✠ ✠

Morning came early. Camp was alive as Lone Person once more called for the people to gather their belongings. Once more Liza followed the Pikuni as they moved farther north, farther from her past. She had decided to postpone her decision about leaving, if only because she could not bear to leave her father. She had almost lost him once; how could she choose to lose him forever?

She walked in a daze, placing one foot in front of the other. It was difficult to speak, so she merely kept her eyes on the trail. Her father, riding his travois, tried to converse, but she could not.

The day was chilly and dark clouds crossed the horizon. Autumn had come to the northern territory and soon winter would follow. *Would she still be here,* she wondered.

A stiff wind slowed the progress of the tribe. Even the children slowed their step, keeping their heavy capes drawn over their shoulders.

Crying Wind called for a rest halfway through the day. It was clear a storm was moving in quickly. The women unpacked their lodge poles and set up camp. This time the children were instructed to gather wood and buffalo chips-anything that would burn. The fires were built inside the lodges, the smokey air stifling as Liza helped organize the family's possessions.

Her father's willow rest was placed inside the lodge. Crow Woman clucked over him, covering him with an extra robe. Liza mused how mothers everywhere were very much the same.

Come Running had already begun to boil a small amount of pemmican. The soup would be flavored with onions and small round roots which Liza had come to like. She offered to help the young woman. Picking up an onion, she peeled it and dropped it into the kettle. Come Running smiled her thanks, then excused herself and followed Crow Woman outside.

Liza stirred the soup, her mind wandering. She had not seen Red Eagle all day and had to slip away to avoid Running Antelope several times. Obviously angry that she had refused and humiliated him in front of the tribe, his insolent stares had provoked her to silence. She only hoped he would not seek her out again.

Even now, two lodges away, she could hear the stern warrior's thundering voice, ordering Black Quail to hurry with his food. Frowning, Liza turned to her father. "Running Antelope is vile and arrogant!"

Her father spoke softly. "Liza, is this still troubling you? Running Antelope? I have already told you that no one, least of all Crying Wind, is considering his proposal! Just last night during the feast he told Running Antelope not to approach you again."

"Too bad Black Quail didn't have someone to protect her."

"Yes, the poor girl is frail. Crying Wind said that her father had promised Black Quail to Running Antelope when she was but a child. Then again, she has someone to care for and feed her. Her own mother and father are dead. And

Running Antelope is a good provider. That's an important trait in the Pikuni world."

"Umph," grunted Liza. "So Indian women are just sold or purchased, like slabs of bacon or a pound of beans?"

"Life is hard. That's why many Pikuni men have several wives. But I would never want you to marry for anything except love."

"Well, I am pleased we agree on one thing," quipped Liza, "for I wouldn't marry unless I was deeply, madly, irrevocably in love. Otherwise, life would be unbearable."

Her father smiled. "Yes, men are savages—"

"They are!" she snapped. "All men!"

"Not just heathens?"

"All men," she repeated, slapping her hands against her dress.

"But especially heathens?"

Liza only half listened to her father. A sudden movement caught her attention and she turned just in time to see that Red Eagle, not Crying Wind, stood outside the lodge opening.

She colored instantly. *How much had he heard?*

His voice held a note of impatience. "Crying Wind sent me to find you, Many Words. A council is to be held and he has asked that you come."

Her father stood up, pushing the robes off his lap. He nodded. "Of course."

Liza's eyes widened in surprise. "Many Words?"

Red Eagle turned to her, a distinct hardening in his tone. "Your father is considered to be a man of many words. Good words," he added.

She detected a hint of censure in his voice. "I didn't realize—" she said.

His steely glance seemed to accuse her of more than not understanding. She clenched her fists and turned away. "Don't forget a cape, Father, the air is brisk."

As the two men left, Liza frowned. *Why was it, that every time Red Eagle approached her, she was in a befuddled state of mind?*

122

She picked up another onion. Perhaps she should leave before winter came. Go back and begin her life again.

What life, she thought miserably, *what life*?

Dinner was eaten in silence. Crow Woman, distracted because Crying Wind and Many Words had not returned, played with her food. Come Running, always timid, ate sparingly. Liza, forlorn over her own troubled spirits, finished her soup and quickly found her way outdoors.

The wind continued to whip through the village but no rain had yet fallen. The camp, set not far from a copse of young cottonwoods, was protected only on one side. Liza moved toward the trees, an icy fear twisting around her heart.

As she left the gathering of tipis she heard her father.

"Liza," he called. "It's too cold to be out. Why aren't you inside with Come Running and Crow Woman?"

"It's stifling. I need air."

He approached her, his face etched in worry lines. "It is a worrisome time for Crying Wind, I'm afraid."

She turned. "What has happened?"

"It's what has not happened that concerns him," returned her father. "There has been no sign of buffalo."

"Buffalo? Is that all?"

Her father's brows narrowed and his tone became derisive. "Daughter, without buffalo, these people cannot survive. Buffalo is their life. It provides shelter, clothing, food, everything."

Liza paled at the seriousness of her father's words. "I had no idea—" she blurted.

"Of course not. How could you? But it is a matter of grave importance. Right now they need to be killing buffalo so they can prepare for the long, dark winter."

She shuddered. "Father, you can't stay here through winter. Your health. You're not strong enough. Please, reconsider."

"Elizabeth," he sighed. "Whatever time I have left on earth will be spent with the Pikuni. There is a great battle to be won

123

here, not just for me, but for them. Do you have any idea of the fear and sorrow these people live with? Their land is being taken by miners and settlers and the buffalo are being slaughtered. Crying Wind fears his people will soon go the way of the buffalo. I pray he is wrong. There must be some compromise that can be reached. Unfortunately, the army does little to stop settlement, in spite of the treaties signed."

"Why should it? The soldiers are here to protect Americans."

Her father frowned. "The soldiers are here to keep the peace. There is a difference."

Again, Liza bit her lip. There was so much she did not understand. "Think of the settlers murdered by Indians. Surely you don't condone that, Father!"

"Of course not. But men like Mountain Chief are no worse than the Americans who think nothing of killing Indian women or children. Mountain Chief is an outlaw, to be sure, but Crying Wind and other Pikuni leaders do not approve of him, any more than we would. Don't you see, that's exactly why I can't leave."

She drew her robe up. The wind had picked up and seemed to whip around her, slapping her face and hands with icy fingers.

"Liza, Crying Wind has told me you must decide what you plan to do. He cannot afford to lose a single brave if more time passes and the buffalo aren't spotted."

"Without you—" said Liza, but only half aloud. For though she knew the answer, she could hardly blame him now, especially after seeing him with Crying Wind, watching him struggle to repeat Crow Woman's instructions, and listening to his plea for the Pikuni.

She pressed her hand against her father's arm. "I understand, Father, more than you might think, and I'll give you my decision soon," she whispered.

He smiled. "Please don't stay out in this wind long. The rain is coming soon."

Liza nodded, then snuggled under her robe as she wandered into the grove of cottonwoods. The wind spiraled down through the limbs and amber-colored leaves spun like whirligigs before falling to the ground.

The trees arched together and many upper branches overlapped, almost shading the soft earth below. Enchanted, Liza walked to the center of the grove. She felt as if she'd entered a church and sat down on a small stump.

For some reason, she wasn't surprised when she saw Red Eagle standing in front of her, his own cape hanging over his shoulders and down to his knees. His expression was cool.

"The rain will come soon," he said flatly.

"Not soon enough," returned Liza.

Red Eagle frowned, his dark eyebrows knitted together. Liza studied the small scar that creased his bottom lip. It was the single flaw in his otherwise perfect face. "I do not understand," he said.

"It means nothing, except that it doesn't matter to me if it rains, or snows, or blows." She shaded her eyes with one hand and looked up at him. The dull ache, which had begun deep in her heart, spread quickly to every part of her body.

"I do not understand."

She shrugged. "Why should you? You are what you are, and I am what I am. What does it matter?"

There was a stilted silence then, and Liza watched the change in Red Eagle's face. The hurt and longing was reflected in his eyes as he dropped to one knee. "Because," he began.

Liza felt him shudder as he drew in a sharp breath.

"It matters," he said then. "Everything matters."

She shook her head. "You don't understand."

A small smile crept across his face. "No, I don't understand many things."

She frowned.

He said nothing more but sat, one arm against his knee, his dark eyes travelling over her. She tried to keep her thoughts still and wondered if she were more afraid of herself than of him.

As always, his expression communicated little, except that it alternately thrilled and frightened her. *What was it he was waiting for? What was it he had started to say?*

"Did the dog-faced soldier hurt you?" he asked at last.

Liza jumped. "What?"

"Did he hurt you?"

She inhaled slowly. "No, he didn't hurt me. He took everything though, all our food, our clothes, even bibles my father had brought with him. Why do you ask?"

He faltered in the silence that engulfed them. "He will never bother you again."

Liza's nerves tensed immediately. "I don't understand."

"The soldier is dead."

"Dead? You mean—" A cold knot formed in her stomach.

"I put my knife through him because I imagined him—hurting you."

"Dear God, why?"

"He would have killed me."

"But when?" Liza's heart skipped another beat as she tried to digest it all. "When did you see Private Scott?"

"Two days after I left you. On the trail. He said—he said he—"

Liza stared, wordlessly.

"He said he hurt you—badly," finished Red Eagle.

His words lodged in her brain. Hurt her, badly?

Red Eagle's dark eyes were like shadows in the graying light and the wind twisted his black hair into long spirals. "I would kill again." His gaze was steady.

She stared at him, amazed and shaken.

He seemed to await a response, but she was too stunned to speak. Leaning forward, his breath a whisper against her cheek. His sweet, leathery smell was intoxicating. *Why couldn't she talk? Why couldn't she move?*

"But, you never came back," she whispered at last. Had she somehow thought he would?

"A trapper found me. I was bleeding. When I was able to go on, you were gone. But I followed your tracks."

"You were hurt?"

"The wounds healed quickly. It was not my wounds that

126

worried me," he added.

Liza's heart hammered in her chest, even as her fingers ached to reach out and touch him. She pulled back, then watched as the corners of his mouth tipped up. Was he smiling at her, laughing at her? She blushed.

Red Eagle's smile disappeared. "Your father, Many Words, says you are to leave." There was no question in his voice.

Liza stammered, "I—I don't belong here."

"Where do you belong?"

She waited until her pulse quieted. "I don't know. I—I seem to be—lost." She sighed, eyes wet with the tears she had fought all day. "I think of going back, and then—" She shrugged. "But my father is happy here. He will not leave."

"Many Words is a good man. Crying Wind thinks much of him."

"My father thinks much of Crying Wind."

"Crying Wind says your father is a man of much medicine, a holy man. He says the people should listen to him. But I fear they will not."

"Why must they listen to my father?" Liza's eyes returned to the scar that moved with Red Eagle's words. She wondered what it would be like to touch the scar. To touch his lips.

"There is much that is coming to the Pikuni people, much that they don't understand. There are many warning signs."

"But what can my father say that will make a difference?"

"He understands the ways of those who write the treaties."

"You can understand that, too. After all, you're white."

Red Eagle nodded. "Yes, I am my father's son. But I have never lived much among the whites. I have not lived much among the Pikuni. I have lived most of my life in the mountains."

"But my father is not strong."

"He has a strong mind and heart."

Liza sighed. "Yes, he's stubborn."

Red Eagle chuckled then and Liza felt a current race

through her. The sound of his laughter was like a cool drink on a hot day.

Neither spoke for a long moment.

Finally, uncomfortable and fearing her racing heart would give her away, Liza jumped to her feet.

"I wish there were other things I understood," she said spontaneously.

Red Eagle had moved to her side and his nearness was like a draught. "Ask me," he said.

She struggled to find a question she dared to ask, for her deepest questions only she could answer.

"Well," she said, turning to face him, "why do we keep moving? Is it to find the buffalo?"

He raised his eyebrows as he considered her question, then smiled. "Yes. But after we do, we will join with other tribes until we reach our winter camp."

"Why haven't we found the buffalo?"

"Only He That Knows All can say. Red Quiver says this is to be a good year."

"You don't believe it?"

His broad shoulders heaved as he breathed his answer, "No."

She studied his dark, brooding eyes. "Why?"

"It is hard to explain. In my dreams an old woman comes to me. She tries to warn me. But I cannot understand. I cannot see what she is hiding."

"Hiding?" Liza shivered. "It sounds more like a night-mare than a dream." She clasped her arms about her chest. "I have troubling dreams, too, but when I wake up the dream is gone."

Red Eagle shook his head. "I only know what I see. What I see is not good."

The first rain drops fell then—fat drops that bounced as they hit the dry ground. Liza flinched as one landed on her nose.

Red Eagle smiled. "The rain comes soon enough?"

She giggled, dropping her eyes to the ground. "Perhaps

too soon."

Red Eagle reached out carefully, wiping the raindrop from the tip of her nose. The mere touch of his hand sent a shiver through her. "I should go now. Father—"

Red Eagle shook his head and Liza felt weak all over. Putting a large hand to her waist, he drew her to him, his breath hot against her neck. "The rain is a sign of blessing in the Pikuni world. Perhaps it blesses us."

She trembled. Another raindrop touched her face.

Gently pressing his lips to her ear, his words were like a caress. "I would never hurt you. I am not a savage."

Tears slipped down her cheeks as she dropped her head. Then she reached out to wrap her arms around him.

But he was already gone.

CHAPTER 15

*T*HAT NIGHT, AND FOR MANY NIGHTS, LIZA AWOKE TO the eerie songs and chanting of the men. Her father said it was the men calling the buffalo, asking them to pass this way.

Each day small hunting parties were sent off in several directions; though they brought back deer, antelope, and other, smaller game, no buffalo were sighted.

The women busied themselves treating the hides of the deer and antelope. At first Liza was repulsed by the job, but as the days wore on she found herself helping Crow Woman without complaining.

The work seemed to settle her troubled mind and busy her restless hands. She had not told anyone of her encounter with Red Eagle, but the memory thrilled her even as she labored. It also alarmed her more than she could admit.

Her decision to leave or not, however, was postponed because of the urgent need to find buffalo. Liza didn't admit how relieved she felt. At the same time, she worried: *would she stay all winter?*

By the end of the second week on the trail, Liza's father was well enough to ride horseback. He also walked everywhere, using a cane Red Eagle fashioned for him, visiting the older braves who could no longer ride fast or hard.

"Well, perhaps I'll be able to join the hunters soon," he announced to Liza.

She looked up from her work at the thin man who stood there. He hardly resembled her once robust, almost hulking father. His face was clean-shaven and his long hair groomed, but his cheeks lacked color and his shoulders seemed shrunken. Still he had enthusiasm and energy.

131

"Father, you're getting stronger every day."

"I feel better. Crow Woman keeps feeding me every time I open my mouth."

Liza smiled. Crow Woman doted on her father just as she doted on Red Eagle. Just as she would dote on Liza.

Liza turned back to the deer hide she was tanning. With the blade Crow Woman had given her she feverishly cut and scraped away the strips of flesh and chunks of fat. The hide had already been stretched and staked, hair side down, as Crow Woman had shown her.

Her father hobbled out past the lodge area and found a granite stone where he could sit. He leaned forward, smiling. "It feels good to be moving about so easily," he said.

"I'm glad, too." Still, she wished he were not so thin and pale.

"Liza," he said, tilting his head. "All things take time. And things do work out—"

She glanced up from her work, one hand still wrapped around her tool. She wiped the sweat from her brow. *Yes, time,* she mused. *Everything takes time—but does it work itself out? Really?*

She bit her lip.

Crow Woman, who was working on a second hide just inches away, leaned over to where she was working. Clucking her tongue, she pointed to a spot where Liza had cut the hide too deeply.

Liza apologized.

The old woman smiled as she studied the rest of Liza's handiwork. She said something Liza couldn't understand, then stood and lifted up Liza's hide.

"Come!" she said.

Obediently Liza followed Crow Woman to a long log Red Eagle had brought earlier that day. She motioned to her, repeating her favorite English word, "Come."

Liza couldn't help but smile at Crow Woman; she was a patient teacher and Liza grew fonder of her every day.

Spreading the hide, hair side up, over the log, Crow

132

Woman showed her how to remove the hair with a scraper. "Come," she said, for the third time.

Liza nodded. Though Crow Woman knew few words they were enough.

Taking the primitive tool from the old woman, Liza tried to imitate her movements, but this job was even harder than the first. Fine hairs grew up under the longer ones; who would have thought there were so many? Several times she stopped to take a breath, dissatisfied with the poor quality of her work.

The afternoon passed slowly. Finally, a cool breeze began to blow—a welcome relief as perspiration rolled down between her shoulder blades. Her back ached and she complained to Crow Woman. But the older woman would not let her rest; each time she sat back, Crow Woman nodded and said, "Come!"

Come Running was also busy tanning a hide but she did not join Crow Woman or Liza. The younger woman had continued to remain aloof, causing Liza to wonder if she disliked her. Her father had said that Come Running was shy and, as second wife and younger sister to Crow Woman, she had fewer privileges.

By evening, Liza was ready to quit. She plopped down on the ground. "That's it!" she declared.

Her father ambled over to inspect her work. "I'll be. Look at that. It's not half-bad. You may make a good Indian wife after all. I could call Running Antelope back—"

Infuriated, Liza threw her stone tool down. "That is not funny! And I'll not be staying here any longer than I have to, thank you!"

Her father reached out his hand. "Elizabeth! I was only joshing. I'm proud as punch. Don't get fired up about a little teasing. You used to have a better sense of humor."

She stood. "I guess I don't find such taunts funny."

"In the future I'll remember that."

"The future. Hmmm," she said only half-aloud, "what's that?"

Her father frowned. "The future is not ours to know. But I suspect that even if we could glean a little of it, we would not know what to do with the knowledge."

Liza shrugged. Perhaps knowing what her future held would give her a better outlook on life. But then, what was it Red Eagle had said? He had beheld a piece of the future in a dream and it terrified him.

Hopefully her future would not prove so grim.

The last of the hunting parties returned just as the women in the camp were preparing the evening meal. Many of the children had gone off to gather roots and wild greens, which were added to the evening soup. Come Running was busy roasting a chunk of venison and there were fried cakes, as well.

When Crying Wind arrived, he slipped into the lodge without speaking to his wives, and Liza's father followed him. Crow Woman took their meal into them, but her face was dark with worry when she emerged. Liza watched, hoping for some clue as to what was happening, but Crow Woman said nothing. Eventually, Crying Wind left again, his medicine bundle in one hand.

Liza, sensing the tension, stayed out of the way. Perhaps her father would explain later. She filled her own bark plate and settled down next to the fire.

"Crying Wind is worried," her father said, coming up behind her. "The buffalo still haven't come."

"Will we move tomorrow?"

"I don't know. That will be decided by Crying Wind, Red Quiver, and the others."

"It must be terrible to think that winter could come without finding the buffalo."

Nodding, her father walked away and disappeared around a corner.

"I see your father has gone to join the others."

Liza jumped when she heard Red Eagle's deep voice. "Uh, yes," she returned quietly. "He didn't say why. Will Crying Wind object?"

Red Eagle shook his head. "He invited your father earlier to sit with him."

She nodded. This friendship between Crying Wind and her father was an amazing thing. *How could two people with such different ways come to share such harmony?*

She glanced up at Red Eagle and blushed. "Please, sit down," she said.

He dropped to the ground beside her. She fumbled with her food. "Father says there is still no sign of the buffalo."

"Red Quiver says the buffalo do not hear the cry of the warriors. We will move camp again if they do not come soon."

"So when will we find them?" She nibbled at a fried cake.

"I do not know. Red Quiver says that only the Above Ones have the answer to that. But then, is not all life a mystery, except to the Creator?" whispered Red Eagle, his dark eyes on her.

Not since that night under the trees had Red Eagle come so close or spoken so earnestly to her. Liza had feared she'd offended him and she was glad he sought her out tonight. His presence was soothing.

She turned her attention to his moccasins. They were beautifully crafted. Had a woman or lover made them for him?

She dropped the fried cake back on her plate. She wasn't very hungry.

"Life is full of things we can never understand," said Red Eagle suddenly, pointing to a tree growing at the bottom of the ravine. "Do you see the wind? The Pikuni believe that wind comes from a great animal who lives in the mountains. He moves his ears backwards and forwards and the wind blows."

Liza smiled. "Do you believe that?"

"It's possible, right?" he said, returning her smile with a wink. He shrugged. "I do not know exactly what I believe. I do know that the world is changing for the Pikuni and the things they have always known are no longer true. But I was not raised with my mother's people. My mother and I only visited during the summer months when they crossed over to the Sweet Grass Hills."

"The Sweet Grass Hills?" whispered Liza. "What a lovely name. It must be a wonderful place."

Red Eagle smiled softly and his dark eyes narrowed. "It is a place of great beauty and promise. Plenty of food and sunshine. It is also a place of peace. Each year the people return to it."

135

"A little piece of heaven?" said Liza. She held her breath. What was heaven really, she wondered, her gaze drawn to Red Eagle's mouth.

Red Eagle smiled again, then drew a circle in the dirt with his fingers. The very air around them crackled as if on fire and his nearness made her senses spin.

She studied his lean, dark-skinned face. As Indian as he looked, it was hard to remember that he was half white. Perhaps he had questions about his father's world. Like her, maybe he was lost between two different worlds—

The thought startled her. Until this moment, she had never thought of her own Indianness as something real. Looking down at her hands, she wondered if it was real. Did it change anything?

Carefully she set the rough bark plate on the ground. Everything about the moment seemed to be wrapping itself around her like a blanket: her scattered thoughts, Red Eagle's voice, his smell, his very presence.

Oh, what was happening to her?

Her gaze travelled boldly up and down Red Eagle. He didn't seem to notice and she realized he'd closed his eyes. Her heart pounded erratically as her eyes found the small soft spot just below his Adam's apple. It throbbed gently and its very throbbing filled Liza with her own, deep, fluttery ache.

His eyes opened slowly then, and she cleared her throat, pretending not to have been affected. But his eyes, glittering like obsidian flakes in the long shadows of the evening, seemed to ask a question.

He said nothing as he moved near. Reaching out, he brushed the side of her face with his fingertips. A delicious tingle rushed down her spine as she moved closer. Her eyes searched his face.

Without hesitating, he slid his fingers down the side of her neck, tucking several strands of hair behind her ear. Liza trembled.

His fingers grew more possessive then, curling around her ear and dropping to her throat. She let her buffalo robe

136

slide off her shoulders, exposing her open neckline, inviting him to look, touch, caress. Slowly he moved his hand over her shoulder and down her arm.

Red Eagle pulled Liza towards him, drawing her to him as if they were moving through water. Cautiously, curiously, she pressed two fingers to his parted lips.

She had never known a man. Any kisses she'd experienced had been brief and hollow. But Red Eagle's very nearness was like a brand and she shivered all over as he stroked her face and chin and neck.

She couldn't understand the passion that drove her but she responded to him eagerly, without embarrassment. Instinctively, she moved both hands over his leather-clad chest. The feel of his muscles and his musky scent aroused her.

Liza heard her name whispered and she sighed, wondering if he could taste the desire that filled her.

He whispered something else, but it was in Blackfoot. Haunting and lyrical, she opened her own mouth to speak, to ask what he was saying, but he quickly stopped her words with his fingers. Then, before she understood what was happening, he jumped up and was gone.

CHAPTER 16

*E*ARLY IN THE MORNING THE ENTIRE CAMP WAS ON the move. But today, instead of the usual chatter and laughter, voices were hushed and children subdued.

Everyone was worried and Liza was, too.

Before putting out the last of the fires, the fire carrier took out his fire horn, a large buffalo horn with the center burned out. Into this he slipped a live coal and piece of punky material. He then plugged the horn with a stopper. The punk, Liza knew, would smoulder indefinitely, and the fire carrier would feed in more on the journey. When camp was finally set up he would light the village's fires.

Her father now rode one of Crying Wind's horses. Liza wanted him to ride the travois, afraid that if the horse stumbled or shied he would be thrown. Red Eagle rode alongside him for several miles and she was grateful that he sensed her concern.

She walked with Crow Woman as always, but today she wore a new pair of moccasins. They were made with high buckskin tops and rawhide soles and had been smoked to protect them from moisture. Surprised when Crying Wind's wife gave them to her, Liza had fondled them for many moments before slipping them on.

Crow Woman, pleased with her response, smiled and nodded. Liza glanced only a moment at the tattered, hardsoled shoes she'd worn for weeks before discarding them. The moccasins fit like a fine pair of kid gloves and she could move easily in them. A young girl, perhaps eight or nine, shyly asked for her old shoes, then paraded around in them as if they had been cut from fine cloth.

Late in the day the tribe finally halted. Liza's father was moved to a travois.

Dismounting, Red Eagle came over to Liza. "You will ride," he said. "I will walk beside your father."

She shook her head. Red Eagle's black horse was one of Crying Wind's finest. He had presented it to Red Eagle the night of the celebration. The animal was young and spirited, and Liza feared she could not ride it capably.

"Are you afraid?" asked Red Eagle, placing his open palm against the horse's neck.

Liza bristled. She was still angry that he had left her so abruptly the night before. Confused and hurt, she had spent a restless night trying to quell her emotions. He had given no explanation; indeed, he seemed more cheerful today than he had in a long time.

"What's the matter?" teased her father. "You're an able rider. You haven't lost your spark, have you?"

"Of course not." She glared at him. "Tell him I have always been a competent horsewoman."

"You tell him," he returned jovially.

"Humph!" she snapped.

There were no stirrups and the saddle was a simple frame covered with hides. Hoisting herself up, she tried to straddle the horse but fell backwards onto the ground.

Red Eagle chuckled and Liza turned on him. "This is not a proper saddle."

He helped her to her feet, then bent over. Pointing to his left shoulder, Liza stepped up and jumped easily onto the horse. The black mare was anxious to be on her way and swung her head impatiently.

Crow Woman laughed delightedly. "Come!" she cried.

Liza laughed then, too, suddenly enjoying being atop a fine horse. It whinnied and pawed nervously so she pulled on the reins until the horse was quieted. She glanced down at Red Eagle and blushed. His smile was broad and infectious, his pleasure evident in his twinkling eyes.

"Take her for a run," he said. He pointed to the handful

of adolescent boys waving to her.

She barely hesitated before putting her moccasined heels into the horse's flanks. Instantly, the mare broke into a trot.

Liza rode hard for a hundred yards before easing up, the air lifting her long braids and burning her cheeks. The moment was one of incredible freedom and she found herself reluctant to turn back to the crawling parade of travois and people. The pack of boys urged her to race back to Red Eagle and the others, but she declined. It was one thing to take the mare at a gallop, quite another to let her race unfettered.

Liza was still laughing as she returned to Red Eagle and her father. Red Eagle's nod of approval was almost as thrilling as his touch had been. She blushed and looked about awkwardly.

Suddenly, however, the horse began to stamp and shake her head nervously. Liza turned in the saddle, just in time to see two riders moving at a hard gallop.

At first she didn't recognize them, but soon she saw the dappled horse and realized that Running Antelope and Little Otter were approaching.

It was easy to see they brought good news, for they whooped loudly as they cantered up to Crying Wind. Running Antelope drew up alongside her; nodding, his gaze raked over her boldly. His eyes flashed and even his horse trembled in response to his irritability.

Liza did not waver under his steady gaze but Red Eagle moved quickly. Taking the mare's head he held it steady, his own dark eyes on Running Antelope.

Running Antelope grunted and said something to Red Eagle in Blackfoot. Red Eagle held his tongue but his face turned red with repressed anger.

The tension was muted, however, as the news of buffalo spread quickly through the band. A herd was grazing only a few miles to the east.

As if a wild prairie fire had been lit, the people set to work. The women unraveled the travois and lodges. The children scampered wildly, imitating the buffalo and the great hunters.

Jumping off the mare, Liza handed her reins to a young boy who would hobble the spare horses in a ravine nearby. She hurried to join Crow Woman and Come Running as they set up Crying Wind's painted lodge.

But it was the hunters that captured Liza's attention.

Slipping off their tunics and any ornamentation, the buffalo hunters discarded everything except their breechclouts. Frame saddles were removed from their best buffalo horses, leaving only simple pads that freed the riders from any constraints. She watched Running Antelope slip a buffalo hide around the belly of his dappled horse, cinching it down with a buckskin cloth.

Not every horse was capable of becoming a prized buffalo horse. Only those trained with precision could run down a buffalo within a mile or less. A good horse was able to move through a mass of stampeding cows and bulls while the rider communicated with just his knees.

A war bridle, or rawhide thong, was tied to the horse's lower jaw and a single rope, often fifteen to twenty feet long, was tied around its neck. The free end of the rope dragged behind the horse so that if the rider fell, he could grab hold of the rope and stop the horse instantly.

Several hunters were selecting quivers of six or seven arrows while others chose rifles. One brave shoved a handful of bullets into his mouth; Liza had heard tales of warriors who could load their rifles at full speed by spitting bullets into the barrels of their guns. She wondered if it was true.

The hunters, including Red Eagle, were ready in an amazingly short time. Crying Wind had insisted his nephew ride his buffalo horse. Mounted and ready, Red Eagle was more handsome than Liza had ever seen him. The oiled muscles of his bronzed legs and bared chest were taut as he held the nervous animal at bay; the animals were every bit as excited as the riders.

As he turned to join the rest of the hunters, Red Eagle nodded to Liza. She smiled, feeling a thrill of pleasure that he would take the time to acknowledge her. *Did he know how magnificent he looked?*

Exhilarated and animated, the hunters fell in line behind Running Antelope and Little Otter who kicked their horses savagely and galloped across the open plain. The line of hunters stretched for half a mile and several women trilled with delight as they watched their men depart.

Meanwhile, the women finished setting up camp. Then, taking up their knives they followed the dust trail left by the men. Some were mounted but most went on foot. Their elation was contagious.

Liza's father smiled. "I am glad we've finally come across the buffalo. I was beginning to fear we had brought them bad luck."

"I didn't think you believed in luck," she said.

"I don't," he said. "It's clear the good Lord shines His light upon these people."

"It almost feels like the fourth of July," she said. "Give them a few rockets and I'd think I was back in St. Louis!"

"Follow them," he broke in, pointing in the direction of the scurrying women.

"I don't know. It could get bloody."

"I'm sure it will. So what? I would, if I could," he added, almost wistfully.

She glanced at her father. He had changed so much, inside and out, that he hardly seemed the same man. His face, though lean, was less pale; his hair, long and loose, hung over his ears. Each day he grew softer, kinder. He laughed over small things, a wonderful, child-like laugh that transformed him instantly. Obviously something here had brought him peace.

It didn't take her long to catch up to the women. She held up her skirts as high as she dared, letting the air blow through her legs. She wished she could cut several inches off the heavy fabric since it dragged at her legs and slowed her down.

Crossing a rolling expanse of land, she found the women hunched down hiding below a long ridge, waiting with their knives poised. They were giddy with anticipation but held their tongues, shushing one another so that no one moved too quickly.

143

The silence persisted a long time until finally, triggered by some invisible movement among the grazing buffalo, the hunters burst into action, spurring their horses and shrieking wildly. The response was incredible and Liza jumped to her feet to watch. Come Running grinned at her, pointing and waving at the thundering herd.

Twisting this way and that like a fat, black snake, the line of buffalo wound down and around the ridge, but the snake suddenly snapped like a dry twig. Dust boiled up as animals scattered in small groups, cows bellowing, calves bawling. It was hard to discern man from beast through the heavy brown cloud. Only the sounds of the horses and buffalo, laced with the men's high-pitched cries, gave clue as to their location.

The grimy fog moved on and Liza was finally able to distinguish a few of the men's faces. She searched for Red Eagle but could not spot him. She saw Running Antelope and watched him, transfixed. At full speed, he dropped the reins of his bridle and held a gun to his cheek. Liza couldn't tell how many bullets he fired but a reddish-brown cow fell to her knees and Running Antelope swerved past her. Quickly he raced after another enraged animal as it thundered across a dry ravine. Suddenly, it, too, staggered and dropped. Running Antelope moved as if he were an extension of his animal. It was an amazing sight.

The women cheered as other hunters downed more beasts. One young warrior circled a buffalo calf. Pulling his bow back, he drove an arrow into its neck. He pivoted, his horse dropping to its haunches, then shot a second arrow into the calf's side, just behind the left shoulder. The calf bawled as it fell, a hideous cry.

Sickened by the sound, Liza turned away momentarily.

The herd finally outran the warriors, but across the earth a dozen or more animals lay, some still quivering as they suffocated or bled to death. Then the women were on their feet, their tongues trilling rapidly a high-pitched, frenzied cry.

Crow Woman, spotting Liza, called out, "Come! Come!"

Liza followed but felt weak at the sight of such death.

The moment they reached the carcasses, the women

began to strip the animals of their hides. Several braves had already removed inner organs and, bloody and steaming, ate them eagerly. Liza, still overwhelmed by the smells and sights, felt faint. Just then, Running Antelope, his hand wrapped around a piece of tissue, approached her and grinned. Blood running down his arm, he bit off an enormous chunk.

She gasped and ran away.

Before she had gone very far, she vomited.

CHAPTER 17

*F*OR MANY DAYS, THE CAMP WAS ALIVE WITH ACTIVITY. Between feasting and celebrating, everyone worked to get the meat cut and dried. Some was pounded into mash and combined with chokecherries or sarvis berries, as well as tallow, to make pemmican. Flattened into cakes, it would be saved and eaten in winter.

The hides were stretched and scraped. Some were to be left as rawhide, others worked into buckskin. Many were tanned with the fur left on for bedding and robes, while others were softened just enough for cinches, ropes or lodge skins. Some of the hides were smoked so they remained soft and pliable. These smoked ones were wrapped around a set of poles propped up like a small tipi. Various roots and barks were burned to color the skins.

The buckskin would be used for clothing, too, but more for quivers, saddlebags, moccasin soles, and parfleches.

By the end of the third week, Liza was exhausted. She was amazed by the women's ability to manufacture so much from animal hides. Crow Woman, speaking through Red Eagle, instructed Liza at every step of transforming the heavy, stinking hides into soft, pliable leather. She had already been introduced to tanning deer hides, but these hides required great energy and strength. After scraping the hides, the women had to rub them down with oily mixtures of fat and buffalo brains, first with their hands, then with smooth stones.

At first, Liza turned her nose up as Crow Woman handed her the slimy mess, but Crow Woman merely clucked her tongue and shook her finger.

Next, the hides were dried in the sun and rolled up into

large bundles. After a time, they shrank and it took great strength to restretch them. Liza spent many hours rubbing a rough-edged stone over the entire surface of one skin before Come Running showed her how to pass it back and forth through a loop of sinew that was tied to a pole.

At the end of each day Liza's muscles burned and her neck and shoulders ached. Each night she slept soundly.

One morning during the fourth week, Crow Woman woke Liza up early. "Come!" she commanded.

Frowning, she rolled out of bed. But she had learned that it was useless to argue with Crow Woman. Together they went to the river to bathe. Liza hated the early morning ritual, especially now that the air and water were biting and cold.

Today, as she stepped out of the water and up the bank, Crow Woman rushed ahead of her, stealing her shabby dress from the bush where it hung. Surprised, she laughed and hollered, "Bring me my dress!"

But Crow Woman disappeared into the brush, emerging with a bundle in her hands.

Liza, trembling all over, begged, "Please, Crow Woman, give me my dress."

Crow Woman shook her head. A smile lit her moon face as she opened the bundle. From her dark, knotted fingers hung a buckskin dress.

Liza peered up at the older woman, startled. "For me?" she asked. She glanced around, noting that several women had gathered in small clusters, fingers splayed across their mouths, trying to hold back their delight. One old crone, naked to the waist, stood near the shore nodding her gray-black head up and down. She clapped as Liza blushed.

"Come!" cried Crow Woman. "Come!" She shook the tunic out as if shaking out a blanket. Her eyes twinkled and her broad smile revealed several broken teeth.

Liza stepped up to the dress as though she were approaching an altar and reached out slowly, overwhelmed by the gift. Pulling it over her head, she felt its softness as it fell against her wet, steaming body. She looked down and was amazed.

The dress hung to her shins. The side seams had been turned out and the edges cut into fringe. Slightly yellowed from smoking, the two sides of the dress were joined by a yoke carefully stitched and detailed with shells, beads, and colored porcupine quills. The beads, sky blue and white, had been sewn with two threads simultaneously. This, she knew, required more skill and time than the simpler, looser stitches of a single thread. The porcupine quills were long and thin and had been dyed yellow. They lay in two diagonal rows that came together near the front of the yoke.

Liza stared at the quills. She had only recently learned that quillwork was a special craft, practiced only by those initiated. The Pikuni believed that the gift had been given them by Thunder and the women who worked with quills could suffer blindness or sickness due to their innate power. It was a ritual entered into at great risk.

She bit her lip as she continued to study the intricate designs. Rubbing one hand over the soft buckskin, she was amazed again by its velvety texture. The dress was beautiful, more beautiful than anything she had ever owned back in St. Louis.

The thought so startled her that she looked up, trying hard not to cry. "Thank you, Crow Woman," she murmured.

Crow Woman beamed, her smile dimpling her round flat cheeks. Her black eyes glistened and Liza realized the older woman was crying.

Slipping on her moccasins one at a time, Liza felt as if she had stepped into another place, another time. Suddenly she was removed from her old, familiar world. She glanced back at the river and the faces still turned toward her, wondering if they could see the change.

Had she been caught up in a dream? Her very footsteps were restrained and deliberate, and her body moved as if in slow motion. *Was it more than the new dress? Had she emerged from the water a different person? Had she gone through a primitive baptism, where one life replaced another?*

Crow Woman tittered and waved her hands. "Come!" she

clucked. "Come." She pointed to the village, half-bathed in the robin's blue light of early morning, where narrow ribbons of gray smoke curled up the sky. Only the sound of dogs, yapping and snarling, and occasional whinnies of the horses broke the enchanted silence.

Liza followed Crow Woman, her gaze fixed on the long fringe hanging from the edge of her new dress. It brushed her calves like fingertips while tiny cowrie shells tinkled with each step. The rhythms were soft and pleasant, reminding her of a baby's rattle.

Standing outside the lodge, Crying Wind and her father were waiting. Crying Wind nodded as Liza approached, his smile warm and approving. He turned to passersby, pointing and laughing.

But her father spoke in a subdued tone. "You look beautiful, Elizabeth. Incredibly beautiful."

Liza glanced up at him, then turned to Crying Wind. "Please tell Crow Woman how deeply touched I am by her gift. The dress is lovely."

He translated and Crow Woman nodded. Then, for the first time, Liza noticed a broad smile on Come Running's face.

Feeling awkward and shy, she mumbled, "Thank you," to her, too. And, hoping to hide her tears, she slipped into the tipi.

❊   ❊   ❊

Red Eagle also watched Liza return from the river. As she moved, her body swayed as if a gentle breeze propelled her. He smiled. Crow Woman had told him of her intended gift earlier, and in preparation of that moment, he also had a gift. He hoped it would speak to Liza's heart.

He raised his pouch, flipping open the leather flap. Sliding his hand inside, he gently removed a necklace. It filled the palm of his hand. He studied it, feeling proud. It was beautiful, a much prized ornament in the Pikuni world for the bear was an animal of powerful medicine. Normally, only warriors wore necklaces made from bear claws but Red Eagle knew Liza had earned the right to wear it. The claws were not those of the animal she had killed, but they represented the courage she showed the night the bear entered her camp. Many Words had shared the tale with him and since that time he wanted very much to honor her bravery.

He had carried these claws in his medicine bag for many years, a gift from his father. Attacked by a bear while trapping, his father had wrestled it to the ground and killed it. It took many weeks to heal from the deep cuts the bear had given him. One, across his belly, turned into a long, jagged scar. Just a boy, Red Eagle had gone back to the spot described by his father and cut off the animal's claws. His father gave them to him as a reminder of the unexpected dangers hiding in the world.

Now he wanted Liza to have them.

It would be an important moment for him. And in the eyes of the tribe, it would be an important moment for her. But first he would relate the story of her boldness and courage.

Running Antelope had also seen Liza emerge from the brush, dressed in her new buckskin dress. His gaze travelled up and down her slender form greedily. Still angry by her refusal of marriage, he watched her now. If only Crying Wind had spoken for him. After all, the girl should have been his. He had brought her to the village. Running Antelope had saved her life and her father's, and surely, they would not have survived alone.

He considered again the benefits of such a marriage: she was strong, learned quickly, and worked hard. Most of all, she could give him what Black Quail could not seem to—a child.

Adjusting the decorated vest he wore, Running Antelope turned away. Someday he would have her. If only the Above Ones would bless him.

⌘ ⌘ ⌘

Liza rolled over. Her eyes burned from the tears. She wiped the last ones away and looked up through the smoke hole opening to the bright morning sky.

Liza did not understand why she wept or why her heart

ached. The dress was beautiful. Crow Woman had been as kind as any mother or grandmother, and she knew how many hours had been spent on the garment; the old woman's love had been carefully stitched into the dress.

So was it Crow Woman's fondness that had touched her so deeply? She had certainly never expected to experience a bond with these people. They were, after all, from a different world.

Letting go of the old dress, as ragged as it was, was like throwing away the last piece of her old self; surely now, not a thread of her other life remained—nothing except her mother's ivory comb, a lap quilt, and memories.

Perhaps she was afraid she would never go home now, that she had joined in her father's decision to stay with the Pikuni.

But, no! Of course not. She shrugged aside her tears. She was free to choose her own life, and she would.

So, what was it that bothered her?

CHAPTER 18

*T*HERE WAS LAUGHTER AND FEASTING THAT NIGHT. The men had returned with more fresh meat and the women had been busy all day. The children were excited and long after the stars came out the fires burned and drums sounded while stories were told and food was shared.

Crying Wind began by telling a favorite story, the tale of how the deer lost his gall. Liza, as curious as the children, listened as the old man related the story in Blackfoot and English, just for her.

"A long time ago," he began, eyes bright, voice melodic, "a deer and antelope met on the prairie. At that time, they both had dew-claws and galls. They were both braggarts and each boasted how fast he could run. So, they challenged one another to a race, even staking their galls on the race.

"Now the race was run across the prairie. The antelope was faster and won easily, so he took the deer's gall. But the deer complained, 'You may have won, but the race was not fair. We only ran on the prairie. A second race must be run through the forest. Then we will see who is really faster.' On this race the two animals bet their dew-claws.

"The deer easily won the second race, so he took the antelope's dew-claws. That is why, to this day, the antelope has no dew-claws and the deer has no gall."

When Crying Wind finished the story, the children waited in silence, their eyes wide. They clearly loved the fable. It reminded Liza of stories her grandfather had told when she was small. Sitting on his wide, soft lap, she would listen as he spun tale after tale. His ivory-tipped pipe would click against his teeth, tap, tap, tap. Even now she remembered being as fascinated by Grandfather's pipe as by his stories.

Red Eagle, who had been standing behind Crying Wind, stepped through the crowd. Clearing his throat, he cast Liza a long look.

"The story I tell is one that happened not long ago," he said in Blackfoot.

Crying Wind smiled. "Let's hear it."

Liza wriggled uncomfortably but the children clamored for the story. Brown Dog, a small girl with a hare-lip, nestled into her father's lap. His chin rested on her head.

Red Eagle continued. His eyes were bright, his words soft as they rolled off his tongue. "It is about Liza."

Crow Woman raised her eyebrows and smiled at Liza from across the large circle. Running Antelope, who stood on the other side of the fire, moved closer while Black Quail, watching him, frowned.

"What is he saying?" she whispered to her father. He had been learning the Pikuni language and leaned forward to listen.

"Not much," he replied, "yet."

"It was late at night," began Red Eagle quietly. "She was alone, except for her father who was badly wounded and not moving. He slept like those who are not part of this world or the next; she did not know if he would live or die. And then, in the darkness, she heard a sound. She had only a pistol."

At that, many of the children frowned and several warriors nodded to one another. Liza leaned forward, wanting to interrupt, but Red Eagle smiled and rushed on. "She heard a growl and knew it was a bear."

The children's eyes widened and the men grunted.

"It came closer." Red Eagle paused and took a long, slow breath. Brown Dog eased deeper into her father's lap, drawing his arms about her. She looked over at Liza in awe.

"Liza fired once but the bear kept growling." He imitated the face of a frightened woman and the children clapped their hands to their faces. His voice rose. "She shot again, then again, and again. She fired five times, and the gun was finally empty. She was too frightened to reload but did not hear the bear anymore."

154

The children were silent, waiting to hear the end of Red Eagle's tale. He pointed to a tipi that stood fifty yards away. "In the morning when she awoke, she found the bear just that far away with four shots in his chest. Here, here, here, and here!"

All eyes turned on Liza then and she frowned, casting Red Eagle a hard look. She did not enjoy being the center of so much attention, especially when she had no idea why.

"What were you saying?" she demanded.

Crying Wind put his hand out. "He told of how you killed a bear. The killing of *kaiyo* has strong medicine."

"Oh, that?" she said. She waved a hand through the air, embarrassed by the attention. "What else could I do? But he wasn't a very big bear."

Crying Wind laughed and her father, who had been sitting quietly, spoke up. "Elizabeth saved my life by killing that bear. She did not hesitate. She was very brave."

"Father," she hushed him. "It was fear, not courage, that caused me to shoot the bear. I didn't want to be it's dinner."

Crying Wind chuckled again and shared the joke with the people. Everyone laughed and nodded their heads.

The Pikuni loved a good joke.

Red Eagle cleared his throat. "Liza," he said in English. "Ever since I heard of your bravery, I have wanted to give you something."

This time Liza did not squirm. Holding her breath, she looked into Red Eagle's dark eyes, thankful that the moonlight could hide her emotions.

He walked towards her quietly and an eerie silence fell over the gathering. Taking his time, he approached her and dropped to one knee. Then, reaching into his buckskin pouch, he lifted out an unusual necklace.

Five large claws were mounted between beautiful oblong beads that were blue, white, and yellow.

Liza's hand shook as she took the necklace. Her face flushed crimson and, if she could have, she would have run away.

Instead, she held the necklace for a long time, examining it carefully.

"You do not like it," Red Eagle whispered to her.

She raised her tear-studded eyes. "No, I like it very much. It's—it's lovely. Truly, I had forgotten all about the bear. But where did you get these claws?"

"They were a gift from my father. I was only so big. He wanted me to remember how dangerous the world can be—"

Liza swallowed the lump in her throat. "But I can't take—"

"Do not refuse my gift," he said, putting his hand out. "Please put it on,"

She nodded, afraid to look too deeply into his eyes. Crow Woman came forward, took the necklace from her fingers, but rather than placing the necklace around Liza's neck herself, handed it back to Red Eagle.

Red Eagle, smiling broadly, raised it carefully over Liza's head. Instantly, the children cheered and the women laughed.

Crying Wind laughed loudest. "From now on, we will call her Five Shots!" He repeated his words in Blackfoot and everyone clamored their agreement.

Liza shook her head. "Excuse me," she stammered, fighting her way through the crowd. "Please, I'm—I'm tired."

Several children reached out to touch her as she weaved past the fire and fled toward the lodges.

Before she could reach Crying Wind's lodge, however, Running Antelope stepped out of the darkness and stopped her. His voice was sharp as he stood squarely in her path, hands clenched at his sides. "You—Mekotsepetan?"

Liza shook her head, confused by his question. He repeated it, his angry eyes flashing, his lips curled in disgust.

"I—I don't know!" she blurted. "I don't know! Get out of my way!" She tried to push past him but he grabbed her, pulling her closer. "Get away from me!" she sobbed, yanking at her wrists.

Immediately he dropped her hands and, saying something under his breath, turned and stormed away.

She watched him, afraid of the look in his eyes, wondering whether she had been a fool to stay here after all. Then, glancing over her shoulder, she relaxed; Crying Wind stood less than six feet away. And he was holding a knife in his hand.

✠   ✠   ✠

"May I sit down, Elizabeth?"

Liza did not respond. She didn't want her father to see her swollen eyes and tear-stained face. She sat very still and did not turn around.

"Elizabeth, we need to talk. Are you so unhappy here? I had hoped everything might change for you once you got to know the people and especially after Red Eagle came. But I was wrong. It's clear now you can't go on like this. Crying Wind has agreed to send you back tomorrow. His braves can take you at least as far as Fort Shaw. They will protect you."

I don't need an armed escort for protection, she thought miserably, her hand still wrapped around the smooth, cool beads of the bear claw necklace.

"Please, Daughter, speak to me. I know I've made some terrible mistakes. God knows I have apologized over and over, have begged Him for forgiveness. But it seems I haven't succeeded in receiving yours." His voice was barely audible. "I will do this the right way, if you will let me. Crying Wind says that if you leave tomorrow, you can be at Fort Shaw within a few days. From there, I'm sure Lieutenant Cole or one of his men can get you safely back to Fort Benton. I'll send a letter explaining everything."

His voice faded away then and she was left wondering: *was this truly what she wanted? To leave her father? To leave Red Eagle?*

"Elizabeth! Are you so angry you won't speak to me?"

She sat up, wiping away her tears. "Father, don't. It's not what you think. Truly. Two or three weeks ago, I didn't know if I could ever forgive you. Even a week ago, I was angry. Sometimes I thought I would never be happy again. But I'm confused, terribly confused." Liza's lips quivered as she tried to put her tumbling feelings in perspective. "Tonight, I discovered I wasn't angry any more. Not at you. Not at the Pikuni. Not even at Running Antelope. Perhaps only at myself."

157

"I don't understand."

She shrugged. "Neither do I. But you always talk about how God answers prayers. Maybe he answered one tonight."

Her father's smile was immediate. Raising her chin he studied her face. "Praise be to Him, Liza. I feared you would hate me forever. But I will keep my promise. And Crying Wind will keep his. Tomorrow we will send you on the first part of your journey home. Home," he repeated. "I know your grandparents will be delighted to have you. They said I was crazy from the start. Perhaps they were right."

"No, Papa—"

"Don't worry. How could I have expected you to share my dreams? And how could I ask you to give up your own dreams?" He sighed. "I have prayed you would understand, because I believe this is what the Lord sent me to do. Crying Wind, the Pikuni, they need me as much as I need them, even if I can't stop the future from hurting them. Does that make sense?"

Liza nodded. She understood far better than she dared admit. And, now, to go back? What was in St. Louis that wasn't here?

She turned her face toward the tiny opening where the moonlit sky twinkled. Out of the narrow opening a lazy smoke trail wafted up into the blackness and the moon, Old Night Light, seemed to be winking at her. Taking a deep breath, she whispered, "I'm not ready to leave, not yet."

He drew her close. "I'm happier than you can imagine."

She smiled as she looked up.

In the doorway stood Crying Wind. Crow Woman was beside him and a tear shimmered in her eye.

CHAPTER 19

*T*HE WARRIORS HUNTED EVERY DAY. MANY OF THE buffalo hides would be traded to Riplinger, who ran a trading post several days' ride to the northwest. Everyone looked forward to the big man's arrival in camp; more and more Pikuni women wanted cloth and utensils, beads and trinkets.

One day, Crying Wind and Red Eagle invited Liza to accompany them on a buffalo cow hunt. Liza and Crow Woman, both on foot, followed the hunters to a wide, high ridge where they watched as the men constructed the piskin, a funnel-like pathway. Hiding in the brush or along the cutbanks, the warriors kept the animals from breaking away until they finally chased them over the edge of the precipice.

Unnerved by the animals' howls, Liza jumped to her feet and started back for the village. Her stomach churned. The death cries were even more horrific than those in the first great hunt she witnessed.

She heard a horse trotting up behind her and she glanced up at the rider.

"I will take you back to camp," said Red Eagle, pulling up alongside her.

Liza took a deep breath and nodded. "I didn't know death could be so terrible."

"The killing or the dying?" He leaned over and extended his right arm. Gripping it firmly, he swung her around onto the rump of the black mare. She clasped her arms around Red Eagle's middle, feeling him twitch as her fingers pressed against his belly.

He turned slightly, smiling. *Could he hear her heart thumping?*

They rode back to the village in silence.

When they reached Crying Wind's lodge, Red Eagle slid off first, then turned and faced her. His hands encircled her waist, and suddenly, she hoped he would kiss her. She wanted him to kiss her. She felt paralyzed as his dark gaze held hers. She waited breathlessly.

"The children are watching," he whispered, at last.

"Yes, they are." Her cheeks colored under the heat of his gaze.

Stepping out of the circle of her arms, he remounted and galloped back the way they had come.

✠　✠　✠

For several days, the women continued tanning hides and curing meat. Liza worked easily on the tasks Crow Woman assigned her; having done little physical labor back in St. Louis, she felt great satisfaction in the things she accomplished.

She also began learning a few phrases in Blackfoot, though the language was difficult. Crow Woman was pleased with her progress and the two women laughed over her mistakes.

And her father grew strong enough to assist in simple jobs. Wrapped in his buffalo robes, he used an awl and sinew to stitch together parfleches and other small items Crow Woman gave him. When he tired, he read aloud from his small pocket bible as Liza and the other women worked.

Meanwhile, Crying Wind instructed Rabbit, a man known for his artistic skill, to paint a new lodge being built for Many Words and Liza Five Shots. Rabbit painted images of her father and Liza, as well as an enormous bear, along the bottom edge.

"It's far bigger than the real one," she told her father.

He laughed, then said, "Are you sure?"

One morning, Red Eagle stopped by the new lodge. Smiling at several children who followed him, he retold the now famous tale. Liza blushed as Red Eagle raised his arms and growled, pretending to be the bear, and the children applauded when he came to the end of the story.

"You do not need to tell it over and over," she told him, as one of the children grabbed her hand. She smiled down at Red Bird, daughter of Rabbit.

"It is an honorable thing to take on such a powerful animal," he told her. "Courage is important to the Pikuni."

She blushed all over again and protested, "It wasn't courage! I was terrified. And I keep telling you, the bear wasn't so big."

"But courage is a terrifying thing, Liza Five Shots."

As he whispered her new name, Liza felt as if she had been embraced. No longer able to deny the spark that flashed between them, she held her secret desire close to her heart.

With a nod he left her, but the children followed him. *How was it*, she wondered, *that a man reared in a world she didn't understand, should be the one to touch her soul?*

✠ ✠ ✠

Mornings grew colder and several rainstorms passed through leaving the ground wet, leaves damp, and air brisk. One night, a fierce wind swept through the village, forcing Liza and her father inside. All night it howled, a haunting whine that sent chills down Liza's spine. Red Eagle's story of the great beast that caused the winter wind came to Liza's mind. Winter was coming.

Red Eagle left with the hunters for three days. When he returned, he came directly to Liza's tipi with fresh meat and a bundle of interesting objects. Her father had begun a collection of leaves, animal skins, stones, nuts, and cones. In the evenings, as the air cooled and the sky darkened, he took them out to share with Liza, reciting their Pikuni names. He wanted to learn everything he could about this new world, as quickly as possible. Red Eagle seemed just as eager to teach him.

On a morning in the middle of November, a heavy snow fell. It fell silently, the flakes settling across the high prairie like

161

autumn leaves. By midday the entire landscape was white, and the children, dressed in tall leggings, tunics, or capes, ran out to catch snowflakes.

Awed by the white-laced world, Liza stood outside her lodge with one hand extended. The flakes landed quietly, tingling as their icy wetness filled her palm. Never had St. Louis looked as perfect as this. Indeed, she had never thought winter was a season she enjoyed, but now she found herself entranced by it. There was a magic she could not describe.

It wasn't long until preparations began for the tribe's final move. This time the people would travel to the Bear River, the river the whites called the Marias. There they would join other Pikuni bands and spend the winter; when spring came, they would move again, across the Sweet Grass Hills.

On the morning of their departure, the procession moved out smoothly in spite of the falling snow. Liza spotted a curious coyote that stood atop a knoll while several gathering hawks, circling high above, seemed to watch as the snake-like line of bodies and animals passed. Crow Woman rode Crying Wind's big spotted horse and carried his decorated shield. Come Running chose a bay mare and Liza was given a young sorrel. Liza's father rode a stout buckskin.

Red Eagle rode his black mare and Liza thought he looked magnificent in his winter leggings and long cape and hood. Several times he joined them, and they rode, three abreast, in a peaceful, satisfying silence.

The next morning, Running Antelope unexpectedly rode alongside her, a bitter frown on his face. He started to speak, but then glanced over and saw Crying Wind. Without a word, he spun his painted horse around and galloped away.

Red Eagle was soon at her side. They rode comfortably for a mile until he turned and spoke. "It is said that Running Antelope still intends to make you his wife." His voice had an odd tone and she flashed him a hard look. His tense grip on the reins betrayed his placid expression.

"You're crazy."

He seemed to ignore her remark. "It is said that this time

162

he will bring Many Words *three* horses and Crying Wind *three* horses if you will marry him."

She frowned again. *"He's* crazy. I wouldn't marry him! He's—"

"A heathen and a savage?"

"No, cruel and cold. And he treats his wife terribly. I could never, uh, marry—" but she didn't finish her statement.

Red Eagle's eyes were on her, his mouth drawn up in a curious smile.

"Don't ever suggest such a thing again," she snapped, suddenly embarrassed. "Besides, whatever would we talk about, he and I?"

Red Eagle's smile vanished. "It is not for talk that he wants to make you his wife!"

Without saying a word, Liza kicked her horse into a trot.

✠ ✠ ✠

Several larger Pikuni bands were already camped along the four or five miles of the upper Bear River when Crying Wind's band arrived. Crying Wind, nodding to the familiar faces, led his own people past the broad ribbon of tipis to an area some distance away. Their spot hugged a narrow ridge and was protected by a thicket and scattered thin trees.

Alighting from his horse, Crying Wind ordered the children to help construct the village. Brush fences were to be built to keep snow out of the lodges.

Liza was relieved that they were not settling closer to the other bands. She had never seen so many Indians in one place and with the recent conflicts scourging the Montana Territory, she was afraid they may not welcome two whites.

But it did not take long for the men of Crying Wind's tribe to mingle with the other tribes. There would be much gambling by nightfall. For the men and children, winter was the time of storytelling and game-playing while the women repaired and maintained a well-equipped lodge.

Running Antelope, accompanied by Little Otter,

slowed his horse when he spotted Liza standing outside her lodge. He was dressed in his finest robes, his hair tied into a knot on his head, feathers and brass bangles dangling. He wore a quilled vest, several necklaces, and long, intricately-beaded earrings.

"Hello," he said, enunciating the English word carefully. His eyes fastened on the bear claw necklace hanging around her neck.

Instinctively she closed her hand over it and straightened her shoulders. Then she nodded and mumbled a greeting in Blackfoot before resuming her fence building. She didn't want him to see how distasteful and frightening she found his attention.

Over her shoulder she spied Running Antelope and Little Otter kicking their horses into a lope. With a loud warning to some children gathered nearby, they sped through the camp and Liza breathed a sigh of relief.

Later, when she paused to rest, her thoughts turned to Red Eagle. He was never far from her mind anymore, even if she didn't see him all day. Today she imagined what hc might look like dressed in a tailored suit. She laughed, thinking that he wouldn't like the restraining neckline or severe cut of a gentleman's cloth coat.

She also thought about his life before. He had told her nothing of his parents or childhood; Liza did not know if he still grieved over their deaths or whether he did not want to share something so private. Her father had told her Red Eagle's only brother died as a young child.

She understood his reluctance to speak of the dead. She had still not told him about her mother.

Perhaps she would ask him later.

She laughed out loud. There was so much she wanted to know.

Red Eagle watched as Running Antelope and Little Otter stopped to speak to Liza. Busy unpacking his own possessions, he looked up just as they approached her.

It was clear Liza did not appreciate Running Antelope's attention, but the fact that his cousin still pursued her worried him. Perhaps she would give in to his offers. He was a great warrior and could someday become a leader in the tribe. He had much to offer a woman.

Indeed, as boys, Running Antelope never let his younger, half-white cousin forget who was most capable.

Whenever they went hunting, Running Antelope returned with the biggest and best animals. Once, Running Antelope witnessed Red Eagle's futile attempt to kill a lame rabbit with a whole quiver of arrows. Returning to camp first, he told the story over and over, imitating Red Eagle and the poor, injured rabbit. Everyone, including Crying Wind, laughed.

Now, fully grown, Running Antelope was still a favorite among the people. Young women blushed as he walked by, hoping he might choose one as his next bride. Clearly Black Quail was fragile and useless as a wife. He needed a strong and robust woman to bear his children.

And he was not accustomed to being a loser.

Red Eagle threw his buffalo robe across his pallet, tormented with thoughts of Liza in the arms of his proud and arrogant cousin. Running Antelope would not know how to treat her. He did not appreciate her spirit or temperament. She was different, special, and someday he hoped she'd be his!

Only, was she ready to hear that from him? He had to be sure before he spoke what was in his heart.

Feeling the heat of passion rise in him, Red Eagle cursed himself. How he longed to make Liza his. Even now, he could taste the sweetness of her flesh and feel the warmth of her breath across his cheek. He remembered how she had reached out, her hands on his face, how she had moved against him, inviting him to touch her.

Only his fear of losing her had kept him from taking her, from revealing his love too soon.

�֎ ✖ ✖

Within the month, the settlement of tipis covered several miles. The largest camps included Heavy Runner's and Standing Wolf's bands. Both men were respected by Pikuni and whites alike. They were strong and wise leaders; Liza's father assured her that life would be safe and orderly.

Crying Wind spoke out often against Mountain Chief and demanded that his own young warriors resist joining forces with the renegade leader. Crying Wind had managed to maintain the peace between the army and his people for many months, and he had given his word that there would be no attacks on settlers or miners in the area. In exchange, the army promised to protect the Pikuni territory.

But Crying Wind could not speak for all the people camped along the river. He could only hope that reason would outweigh passion.

Such stirrings, however, left Liza wondering if she and her father should leave before trouble broke out. She spoke of her concerns, but he put her off, saying, "I've been too close to death to fret now. But if this is your desire, I will ask Red Eagle to take you back to Fort Shaw. From there I'm sure Lieutenant Cole will escort you to Fort Benton and book passage to St. Louis."

Liza refused. She did not want to leave her father.

She did not want to leave Red Eagle.

One evening her father returned with more news. He sat down, his face drawn. "It seems Mountain Chief and Owl Child have murdered Four Bears, a white man married to a Pikuni woman. The army is looking for them everywhere."

"Why would they murder him?" she cried.

"It seems they were out to avenge the murder of Mountain Chief's brother, who was shot down after rumors spread that Pikunis attacked a wagon train. Later, it was learned that drunken Crows attacked the wagons."

"So did the army arrest the murderers?"

Her father sighed. "No. They were white men. There was

never any attempt to arrest them. In any event, Mountain Chief and Owl Child are dangerous. Even Crying Wind says few Pikuni leaders trust them, but no one will speak against them because they are Pikuni. Unfortunately, I suspect the army isn't going to quit until they're caught."

"What if the army doesn't catch them?"

"I don't know."

"But, Father, will they kill us next? What about Red Eagle? He's part white. What if Owl Child and his men decide to take revenge again?"

"I don't know, Elizabeth. Crying Wind says not to worry, that in most Pikuni tribes half bloods and adopted whites are considered members."

"Most tribes?" snapped Liza. "What about all tribes?"

"Elizabeth, Crying Wind is a good man. I only wish the army would give him, and others like him, credit for keeping the peace. The situation could be much worse."

But in Liza's mind it couldn't get much worse. Crying Wind was a good man but he couldn't keep Mountain Chief or the others out of trouble. He couldn't protect her father or her or even Red Eagle if some renegades decided to take revenge on them.

The prospect of death at the hands of such ruthless men left her weak. She had survived one ruthless attack but she had been able to run and hide. *Where could she go now, during winter? How could any of them escape?*

Rolling onto her back, the dim light and hazy darkness of the approaching winter night filled her with a sense of dread.

She suddenly remembered Red Eagle's ominous, haunting dream. He'd told Crying Wind about it, but what did it mean? Was it a message for all the Pikuni, or just him?

✠ ✠ ✠

Early the next morning, snow began to fall again. The camp was strangely quiet as few people moved about during the gusty storm. Even the dogs were brought inside or given their own shelters, and the horses were hobbled or tethered close to the village.

The storm persisted for three days. Finally the clouds moved on, leaving the sky a brilliant blue. The snow, covering everything in sight, glistened in the sunshine. Liza emerged from her lodge, cupping her hands over her eyes so as not to be blinded by the bright light.

Her father followed her into the daylight. "Ah, this is what my poor bones have needed," he said. "Sunshine!"

"Yes," agreed Liza, drawing her cape around her shoulders. "I think I'll take a walk. Will you join me?"

"Not today. Crying Wind has asked me to accompany him to Heavy Runner's camp. He will introduce me to him today."

"I wish you wouldn't go," said Liza. She didn't add, *"What if Mountain Chief or Owl Child are there?"*

But Liza knew her father would go. She watched him pick his way carefully, lifting his knees with each step so that he wouldn't push through the snow.

She turned in the opposite direction and headed for the riverbank. She had discovered a half-hidden spot where she could disappear. Protected by a rocky outcropping and a large brush area, it even boasted a log where she could sit and dream.

As she eased down the slippery slope leading to the river, she heard a familiar voice. Turning, she smiled. "Hello!"

She bit her lip as she looked up into his dark face. His horse pawed at the fresh snow, tossing its head as he reined it around. He looked magnificent.

Red Eagle slid off the mare and stood two feet from her. "I went to your lodge to retrieve your father, but he has already gone."

"Yes, he and Crying Wind are to visit Heavy Runner today."

"And where are you going?" he asked, leading his horse through the snow. The horse whinnied softly.

Liza took a deep breath, only too aware of Red Eagle's nearness. His wide, dark eyes drew even the last bit of strength from her. "For a walk," she said at last.

He reached out and wrapped a loose strand of Liza's hair around her ear. His touch sent a shock wave through her, and she hesitated, turning her face to his.

Then it happened. He moved towards her and gathered her into his arms. The smell of leather mixed with smoke and his own manliness was intoxicating. Liza's breath came haltingly and, even through his cloak, she felt his heart beating in rhythm to her own.

His mouth was warm and gentle and she returned his kiss. He drew her closer, her body sheltered in his. Suddenly, frustrated by the layers of clothing that separated them, he unwrapped his cape and pulled her inside. She slipped her arms about his neck and buried her hands in his long hair. Her heart leaped as she heard him moan, his hands moving down her back and around her hips.

An explosion of desire left her weak. "Mekotsepetan." His name was like velvet.

Then his lips grazed her earlobe and moved greedily down her neck. She trembled as he brought his lips back to hers and her emotions whirled and skidded inside her, pleasure and pain rolled into one.

She didn't want to move, ever.

She felt tears burning her cheeks. Drawing back, she watched the play of emotions on his face and knew it reflected her own.

"Liza Five Shots," he said slowly. She tingled as he repeated her name, only this time it was but a whisper. "I must go," he said then. "Crying Wind said I must go with him to Heavy Runner's camp."

"Is he waiting for you now?" she asked, fumbling awkwardly with her cape.

Red Eagle nodded and pointed.

Turning, Liza gasped.

On the flat, just beyond the camp, Crying Wind, her father, and Running Antelope were mounted and waiting.

"Dear God," whispered Liza, "did they see us?"

Red Eagle touched his finger to the tip of her nose. "Oh,

169

yes," he said. "I hope so."

"Oh!" she breathed and, fighting her tears, rushed down to the river to hide.

CHAPTER 20

*D*ECEMBER WAS A DARK MONTH. IT SNOWED DAILY and Liza spent most of her days with Crow Woman and Come Running. But as snow piled up, they became more and more confined. It was the worst December anyone could remember.

Still, the women trekked to the river to bathe and the men spent hours in the sweat lodge before and after swimming in the icy water.

Crow Woman had just returned from her time of separation, those days, Liza had learned, when a woman cannot be near a man. Thankfully, Liza was not expected to follow the same tradition.

On the day Crow Woman returned, Come Running called many women together, including Liza.

She entered the lodge and Come Running greeted her with a wide smile.

Crow Woman grinned proudly. "Come! Eat!"

Liza nodded and sat down in the place that was offered her. After filling her bark plate, she looked around the circle. Everyone was happy, content, smiling. She turned to Crow Woman and asked, "Tsanistapiwats?"

The old woman patted Come Running's belly and grinned.

"A baby?" laughed Liza. She turned to Come Running. "You are with child?" She clapped her hands together. "That is wonderful. A baby! May God bless you both."

Come Running, looking keenly at her, nodded vigorously. She rubbed her tummy and said something in Blackfoot. Everyone else laughed.

That night, Liza gave her father the good news.

"Yes, he's struttin' around like a turkey gobbler in a hen pen!" he said. "I understand his only other surviving children, two daughters, are married off and live in other bands. However, Crow Woman is not past child-bearing age, as Crying Wind staunchly reminded me today."

She laughed. "Well, it will be nice to have a baby under foot. The world is always a happier place when babies are around."

Her father cleared his throat. "Elizabeth, are you saying you will be here when it's time? Likely as not, the child won't come for at least seven more months. I thought—"

She shrugged. "I'm just talking about babies in general."

But later, as she rolled up in her buffalo robes, listening to her father's snores and the popping fire, she couldn't help but wonder where she would be come spring.

✠ ✠ ✠

It was late the next day that Riplinger came to trade with several of Crying Wind's braves. Leading two pack mules, he arrived just as Liza and Crow Woman were preparing supper. He hobbled his animals and lumbered through the snow, an enormous sack on his back. This was his second trip in the last month.

Liza liked the big man. She had first met him when they were still at Fort Shaw, so when she saw him again in the village, he was surprised and she delighted. He was a jovial, kind man, in spite of his crude manners.

Sitting back on her haunches, she laughed aloud. "If you don't look like St. Nick himself," she said.

Riplinger smiled, spitting a long stream of tobacco across the white snow. "As a matter of fact, I do have somethin' for you, Miz Ralston. In the spirit of the season, it'll be a gift! I got it in trade from an old cowboy, but where the hell he got it, God only knows!"

Still laughing, Liza led him into Crying Wind's lodge. Come Running and Crow Woman immediately crowded around, anxious to see what the trader had in his bag. He spoke quickly to each of them, handing them a pouch. "Beads," he said to Liza. "All squaws love beads. But for you," he added, digging through the contents, "I have somethin' else."

She waited impatiently. She hadn't received a gift since her twentieth birthday, almost a year ago. For that austere occasion Grandfather had given her a beautiful ivory pen set and sealing wax; her parents had given her a bible and a locket. Thinking she would return sooner than later, she had placed all four items inside the drawer of her secretary stored in Grandfather Poole's home.

Riplinger interrupted her daydream as he dropped the bag to the ground. "Damn mess. I gotta always be carryin' more than I can handle," he muttered. "Ah, here it is!"

Taking out a small package wrapped in burlap and tied with a string, the trader handed it to Liza. "The moment I seen it I said, that 'Lizbeth Ralston oughta have this."

She smiled. "Don't tell me you made a special trip. And in this weather?"

"Nah," said Riplinger. "But it made it a nicer jaunt just the same."

She carefully unwrapped the package. She could tell that it was a book, but when she saw that it was a collection of poems by the finest English poets, she pressed it to her breast and sighed. "This is, without a doubt, one of the nicest gifts I have ever received. Thank you, Mr. Riplinger."

Riplinger, his mouth full of spittle, smiled. "Well, I'm pleased that's so," he replied gallantly. "You are prettier than a picture and deserve somethin' special. Now I better get going 'fore the rest of the squaws come pushin' in here. I told Long Tooth I'd be out here today. He says he's got prime hides for trade and a squaw that's ready to skin him if he don't get her some gewgaws." He grabbed his sack and threw it over his back.

Just like ole St. Nick, she thought.

Crow Woman and Come Running, still wanting to bargain, followed the trader outside but Liza, anxious to be alone with her treasure, dipped out of the lodge and ran to her own tipi.

173

For many nights she read poetry aloud to her father. One evening, while he was visiting Crying Wind, she discovered a poem by Sir Edward Dyer. Entitled "A Modest Love," it stirred her deeply.

By the time her father returned, she knew the lines by heart:
"The firmest faith is in the fewest words;
The turtles cannot sing, and yet they love;
True hearts have eyes and ears, no tongues to speak;
They hear and see, and sigh, and then they break."

✠ ✠ ✠

Rolling towards the fire, she sighed. Why did the poem bring Red Eagle to mind? Was it because his was a 'true' heart, one which spoke volumes without uttering a sound?

And yet, were their hearts, like those in the poem, doomed to break?

✠ ✠ ✠

The next afternoon, as Liza crossed the sun-baked snow, Red Eagle stepped out from the trees to meet her, a smile across his rugged, handsome face. The bright sunlight lit his features, especially his dark eyes, and the whiteness of his new buckskin shirt was as blinding as the field of snow surrounding him. Crow Woman had designed and stitched the tunic, adding a multitude of tiny stitches and colorful beads down the front.

"It's a beautiful day," she said. "I have never seen such snow. I believe it's the whitest thing I've ever seen."

Red Eagle looked out across the wide open plain and then turned to her. "Yes, beautiful."

She blushed.

He raised his eyebrows. "Where are you going?" He pointed to the brush patch ahead. "I have seen you disappear several times into this brush." He smiled. "Are you hiding?"

"No," she blushed again. "It opens up, just enough to slip

inside. I like to read and think here."

"Then I will leave you," Red Eagle said.

"No, please. It's not important."

"Thinking is important. And reading, too."

"Yes, I suppose it is. Do you read?"

Red Eagle turned his gaze to the snow-capped mountains. "My father taught me to read. But I do not read much. What do you read?"

"Oh, anything," said Liza, "but I have only this volume of poetry. Mr. Riplinger gave it to me."

He looked at the book she held out. "Poetry?"

"Poems," she whispered. She smiled at Red Eagle's look of bewilderment. "A poem is like a song."

Red Eagle nodded. "My mother sang many songs. She sang all day long."

Liza wondered what White Weasel Woman had been like. "What kinds of songs?"

"In the Pikuni world, there are songs for almost everything."

"My mother sang, too. She had a lovely voice."

"Your mother is in St. Louis?"

"No, she died. She is buried outside Fort Shaw."

"I am sorry," Red Eagle said quickly. "It is hard to remember."

"No, it's good to remember. I think about her often."

"Was she like you?"

Liza shook her head. "No, she was a quiet woman, and very well mannered!"

Red Eagle smiled. "You do not have manners?"

She stammered for a reply. "Well, yes, but not always when I should. At least that's what my father says." She turned the book over in her hand, suddenly feeling foolish.

"Hmm," he said, taking a step away. "You want to sit and think and read your poems."

Liza shook her head. "No! I mean, I'd rather walk. Would you walk with me?" She stamped her feet against the hard snow. "It's difficult to sit still. The air is so cold."

175

Red Eagle reached down and wrapped his fingers around Liza's. His touch thrilled her and she started walking so as not to reveal her dishevelled emotions.

They walked for awhile without speaking. An eagle, soaring in the distance, seemed to float in the air. In the silence, its immense wings could almost be heard as it turned and flew to the top of a tall pine tree.

"It's so peaceful here," sighed Liza. She had left her hand cupped inside Red Eagle's and the intimacy she felt made her tremble.

"Winter is a good time for the Pikuni," he said. "A time of peace and long nights. And if there is plenty of food, it is a time of celebration."

Their moccasins squeaked on the dry, packed snow. The world around them glittered like a field of diamonds, but it was Red Eagle's presence that filled Liza with contentment—unlike anything she'd ever experienced. Her very contentedness frightened her.

Everything about her feelings for Red Eagle frightened her.

He led her across a frozen pond. Slipping and sliding, Liza began to giggle. Unexpectedly, Red Eagle grabbed her hands and pulled her around in a large circle. Losing her balance, Red Eagle wrapped his arm around her waist just before they fell, laughing, to the ice.

Hearts pounding, they sat, not moving, not speaking. Liza faced Red Eagle and giggled.

"It's cold," she whispered, lips turned up in a smile.

"I'm not cold," said Red Eagle softly. Slipping his hand under her chin, he raised her face to his. "My heart is on fire, Liza Five Shots."

Frightened by the intensity of his gaze and overwhelmed by his confession, she pulled back. She had not expected him to speak about feelings when hers were so perplexing and powerful.

"Must I not talk to you of my heart?" he asked, suddenly serious. His eyes narrowed and he waited.

"It's just that—I don't know," she said, her gaze drawn to

176

his hands. "I'm so confused—"

Red Eagle got to his feet in one swift movement. Extending a hand, he helped her up. The moment was gone.

She tried to speak. "You don't understand. I want-"

"I will walk you back to your lodge," he interrupted, not looking at her.

"No."

"It's cold and getting colder."

"Red Eagle, please. I'm sorry. I—"

"It is for me to apologize. I do not have the right to say more. I have not earned the right," he added abruptly.

"No!" cried Liza, but it was too late. He was moving away, his shoulders squared, dark head bent. She took a step to follow but then stopped.

Holding back tears, Liza pressed the book of poems to her lips, her hands cold in spite of the pounding of her heart. *Didn't he understand that she wanted desperately to love him? That she was dumbfounded by her response to him?*

She wiped away the tears that filled her eyes.

But turtles can't sing.

✠   ✠   ✠

Her father was waiting by the lodge when she returned. He wore a worried expression and did not notice her tear-streaked face.

"Liza, there's trouble with the army."

"Has Mountain Chief attacked?"

"Not yet, but there are rumors a war council has been called. And Heavy Runner and Standing Wolf suspect the army is out for Indian blood."

"No!" She followed her father inside their lodge. "Where's the war council being held? Here?"

"No. But several Pikuni braves, some who trade in whiskey, have left. And Mountain Chief and Owl Child are calling for a war council. No one knows where the renegades are hiding, maybe up north in the British possessions, maybe here in the Montana territory. They have stolen more horses and guns and burned some settlements. One hunter was ambushed on Deep Creek, so the army says it must take action if it is to restore peace."

Liza's stomach rolled. "But if the army attacks, innocent people will get hurt."

"People will die."

Liza paced back and forth. "Perhaps Heavy Runner or Standing Wolf will send someone to talk with the army. Lieutenant Cole—he seemed like a reasonable man. He knows how these Indians think."

"The lieutenant has no authority and General DeTrobriand is as much a pawn as his own soldiers. It's the men higher up making these decisions. The agent at Fort Benton has already been petitioned but Crying Wind fears he isn't willing to listen."

"Oh, Father, the army has to understand that it's not all the Pikuni who have done these things. Owl Child and the others, they're the criminals, even in the eyes of their own people."

"I wish it were that simple, Elizabeth. Heavy Runner and Escape Man already travelled to the Teton agency, but no one there would listen and it's well-known that General Sherman himself considers all Indians fair game."

"How ridiculous!" she cried, throwing her book onto her sleeping pallet.

"Yes, and the army is demanding all renegades be turned over, including those accused of killing Four Bears. If not, there will be trouble. How Crying Wind or the other peace-keeping chiefs can do this, God only knows. A chief is not responsible for those who go their own way, even if he's a holy man like Crying Wind. It's not the Pikuni way."

Liza sat down, fear wrapping around her like a heavy cloak. She studied her father's worn and worried face.

"There is talk of another meeting at Fort Benton. If Crying Wind agrees, I will go. Maybe I can help resolve the situation, get them to listen."

"What?" She turned on her father, heart sinking. "You

can't be serious! You aren't fully recovered. And you have never travelled in weather like this. With the storms and snow, you'll never make it alive. Father, how could you even think of doing anything so preposterous?"

"I have to go."

"No!"

"I won't argue with you."

"But this isn't your fight. The Pikuni have their own leaders."

"Daughter, I will not turn my back on these people. They are innocent and cannot fight this battle alone any longer. How many times did I preach against slavery from the pulpit, yet I never chose to fight in the war. Well, I'm here now. Even if I still had a pulpit, I would step down. My place is with Crying Wind and his people. Elizabeth," his voice dropped almost to a whisper, "each of us has his Macedonia. Mine is here, with these people. If I die standing with them, it would be an honorable death. I couldn't wish for more. As Crying Wind says, a warrior knows that to die for his family and his people is a good death. Isn't that what Jesus preached, and finally did in His life?"

Liza stifled her tears. She had never seen such determination in her father's eyes. "So once more you are choosing to go out on a mission which could, in the end, achieve nothing. What if you die?"

"*We all die*," said her father carefully.

She moved away from him then and turned her face to the fire. The crackling flames curled around a green stick of kindling, trying to devour it. She wondered if it was an omen: would she, too, be consumed by the flames of hate burning around them?

Her father spoke, his words hanging between them. "I must do what I can, Elizabeth. Forgive me, for whatever I am or am not, for whatever you wish I was—"

"Don't, Father," she whispered, holding up her hand.

CHAPTER 21

*T*WO DAYS LATER, ON THE EVE OF THEIR DEPARTURE, Liza learned that Red Eagle would also be a member of the peace party, which now consisted of nine men, including Crying Wind, Many Words, Running Antelope, Little Otter, Long Tooth, and four other warriors from Heavy Runner's band.

When she heard the news, Liza ran to his lodge. Too shy to make her presence known, she hesitated, her left hand resting on the brush fence encircling his tipi.

Suddenly the door flap snapped open and Red Eagle emerged, his dark eyes round with surprise. He was dressed in buckskins and leggings and wore a cape made of rough buffalo fur.

He waited for her to speak, a puzzled expression on his face. They had not spoken since their dance on the ice and now, frustrated by all that she wanted to say but couldn't, Liza blushed.

She slid her hands under her buffalo cape as Red Eagle's glance swept over her boldly. She shivered, but not from the cold. "I see you're in a hurry. I just—I came—uh, to say—good-bye," she stammered. She felt like a schoolgirl as she fidgeted.

Red Eagle pulled his long gloves off and held them in one hand. "I will come back," he said.

She nodded, the tears she had been holding back tickling the corners of her eyes. "It could be a dangerous journey," she said. She glanced around the village, aware of how quiet it seemed. "At first, of course, I was angry with Father for wanting to go but I don't suppose I'm angry any more."

"Crying Wind is a wise leader," returned Red Eagle, "but I fear the army will still not listen to him or anyone."

"Perhaps they will listen to Father. He's a very forceful man. People used to come from miles around just to hear him preach. The army will have to hear him out!"

Red Eagle pushed the hood off his head. His face communicated nothing; he seemed to be deep in thought.

"I know you're in a hurry—" she began.

"Crying Wind has sent for me."

"I don't want to keep you."

Red Eagle smiled slowly and deliberately. "Come, sit. Crying Wind will wait." He pulled open the heavy flap of his lodge.

"I don't know—" she returned awkwardly.

"Are you afraid, Liza?"

She shook her head, eyes clear, voice calm. "Not of you. Never of you," she whispered.

Inside the tipi was dim, the fire but a few embers. Red Eagle squatted, dropping his gloves to the ground. He picked up a long stick and stirred the coals, glancing up at her as he did so.

Her heart skipped a beat. *What did she want to say?*

She stood awkwardly, looking down at him. Bright orange sparks danced between them, floating toward the chimney opening. Finally, her eyes grew accustomed to the dimness. "It's just that—" she murmured, then closed her mouth.

Red Eagle stood up.

Playing with the fur on her cape, she twisted it into tiny ringlets. *What had she hoped would happen?* That he would take her in his arms and kiss away her fear? She shook herself; she was the one who had pushed him away. "I wanted to say that I'm sorry for the other afternoon."

He shook his head. "You do not need to apologize. I am impatient. I did not want to wait."

"But I wanted what you wanted," she whispered.

Red Eagle shook his head. "No, I do not think you know your heart, Liza Five Shots. It is not enough to want me for what stirs you, here." He pointed to her belly, and she blushed. "I do not want you for just a day—"

Silence enveloped them. Liza felt herself breathing in and out, but it was as if she were outside of herself, watching. To hold her own fear in check, she turned away.

"I have said too much," he mumbled.

"No! Not too much. I am just confused. I suppose you are right when you say I must learn to know my heart."

"When I return," he whispered, putting his hands on her shoulders, "we will talk again. Perhaps then you will know what it is you seek."

She held her tears back but the pain in her middle caused her to sigh. Reaching around, Red Eagle drew her into the circle of his arms. His face was illuminated by the amber glow of the fire.

Slowly, with his forefinger, he traced the line of her nose down to her chin, then up to her ear. He wrapped his cape around her shoulders and she relaxed against him, closing her eyes. "I will come back to you, Liza Five Shots. I can only pray to The God Who Knows All that you will be waiting for me."

"Yes," she said, so softly she wondered if she had spoken at all. "Yes."

But he was gone, and his words were only an echo in her ears, his breath still hot on her skin.

Liza opened her eyes slowly and turned to the fire, which flickered, even as the blast of cold air from Red Eagle's leaving moved eerily through the lodge. Strangely enough, for the first time in her life, she felt a sense of belonging that had nothing to do with where she was.

She was in love and Red Eagle wanted her, not just for today, but for a lifetime.

Dear God, but what if—what if?

✠　✠　✠

As the sun sent the morning's first light across the snow, Liza said a strained good-bye to her father. Red Eagle watched from a distance.

A smile tickled the corners of his mouth as he

approached her. "Good-bye," he said, brushing a lock of hair from her face.

"Good-bye," she said. "Be careful."

He nodded. "We will return in two or three weeks."

She inhaled deeply. It sounded like a lifetime. "I will be here."

Red Eagle opened his mouth as if to speak, then closed it. Instead, he put his fingertips lightly against her lips and smiled. He turned and rejoined the party of warriors waiting on horseback.

Liza looked from her father to Red Eagle, memorizing every detail of their faces, their bodies, the way each looked sitting on their horses, poised against the blue-gray skyline. Tears would embarrass both of them, so she bit her lip and straightened her shoulders.

The small troop moved out slowly and those watching stood and waited until the last man's shadow had disappeared into the low clouds. Liza shivered as she turned away; it felt as if the men had been swallowed up by the blue-gray world.

That night she did not sleep. Wind swept through the village, howling and tearing at the stretched fabric of the buffalo lodges. Gusts whistled through her own tipi and Liza covered her head with robes to block out the hideous whine. If this were the cries of a wild animal, she decided, it must be a monstrous beast.

Well into morning the wind whipped and whirled. Liza prayed fervently for her father and Red Eagle, as well as for Running Antelope and the other men.

But as the storm raged outside, a storm of protest reeled through her mind. *If only this meeting could have waited until spring. Certainly the army would not attack in the middle of winter.* Lieutenant Cole had assured Father on their first day in the Territory that the army would never send troops without first trying other means to achieve peace.

But, as her father had pointed out, men like Lieutenant Cole and General DeTrobriand had little power in the face of terrible unrest.

The storm continued. Snow followed wind, and lasted all day and through a second night.

As the dawn of the third day broke, Liza awoke to a world drenched in white. Icicles hung from everything, even the long hairs of the horses' heavy coats. The sky was painted cornflower blue against the pearl white snow, but the people stayed close to the village most of the day. Inside her own tipi, she read from the volume of poetry and began work on a doeskin shirt. Crow Woman had showed her how to design and cut the pattern.

As she worked, she dreamed of Red Eagle. She relived the delicious shudders she had felt when he touched her.

Red Eagle.

Did it matter that they came from different worlds?

✠ ✠ ✠

Time passed painfully. Each morning and afternoon, Liza tramped through the village, her eyes on the distant horizon.

One morning Crow Woman stopped her. "They will come back," the older woman said in Blackfoot.

She nodded. Red Eagle had promised her the same thing. Still, she worried.

The next day was warmer so Liza wandered out to her place beside the river among the willows. There she sat flipping through the pages of her book, the melancholy tone of Dyer's poem haunting her.

But it was only a poem.

✠ ✠ ✠

One week turned into two. Resigned to life without Red Eagle, Liza tried to relax into the rhythm of village life. She enjoyed the familiarity she had developed with Crow Woman. They laughed together frequently, though Crow Woman sensed the state of her troubled heart.

Thankfully, she was also learning more of the Pikuni language and this made the days and evenings less lonely. She better understood the women's conversations and learned of the increasing tension between the whites and the Blackfoot, and the strained relations between the army and the tribes.

The Pikuni people themselves were divided in their loyalties. Most of Crying Wind's people did not approve of Owl Child and Mountain Chief, but others talked of following them into the mountains. Crow Woman confided to Liza that Mountain Chief may have even taken refuge in Heavy Runner's camp. If the army found him, there would be problems for everyone.

"But Heavy Runner doesn't want trouble," she said.

Crow Woman agreed. "It is a difficult thing to keep peace amongst the Pikuni as well as with the white soldiers."

That night Liza returned to her lodge, a new fear settling over her. It had been hard enough worrying about her father and Red Eagle's absence, but now she worried about the presence of this renegade leader and what might happen.

All the next day, Liza thought about the situation facing the Pikuni people. Their problems had now melded with her own, and she found herself frightened for Crow Woman, Come Running, Crying Wind, even Black Quail: what would come their way and how would it all end?

As she walked back from the river that evening, her arms full of driftwood, she noticed several young men grouped together around another man, a stranger. It had been a calm day, though a thin line of gray clouds now covered the highest peaks. The snow was dry and the frost had finally melted off the boughs of nearby trees. But there was something disturbing about the scene that sent a chill through Liza. She looked up to see if the wind had begun to blow.

All was quiet.

Then her attention was diverted by the stranger. He was dressed in furs and from his black hair tassels of animal or human hair woven with beads and brightly-colored trim were draped. He wore earrings of feathers and quills and about his neck hung a quilled and beaded necklace.

His face was unusual, lined and deeply-etched by weather and experience. But it was his glance that caught Liza by surprise. Like two shiny buttons, his black eyes narrowed as they scanned her face and a scowl creased his leathery features. She felt the heat of his disdain even after she was out of his sight.

The next day, Crow Woman reported that a warrior from one of the Blood tribes, a man called Too Fat Belly, had accompanied Mountain Chief to the Pikuni settlements. Both hoped to gather more followers and were encouraging as many young men as would listen to join their band. *Had the stranger been Mountain Chief or Too Fat Belly?* Liza shivered.

A few days later, she overheard Come Running whisper that Heavy Runner himself was growing more troubled, especially since no word of Crying Wind's arrival at Fort Benton had been received.

Crow Woman hushed her sister.

But Liza's dark fears were once more rekindled. *What if the men had never reached the fort?* Perhaps they had gotten stranded or lost. Perhaps her father had fallen ill or, worst of all, perhaps the men had been captured by another tribe. The Blackfoot had many enemies.

Liza went to bed that night sick at heart. Aware of every sound and smell, she shivered, listening to the winds blow through the camp. She jumped when an owl hooted and distant coyotes cried out in the darkness. The smoke of her cold fire burned her nostrils and brought tears to her eyes.

If only she weren't alone. If only Father had not gone. If only Red Eagle were here. *Dear God, what would she do if neither returned?*

Liza pressed her hands to her breasts as the tears continued down her cheeks.

187

CHAPTER 22

*T*HREE DAYS LATER, AS A NEW STORM BROUGHT GREAT flat flakes of snow, Crow Woman came to Liza. Her face was wrinkled with worry and grief.

Not understanding her rapid string of words, Liza could only repeat, "Tsanistapiwats?"

Crow Woman took her by the hand and led her to the painted lodge of Running Antelope; there she hesitated, a question rising in her throat. But throwing open the heavy flap, Crow Woman entered the dark space and she followed.

It was filled with smoke and the odor of herbs and other burnt offerings. As Liza's eyes adjusted to the darkness, she discovered Black Quail stretched across a buffalo robe, naked. Her skin was ashen even in the dim light. Next to her sat Little Otter's sister, Big Horse. Her face held a look of horror and unabashed fear.

Big Horse glanced up at Liza, brows knitted together. Meanwhile, Crow Woman turned to Liza and whispered another long string of words. Liza immediately understood one word: dying.

She knelt beside Black Quail. Touching her shoulder, she realized the frail woman was sweating furiously and her body burned with fever. "She is very ill! She needs a doctor."

Both Crow Woman and Big Horse nodded, tears running down their faces. Frustrated, Liza ran to the water pouch hanging from a horn near the lodge's entrance. She poured a handful of water into her hand, then dripped it over Black Quail's belly. The semi-conscious girl shivered in response to the cool water.

"This is no good," sighed Liza. "She needs medicine. She

189

needs a doctor." She looked around again, noting that the women had prepared some kind of tea. When she pointed to it, Crying Woman frowned and explained that Black Quail had not been able to drink it.

Liza moved closer. If only she had some of her mother's laudanum; her mother had often used it to quiet a fever or headache.

Just then Black Quail rolled over and vomited. Liza jumped back, the putrid odor causing her own stomach to roll. The poor girl vomited a second time and then began to moan. Big Horse cried out, her words lost in Black Quail's growing agony.

Crow Woman slipped out of the tipi as Liza mopped up the pool of bile and spit. Big Horse continued to fan Black Quail, though Liza feared it futile. Without medicine, the girl might not recover.

Almost immediately, Crow Woman returned with the sun priest, Red Quiver. He entered the lodge, rattling with each step. Liza noticed the tiny bones and odd bangles tied to his wrists and ankles and quickly moved out of the old man's way. She knew very little about the sun priest, but his severe expression, ancient sunken eyes, and strange appearance frightened her.

From an animal skin bundle, he removed an assortment of items. He began to sing and chant, moving up and down the body of Black Quail. He then shook a large rattle made of bones and teeth and he sprinkled a fine powder in a circle around the lodge. The dust gave off a musty smell that made Liza wrinkle her nose.

Feeling the outsider, she left the lodge. The fresh air was like a slap on the face and it was still snowing, but the flakes were smaller and wetter. She inhaled deeply and returned to her own lodge.

Within a few days, it was clear that the tribes along the Bear River were battling smallpox. Black Quail was the first victim in Crying Wind's band and she died a slow, agonizing death. By the second morning, another woman was violently ill.

Liza was stunned. The Pikuni people were powerless

against such a disease. They had no proper medicines, no doctors. They didn't understand how the sickness, what the Pikuni called the white scabs disease, could spread and she was at a loss to explain it to Crow Woman. Red Quiver, of course, would not listen to her; after all, she was not one of them.

Most of the deaths were occurring in Heavy Runner's and Standing Wolf's bands, where larger numbers of people were struck. Unfortunately, the disease was still in its early stages.

Night and day, Red Quiver travelled from lodge to lodge. By the end of the first week, in spite of his efforts, a half dozen people were dead. In the meantime, Liza and Crow Woman made broth from the meat the hunters brought in. Seasoned with herbs Crow Woman kept stored in parfleches, she and Liza carried the soup to those too ill to eat anything else. Come Running was not allowed to accompany them for fear she would endanger her unborn child. Each evening, Liza dropped exhausted onto her buffalo hides, sometimes not even removing her moccasins.

Then, as if the people had not suffered enough, on the ninth day of dying, Crow Woman told her that a group of young warriors had finally deserted. Afraid of disease and anxious to seek revenge, they had followed Mountain Chief and Owl Child into the mountains. Three were from Crying Wind's band, including Fast Walker, a happy, smiling young man.

"Oh, Crow Woman, surely Fast Walker will come back!" she said. "He is not old enough to be turned into an outlaw."

Crow Woman nodded. Fast Walker had been a favorite of Crying Wind's. "This is a sad time for the people," she said. "Perhaps there was more in Red Eagle's dream than Crying Wind and Red Quiver understood."

Liza put a hand on the older woman's shoulder. A dream could not have protected any of them from this disease. It was an enemy without a face.

Crow Woman reached up and patted her hand softly. "But you have brought us all much gladness, Liza Five Shots."

Startled by the words, Liza blinked back her tears. When

191

had she stopped being Liza Ralston of St. Louis and become Liza Five Shots of the Montana Territory? When had she gone from being a stranger to a member of the tribe?

She slipped out of the lodge, deeply moved, yet deeply troubled. *If she were one of them, why wasn't there something more she could do?*

✠ ✠ ✠

The days and nights became interminable. A terrible blow fell when Red Quiver was struck down by the pox. Within three days, the shrunken old man was reduced to skeleton-size; his dying was accompanied by much grieving and wailing.

Yet Liza and Crow Woman seemed immune to the disease. They ministered to others, bringing water or broth, collecting wood for fire, or taking care of motherless children.

Liza, sure that there was medicine that could help, petitioned Heavy Runner to send a few of his strongest braves to Riplinger's Post. Heavy Runner refused. He spoke angrily, haltingly, so that she might understand. The young men would end up with a bullet for their trouble; not even Riplinger would accept Indians coming in with the threat of smallpox hovering over them.

Liza decided she should go. Perhaps she could do what the Pikuni could not. She asked Crow Woman to loan her one of Crying Wind's horses. The older woman frowned.

"Can't I try?" wailed Liza.

Crow Woman shook her head and replied in Blackfoot, "How would you find your way? Who could go with you? Who is left to go with you?"

Frustrated, Liza stormed out of the lodge, taking one of Crying Wind's bridles. Slipping over to the horse enclosure, she found the young bay she had often seen Come Running ride. She led it out of the corral, climbed onto its shaggy, bare back, and rode it down to the river. Winding like a coiled snake across the desolate plain, the cold water lay gray against the white earth, barely moving past chunks of ice. Only remnants of grass and reed, bent over or broken off, stood along the banks. Little remained of the shore's lush growth and Liza could only imagine what this place must be like in spring.

It was no use. As she scanned the rolling white swales and cutbanks, she knew Crow Woman was right. She knew nothing of this wilderness and would only get lost, bringing another disaster to Crow Woman.

If only Red Eagle and the others would return. If only Crying Wind and her father would come, surely, they would know what to do.

That night, a terrible gnawing attacked, a dull pain deep within her spirit. To counteract it, she repeated Red Eagle's last words over and over. "I *will* come back."

☩ ☩ ☩

More days of sadness passed. Too tired to pray, too spent to even change her clothes, Liza returned to her lodge each night worn out and tormented. A terrible thought began to haunt her; if the illness was not contained, there would be no reason for the army to negotiate peace, no reason to resolve the conflicts boiling beneath the surface. The army would not lose a single soldier in this battle.

Even her treasured volume of poetry did nothing to salvage her emotions. One evening, in a fit of rage, she threw the book across the fire. The cover, hardly intact, separated from the pages and was devoured by the dancing flames. The pages curled up, one by one, until they disintegrated into gray ash.

But she felt nothing. She was too numb, too heartsick.

What good were words of love, anyway, when people were dying, helpless against something they could not see or hear coming? Worse than any enemy on the horizon, the Pikuni would be destroyed, one by one.

Liza looked down at her own calloused hands as if they were another's. Her fingers trembled and she gulped hard, hot tears.

Would life ever be simple again?

193

CHAPTER 23

*T*HE SMALLPOX EPIDEMIC CONTINUED. ENTIRE FAMILIES were eliminated. Often, only a grandmother or single sibling was left untouched; in one family, four members were struck down, leaving one adolescent girl who, in Pikuni tradition, cut off her long hair and several finger joints. Liza was horrified but helpless to do anything for her.

Still there was no word from Crying Wind and his party. Scouts were dispatched but they returned after three days, eyes downcast, words clipped.

One morning, a group of men left the settlement. Huddled under her buffalo cape, Liza watched them ride away, their faces hard as stone. They represented the strongest of the bands but, realizing there was no other choice now, Heavy Runner and Standing Wolf sent them to trade with the whites: buffalo hides for precious medicines, medicines everyone prayed would stop the dying.

The party of men set off in the direction of Riplinger's Trading Post. But if word reached the whites before the men did, they could be ambushed or captured or sent back, empty-handed. But to fight or die as a warrior was far better than at the mercy of evil spirits and illness. It was every warrior's desire to die bravely. This enemy, the insidious white scabs, was not an enemy any honorable brave wished to face.

The parade of warriors was quiet, the women and children who watched them, drawn and sad. No one smiled or spoke as the heavily-cloaked men passed by, and the haunting cry of a red-tailed hawk circling above was the only thing to break the awful stillness.

Liza grasped the folds of her cape as she noticed Crow

Woman beside her own tipi, face pinched, eyes hollow and sunken. Concerned that the old woman might be ill, Liza rushed to her.

The older woman raised her face and whispered, "Piik."

Liza nodded and followed her into the familiar lodge. Letting the heavy flap door drop behind her, she caught her breath. There, bent over, was Come Running, vomiting into the dirt. She looked up, only briefly, then turned away.

"Oh, dear God," she moaned, "she has the pox." She touched Crow Woman's arm, tears burning her eyes.

Crow Woman did not respond except to stare blankly. Only her hands trembled.

Liza leaned over Come Running, but the sick woman turned away. She did not want Liza to come near.

Waving her hands above her head wildly and mumbling something unintelligible, she signalled for both of the women to leave.

Crow Woman bit her lip as she tried not to cry. Taking Liza by the arm, she led her out into the gray morning.

Later in the day, Liza returned to help nurse Come Running. Covered in sweat, the young woman passed into delirium several times. Crow Woman had made an herbal tea that Come Running was able to sip but she refused any broth.

By nightfall, Liza stumbled back to her lodge. Her cooking fire was nearly dead, but with numb fingers she took some pitch pieces from her meager store and stoked the coals. Within a few minutes, the fire blazed and Liza huddled over it; nevertheless, the heat could not penetrate her chilled bones.

Nothing seemed to ease her shivering and as she tried to sleep, she wondered if it was her turn to fall ill. She rolled her head from side to side, mind whirling with a thousand disconnected thoughts. How sad that she should die alone without her father, without Red Eagle. Was it some wicked trick being played on her by God? She tried to laugh but the sound came out a hoarse cough.

Liza barely had the strength to pray, so she recited old, familiar prayers, childish prayers her mother had taught.

Then she started praying to be released from her death sentence. "Please," she whispered as she listened to an owl hooting in the night, "let me live. Let me have a chance to love, to walk with Red Eagle by my side."

As the night deepened, she continued to tremble. Drawing her arms and legs up against her body, she wondered if this was the end. In desperation, she crept over to her stash of cooking wood and placed two small limbs across the red-orange flames, an extravagance she could not afford.

"The world be damned," she said out loud. "I'll not pass into oblivion freezing cold."

She closed her eyes. Perhaps death was not so bad. At least she would no longer struggle with the emotions that had plagued her since entering the wilderness.

⚜   ⚜   ⚜

Red Eagle pulled his buffalo robe over his head and shoulders. His hands were so cold he could barely move his fingers and his eyes burned from the raw wind ripping through the small group like a whip.

Looking around the fire at the rest of the heavily-cloaked men, his glance fell on Many Words. No doubt the big man suffered more than anyone, though he tried hard not to show his exhaustion. He had valiantly followed them, not complaining, even though it was clear he was growing weaker and weaker. Red Eagle only hoped he could finish the journey.

The trip had been a failure. They had reached Fort Benton after two weeks on the trail where they became stranded in a snowstorm that claimed two horses, then slowed down by sickness, which nearly claimed two of their ablest warriors.

When they finally reached the fort, Lieutenant Pease ordered his troop's physician to tend the sick men first. Days later, the lieutenant reported that another attack by a renegade Blackfoot band had made negotiations pointless. He called in soldiers and, without offering an explanation, arrested Crying Wind.

As Red Eagle recalled the incident, his face burned with rage. It had been a horrendous mistake. Many Words, overwhelmed by the lieutenant's charges, protested but Pease walked away, refusing to listen. Many Words followed him, demanding to see the general, but the lieutenant laughed and called him a stinkin' Injun lover.

Running Antelope nearly got himself killed after that as he ran after two troopers, his knife drawn. Three other soldiers cornered him, confiscated his knife, and threw him into another jail cell.

Red Eagle and the others could only retreat, returning to their makeshift lodge outside the fort. They were stunned.

Many Words insisted the mistake could be corrected, that the army caved into pressure from settlers. Little Otter didn't care; he wanted to break in and rescue Crying Wind and Running Antelope. He would prefer taking a few scalps on the way out.

Many Words sternly disagreed. "Do you want to get them both killed? Maybe strung up from the nearest hanging tree? That's what will happen. You've got to listen to me. It'll take time, but I will get the general to hear me out. Please, trust me, all of you."

It was difficult waiting. Day after day, Many Words went to the general's office, only to be turned away. Finally, the general agreed to see him alone. Many Words rushed in, confident he would be heard.

But when he returned his face was grim. The general had listened but refused to respond, so action was postponed. Many Words sat for hours, his head in his hands, refusing to eat or drink.

Red Eagle left the lodge then and headed out to the Indian village that stretched for a mile around the fort. There he saw hungry women and poorly-clothed children sitting beside campfires, their faces blank and spirits heavy. He wondered if this was the future he had glimpsed in his dream.

As if beckoned, an old woman emerged from the nearest lodge, her mouth caved in, her skin pitted and scarred. Red

Eagle drew back, afraid that this was the dream woman herself. But the woman only wailed, "Feed the old and dying!"

"Woman," asked Red Eagle, "where is your family? Where are your sons?"

"My son is dead and so is my husband. All but my son's wicked wife. She has found a lover and sent me away. Abandoned me. She says it is my time to die."

Red Eagle opened his pouch and removed several pieces of pemmican. "Were I your son, I would feed you—"

"And I would weep over your grave. There will be many mothers weeping soon," she added, grabbing up the dried meat and hurrying away.

In her wake Red Eagle stood. He returned to his lodge, but did not share with the others what the old woman had said. But that night his dreams were filled with death and horror, burning tipis, screaming women and children.

Two more days passed before Crying Wind and Running Antelope were finally released. The lieutenant did not apologize; he only nodded his head and said, "Our Indian agent says that Crying Wind is a trusted leader and friend. For that reason, he has been asked to meet with the general. Have him here at 8:00 sharp, tomorrow morning."

The next morning, talks continued. Crying Wind explained repeatedly that the Pikuni camped along the Bear River had not befriended Owl Child or Mountain Chief. Heavy Runner had given his word, as had Standing Wolf and Crying Wind.

"Then why," interrupted the army general, "could no leader stop the murdering renegades like Peter Owl Child and Mountain Chief?"

The general frowned; he did not like what Crying Wind or Many Words told him, that a leader could only influence his people through wise counsel and, if a warrior chose to go his own way, there was little anyone could do to stop him.

The general would not be appeased. "The renegades must be stopped! Do you understand? Heavy Runner, Crying Wind, and the others must return the horses that were confis-

199

cated *and* bring Owl Child, Black Weasel, and Mountain Chief to be tried for their crimes. Short of that, there is nothing else to discuss."

Crying Wind shook his head, discouraged.

The general then read from a piece of paper the names of others known to be following Owl Child. When he read Fast Walker's name, Crying Wind dropped his chin, shamed by the young man's foolish act of betrayal.

Many Words broke in. "General, the leaders of the Pikuni are only as strong as the warriors allow them to be. They cannot force men to act reasonably!"

"Then our negotiations are over," returned the general abruptly.

"But, sir, the people support Heavy Runner's and Crying Wind's desire for peace. They do not want a war, any more than the army. Believe me."

The general carefully rolled a cigarette as he watched Many Words. His manner clearly indicated that he found the minister irritating.

When he stood up, he glanced down at Crying Wind. "It is the Pikuni who cannot believe what is in store for them," he said carefully. Without another word, he turned and left the room.

Two more days passed before the general called Many Words and the others back to him. "I'm afraid," he announced, "that nothing you have said adds a whit of support to Crying Wind's claim that his people have not aided the criminals. We have reason to believe otherwise. Indeed, at this very moment, members of Mountain Chief's raiding band are being protected in Heavy Runner's camp!" He turned to Red Eagle and added, "The only way to win the confidence of the army now is to assist in the arrest of Mountain Chief, Owl Child, and their followers. Short of that, there is nothing I can do to change the coming events—"

Red Eagle understood then that the dream woman had spoken the truth, without uttering a word.

"Go home," the general said finally. "Go home to your

people. Tell them that the action of one represents the actions of all."

Disgusted, Crying Wind stumbled to his feet, his black eyes blazing. Red Eagle had never seen his uncle angrier or more determined. Perhaps never more disillusioned, either.

Early the next morning, the peace party left. Before the day was over, Red Eagle knew that Many Words was ill. His heart and spirit had been battling and now they were broken. Red Eagle asked him if he should return to the fort and the white man's doctor.

Eyes wide and brows furrowed, he refused. "Never," he whispered to Red Eagle. "There is nothing for me there."

The men returned by the same trail they had come, only they were spent, emotionally and physically, so the journey became more arduous with each passing day.

⊗ ⊗ ⊗

Crying Wind's peace mission had been a failure, just as Heavy Runner's had been before. So much for justice, sighed Red Eagle. So much for negotiating with the army. The army heard only what it wanted to hear, and it would do what it wanted.

The wind howled all day and snow fell at intervals. *If only the sun would shine for more than an hour or two a day, the men could move faster,* thought Red Eagle. But Many Words moved ever more slowly and Crying Wind moved cautiously, too, calling for another stop even before nightfall.

Turning his back to the icy gusts slapping his face, Red Eagle drew a long, steadying breath. He buried his muffled head into his arms to keep the swirling snow out of his eyes. The shelter they had constructed lasted not more than a few hours, leaving each man to huddle under his own robe, fighting off the wind as best he could.

Hoping the storm would pass as quickly as it had come, Red Eagle closed his eyes. Without calling her to mind, the calming image of Liza flashed before him. Gazing wide-eyed at him across the fire the night before their departure, the yearning in her eyes stirred him deeply. *Did she know the power she possessed?*

Her mouth had quivered nervously as she wished him good luck on his journey and only by sheer determination had he held her at a distance even though desire burned in his loins. Had he taken her then, however, he would have lost her forever.

Forever. That's how long he wanted her by his side.

Like the Seven Sisters stretched across a clear night sky, their lives had become connected and he could no longer imagine life without her. She was strong and he admired that. She was soft and alluring, a softness he wanted to protect.

She would be a good friend, companion, wife; he was sure of it. He would build a home for her, just as his father had built a large, square house for his own mother. Or perhaps they would return to his parents' house. Either way, a house with flowers and a garden. Even a few chickens. She would like that. And he would buy many books of poetry which she would read aloud; perhaps he'd read some to her.

He pulled his robe more tightly about him. There would be time, in the spring, as they travelled to the Sweet Grass Hills. He would go to Many Words and speak his heart. Until then, he would dream of chestnut hair and flashing brown eyes.

CHAPTER 24

*T*HE AIR WAS BITTERLY COLD AS LIZA STIRRED. REVIVED by the night's sleep, she examined herself carefully. There were no unsightly scabs and she seemed to have regained a good deal of her strength. She wondered at her wild, desperate imaginings.

She stood up and shook her arms and legs, as if to test each limb. Relieved, she knelt beside the firepit and stoked the embers. The flames jumped up and she quickly placed a piece of pitch across the fire. She would be more cautious about burning up her meager supply of kindling.

She heard a strange commotion outside. Reaching the door of her tipi, she pulled back the flap but nothing moved outside. The world was deathly still.

Perhaps a gust of wind.

Liza returned to her small fire but an eeriness had filled her lodge. Once more she was drawn to the door, but once more, she saw nothing in the bitter blue dawn.

But something was amiss.

She quickly pulled on her leggings and moccasins, then wrapped a small, fur cape about her. Last night's storm had abated, but clouds lingered and the world seemed frozen, laced with icicles and hairy frost.

She walked out past her own lodge and scanned the riverbank. Nothing stirred. The trees near the water's edge were covered in white, limbs hanging low, branches strung with gossamer crystals. A foggy mist clung to the water like wispy shreds of cotton and the heavy brush dripped with the white mist. Even without the sun's rising, the crystalline landscape was brightly lit.

Shivering but still curious, Liza decided to investigate. She padded through the snow, circling the village once. Even the camp dogs had found hiding places. One old horse who had wandered into camp stood like a frozen statue. Its long, shaggy mane and winter coat were painted with frost. She nuzzled its cold nose and wiped the ice from its eyelashes.

She moved on. A new fire had been built in the lodge belonging to Yellow Dog's wife, for a fresh curl of dark smoke rose from the smoke hole. Yellow Dog and his son, Two Son, had died just a few days apart. Shot-in-the-Foot, Yellow Dog's wife, and a young daughter were all that remained of his family.

By the time Liza reached the boundary of the circle of tipis, she chided herself for her apprehensions. Yet the cloud of foreboding still hung in the air. *Was it because this had become a camp of death, a village of dying people? Was it the last gasp of a sick people that had curdled her thoughts?*

She sighed and looked downriver. She could see the tops of lodges in Heavy Runner's and Standing Wolf's camps. All was silent and still, deathly still.

Just as the yellow-orange rays of daylight broke through the clouds along the eastern horizon, Liza caught sight of an elderly man running across the snow. He was familiar but at this distance, she could not see who he was. *Was it Heavy Runner himself? Why was he running?*

A terrible fear gripped her as she turned to scan the rolling landscape beyond. Then she shivered, as if she knew what she would see.

She gasped and stumbled backwards.

Stretching from one end of the far hollow to the other, barely discernible above the waves of white ravines, was a blue-black line of men, some on foot, others on horseback. Dozens stood waiting, but the only movement was the stamping of their horses' feet.

Frantically, Liza's gaze returned to the old man still moving forward, one hand above his head. She wanted to call out, warn him. But he was too far away.

It was too late.

A single shot rang out and the old man staggered. In slow motion, he stopped, then swayed, falling to his knees. His cry was lost as a hail of cheers and shouts erupted from the line of men.

Suddenly, women and children were stumbling out of the lodges. Some ran forward to investigate the shooting, while others fled in all directions.

Liza did not wait to see anymore.

Dashing back through the encampments, she screamed, "Soldiers! Run!"

She swerved to avoid the children and hysterical women floundering out of their tipis and across the snowy plain, some only half-dressed. Several old men, grabbing their rifles and bows, ran forward toward the approaching line of horses.

Liza could not look back. The muffled hoof-beats, like a chorus of drums, pounding, thumping, beating against the snow-packed earth, grew louder. Slapping against the tipis as she ran, she sobbed over and over, "Soldiers!"

Two elderly women, peeking out of their lodge, spied Liza's face, then spotted the ragged columns of men approaching in the distance. Grabbing up their robes, they hobbled off after the horde of figures flooding to the river.

Liza did not stop until she reached Crow Woman's lodge. Panting, almost unable to speak, she ducked inside, snatching a parfleche of pemmican and a gourd that hung from one of the lodge poles. "Quickly!" she cried. "Soldiers! They're here! Come! Now!"

Turning to Crow Woman, who had not responded to her commands, Liza realized the older woman sat, mute, resolute. Beyond her in the dim light lay Come Running, who was deathly pale. Only the scabs which covered her face and limbs marred her fine features.

Liza yelled again, ordering Crow Woman to move, but Crow Woman regarded her only for a moment before turning away. Desperately, Liza screamed. "We must get away! There are soldiers, with guns! Please. We'll take Come Running with us. We'll hide. Now!"

Crow Woman shook her head, then flipped open her buffalo robe to expose her naked body. Liza gasped. Like her sister Come Running, Crow Woman's belly was covered in the all-too familiar blisters.

Liza froze, not knowing whether to stay or flee. As with her father on the night of the attack, she could not imagine leaving Crow Woman behind.

The confusion outside was growing. People were screaming and guns were being fired all around them. Horses stampeded through the village as the soldiers began to sweep through.

Liza jumped. "Please! I know a hiding place!"

Crow Woman shook her head again. Then she stood up and walked over to Liza, a frown creasing her potato-brown cheeks, her dark eyes wet with unshed tears. She slapped Liza so fiercely across the face that she stumbled backwards, shocked. Next, the older woman screeched at her—unintelligible sounds in Blackfoot.

Liza stared at her, then ran to her, throwing her arms around her. "Please! I love you," she cried. "You are my near-mother. You are my friend, nita-ka."

Crow Woman pushed her away and the two stood in silence for a moment, their eyes locked, their hearts breaking.

Then Liza fled from the tipi, fighting the desire to return to Crow Woman and die with her. But the instinct to live was too great; the will to survive catapulted her towards the upper banks of the river, to her secret hiding place.

She ran, crouching, from lodge to lodge, then from tree to rock. She did not look back, fearing that if she did, she would never be able to go forward. The screams of terror followed her, while pounding hooves sent tremors across the frozen earth, a cacophony of death and terror.

Liza's throat burned as she pushed on. She dared not stop, not even for a breath. Every step was another step towards safety and she started counting the number of steps she took. *Ten, eleven, twelve*—

She saw her hiding place and quickly dove into the heavy

brush, crawling until she was buried in brambly vines and tall, dead reeds. For the first time she was grateful for the heavy snow even though it filled her moccasins and leggings, sending shivers up and down her legs and body.

As the sounds of horses and gunfire moved closer, she stifled the hot tears of fear and grief that could betray her. She willed herself not to think of Crow Woman or Come Running or all the others.

There would be time for that later, if she survived.

More gunfire exploded only yards from her. Stuffing a fist into her mouth, she squeezed her eyes shut and swallowed her cries.

Minutes or hours later—Liza could not tell—the gunfire became sporadic. Still she remained, paralyzed from fear and cold. Suddenly she heard footsteps. She pressed her eyes shut again, fearing they could be a lantern, signalling her presence.

The men's voices were hushed as they approached her hiding place but their words were clear and harsh.

"Stinkin' Injuns," muttered one.

"Filthy," returned the other.

Liza burned with rage, wishing she was a man or at least possessed a gun. *She'd blow them both to kingdom-come.*

They moved closer, the tips of their boots only a stone's throw away. She took a shallow, quick breath even as she shoved her fist deeper into her mouth.

"They're like a pack of squalling pups," whined the first trooper. "But ole Smithy, he couldn't take it! He high-tailed it, cryin' like a baby."

"Smithy's jest an Injun-lover," grumbled the second soldier. "Sure wish we had time to take some scalps, though. You can get two bucks for a good one! But Cap'n Baker, he don't want no scalping. Says this one's official, only lookin' for those that been doin' the horse stealin' and murderin.'"

"I think he's jest scairt of what'll come back to haunt him...like the ghosts of these Pikuni."

"Well, the scuttlebutt is that ole Sheridan hisself told DeTrobriand to strike and strike hard. You think this was hard 'nough?"

Liza's eyelids fluttered open but she quickly pinched them shut. *Could they hear her heart pounding?* Still gasping for breath, she was afraid her lungs would explode.

"'Cept for killin' the children, this was the best huntin' I've done," laughed the first trooper. "The babies squeal, though. Like coyote pups. But I seen one little squaw I wouldn't a'minded givin' a poke. Curtis put a bullet through her. Told him he was a fool. Most of these squaws are pock-marked and dirty as rats. Here, gimme that bottle. Where'd you get it anyways?"

"I got it from Spence. He got it from them runners that come through a week or so ago. It's some of the rotgut they been pawnin' off on them lunatic Blackfoot braves. Tastes like horse piss. No wonder so many of them is as crazy as fleas. It'd make anyone's arse pucker. We better move. Colonel said he wants some prisoners to in-ter-o-gate."

"Well, I gotta admit that kickin' 'em when they's all huddled down for the winter is the right way to put the bee-jeezus into 'em!"

The two drunken troopers stumbled away then and Liza spit out her fist along with her hot breath. Tears escaped and were running down her cheeks. They burned in the cold air and she struggled to wipe them away.

If she didn't, she might never stop crying.

Liza had never felt so enraged or so frightened. She whimpered, bile rising up to her throat. *How could this be happening?*

Time passed painfully but she was too afraid to move. Occasional pops of gunfire could be heard, indicating soldiers were still in the area. The sound of horses had long since faded into the distance. No doubt the army had taken the Pikuni horses as well. Without them, the people would be helpless.

Thinking of their helplessness, Liza wondered how many had been slaughtered. *How many, already sick or dying, had been cut down?* Even now, smoke drifted to where she lay and Liza knew the soldiers had burned the villages.

She shut her eyes again, resisting the pain that had settled over her. She had to focus her energy on overcoming the cold and the wet. Moving her shoulders, she found it almost impossible to raise either arm. But as she wiggled her near-frozen toes, she felt them tingle.

The pain was at least a reminder that she was alive. It seemed a welcome feeling and filled her with renewed determination to survive. She would shed no more tears today. Instead, for those who had lost their lives, she would live. She would live to be a witness to everything that had happened here this day.

CHAPTER 25

NEARLY FROZEN, LIZA PULLED HERSELF OUT OF THE heavy brush. The day was almost gone.

She struggled to her feet, shaking so terribly she could hardly stand or move. The muscles of her neck and shoulders burned like hot irons and her hands and feet were almost beyond feeling. She fought to ignore the pain as she placed one foot in front of the other.

The village no longer existed. What she saw was more paralyzing than her physical predicament and, as she blinked back tears, she felt her stomach rise up. She turned away and vomited.

Where people once walked, bodies were strewn like rags across smoking, littered debris. Lodges had been torn down, then burned. The smell lingering in the air was so nauseating she could hardly move.

But she did. She staggered along the once-familiar path leading to Crying Wind's lodge.

Where once his enormous tipi stood, beautifully painted, nothing but ashes and smoking lodge poles remained. She held her breath and took a step closer. "Dear God, no!" she wailed, spotting the remains of Crow Woman and Come Running. The two sisters had died in each other's arms.

She dropped to the ground, pounding her fists against her thighs, and cried.

Her thoughts numbed: *Were there no other survivors of Crying Wind's camp? Had everyone perished?* Finally, she heard a sound, the voice of a child. A young child cried out as Liza dug through the fallen timbers.

"I'm here!" she screeched, pulling at the rubble. Pieces of

a lodge pole fell apart in her hands, the fragments still warm against her cold fingertips. She reached out for the little girl's hand, tiny and limp, and sobbed, "I've got you! I've got you!"

She glimpsed a small face. Though the girl was covered with blood, Liza recognized Bull Child, the youngest daughter of Basket Dancer, a woman not much older than Liza herself.

Liza tugged at the last pole, shoving it to one side. She laughed as she felt the child move, and tears ran down her cheeks. Miraculously, except for a few bruises and a cut to her face, Bull Child was not harmed.

The girl allowed Liza to lift her and Liza immediately carried her away from the smoking tipi. Wide-eyed and solemn, Bull Child clung to her.

"We'll be fine," whispered Liza. "I promise you." But she had to harness her own fear as the child pressed her small face to her shoulder. "I'll not leave you," she added, hoping to ease the child's trembling.

Bull Child closed her eyes and her tiny whimpers subsided. They moved on past another lodge where an old woman and her dog lay side by side in the ashes. Blood had pooled around them giving them each a crimson halo.

"How could anyone do this?" she moaned. *"How?"*

Hardly able to see through her tears, Liza carried Bull Child to the river, where she tended her wound. It had stopped bleeding, the dried blood collecting on her scalp and along her cheek. Gently Liza rubbed her fingers across the little girl's soot-stained cheeks, smiling as she wiped away as much crusted blood as she could.

Then she wrapped her arms around the child and pulled her close. Their soft breathing was the only sound in the oppressive silence that clung to the remains of Crying Wind's village.

By early evening, at least two dozen survivors had appeared, some sooty from ash, others black and drenched from the mud holes they had dug along the riverbank. All were chilled to the bone and some shook uncontrollably. They moved like dummies, eyes empty, speaking little. Only the chil-

212

dren sobbed as the old men and women rifled through the ravaged camps, looking for something or, perhaps, nothing.

Several reported that they had seen a large number of Heavy Runner's people escape, while some were taken hostage. No one knew where those were headed, nor who had been captured and taken away. And no one knew if the army would release them or lock them up. But when they realized the people had contracted smallpox, would they do something even more terrible? How many had survived?

Liza clasped Bull Child's hand. They were the only survivors from Crying Wind's small band, unless others had been taken or escaped down river. Feeling lost, she approached a small gathering where one woman she vaguely remembered as a member of Heavy Runner's camp and friend to Come Running stood next to a bedraggled, elderly man. Toward her familiar face, Liza moved timidly.

The woman's name was Cut Finger. She was covered in soot but her lovely face was like a torch light for Liza. At the same time, the man beside her was so frighteningly austere and intimidating that Liza almost turned away. His long gray-black hair was matted and filthy, his face scarred and pitted. One scar was shaped like a half-moon, encircling his left eye. Spotting Liza, he frowned and grunted then drew his left arm, which appeared broken, firmly to his side.

His steely gaze raked her face with angry intensity as she stepped up to Cut Finger.

Cut Finger greeted her and Bull Child. Pulling the child into her arms, she gave her a hug. Tears were in her eyes as she stood and spoke to Liza. She indeed remembered Liza Five Shots, whose near-mothers were Come Running and Crow Woman, and whose father was Many Words, the holy man who came to live among the Pikuni.

Liza's tears matched hers as the woman hugged her again.

The grim, old man said nothing.

At last, Cut Finger turned to him and spoke so rapidly that Liza could not translate. The old warrior swung his free arm in large, wild circles. She tensed, wondering if he would refuse to help her; he seemed to be protesting something. *Did he blame her for what had happened?*

Cut Finger interrupted him, saying something stern in response to his remarks. She turned back to Liza and led her and Bull Child away. The three walked down to the river where other women were filling up paunches with fresh water.

Even from a distance, Liza could feel the man's bitter hatred and she tried not to shiver. Perhaps it would be better if she left and made her own way.

She fought back the fearful thought. Where would she go? She had no idea where her father or Red Eagle were, and she couldn't travel very far through the wilderness. Most importantly, when they returned, she wanted to be where they could find her.

A handful of women continued to gather what items they could from the ruined villages. As they worked together, Liza learned that the man's name was Mad Horse and that he and two women, Fat Dog and Sharp Hand, had eluded the soldiers by hiding under corpses.

By the time darkness fell, the small group had gathered all the supplies they could. The group included seven children, two young mothers, three older women, Liza, and two adolescent boys. Most had escaped by carving out holes along the river's edge; one of the younger women, Yellow Grass, had suffered frostbite on her fingers and toes, while the other, Rides-a-Horse, was limping after the falling lodge poles of her tipi pinned her. She walked aided by a cane Cut Finger fashioned from a stick.

It was Mad Horse, however, who took charge of the wizened band. After confiscating the collected rations of food, he ordered the women to search for more. Liza did manage to find some, but this she tucked inside her dress. She also retrieved two pairs of moccasins, two more blankets, and a large buffalo robe.

Other tattered groups, most from Heavy Runner's band, had already melted into the landscape, some moving north, others east or south. Knowing it would be dangerous to remain in the area unarmed and without warriors for protection, no one thought to stay.

Liza followed Mad Horse reluctantly. It was clear the old man resented her. Had it not been for Cut Finger, she would not have followed him at all. Holding Bull Child's tiny hand, she kept her eyes on the trail ahead. Where they were headed, Liza had no idea. She only hoped her father and Red Eagle would read their tracks and come soon.

Silently the ragged party moved upriver. The familiar landscape began to change, making Liza more unsure of her destination. Biting back her fear, she decided she had to do something and was as well off with Cut Finger as with anyone. Or so she hoped.

Liza bowed her head against the stiff breeze that suddenly swept down the cutbank. There would be time to consider her plight later.

✠ ✠ ✠

Crying Wind called a halt. The party had travelled late into the evening and everyone needed rest. The horses were exhausted from plowing through the deep snow and the men were hungry. Two braves immediately set out to trap a rabbit and gather more willow brush for the fire. The other men settled in around the fire, each one wrapped in heavy robes.

Red Eagle dropped to the ground beside Crying Wind. "A strange feeling has followed me since we left the fort," he said, so softly no one else could hear. Between the haunting memory of his dream and the strange words the old woman in the village, he sensed that something was wrong. *Could he trust the feeling?*

"Go on," encouraged Crying Wind. "A warrior must always listen to the voices that direct his footsteps."

Red Eagle nodded. "A darkness, a strange fear, passes over me whenever I think of the people," he said. "I do not understand it, but it follows me like my shadow."

215

Crying Wind sat without speaking for several minutes. His eyes were half closed, as if contemplating something deeper than could be seen. Finally he opened them and nodded to his nephew. "I, too, have had a terrible feeling," he said. "I had hoped it was only an old man's fear." He cast a glance at Many Words, who was wrapped in his own robe a few feet away. The holy man had grown weaker with each mile and Crying Wind and Red Eagle both knew there was not much strength left in the frail body. Perhaps it had been a mistake to bring him. But who could have known how the journey would end?

Crying Wind turned back to Red Eagle. "Your dream. It still haunts you? And the old woman. Has she revealed what is coming?"

"No," sighed Red Eagle. "In my dream her wailing was like the cries of a hundred women. But at the fort, an old woman came and spoke to me, in riddles."

Crying Wind nodded again and a deep sigh escaped his pursed lips. "It is enough." The old man dropped his chin and Red Eagle wondered if he was praying or was just worn out. He waited patiently. He knew his uncle was wiser than a hundred men, trusting him more than he trusted himself.

Many Words, suddenly raising his face, caught sight of the old Indian's hunched position. "What is it, my friend?" he asked breathlessly.

Crying Wind was slow to answer. His eyes were still closed. Taking a slow, careful breath, he said, "Perhaps nothing. Perhaps only an old man's fear." He glanced at Red Eagle sharply.

Many Words reached out, fingertips brushing Crying Wind's blanketed arm, his dark eyes bright in the hollow of his pale face. "Elizabeth?" he whispered. "The village? Has something happened? Is my daughter in danger?"

Red Eagle's expression grew dark. "I do not know." He wished he could put the holy man's mind at ease but they were all past pretending that life was as it had always been. *Hadn't their reception at the fort shown them all that the future of the Pikuni was bleak, that their days of freedom were in jeopardy?*

216

"Nor I," added Crying Wind solemnly. "Old men think strange things when the cold comes into their bones." He shook his head at Red Eagle.

Many Words was already alarmed. Raising up on his haunches he cried out, "Dear God. Do not let it be my Elizabeth. She has no part in the craziness that is descending upon this land."

Crying Wind grunted. "And who has chosen to take part?"

Many Words apologized.

"Your words are those of a father," returned Crying Wind. "But Red Eagle will go on. He will travel to the village and bring word if he can." He turned back to his nephew. "Tell the others, then begin at once. You can make your way quickly without the rest of us."

Red Eagle jumped to his feet.

Crying Wind held up his hand. It looked thin and yellow in the gray light. "Take Running Antelope with you. You are both young and swift. We will follow as quickly as we can."

Red Eagle nodded and turned to go but Many Words cried out to him. "Wait!"

Squatting once more, Red Eagle put his head close to Many Words. The face of the holy man was a dead man's face, pale and nearly empty. "My daughter, Red Eagle. She is all I have. Do not let any harm come to her."

"None will come to her."

"But promise me!" moaned Many Words, his out-stretched hand now shaking uncontrollably. "Never, never, let anything hurt her again! I have failed her. I was wrong, Red Eagle, to bring her—"

Red Eagle shook his head. "Liza Five Shots is strong."

"Yes, perhaps," mumbled Many Words, his voice fading.

Red Eagle squeezed the older man's shoulder. "I would give up my own life before I let anything happen to her," he said. "I love Liza Five Shots. I intend to make her my wife."

Many Words nodded, a smile touching the corners of his sallow lips. "She is a sharp-tongued, strong-willed young

217

woman," he said after a moment. "She may make your life difficult. But she's honest and good and has a heart made for loving."

Crying Wind slid closer to his old friend. "Old man," he
teased, "Red Eagle will never be able to take her as his wife if
you do not turn loose his arm. The night grows darker and you
must gather your strength if you hope to witness Five Shot's
wedding!"

"I do not worry about my future," he said softly. "I know
where I am going. But take this. Tell her it is hers. It was once
her mother's. It is all I have to give her in the way of a blessing,"
he muttered, fumbling inside his robe. His hand shook as he
extended it once more to Red Eagle. Looking into the young
man's eyes, he added, "Make her a good husband,
Mekotsepetan. A loving and kind husband. A husband who
serves God and protects his wife. Tell her that, in case I do not
live to tell her myself."

Red Eagle picked up the dainty cross that hung from a
long silver chain. "I will do so, Many Words. I promise."

"Now go," interrupted Crying Wind, his hand stretched
out in farewell. Turning to Many Words he added, "We will not
let you die yet, old man, so do not sigh your last breath."

As Red Eagle got up, Many Words said, "Who knows the
will of God? If I am to die, it is well. Go with God, my son."

Turning on his heels, Red Eagle immediately went to
Running Antelope. Packing only a few things onto the backs of
their horses, the two men set off just as the heavy cloak of night
enveloped them. Under the canopy of blackness, however, the
white landscape lit the trail enough for them to follow.

The two men did not speak as they journeyed. Each was
lost in his own thoughts and Red Eagle knew that the jealousy
that had kept them distant for so long stood between them
now. Only their shared commitment brought them together.

For Red Eagle, a new heaviness had been added to his
burden. He would probably never see Many Words again and
he would have to tell Liza if her father did not return. He patted
the pouch that held the cross, knowing it would mean a great
deal to her in any case. *But would the loss of Many Words be too*

much for her? Would she choose to leave rather than stay if her father died?

It took all night for the two riders to reach the upper portion of the river. The horses, panting heavily as they slid down a coulee, needed a rest and finally Running Antelope pulled his horse around.

"We must stop," he said. He ran his hand down his horse's mane. The animal shuddered under the weight of his rider.

Red Eagle nodded. It was a foolish man who allowed an animal to exhaust itself. They rode to the bottom of the ravine, to where the river made a wide bend. They dismounted and led their animals to water, then shared their rations of pemmican. Little else was said until it was time to leave.

Running Antelope, his hawk-like eyes clear and narrowed, placed his gloved hand on his cousin's arm. Speaking softly, he said, "I do not any longer carry anger. It is time to put it aside."

Red Eagle, grateful, smiled his thanks. "That is good," he returned, "for I fear that whatever has come may require more from us than we have ever given. We are the same, you and I. We are as brothers. We are Pikuni. We must take care of our people."

Squeezing his arm, Running Antelope nodded. "Never again will I shame my little cousin," he said, his mouth turned up in a rare smile. "He does his people honor."

Hesitating for another moment, the two men resumed their trek in silence. If they were lucky, they would reach the villages sometime in the late afternoon.

It was as the pale winter sun peeked through the layers of gray cloud that the two recognized the outskirts of the Pikuni settlement. A dismal fog had settled over the area, so it was impossible to discern more than a darkened place in the landscape. They pushed their horses on.

After tramping through another stretch of wind-blown ridges of snow, Running Antelope yelled over his shoulder. "I do not like this! I smell death!"

Red Eagle said nothing, but his eyes flitted anxiously along the horizon. Turning to glance across the river, his spine tingled; an almost haunting haze had settled over the ice-tinged water and snowy banks. He kicked his horse, forcing it into a trot, and the animal lunged through the drifts, panting hoarsely. Wet snow flew up like clumps of mud around them.

Red Eagle pounded the flanks of his horse again. "Ha!" he cried.

The smell foretold all. Even the horses whinnied, eyes round with fear, ears flat against their heads. Red Eagle's black mare pulled back but he urged her on.

"Is this the work of the Sioux or Crow?" said Red Eagle, his voice hardly a whisper.

"No!" boomed Running Antelope, his black eyes blazing with hatred. "This is the work of dog-faced, yellow-haired soldiers!"

They had reached Standing Wolf's and Heavy Runner's campsites and the smoking odor of death hung about them. Horrified by what loomed ahead, the men fell silent.

Running Antelope was the first to dismount. Sliding off his horse, he dropped his buffalo cape and rushed through the burned debris, a look of fury across his face.

Red Eagle stifled a cry of grief as he spotted a body half buried by charcoaled timbers. It was the body of a young girl. The toes of her moccasins stuck out of the inky remains, bright, cornflower blue beads stitched across their width, a stark reminder of a loving mother's attention.

Running Antelope turned, his eyes filled with tears. Through tight lips he said, "There will never be an end to the conflict. There is no such thing as peace with these animals!"

Mounted again, the two men rode directly to Crying Wind's encampment, their faces hard. Red Eagle's stomach rolled over. *Would he find Liza half buried, half burned? What about Crow Woman and Come Running, Black Quail, and all the others?*

In minutes they reached what should have been the tiny village. Destruction lay before them. In stunned silence, they jumped down and stumbled through the litter. Red Eagle quickly found Liza's lodge, but it had been razed. And there was no Liza! He ran immediately to the remains of Crying Wind's lodge, where he found the entangled bodies of his uncle's two wives. Dropping to his haunches, tears of rage welled up. *How could this have happened?*

He heard Running Antelope's anguished cries and turned to see the warrior thrashing through the charred remains of his own tipi. He picked up a half-empty paunch of water still hanging from one of the lodge timbers and stared back at Red Eagle. His eyes burned brightly, two black embers in his long, stern face.

There was nothing left. Not a single lodge had been left standing. Corpses and treasured possessions were scattered across the snow like scraps left by a pack of renegade dogs.

But where was Liza?

Searching everywhere, Red Eagle found not a trace of her. *Had she been captured? Had she been spared by the soldiers and taken back because she was one of them? Would Liza have let herself be taken away?*

No, Liza would not leave the people. He knew the deep love she had for Crow Woman and she would not have willingly left her or Come Running behind.

As if led by a scent, Red Eagle headed to the only hiding spot where Liza might have retreated, her secret place, where she had gone to be alone and read her book of poems. He crashed through the soft snow as he retraced the familiar path.

Once there, he dropped to his hands and knees and, in spite of the heavy brush, felt the depression someone could have made if they'd been half buried in the snow. It was smooth to the touch, worn away as if someone had huddled there.

His heart leaped. Liza had to be alive. Perhaps she escaped into the mountains with others who survived. *How would he find her now?*

Truly frightened, Red Eagle clenched his fists. Turning his eyes south, he cursed the soldiers and their generals, the evil hearts that led men to destroy others and the greedy stomachs of those who could never possess enough.

Then he wept.

221

CHAPTER 26

*R*ED EAGLE AND RUNNING ANTELOPE SAT TOGETHER in front of a small fire. Neither spoke of the other's grief. There was no need for words. Such sorrow was borne in silence.

They had spent more than an hour wandering through the village, hoping to find clues as to the whereabouts of Liza and Black Quail.

"The people were run down like vermin," cried Running Antelope.

"We must bury them."

"Not until we have taken revenge on those who did this. The spirits of the Pikuni will not rest so long as their butchers live."

Red Eagle said nothing. His hatred was tinged with the knowledge that revenge only would bring more death. *Yet how could they not retaliate?*

"I will never sleep again until I have taken the scalp of every Napikwan I find. Until we have rid our land of these animals."

Red Eagle nodded. He knew Running Antelope was right. There would be no peace. But there would be no peace for the people, either, if they made war on the army. There were too many soldiers and more who would come after. Red Eagle had been to many forts with his father. He had seen the soldiers with their guns and cannons. Whenever soldiers left, others took their place. Even his father, who hated having more and more settlers move into the territory, had admitted that the whites were here to stay, that nothing would stop them from taking the land. He had often wondered if it was best for the Pikuni to share. But he had also said the whites were too greedy.

Red Eagle thought of Crying Wind and Many Words and the others who would soon arrive. Their impending pain rekindled his own and suddenly he hoped that Many Words would not live to see what the white men had done. Indeed, if Liza was dead, the holy man would die with a broken heart.

And what about Crying Wind? With Crow Woman and Come Running, who had been carrying his child, dead along with most of his band, his uncle was alone.

"My tears will never be finished," moaned Running Antelope, hurling his knife into the snow. "I will never be at peace with the Napikwans."

He grabbed the knife and slammed it into his scabbard. Then, jumping onto his horse and wheeling around, he rode across the open meadow. Raising his arms wildly above his head, his voice raised in a battle cry, he galloped back toward the ruined village. Round and round he raced until Red Eagle went out and stopped him.

It would be no good to run his horse to death.

As the shadow of the winter sun spread its blue-gray fingers across the horizon, Red Eagle heard the muffled sounds of approaching horses. Signalling Running Antelope, the two men rubbed out their fire and led their horses stealthily down to the trees near the river. Neither carried a rifle, their only weapons long knives. Red Eagle positioned himself behind some heavy brush, a few yards from his cousin.

A score of men appeared, their voices harsh and loud. They dismounted and wandered through the scattered remains, kicking at the timbers as if seeking something. One of the men, yelling to the others, picked up an ornamented breastplate. Twirling it over his head, he let it sail through the air. Immediately, another soldier took aim with his rifle, shattering the hairpipe breastplate into pieces. The rest cheered.

"Look at this!" cried a second soldier, lifting up what was left of a small boy. Only a head and body and parts of two legs dangled from his fingers. Both arms had been burned away. "Damn, this place is beginnin' to really stink!" he hollered, tossing the corpse aside.

"What Injun don't stink?" returned a third soldier.

Red Eagle's bowels churned and he thought he would be sick. His hand shook as he placed it on the butt of his knife. He had killed one man. He would not regret killing these. *But could he and Running Antelope take them all?* Without guns, it was impossible.

He glanced over to where Running Antelope was crouched and even through the tangle of brush and trees that separated them, he could feel the rising intensity of his cousin's hatred. *Revenge would be sweet, but was it wise?*

As his thoughts waged battle in his brain, Running Antelope bounded out of the thicket. Like a madman, shrieking and screaming, he rushed at the surprised trooper nearest him, driving his knife into his soft belly. Grabbing the gun in the soldier's belt, he turned on the other men.

One shot was all Running Antelope could fire before two shots in rapid succession brought the warrior to the ground. Blood erupted from his head and Running Antelope howled as he writhed in pain. Trying to get up, he teetered for a moment, then fell to the snow in a heap. He jerked as another bullet tore through his shoulder. The white snow was flooded with his red blood.

Red Eagle, overcome with rage, rushed forward wielding his own knife. Tears filled his eyes as he ran to where Running Antelope lay. His words were clear as he cried, "You dog-faced murderers!"

His face contorted and he swung the blade through the air. "You are filth, less than the insects that crawl through a dead man's body! Go ahead! Kill me. But even then, my spirit will come back to hunt you down! Just as the spirits of those lying here will haunt you forever."

"Don't shoot!" came a clipped command. "Don't shoot!"

"Yes, shoot me!" challenged Red Eagle, whirling around again. "This was Running Antelope. He was a strong warrior. I am Red Eagle! Kill me!"

"I said, don't," growled the voice again. Red Eagle turned to face his enemy.

A tall lieutenant stepped through the rubble, one gloved

hand raised. His eyes, like chips of blue ice, glistened under the cavalry hat pulled down low over his face.

The other soldiers glanced from their lieutenant to Red Eagle. One nervously fingered the trigger of his gun.

"No one shoot, goddammit. Put your guns away. This one speaks English. He might just have some answers for the general." The lieutenant turned to Red Eagle, squaring his broad shoulders.

"It is dangerous to let me live," whispered Red Eagle. He had never experienced such hatred as he did then, staring into the man's cool eyes. *These eyes had seen his mother's people die,* he reminded himself. *These eyes had grazed over their dying faces as if they were dogs. Women and children. Old people.*

The lieutenant pushed his cap back, revealing sandy-gray hair. He laughed sardonically as he pointed his gun at Red Eagle's head. "Ha! You're wary. That's good. And it would be good if you'd talk," he said in halting Blackfoot. In English he added, "We know about Mountain Chief and Owl Child. We know the others, too, Crow Top, Black Weasel, Eagle's Rib—all were seen here, part of this winter camp. Where'd they run to? Were you and your friend here off to join them somewhere? Don't try to protect them. They're murdering thieves."

Red Eagle felt the hair on his neck stand up as he stared back at the man with the gun. "Who is it that murders women and children in their beds?" he demanded in Blackfoot.

The lieutenant waved the barrel of his pistol in a circle. "Start moving," he said carefully. "I got a half dozen men who'd like nothing better than to pump you full of lead."

Red Eagle's eyes narrowed as he watched the officer's long-barrelled pistol. The man was big and shrewd. No doubt he handled a gun well.

"You won't do those people any good lying face-down in the snow," added the lieutenant. He nodded his head in the direction of the black remains that were once Crying Wind's village.

At that moment, Red Eagle decided it didn't matter. Liza was very likely dead. His mother's people were dead. Running Antelope lay bleeding, having died a warrior's death.

Spinning on his heel, he pulled his knife. But before he realized what was happening, he felt the crushing blow.

In the next instant, the world went black.

✠　✠　✠

When Red Eagle opened his eyes, he could see he had been bound and gagged. His hands were tied behind him, as were his feet. He lay sprawled on his belly in the trampled snow, not far from the soldier's horses.

Cursing his foolishness, Red Eagle wished he had died. *Why hadn't they put a bullet to his head?* He thought of Running Antelope and groaned. At least he had died nobly.

He glanced at the line of tethered horses. With their heads lowered, they stood in the gathering darkness quietly. Steam clouded their nostrils and one stamped its foot. Beyond them, Red Eagle could see the curling smoke from the troopers' campfire.

Drawing his feet up behind him, Red Eagle fidgeted, but found he was bound tightly. He could not reach the twisted rope that held his feet. He tried rolling into a ball and rocking back and forth, but was still unable to reach the twisted knot.

Frustrated, he dropped his chin to the wet, icy snow under him and closed his eyes. Instantly, he opened them as he heard the deep voice of the lieutenant's boots crunching across the snow.

"What the hell?" A boot swung into his ribs and Red Eagle coughed as pain shot down his back and through his head. "Go ahead, try it! You wiggle another inch and I'll take off one finger at a time. You got me, breed?"

Red Eagle's nostrils flared and he growled instinctively, but held himself taut even as the lieutenant swung his boot a second time. "Maybe I should turn you over to those potlickers over there," taunted the big man. "They're half-drunk but they'd cotton to taking turns at you." He pointed to where the blue-clad men were gathered around the fire, their faces concealed by the wall of horses. "Whether you live or die means nothing to me," continued the lieutenant, his blue eyes hard and cool. "But it might just mean something to you—"

One soldier, hearing the taunt, clambered to his feet.

"Come on, Lieutenant," wailed another as he stumbled forward. "Look at 'im. He'd sooner piss on you!"

The lieutenant grumbled, "You idiot. DeTrobriand wants a few healthy ones to interrogate. Sick women and squalling papooses aren't what he wanted."

"This one's better dead," snapped a third soldier. "He's too damn wise."

"I'd just as soon put a gun to his head myself," came the lieutenant's reply. "But for now we're doing just as we were told. There'll always be another time to even scores," he added, gaze fixed on Red Eagle.

"Yea," added a tow-headed soldier who had moved within range of Red Eagle's head. "Lieutenant Cole's thinkin' all the time. He's got all kind of plans, don't ya, Lieutenant?"

Lieutenant Cole glared at the young, mouthy soldier. Swinging his boot once more, he turned on Red Eagle. "See how much they'd like a reason to finish you off? Think you really want to break free?" He laughed loudly then. "Hell, let's mount up. I'm tired of the stench and we've got a long way to ride before we reach the fort." He feigned a sigh. "Sorry there just don't seem to be any extra horses. I guess that means you'll have to stumble along behind!"

The soldiers mounted quickly, grumbling that they'd sooner shoot the dirty Indian as look at him. The lieutenant, removing the rope from his saddle, slipped one end through and around Red Eagle's bound wrists. He tied several knots before drawing it up tight.

Mounting, he wrapped the other end of his rope around the saddle horn. Clicking his heels against the horse's flanks, he bellowed, "Move out!"

Red Eagle grit his teeth, pulling against the rope that jerked him forward. He was not about to reveal that there were two good horses hidden down by the river. He would need those when he returned.

✠ ✠ ✠

Liza could not take another step. Her hands were swelling and her legs felt as heavy as stumps. She had to rest, and she suspected the other women and children needed it, too.

She dropped her buffalo robe to the snow and cried out, "Stop! Please! The children must have food and rest."

Bull Child, climbing off of Liza's back, squatted beside her in the snow. She had not left Liza's side since the massacre.

Mad Horse, turning on his heel, glared at Liza. He shook his head and said something to Cut Finger. Liza yelled back at him, mindless of the risk. "I don't know what you're saying, but I don't care! I need to sit down and so do the children. And we're hungry!"

Pushing a hand into her sack, Liza pulled out two strips of jerky and handed one to Bull Child. The girl chewed happily, saliva trickling down her upturned lips.

Cut Finger spread out her own buffalo hide and sat down a few yards from Liza. Pulling out a pouch, she handed her two sons some pemmican.

Mad Horse, growing angrier, stomped back and forth, to no avail. The women had all squatted on the riverbank, the children beside them, their hands out. One of the older boys, Skunk Cap, took a paunch and filled it with water and carried it around to the women. Mad Horse sat down, still angry, his steely gaze on Liza. Liza merely smiled, not caring any longer what the warrior might do to frighten her.

Suddenly remembering, she pulled out her bear claw necklace. It gave comfort to stroke the satin edges of the claws and bright beads and brought Red Eagle to mind. *Oh, that she had not wasted so much time on being stubborn, resisting getting to know him.*

Feeling Mad Horse's gaze upon her, Liza slipped the necklace back inside her buckskins. She turned to face the old man and his scorn burned her, even at this distance. The man was a demon, she thought, a shiver of foreboding running down her spine. He was not to be trusted.

Liza returned to her food, pulling Bull Child closer for comfort. Bull Child smiled up at her, moon face soft in the afternoon sunshine. The child was exhausted. They had walked for almost two days, sunup to sundown, with little food and less rest. They couldn't continue at this pace. It would be a death march.

Turning her eyes back on Mad Horse, Liza wondered if that was what he had planned.

If only Liza knew where they were going. She had tried to ask what lay ahead, but communication with Cut Finger was not simple. Cut Finger spoke more rapidly than Liza could follow; Crow Woman had helped Liza by speaking slowly and carefully. But Liza had understood that they were headed to Mountain Chief's village. And that must mean they were going to cross over into the British territory, north of the Medicine Line. *Would Red Eagle and her father figure it out?*

Time passed all too quickly. Unexpectedly, Mad Horse jumped to his feet and began beating Yellow Grass and several of the younger children with his walking stick.

"Stop it!" cried Liza, getting to her own feet. Mad Horse looked startled, his weasel eyes narrowed and bright. He waved his stick once more past Yellow Grass's face.

Liza spoke up. "We're getting up! All of us." She reached out and helped Bull Child to her feet. The sleepy little girl pulled her cape over her shoulders as she picked up her small bundle.

Immediately, the women and children fell into line. Liza and Bull Child took their places near the rear. Stepping carefully around the obviously icy spots near the water's edge, she trudged on. Only her mind escaped the terror that threatened to overwhelm her, taking her back to those last encounters with Red Eagle. *Were they the last she'd ever have?*

Why had she never told him how she felt? Why had she waited so long to reveal what burned within her? Would it now be too late? Liza bit her lip, refusing to give up hope. His memory was a tonic. If only she could drown herself in it.

That night the group found shelter beneath a rocky ledge. Enormous boulders, rolled together as if to form a rampart, provided a walled-in space with a roof that jutted out several feet. After building a fire, Cut Finger boiled some pemmican for soup, while Skunk Cap and several younger children tried to dig out roots from the icy shores of a creek.

The food tasted delicious and everyone spent the evening around the fire. Everyone except Mad Horse. Taking his share of the soup, he wandered off into the brush. For a long time he could be heard mumbling to himself. Rides-a-Horse said that he had some of the white man's whiskey. If so, sighed Liza, he could become even more dangerous.

Throughout the night, Liza trembled. In spite of the fire that Cut Finger kept burning and Bull Child's warm body curled next to hers, Liza could not sleep. Strange dreams and a thousand fearful thoughts tormented her, and Mad Horse's last hard looks sent shivers down her spine. She could not block out the last image of Crow Woman and Come Running dying in each other's arms. She wondered if it had been foolish to wander off with Mad Horse. *Would her father or Red Eagle ever find her?*

If she didn't know where she was going, how would they?

As dawn approached, the temperature dropped. The icy air was like a thousand tiny needles piercing her skin all over. Her face burned. She pulled her cape up over her head, wishing she'd not given her hood to Blue Willow. But Blue Willow had less to keep her warm than she did, she chided herself. Indeed, the girl was so slender Liza could have wrapped a buffalo robe around her three full times.

It was as first light touched the stone ceiling that she noticed something stretched out across the snow. She gasped. Slipping out of her robes, she headed away from the sleeping forms.

It was a naked body. Yellow Grass. She stopped in her tracks, a lump forming in her throat. "Oh, Lord," she stammered, taking a steadying breath. *Had the woman chosen to end her own life or had Mad Horse taken his first victim?*

Forcing herself to cross the open space, Liza knelt down

231

in the snow and drew the lifeless corpse to her. "Did he do this to you?" she whispered. She ran her fingers over the woman's cold flesh looking for wounds; her skin was as cold as the frosty air. "The animal," Liza snarled after spotting several bruises. *But why had he done it?*

Suddenly, Liza heard the warrior's heavy tread. Without a word, he leaned over and pushed Liza out of the way, then pulled Yellow Grass out of her arms and dragged her over the frozen ground. Her body thumped like a doll across the exposed, rocky knoll and Liza had to look away from the coffee-brown eyes staring back at her out of Yellow Grass's empty, sallow face.

Oh, she thought bitterly, *was this the beginning of the next nightmare? Would Mad Horse eliminate them all, one by one? The weakest first?*

Liza stumbled back to camp, where Bull Child was beginning to stir. Cradling the small, ebony-haired girl in her arms, she rocked back and forth. She couldn't lose her mind, she thought, nearly saying it out loud. She couldn't let Mad Horse or her own despair destroy her and the will to live. She couldn't end up like Yellow Grass.

And she wouldn't let anything happen to Bull Child or Cut Finger, or the others. She had already lost Crow Woman and Come Running, perhaps even her own father, Red Eagle, and Crying Wind. God forbid, but it could be so. *Dear God, and if it were?*

Kissing the top of the little girl's head, Liza stroked the tangled strands of hair as she chided herself. *How could she abandon hope? Wasn't each day a day closer to finding Red Eagle and her father?* That tiny seed of promise would have to be enough to feed her heart.

It was out of the eerie stillness that a sudden wail split the air. Cut Finger rushed back toward camp, a sorrowful expression across her face.

Mad Horse returned a short while later, his face sterner than ever, eyes more wary and nervous. He stared at Liza several times, as if to warn her. Liza did not turn away, knowing any shadow of fear would make her more vulnerable than she already was. Instead, she fingered her bear-claw necklace as if it had the power to restore her confidence.

Mad Horse's glance fell on the necklace.

And with a heavy blow to her head, she fell face-first against the wet earth.

CHAPTER 27

*F*ORT SHAW WAS SWARMING WITH SOLDIERS AS THE ARMY patrol entered the parade grounds several days later. Red Eagle, riding double with one of the privates, stared at the blue-clad men lingering nearby. He couldn't help but wonder how many had been on the march to the Pikuni camps.

The small group pulled up in front of a line of familiar white-washed buildings, several that housed officers and one that served as headquarters. Recalling visits to the fort as a child with his father, Red Eagle also remembered that there had been a greater sense of peace then; Indians and traders freely came and went. He recollected, too, how some of the soldiers teased him and taught him to play cards. One lieutenant, Davis Roberts, had also read stories to him. A stocky, gray-haired man, he had been laughed at by many of the younger soldiers for being soft on the half-breed son of Caine McCullough. But Roberts had simply ignored their remarks.

Red Eagle wondered what had happened to the smiling lieutenant. Had he been replaced by this blue-eyed soldier who drove his men and animals like a whiskey-peddling bullwhack-er? He caught the lieutenant's glance and turned away. *Did the man even have the power to read his thoughts?*

An abrupt stop caused him to flop against the back of the young private riding in front of him. The soldier was not much older than him, perhaps younger. He was yellow-haired and his face was long and pink and reminded Red Eagle of the hairless pigs he often saw running around the barns of the white set-tlers. The soldier had said nothing to him, even held himself stiff so that he wouldn't have to feel the pressure of Red Eagle's legs. But with his hands tied behind him and feet bound to the

235

leather of the soldier's saddle, Red Eagle was helpless. The lieutenant had even bound his mouth.

The private waited for his lieutenant to come and rescue
him. The grizzled lieutenant, grinning his sardonic smile,
approached Red Eagle. He ordered another soldier standing
nearby to release the breed while he kept his gun on him.

Red Eagle was yanked to the ground after his feet were
untied. As he fell forward in the snow, he heard the lieutenant
chuckle. He knew the big man was itching to rough him up
again and his ribs were too bruised to take another hit. He
would be no match, bound and sore as he was.

"Over there," the lieutenant commanded, pointing to a
low-roofed, long white building.

Red Eagle moved forward slowly. All eyes were on him
now, the crowd surrounding him growing in size as curious
men eyed him.

"These days, the men don't know whether to smile or
shoot when it comes to dealing with the Blackfeet," bellowed
the lieutenant. "Been too many double-talking Indians!"

Red Eagle held his tongue but his anger was evident by
his flashing eyes. The big lieutenant laughed his hideous laugh
again. "Can't wait to see what the general does with you! He's fit
to be tied these days. He might even hang you after he finds out
what you know."

Holding the door open to the general's front office, he
whispered to Red Eagle, "Walk softly, breed. You'd make good
buzzard bait if'n the buzzards could stomach you!"

The lieutenant gave him a push then and Red Eagle had
to resist the desire to turn and lunge at him. A private, standing
at attention, stepped forward. He kept his eyes on Red Eagle as
he spoke to the lieutenant. "This ain't Mountain Chief, is it,
Lieutenant? Or Owl Child? He's a half-breed—"

"Idiot, of course not! Hell, it'd be a wonder if you could
track a fat squaw through a snowdrift, Private!"

The private flushed, his tongue wiping his lips in an
exasperated sweep.

"Where's the general?"

"Takin' a smoke. He'll be back directly. Guess you could take him in." The private, still flushed and embarrassed, opened the general's office door.

Red Eagle turned his stare on the private as the lieutenant shoved him ahead. The private grimaced, his Adam's apple bobbing up and down in his long neck. Had it been another time and place, no doubt Red Eagle would have found the young private a friendly fellow. He didn't seem to have any real gall to him. But as it stood, Red Eagle saw him as one more of his enemies.

"Sit here," growled the lieutenant, as they entered the empty room. He pushed Red Eagle down onto a straight-backed chair placed not far from a desk.

Simultaneously, a man entered the room from another door. The lieutenant, standing quickly at attention, saluted. The general saluted in return, then waved his hand through the air. "What's this all about?" he said, his eyes on Red Eagle.

"A prisoner, sir. We caught up to him at the—uh, near the settlements," he added quietly.

The general frowned.

Red Eagle remembered him from days spent at the fort with his father, but said nothing. That was another lifetime ago.

"I don't understand. Who is he? Why have you trussed him like a pig?"

"Sir, he and another brave attacked us. We killed the other one after he stabbed O'Grady."

The general frowned. "Will this mess never end?"

He stroked the end of his narrow beard, which reminded Red Eagle of a patch of porcupine quills. His eyes were small and round, but not hostile. Rather, the man looked tired.

"Well, Lieutenant Cole, the scout said that you had apprehended one of Mountain Chief's bucks. So, what does he know?"

"Don't know, sir. He speaks English damn well. A half-breed. Attacked us with this." Pulling out Red Eagle's long knife, the lieutenant slid it across the general's desk. "Quite an Arkansas toothpick, I'd say."

The general glanced at it. "Yes, quite a knife. Where'd you get it?" He turned to Red Eagle, his eyebrows raised in two half-circles above his button eyes. "Have we ever met? You seem vaguely familiar."

Lieutenant Cole chuckled. "All breeds look the same."

"That's enough, Lieutenant," mumbled the general impatiently.

Red Eagle said nothing, but Lieutenant Cole prodded him with the end of his gun. "Answer the general's questions, or the next poke will have some lead to it," he whispered.

Red Eagle grit his teeth before responding. "The knife was from my father," he said abruptly. "Caine McCullough."

"McCullough?" growled DeTrobriand, getting to his feet. "Damn! Didn't you interrogate this man at all, Lieutenant?"

He pushed his chair back and walked to the window. "No wonder you looked familiar! Don't you realize what you've done, Lieutenant?" His eyes were on Cole, who shifted nervously. "You arrested the son of one of the army's most loyal traders. A man of integrity, he could walk into any Indian encampment throughout this territory. It's too bad he isn't alive today. Maybe some of this bloodshed could have been avoided. Now release this man, for God's sake!"

"Sir, if he'd had a gun—"

"I don't care, Lieutenant!" interrupted the general. "This man's father still has friends all over the country. Besides, we are not trying to take the hide of every Indian. At least not while I'm in charge. We've got enough problems to settle after Baker's bungled attack! I won't repeat myself, Lieutenant, untie him. You do take your orders from me."

Lieutenant Cole, slipping his own knife from its sheath, cut the rope binding Red Eagle's wrists. His round face was beet red and his blue eyes seemed to bulge from their sockets. Anger and hatred blazed in his eyes.

Red Eagle said nothing but he followed the lieutenant's every move. When the cords fell to the floor, he wrapped his hands around his wrists, massaging them until needles of feeling returned. The flesh had been rubbed raw and welts, like pale pink ribbons, circled his wrists.

DeTrobriand sighed. "I didn't recognize you. I guess it's been a few years. I would apologize, but I don't suppose it makes much difference. Take him to the infirmary, Lieutenant, and get some salve. Get him some food, too, for God's sake! He looks half-starved." He turned to Red Eagle. "The least I can do is give you a horse and provisions." He sighed, the tiredness returning to his face. "I have no desire to start a war," he said. "I had hoped to keep the peace, as much as the Pikuni leaders. Unfortunately, the situation with Mountain Chief and his son has people running scared. Settlers are afraid to move out of their houses and the army can't be everywhere. Perhaps, if we'd had the support we needed from Heavy Runner and the others, none of this would have happened." He frowned.

Red Eagle drew a deep breath. "Those who have survived will never believe you."

Lieutenant Cole growled, but the general held up a hand. "I daresay, enough blood has been spilled. Believe me, if and when we finally get Peter Owl Child and the others, the situation will be resolved."

"For who?" snapped Red Eagle.

DeTrobriand shook his head. "It could have been worse. We had fair reason to suspect that Heavy Runner was harboring the murderers. Action was required which would convince every Pikuni that we meant business."

Red Eagle straightened his shoulders, the blood racing to his face. "Murdering women and children?"

DeTrobriand sighed again. "Please, I don't remember your name—" When Red Eagle didn't respond, he placed his hand on Red Eagle's knife and picked it up slowly. "You are free to go," he added graciously. He raised his eyebrows as he held the knife out to Red Eagle.

"Mekotsepetan."

"Your Christian name?" returned the general. "Surely McCullough gave you a Christian name."

"It is buried with my father," replied Red Eagle, his eyes blazing.

The lieutenant took a step forward. "General, I'm begging your pardon, sir, but you're making a mistake. This man—"

DeTrobriand raised his hand as he turned his dark stare on the lieutenant. "I fear, Lieutenant Cole, you will be the one to end up in the cooler if you contradict me again. I have had enough confugalties and bloodshed. I intend to stop outlaws, not eradicate an entire people!"

Lieutenant Cole closed his mouth, but his blue eyes narrowed as he brought himself to attention. Red Eagle could feel the heat from the man's cold stare.

"Well, Mekotsepetan," continued DeTrobriand, "once again, you are free to go. I suppose you have no useful information as to the whereabouts of these renegades? Clearly, the sooner we catch them, the sooner life can return to normal for everyone, including the Pikuni."

Red Eagle could not speak. What point was there in telling the general that Crying Wind and his people had had no love for Mountain Chief or his son, that the man had taken to the warpath without sanction of the various tribes' leaders? The generals at Fort Benton had not listened to Heavy Runner, nor had they listened to Crying Wind and Many Words. Surely nothing could be gained by speaking his mind to this man. He turned his eyes to the floor, attention focused on the legs of the general's desk.

DeTrobriand shrugged, his voice droning on, "Of course the hunt will continue. More people will die on both sides. And, as I understand it, many of the Pikuni are suffering from smallpox—"

Red Eagle glanced up. This was new information. "The white scabs disease?" he said softly.

"Yes, and no doubt they could use some medicine. Indeed, I have already ordered medicine to be delivered to the villages along the Marias and Two Medicine, in exchange," he added carefully, "for information."

Red Eagle clenched his fists. Another battle had only just begun for the Pikuni. Without medicine, they were helpless.

"Yes, well," continued the general, "we know there are

those who know something. After all, the bodies of Red Horn and Big Horn, both outlaws, were found not far from Heavy Runner's. Sadly enough, this news will add more heat to the fire, so to speak. But this is purely academic, isn't it? You have no intention of helping us and I have no intention of forcing you to speak. Lieutenant, show our visitor out."

DeTrobriand pivoted away then, his gaze redirected out the window that overlooked the parade grounds. His slender hands were on his hips. Red Eagle, turning away, hesitated.

"Remember," said DeTrobriand softly, "if Mountain Chief does not turn himself in along with the others, all of the Blackfeet, including the Pikuni, will suffer. I am only a pawn in this larger game," he added. "Only a pawn. And if my men ever encounter you on the field of battle, any friendship I had with your father will mean nothing. Nothing."

Lieutenant Cole, his blue eyes flashing at Red Eagle, held the plank door open wide. The young private, still standing at attention, cast nervous eyes on Red Eagle. But neither trooper said anything as Red Eagle strode past them. Only when he stepped outside did the lieutenant speak.

"I'll be following your every step, breed. I know you know what the general wants. And I know you'd love to stick that blade through my guts. I get around. I get around and I have eyes everywhere. So don't think you're free of me! The general may be a fool, but I'm not. I've got plans, so be watching your back—" he added before calling out to a private nearby. "Get this breed a horse and some food! Then escort him through the front gate!"

Red Eagle glanced over at the big man. "I will be waiting," he said quietly.

"The next time we meet," promised Cole, "I'm going to slice you open and leave your stinking guts for the coyotes. So watch your step."

Once mounted, Red Eagle rode quickly out of the fort. The soft snow flew up around him like mud and even after he had gone a mile, he continued to spur his horse on at a trot. But his mind was not on the soldiers who stood staring after him, nor on the conversation he'd had with the general or Lieutenant Cole. It was on Liza and those who had survived the massacre.

Where were they now? Had Liza actually died from the pox? Is that why he'd not found any trace of her? Such a disease would spread like fire through the camps.

He would return to their camp and then set out to find her. If it was the last thing he did, he would find her.

Back at Fort Shaw, three men gathered on the outskirts of the parade grounds.

"The bastard," murmured Cole, his eyes on the horizon. "Before this thing is over, I'm going to skin him alive."

"Lieutenant, let it go," said Edelstein, the private who'd ridden double with Red Eagle on the long ride back to the fort. "Maybe you shouldn't be lookin' for a hog to kick—"

"O'Grady is dead," snapped Cole. "Don't forget that. And if that breed had his way, we'd all be stretched out on the snow. Nah, I've got a score to settle with that one."

The third soldier scratched his head. "Well, all I know is we got to get on with our plan. That detail is scheduled to go out first thing in the mornin'. You talked with the gener'l, yet, Lieutenant?"

"Yeah," Cole said, his eyes still hard, "it's taken care of. He knows I'm the man. Hell, I even speak a little of the language. Anyhow, it's all cleared, and you two yahoos are assigned to me. But we'll have to ditch Potter somewhere along the way, cause I have a feeling he won't agree to anything. Keep your mouth shut, though, Schluter. I know you like to talk."

"Well," sighed Schluter, "I'm not about to squeal. An' if you jest give Potter a jug, he'll be grinnin' like a possum eatin' a yellow jacket."

"True 'nough," added Edelstein.

"Let me handle it," said Cole, looking around. "We better split up. Get your gear packed. Don't try to haul too much or someone'll get suspicious. You got the guns hidden?"

"Sure do, Lieutenant. Ready and waitin'," said Schluter.

The lieutenant watched as the two privates ambled away, a scowl across his face. They were both as useless as tits on a boar pig, but he couldn't manage this without them. Besides, they were loyal, and he was counting on that loyalty to get him through the toughest spots. Potter was another story; he had a conscience.

Turning on his heel, he moved towards headquarters. DeTrobriand would need some soothing after the encounter with the half-breed, and he certainly didn't want to raise the general's suspicions. After all, the old man had agreed to let him lead the detail up into the British territory. And it looked like this might be the only chance he'd have for a long time to make a move.

CHAPTER 28

*R*ED EAGLE REACHED RIPLINGER'S EXHAUSTED. THE old man, hearing a horse approach, came out. He rushed to help Red Eagle off the yellow dun.

"Damn, you're all in," he said.

Red Eagle shook his head, but his body was stiff from the cold and the beating his ribs had taken hadn't helped his disposition. The trader led him into the back room of his post.

"I'll see to the animal," he assured Red Eagle, eyeing him carefully. "Where the tarnation have you been all these weeks, anyway? I guess you been there, seen it? Yea, it's bad. Worse than anybody figgered it would get. Still cain't believe it—"

"What about Liza?" said Red Eagle. He rubbed his legs to get feeling back into them. Three days and nights in the saddle had left him half-frozen.

"I don't know," said Riplinger sadly. "I've had my ears open. I know she was alive before the attack. I talked with her, 'course that was before the pox. But a bunch of Heavy Runner's men came along; man, they looked bad. They was lookin' for medicine but I ain't got that kind of stuff. Oh, a little laudanum, but that's all. That won't cure no scabs. Anyway, I asked how she was farin' an' they seemed to think she was all right. But since the attack, hell, visitors have been as scarce as hen's teeth."

"How about the others?"

"Well, I know there's a settlement downriver aways. I could take you there but you can find it. I wouldn't step foot in the camp, though. Never can tell who's carryin' the scabs disease."

Red Eagle got up to leave.

"Eat somethin' first. You won't do nobody no good if

you're flat on your face. I got a pot of stew and some hardtack. Got some canned goods you can take with you, too. Mebbe some canned milk for some of them babies—"

Red Eagle put his hand on the older man's shoulder. "Yes, that would be good." Then he asked, "Crying Wind? Have you seen him?"

Riplinger shook his head. "No, but I'll send one of these fools I got hangin' round out after him. A couple of 'em are thinkin' of joinin' up with Mountain Chief, but I've been tryin' to dissuade 'em. Hell, that'll only bring more bloodshed. Not that I can blame 'em."

After eating, Red Eagle hit the trail again. He glanced back over his shoulder, hoping he wasn't headed in the wrong direction. It would be wasted effort if he was, but with no better destination, he moved on.

Thick gray clouds gathered along the northern horizon and a stiff wind blew. The weather had been tolerable, in spite of the freezing nights. But if the weather changed, travel would be more difficult. He spurred the yellow dun into a soft lope. He had to reach some kind of settlement soon.

As early morning light broke through the purple dawn, the party of survivors moved out. The air did not seem as cold to Liza as it had been, perhaps because they had kept a large fire burning all night. Even Mad Horse had welcomed the heat, crowding closer to it than he normally did.

Liza trudged on, her mind whirling with the confusion of the last few days. Day and night, Mad Horse kept her with him. Keeping her hands bound, he'd also tied a noose around her neck, which he seemed to enjoy pulling on unexpectedly. Bull Child had been taken away from her, so the child clung to Cut Finger, her dark eyes wide with fear. Whenever Liza tried to console her, Mad Horse kicked or knocked her down. If only she hadn't decided to follow the angry, old warrior.

It was clear he blamed Liza for their misfortunes. Yellow Grass had been the first to die, but not the last. A young boy, Walks-with-the-Moon, did not wake up the morning after

Yellow Grass died. And Rides-a-Horse had fallen through ice, forcing the party to stop and build a fire, delaying them further. Finally, Mad Horse himself nearly sliced off two of his fingers cutting some tall stalks they were collecting along a stream-bank.

All this the old warrior blamed on Liza, and he refused to let anyone come near her. He alone fed her and Liza found it increasingly difficult to swallow the bits of food he shoved in her mouth. His ugly, scarred face and foul-smelling body caused her stomach to rebel. Already, she had thrown up the last meal he'd forced down her. And he rarely gave Liza privacy, forcing her to squat whenever she had to pass water. It was a humiliation she could hardly endure.

He also coveted her necklace. Not understanding why it carried such power, she caught him eyeing it whenever they stopped to rest or eat. She wondered when he might try to take it and why he hadn't yet. Most of all, she wondered what he'd do to her after gaining possession of it.

Thankfully, he had not molested her. Not yet, but Liza wondered if he eventually would. Fortunately, the man feared her as well. Was it the bear-claw necklace?

She tromped on, growing numb to the cold and wet. *It would almost be a relief to die*, she mused. After all her struggles to live, it would be the greatest irony to submit to death now. But perhaps it would be her escape.

She shook her head and took a steadying breath, carefully placing her right foot in front of her left. As she did, she whispered his name. "Red Eagle." Even the sound of his name gave her hope and she could not let that thin thread of faith go. Her very life seemed to hang on it.

But it was not just his name that gave her strength. It was the memories of him that she relived day and night: the warm smiles flashed whenever he saw her in Crying Wind's camp; his smiling, taunting eyes the first afternoon he caught her half dressed by the river; his gentle touch and sweet breath upon her skin when they were alone; his words of love and willingness to wait on her; even his regard for her father and Crying Wind.

Oh, Red Eagle! No longer torn by conflicting emotions, her love had become painfully clear. It didn't matter that their worlds had been separated by time and invention. It only mattered that she would never, could never, love any man as she loved him.

And her father. He had been right. *To understand one's past was part of choosing one's future.* If only she'd understood that before. If only she'd understood all of it before now.

If only she'd shared her love.

She hesitated, taking the next step carefully. Mad Horse, impatient, pulled the rope that bound her.

She cried out, wishing she had the strength of a wild cat.

He grunted and tugged the leash again.

She yanked back, hoping to catch him unaware. Instead, he reached out and slapped her across the mouth. He growled a curse.

Holding back tears, Liza moved on. All she had now was memories, and the strength that came from loving Red Eagle. It filled her with the will to survive. It sustained her as she pressed wearily on, legs so stiff she could hardly feel them. It sustained her as Mad Horse drew her beside him at night, his eyes burning her with hatred and even desire.

If she could get a knife she could try to escape. But Cut Finger and the other women were afraid, too; they feared for their own safety and for that of the children.

Toward evening, Mad Horse called a halt. It was still light enough for the younger children to forage for wood and he sent one of the older boys off to set a snare. Dragging Liza to a tree, he tied her to a branch that hung high above her head. With his mouth set in a grim frown, Skunk Cap followed Mad Horse into the trees, a roughened spear slung over his shoulder. Only Cut Finger, Sharp Hand, Fat Dog, and Rides-a-Horse remained.

Liza tried to coax Cut Finger to help her. The woman hesitated, her eyes flitting nervously left and right. The area was heavily wooded and Liza knew it was risky. *What if Mad Horse was watching them, even now?*

Whispering too softly for Liza to understand, the women

edged closer. Finally, without warning, Cut Finger rushed to her, a small boning knife clutched in her hand. Shaking, she tried to cut through the heavy sinew thongs. She whimpered and tried again.

"Hurry," whispered Liza, her eyes fixed on the spot where she had last seen Mad Horse. "Oh, please!" Her hands shook with fear and foreboding.

Cut Finger mumbled something unintelligible but Liza knew she was working as fast as possible. She bit her lip so hard she tasted blood.

Just then, Mad Horse came thrashing through the snow, his own knife raised. Skunk Cap stumbled after him, fighting to keep his balance. Seeing blood running down Skunk Cap's face, Liza screamed. So did Rides-a-Horse and Sharp Hand, who ran to help him. Trembling uncontrollably, the boy collapsed in the snow only a few feet from the horrified women.

"Watch out! Cut Finger, get out of the way!" shrieked Liza. "Dear God! No!"

Enraged, Mad Horse turned on Cut Finger, screaming and threatening her. She spun and faced him, cursing him, calling him a 'mad dog' and 'one who had disgraced the people.' Her eyes blazed, hard and dark, and her voice was shrill and loud. Cursing him again, she swept her blade through the air. He stopped in his tracks, panting like a wounded animal.

Liza feared he would kill Cut Finger. He didn't. Instead, backing away, he eyed the group of women and children crowding behind Rides-a-Horse. Sharp Hand, helping Skunk Cap to his feet, turned and spoke to Cut Finger. The air crackled with tension.

Hanging from the limb, Liza was useless, helpless. She was also terrified.

❊　❊　❊

Lieutenant Simon Cole raised his hand. "We'll camp here."

Edelstein looked around, clearly disturbed. "Shouldn't

we find someplace more protected, Lieutenant?"

"What better spot is there than one where you can clearly see the enemy coming?"

"What about over there, in those trees?" piped Potter. He pointed to a small grove of cottonwoods.

"I like it here, Private," snapped Cole. "Set up camp."

The three privates dismounted, each taking a pack horse and leading it to a central area.

"Only unpack the essentials, Schluter," directed Cole. "We'll be up before sunrise and I don't want to waste any time repacking those animals."

Schluter nodded. "Hear that, fellahs? Just the gear."

Potter mumbled something under his breath.

"You got a problem with the order?" The lieutenant's bright blue eyes flashed as he stepped around the mule.

"No, sir," grumbled Potter.

"Edelstein, build a fire. Not too big, cause if anybody's passing through, we don't want to alert them to our presence."

"Sure, Lieutenant."

With camp set up, Lieutenant Cole wandered off. Potter, curious, asked, "Where's he headed?"

"How the hell do I know?" said Schluter, shifting uncomfortably.

"Taking a piss, most likely," mumbled Potter. "He must think he's got somethin' the rest of us don't." He laughed at his own joke, but Schluter only frowned.

"I wouldn't be makin' too many jokes at the lieutenant's expense," suggested Edelstein. He nervously looked for any sign of Cole. The man gave him the willies. In fact, he didn't know how he had ended up as a part of this crazy scheme. He really hadn't had much to complain about. The army had been good to him. Sure, it was beans and not much else, but that was as good as he ever got back home.

No, he was nervous about how Cole's plan was going to unfold, and where they were headed. Probably to jail or maybe the end of a rope. Deserters and thieves were not tolerated.

Potter was still grumbling. "At least we could throw on

some extra wood. Not every day you can find enough kindlin' to build a good fire. I'm headed over there, get us some big limbs. You wanna come, Edelstein?"

Edelstein shook his head. "Better forget it. I'm tellin' you—"

Potter got up, disgusted, and he ambled across the open meadow.

That second, the sound of a gun reverberated through the emptiness. Jumping to his feet, Edelstein watched Potter as he fell, dropping like a sack of grain against the snowy earth. A blood-curdling howl was his only protest.

"Damn!" cursed Schluter, turning to Edelstein. "Was that the lieutenant?"

Edelstein swallowed the lump in the back of his throat. His hand was on the butt of his knife. "I don't know, but it came from over there." He pointed to the trees, the place they'd last seen Cole. "Jeez," he added, beads of sweat already forming across his brow, "what's he up to?"

"He said he was gonna take care of Potter, but I didn't think he meant to kill him."

"What d'ya mean, take care of him?" whispered Edelstein, choking back his spit.

A shout brought them both to attention. "Come on, you fools, get over here! I can't do this by myself!"

Edelstein followed Schluter reluctantly. He didn't like this turn of events but knew he was stuck, at least for the time being.

Cole stood over the fallen body of Potter like a hunter with his prey. He was smiling, taunting. He kept his eyes on Edelstein. "Take his scalp, Private," he said, slowly and deliberately.

"Wha—?" squeaked Edelstein.

"Don't gawk," said Cole. "We've gotta make this look like an Indian attack. They'll blame ole Owl Child sure enough. Now take his scalp and make it a clean swipe!"

"But, Lieutenant—"

"Edelstein, I am not about to let you leave us in a pinch here. I told you we're out of here, and we've got to make it look

251

good, like we just escaped by the skin of our teeth. Right, Schluter?" He turned his cool stare on Schluter.

Schluter was quick to respond. "Hey, don't think I ain't grateful! I've had enough of this poor man's army." He laughed nervously, rubbing his thin fingers through his thin moustache. "Edelstein," he said, "you better wise up. The lieutenant is offerin' us the chance of a lifetime. They'll just figger Potter got kill't off by them renegades. Maybe we'll even be heroes, only we won't be around to hear the cheerin'! It's a devil of a plan," he said brightly, turning back to Cole.

Edelstein's heart pounded against his ribs. He knew he didn't have many choices, but he wasn't sure he could do this terrible thing. He pulled his knife out and looked at it, his hand trembling almost uncontrollably. *Wasn't there some other way to take care of the man?* He looked up at Cole.

It was then he realized he had waited too long. The bullet sung out and he wondered if someone had stabbed him with a hot poker. He was on his knees but he wanted to get up. It was impossible. He opened his mouth to speak but the words were lost in saliva that bubbled out between his lips.

"Damn," was all he managed before he fell across the snow.

CHAPTER 29

*E*ARLY THE NEXT MORNING, RED EAGLE FINALLY SPIED THE coulee where many of the Pikuni survivors had settled. A short distance from the river, they were sheltered by a line of granite rocks. To the west was a grove of elms, bare and black against the cold gray landscape. But the sky was clear and blue and the air crisp.

Several army tents had been arranged in a large circle, forming the center of the tiny village. Fires burned and people milled about but the scene was almost haunting; the people were as expressionless and hollow as ghosts. No dogs barked and there were no children running haphazardly through the village. Only a handful of pitiful horses and two scrawny mules were hobbled near the farthest tents.

Red Eagle approached the camp slowly. As he passed the first tents, several old women stopped and gazed up at him. They neither smiled nor greeted him. Moving on, they seemed intent on hiding themselves.

He drew his horse up to a tent where he noticed a tall, dark warrior emerging. Without dismounting, he waited for the middle-aged man to speak. The man did so after studying him closely.

They exchanged brief greetings and Red Eagle slipped off his horse. The horse was so tired it did not seem inclined to wander. A boy, perhaps eight or nine, suddenly appeared and touching the muzzle of the animal, smiled up at Red Eagle.

"Watch him for me?" asked Red Eagle.

The boy nodded eagerly. Red Eagle reached inside his pouch and handed him a piece of Riplinger's beef jerky. The boy grinned.

"I am Stands Down," said the man, pulling aside the tent's flap to let Red Eagle pass inside. The two men sat down beside his fire. "I am a member of Heavy Runner's band."

"And I am Red Eagle, nephew to Crying Wind."

Stands Down nodded. "Ah, Crying Wind! He is here!"

Red Eagle jumped to his feet. "He is here? Where?"

The warrior got up and led him back out of the tent. "He was found five days' ride from here. He was with three other men who have since left our village to locate their own people."

"But Crying Wind?"

"It is not well with him. He does not speak nor does he move. I fear his heart cannot bear the pain. He will die soon."

Red Eagle swallowed. "He saw the villages—"

"Yes."

Red Eagle cursed, then sighed. "It is too great a sadness. I understand his desire to die."

"And I," agreed Stands Down. "It would be far better to die in battle than to sit and rot." He pointed to his head and then his heart. "Even I have thought of letting go of this life. It would be much better to cross over to the Sand Hills."

Red Eagle nodded, acknowledging the other man's grief. "Tell me, was there a man, a white holy man, Many Words, who was found with Crying Wind? Perhaps weak, also near death?"

"I have not seen or heard of anyone by that name. The others who came were not he. But, truly, the young warriors might not have let him live," he added carefully. "Many are bent on revenge."

Red Eagle nodded. "He was very near death when I last saw him. Perhaps it is better." His eyes brightened. "But what about a dark-haired, white Pikuni woman, Liza Five Shots? Have you seen or heard of her?"

Stands Down shook his head. "A white woman in this place would not be safe. There are so many ready to join Owl Child, Black Weasel, and Mountain Chief. Me, I am too old, and I fear the strength of the white man's army with its wagon-guns. But if I were yet a young warrior, I would take up my war shield. The peace the Napikwans promised has come to nothing. Nothing."

How could anyone argue with such a hard truth? Both men stood without speaking.

"I would like to see Crying Wind—" Red Eagle said at last. His heart was fearful, but anxious.

Stands Down pointed to a tent standing at the far edge of the ring. Red Eagle nodded and moved towards it, his hands clenched tightly.

He had known the sight of the massacre would destroy Crying Wind. A man of such great kindness and fairness would never understand the cruelty of those he had once trusted. Red Eagle only wished the old man had died before seeing the village. Like Many Words, it would have been better for him.

Crying Wind was not alone. An old woman sat to one side of the gray-haired warrior, her mouth moving silently, small, black pearl eyes lost in the folds of her brown face. She nodded to Red Eagle and he nodded in return. Then he turned to his uncle. Stretched out on a bed of leaves, covered by a buffalo robe, his pale face was empty of expression while his wrinkled hands lay mute upon his shrunken chest.

This terrible thing has destroyed him, thought Red Eagle.

He is nothing but the hollow shell of a stranger. Perhaps his larger-than-life spirit had already departed this world. If so, he was in a better place.

"Uncle," said Red Eagle, dropping to his knees before him, "it is Red Eagle." He felt for the soft pulse of the man, startled to feel it against his fingers. "Oh, I hoped you would be spared the evil that has come upon the people." He fought back a stabbing pain which gripped his belly.

Taking a deep breath, he tried again. "But I pray now that He Who Sees All frees your spirit quickly so that you can walk away and join your wives and children. I wish you a good journey, Uncle."

He dropped his head then, unable to say more. It was too terrible to see what had become of this good leader, a holy man, his mother's brother. If only he could have died as a warrior, on the trail or on a battlefield.

Tears of anger suddenly filled Red Eagle's eyes, and they

dropped unashamedly onto Crying Wind's neatly folded hands. He stumbled to his feet and rushed outside. He did not stop to speak to the old woman.

Stands Down was waiting for him. In silence, Red Eagle followed the somber warrior to his tent, where a young woman gestured for them to sit. Red Eagle obliged, taking the seat beside Stands Down, and the girl smiled shyly. Stands Down introduced her as Blue Feather, his only remaining daughter.

She was lovely and Red Eagle wondered if she was married, or, perhaps, widowed. She did not conduct herself as a maiden, but Stands Down seemed intent on showing her off to him, calling her to wait on Red Eagle again and again.

Red Eagle was polite. It would have been unthinkable to be otherwise. But he did not want his gestures or actions misunderstood by Stands Down or his anxious daughter. He dared not venture into conversation with her.

After the meal, Blue Feather retreated to the far end of the tent. Stands Down took out his pipe and offered it to Red Eagle. They smoked for several minutes in silence. Then Stands Down invited Red Eagle to stay on with them.

Glancing momentarily at Blue Feather, Red Eagle said, "It is very kind of you. I have travelled many days without rest. You have fed me well but there are those I still seek and I cannot rest until I find them."

"We have heard that many turned north, into the territory that belongs to our brothers. There they will find shelter and protection."

"Yes, but still I cannot stay. You are gracious and your kindness will always be remembered."

Stands Down grunted. "Blue Feather will prepare food for your journey and, if you choose, she will accompany you. It is cold these nights." He leaned forward to add, "There are few men here who need a young wife, although many make their requests. She has refused them all. But I see she likes you."

Red Eagle tried to avoid the look in Blue Feather's dark eyes.

Stands Down continued, "I would also like to send Blue Feather away from here, before the white-scabs sickness reaches her. Those afflicted have set up their own village but I fear, as do many, that it will come and take our remaining children. The army promised medicine but it does not come."

Red Eagle recalled the lieutenant's and general's casual remarks about trading information for the much-needed medicine. He wondered if he should have obliged but shook his head. It was likely a deception and what could he have told them that they didn't already know?

"It is a bitter joke," continued Stands Down, "that the white scabs disease continues to spread. It is the army's best weapon. But perhaps it will turn on the soldiers, those who steal the Pikuni horses or possessions?"

Red Eagle nodded, then rushed to explain, "I wish not to offend you or your daughter, Stands Down, but I can not take a companion. I will be moving quickly. Blue Feather is young and lovely. It will not be long before she finds a good husband—"

"I am sorry you have refused," said Stands Down. "She is strong and has a keen mind. She would make an excellent wife. She is also a capable warrior and has learned to use a rifle, as well as the bow. She would make a mighty warrior's wife."

Once more Red Eagle declined. "Please forgive me, Stands Down. I do not refuse because she is not attractive enough. But I must refuse. I hope I do not dishonor her or you, in any way."

At first the old warrior did not respond but finally said, "I do not understand. Even if you have a sits-beside-you-wife, Blue Feather would make a good second wife. She is not boastful or noisy and I care not for horses or gifts, but," he shrugged, "I can see that you are sure of your answer. I wish you well on your journey, my friend. Perhaps another young man will come along soon."

Red Eagle nodded. "I am sure of it."

Stands Down slapped his thigh then, signaling that the conversation had come to an end. Red Eagle stood.

"Food will be provided you," said Stands Down. "Take it.

257

It is our gift. And do not worry about Crying Wind. His greatness is well known and we will care for his body."

Red Eagle tried hard not to reveal his deep sadness. "Thank you. Both gifts are received with many thanks. I also have a gift for you and your people here. Cans of food and milk for the babies and whoever goes hungry."

Stands Down followed him outside. He took one of the parcels Riplinger had packed for Red Eagle. In exchange, he tied on the leather sack of provisions Blue Feather brought him. She then disappeared into the tent without another word.

"If I pass this way again," said Red Eagle suddenly, leaning close to Stands Down, "and I have not taken a wife, nor Blue Feather a husband, we will talk."

Stands Down smiled and Red Eagle was glad he had pleased his host. The two men then exchanged farewells and Red Eagle mounted his animal, anxious to be on his way.

✠ ✠ ✠

The trail leading north wound along the river. Cole, in the lead, whistled brightly. He led two of the four pack mules. Casting a glance at Schluter, he chuckled.

"Don't take it all so damn hard," he said. "Potter was a problem from the beginning and Edelstein was a coward. Better to get rid of such triflings before we hit any real snags."

Schluter found it impossible to speak. The memory of what they'd done haunted him but he knew better than to reveal that to the lieutenant. No doubt the man would slice his scalp off next, without batting an eye. The two bloody pieces, one blonde and one brown, hanging from the pack box ahead of him, were a pretty clear warning.

A warning he took to heart.

He tried to think of something to say. He looked around at the changing landscape. The area was more wooded here, which was nice, but the snow was deeper, harder to move through. They'd been pushing the animals for two days now, stopping only to sleep and eat. But he wasn't going to complain. He had seen the meanness in Simon Cole, the cruel hardness in his eyes. He'd never known anybody so mean.

If only there'd been another way out. Like Cole, he'd grown weary of the monotonous, pitiful conditions at the fort. DeTrobriand was worthless and most of the men nearly so. If he could just forget the look in Cole's eyes, and the bloody, empty face of Potter and Edelstein, he could maybe look forward to the money. Maybe, but maybe not.

He sighed audibly. With the money they got from pawning medicine, whiskey, and the stolen rifles, the two could make a handsome sum. Then they'd high-tail it to California.

Holding his gloved hand in the air, Cole signalled a stop. Schluter reined in his horse. "What's up, Lieutenant?" he said, his voice coming out in a thin squeak.

"Tracks," said the lieutenant quietly. "Lots of them. Little ones and big ones. I'd say we have us a party of women and children up ahead." He turned around and grinned. "Keep your eyes wide open. I wouldn't want us to miss anything so interesting!" He laughed then and the sound echoed in the dome of silence that surrounded them. "A man gets lonely out here, doesn't he, Schluter?" he added.

Schluter kept his thoughts to himself, grunting a simple 'uh huh.' He tapped his horse lightly and fell into line. Immediately his eyes fell across the scraps of Edelstein and Potter flopping against the pack saddle ahead.

"God a'mighty," he cursed silently, "the man's crazy. Meaner'n a rattlesnake on a hot skillet."

※ ※ ※

Liza worried that Mad Horse might find a way to retaliate against Cut Finger and the others. Having freed her after the encounter in the woods, Cut Finger ordered Mad Horse to leave. Glaring at each of them in turn, he had finally left.

At first everyone was relieved.

After two days of pressing on, however, the group realized they had wandered from the trail and found themselves forced to cross a part of the river that was wide and perilous. Rides-a-Horse wanted to turn back and find Mad Horse. Cut Finger staunchly refused, saying they could manage without him.

The river was wide and the banks steep; in several places craggy bluffs stretched out over the water. There seemed to be no easy crossings anywhere. At the same time, there was no way to be sure it was frozen clear through. Liza could hear the rush of water beneath the iced surface.

Skunk Cap continued to limp along, but it was Cut Finger who was leading the group now. Sadly, they all grew weaker every day.

They spent a day deliberating over the best way to cross the water. The children, delighted to have some freedom, ran up and down the banks digging for roots and wild onions that had survived the winter or greens and stems, which could be added to a soup.

On the second day, Cut Finger managed to trap a snow-shoe rabbit and the children devoured the roasted meat eagerly. It was a welcome change from pemmican and dried meal. Without Mad Horse, there would be little fresh meat.

Rides-a-Horse continued to worry about food. "My stomach growls day and night," she whined. "We need more food! I could eat an entire rabbit—"

Sharp Hand shook her head. "The Sun Chief watches over us, woman. See how he has provided for us already?"

Rides-a-Horse quipped, "Then let the Sun Chief provide us with more meat. My belly is too empty! At least Mad Horse was a hunter—"

Fat Dog, one of the older women, stepped forward. She had said very little in the days they had travelled together. "We all cry for food," she said. "The children are hungry but they do not growl. See, even now they are cheerful."

"They do not have bellies that require as much as mine," snapped Rides-a-Horse.

Fat Dog frowned. Rides-a-Horse was a difficult woman

and sniffed about everything.

Suddenly, a cry came up from the water. Cut Finger was waving to them. "Come! Come quick! Look what we found!"

Rides-a-Horse and Sharp Hand were immediately on their feet. Liza and Fat Dog followed. Even Skunk Cap hobbled down to see what the commotion was about.

"Ha! Do not eat it until we get there!" cried Rides-a-Horse. She slid down an icy embankment, her fat arms waving through the air.

There, along the frozen edge of the water, Cut Finger and the children were struggling to hold onto something. At first, Liza could not see what it was, but it thrashed wildly in the weeds and grass.

"Ach!" shrieked Rides-a-Horse, clapping her hands.

"Tsanistapiwats?" asked Liza, trying to see over the heads of the children. Bull Child had joined Liza, her eyes dancing with mischief.

"Can you not see it?" cried Rides-a-Horse. "It is a young beaver!"

Liza's eyes widened.

"He did not spot us as he swam under the ice!" shouted Cut Finger, triumphantly. "See, his lodge is downstream."

"Foolish pup," clucked Rides-a-Horse. "His foolishness has provided us with our next meal."

"The beaver is strong medicine," ventured Skunk Cap, who had stepped forward. "What do we have that would make a gift for the Underwater People so that they will not be angry?"

Rides-a-Horse shrugged. "Perhaps Five Shot's necklace!" she cried. "It also has strong medicine—"

Liza wrapped her hand around the beads and claws hanging from her neck. "No—" she said, stepping back.

"Well, I am too hungry to worry about it," snapped Rides-a-Horse. "Even a hungry warrior has eaten his brother the beaver. Surely he does not begrudge hungry children a meal?"

"Help me!" cried Cut Finger, as the animal twisted in her hands. "We're going to lose him!"

"Get a club," laughed Sharp Hand.

Fat Dog and Sharp Hand scrambled to find rocks or sticks large enough to knock the beaver out. Skunk Cap, taking the largest stick, stunned the animal with three good swings. He then slit its throat.

"I want its claws," he said, as Fat Dog and Sharp Hand dragged it back to a level place in the snow.

Fat Dog nodded. "You killed him. You are welcome to them. But for that, you can also help me skin Mr. Beaver."

Skunk Cap and Fat Dog skinned the animal and in no time, they had cut the meat away and sliced it into thin strips.

"We will boil the meat and eat our fill tonight," said Fat Dog to the children, "then dry what we do not eat. Tomorrow we will move on. We will cross the water and be on our way. See," she added jovially, "the Above Ones heard our cries."

In the morning, however, Liza woke to the sounds of worried voices. Skunk Cap, in conference with Cut Finger and Sharp Hand, was obviously concerned about something. Liza approached them quietly.

Cut Finger turned to her. "Skunk Cap says there are riders coming from that direction." Pointing to the south, she frowned. "He fears we angered the Underwater People because we did not leave a gift. It was bad medicine." She shook her head, her lips pinched tight.

Rides-a-Horse, joining the group, protested. "It is not wrong to take such an animal when there is hunger."

"How does Skunk Cap know there are riders coming?" Liza asked as she scanned the horizon carefully, seeing nothing.

"He went off during the night," explained Sharp Hand. "He saw the pale glow of a campfire and smelled the animals."

Liza looked over at the boy, impressed by his abilities, especially in light of his injuries. He would be a strong warrior someday. "What does he think we should do?"

"What can we do?" moaned Rides-a-Horse. "We cannot cross the river without knowing where it is safe! We will be swept under and frozen in the water. And what about the children? Oh, if Mad Horse was with us, he would know what to do."

Cut Finger frowned. "We will just have to find a way," she said. "We must not whine or it will frighten the children."

No one argued with her.

CHAPTER 30

SKUNK CAP AND CUT FINGER FINALLY AGREED ON A place to ford. It was high noon and the sun, though brilliant in the blue sky, shed little warmth. A strong breeze was blowing and everyone huddled together in silence, contemplating the fearful obstacle.

"I will go first," said Skunk Cap. "Watch me carefully. Put your feet where I put mine. Do not move too fast and do not wait too long. We must follow each other closely."

Cut Finger nodded but Liza could see the apprehension in her eyes. No one knew if the ice would hold them. In places it was thin enough to see the water underneath. If it could hold them just long enough—that was all they could hope for.

"Send the children after me," continued Skunk Cap.

"What if one falls in?" demanded Rides-a-Horse. "I shall go after you," she said, "and help the youngest ones."

"But you are heavy," protested Sharp Hand. "Let me go. I am smaller, faster, and stronger than you!"

Cut Finger frowned. "Sharp Hand is right. She will go second and the children will follow. Then Fat Dog will cross. You will go after her," she said, turning to Rides-a-Horse. "Five Shots and I will go last."

Bull Child pulled on Liza and shook her head. Liza kissed her. "Perhaps Bull Child can go with me?"

Cut Finger glanced over at Skunk Cap before answering. "Yes. Very well. Now we must strap whatever we have to our backs. Do not carry anything in your hands, for you will need them if you slip!"

Everyone quickly prepared their own packs. It would be impossible to take everything and as Liza stood looking across

265

the crystalline slab of water she wondered, not for the first time, if she were making a terrible mistake. She should never have left the village site. Surely Red Eagle, her father, and Crying Wind had returned by now; they were probably looking for her. She turned and faced south. *What if they thought her dead? Would they venture this far?*

And what if the riders Skunk Cap had spotted were actually Red Eagle and her father?

She grabbed Cut Finger by the hand. "I cannot go," she announced, taking a deep breath. "I cannot go any further. What if Red Eagle loses our trail? If the men Skunk Cap spotted is them, I must wait here! Don't you see?"

Cut Finger shook her head. "Skunk Cap said the riders were dog-faced soldiers. He saw them well enough to see that they were not Pikuni!"

Liza bit her lip. Her heart fluttered and she felt sick. *Oh, that she had never left at all.*

"We must go," said Cut Finger softly. She patted Liza on the shoulder. "Now."

Liza turned around. She shook off her fear and fought tears. *What other choice did she have?* She straightened her shoulders and nodded.

Skunk Cap had already started across the ice. Stepping carefully, he placed one moccasined foot in front of the other. Sharp Hand followed closely behind, stopping to direct the footsteps of the silent children, who almost seemed to skate over the ice. Fat Dog was next.

It was as Rides-a-Horse stepped out on the ice that Liza shivered. The woman lumbered awkwardly, first one way and then the other. Liza stifled a scream when Rides-a-Horse slid and fell to her knees, but the woman quickly got to her feet. Turning to show them that she had recovered, Rides-a-Horse didn't realize the ice was cracked. Liza instinctively threw her arms out.

But the woman was in the river. With a harrowing scream, she catapulted into the still, black water. Cut Finger, moving like a flash, ran to the bank and slid across the thickest piece of ice on her knees. Rides-a-Horse gasped, the frigid water sucking the screams right out of her. Skunk Cap, on the far shore, stood yelling to Fat Dog to hurry. Meanwhile, he, too, scrambled out onto the ice.

Liza, paralyzed at first, stumbled to the shoreline. Bull Child tried to follow her but she ordered the child back. Trembling, she approached the ice carefully. "Let me hold onto your hand!" she called to Cut Finger.

Cut Finger ignored her as she inched farther onto the ice.

"Oh, dear Lord," Liza whispered as she heard the ice cracking all around her, "save them!" She waited, holding her breath.

Suddenly she heard a child's tiny voice raised in a muffled scream. Spinning around, she gasped.

It was Mad Horse!

He had Bull Child by the hair, his long knife at her throat. Liza, throwing herself back to shore, scrambled after him. He laughed, the black pool of his mouth opened wide.

"Damn you to Hell!" Liza heard herself screaming. "Let her go! Let her go!" She closed the distance between them yelling, first in English, then in Blackfoot. With each cry, the wizened warrior laughed louder.

Bull Child's screams grew more frightening and Liza, once more faced with the loss of someone she loved, realized that nothing else mattered except rescuing Bull Child. She approached the leering Mad Horse, her eyes fixed on the terrified child wrapped in his grip.

"Please," sobbed Liza, her hands stretched out in supplication. "Don't hurt her!"

Mad Horse yelled something, his scarred face twisted in fury, but she had never been able to understand him and his words were even more indiscernible now. His haggard shoulders shook, lips curved in an ugly scowl, and his eyes flashed vengeance.

"Dear God, you can't do this!" cried Liza over and over. "Take me! Do what you want with me! But let her go—she's just a child—"

Liza took a faltering step forward. *What if Mad Horse ended Bull Child's life before she could stop him?* Already he was pressing the tip of his blade into the soft flesh under Bull Child's chin. The child bravely stifled her cries. Only her eyes pleaded for help.

In a frantic gesture, Liza yanked the bear-claw necklace off her neck, losing several beads in the water-softened snow.

It was enough to tempt Mad Horse, who smiled slowly.

"They're yours!" yelled Liza. "Yours!" She held them out, nodding and gesturing.

Mad Horse grumbled something unintelligible; almost, as an afterthought, he tossed Bull Child to the snow at his feet. He hurried forward to retrieve the necklace.

But Mad Horse had not seen Cut Finger moving towards him. Her face was red with fury as she lunged wildly, knife poised, voice a vicious growl. Mad Horse moved but too late and she plunged the knife into him.

He let out a spine-tingling cry as blood streamed from his abdomen. Still on his feet, he swung his own knife ferociously at Cut Finger. The woman, not fast enough to move out of its path, fell to her knees. The long blade had cut through her cheek like a butcher's knife slicing bacon, into the flesh of her collarbone and shoulder.

She howled but steadied herself as she struggled to her feet. Blood flowed down her face. Mad Horse, circling as if Cut Finger were a wild animal, was still smiling.

Out of nowhere, screeching as loudly as he could, Skunk Cap came forward, spinning his blade through the air like a silver sword. Mad Horse, one hand still pressed to his bloody stomach, dodged it expertly.

Meanwhile, Bull Child had run to Liza, her own small knife extended. Liza grabbed it from her, then pushed the child to safety, mumbling something to console her. Mad Horse, spying the tiny blade, laughed wickedly, but the diversion gave Cut Finger and Skunk Cap an opportunity to regain their footing. Immediately they ran at the old warrior. Cut Finger, her face ashen in spite of the blood oozing down her neck, slashed at his chest, while Skunk Cap sliced open his right shoulder.

Stunned by the turn of events, Mad Horse fell to the ground, curling round and round like a snake. In unison, the three of them—Skunk Cap, Cut Finger, and Liza—moved in swiftly and bitterly.

✠ ✠ ✠

They did not bury Mad Horse. Leaving him for the birds and coyote, Skunk Cap, Cut Finger, Bull Child, and Liza crossed the river to rejoin Fat Dog, Sharp Hand, and the children. Liza had not realized that Rides-a-Horse was still missing until after everyone gathered around a small fire. She started to say something, then held back. Sometimes silence was the only solace.

Though she had lost much blood, Cut Finger insisted they move on. She refused to camp near the river and Mad Horse's body, which lay humped on the snow like an old bear. Skunk Cap, too, felt they must find a different place to rest, one with sufficient shelter. The wind had begun to gust and dark clouds were rolling across the gray horizon.

Liza was still reeling from the attack on Mad Horse. Though she knew she had had no choice, what she hadn't expected was the animal satisfaction she experienced watching the man writhe. Willing herself to wipe out the terrible memory, she pressed a handful of cold, wet snow to her mouth. It melted quickly against her lips.

Bull Child edged in as close as she could.

"It's all right," Liza whispered, hugging her close.

Skunk Cap approached Cut Finger and frowned.

Liza knew he wanted to move. Cut Finger wrapped a thong around her cheek to keep the chunk of bloody flesh in place, climbed to her feet, and moved slowly out. It was clear she was weak. It would not be long before she was too weak to travel.

Reluctantly Liza and Bull Child followed.

Skunk Cap turned and spoke harshly. "Not so slow!"

Liza wanted to scream at all of them.

After an hour or more, Skunk Cap spied a rocky bench. A stand of conifers would provide much-needed shelter and they were protected by a ring of bare trees whose limbs hung almost to the ground. Skunk Cap, aided by two of the older children, hacked off several thick evergreen branches and three heavier limbs. In minutes, they built an overhang under which everyone could huddle.

Cut Finger, however, was hardly able to move in out of the wind. She had lost enough blood to saturate her buckskin dress and cloak, and the flesh of her cheek hung over the rawhide string like a dried chunk of meat. Liza and Fat Dog cleaned the wound, but it was deeper than any wound Liza had ever seen and needed surgical care. The gash to her shoulder was also deep and Liza grimaced when she realized that the bone lay exposed. *How had Cut Finger managed to move at all,* she wondered through her tears.

It was late when everyone finally settled in to sleep. Cut Finger lapsed into a stupor and did not respond to Liza or Fat Dog's ministrations. The woman's almond eyes remained fixed on Fat Dog's fingers even as she gripped the elk horn handle of her own knife.

Settling Cut Finger under their warmest robes, Fat Dog tried to soothe her. Liza, too, wanted desperately to thank her for her incredible bravery. Instead, she held her friend's hand, gently stroking the calloused fingers.

"Dear God," Liza prayed later that night, "do not let this woman die! This kind and good woman! It's not fair—"

Without understanding why, Liza's prayer seemed to hang heavily in the bitter cold air. She glanced heavenward. *Was God even listening?*

Liza was not surprised when they found Cut Finger dead the next morning. The young woman had passed away after everyone had fallen asleep.

For a time, no one said a word.

But a deep pain lodged in Liza's heart. It was an ache she knew would not subside for a long time. How could it, now that she had once more lost someone near and dear? Someone who had sacrificed her own safety for others.

Getting to her knees, Liza rocked to and fro. There were too many unanswered questions, too many painful memories to bear. *Where was God to hear her? Where was her father to protect her? Where was Red Eagle?*

Skunk Cap took charge of the burial. They would not leave her body unattended. Fat Dog wrapped her carefully in a buffalo robe and together they half-dragged, half-carried her to the highest place on the granite bench.

Easing her between two rocks, each person then placed next to her a token, some item she might take with her into the next life. With silent tears in her large round eyes, Bull Child placed a bouquet of weeds and grasses across Cut Finger's body. Fat Dog lay a pouch of herbs and ashes near her feet. Skunk Cap folded the skin of the rabbit Cut Finger had caught for the children next to the pouch, and Sharp Hand slipped a pair of ragged moccasins under her robe. Finally, each of the youngest children lay a fir bough across her chest.

Then it was Liza's turn.

Taking the bear-claw necklace she had rescued from the snow after Mad Horse's attack, Liza pressed it into Cut Finger's fisted palm. She had no need of it any longer. Her memories of Red Eagle were stronger and more powerful than any amulet, her love for him the greatest talisman.

"For protection as you depart this world, nita-ka," whispered Liza, her face close to Cut Finger's. "It is strong medicine."

The group returned to their shelter, dazed and grief-stricken. Not only for Cut Finger, it seemed to Liza, but for all those they had been denied the right to mourn.

Then Fat Dog and Sharp Hand disappeared into the

271

trees. Before long, a wailing rose up such as Liza had never heard before. It gripped her and her own pain rose in her throat. She stepped out into the softly falling snow and lifted her voice, even as warm tears trickled down her chilled cheeks unheeded. She cried for Cut Finger and Crow Woman, Come Running and her unborn child, Black Quail and Rides-a-Horse, Yellow Grass and Walks-with-the-Moon, even for Giles and those she had hardly known in the villages of Crying Wind and Heavy Runner. Then she cried for her mother and father, for Red Eagle and Crying Wind. Finally, she cried for herself and her aloneness in a world that demanded more strength than she had.

Bull Child came to her then and slipped her small cold fingers into her knotted fist. The child was like the breath of life.

Sighing inwardly, Liza closed her eyes. *Was she the same woman who had come west only nine months before? Was she the same young woman who used to stamp her foot or pout when things went wrong?* She choked back her tears. That silly girl had vanished. In her place stood a different person, a woman of complicated emotions whose life had become like one of Grandmother's festoon quilts, bound together only by time and place.

CHAPTER 31

*R*ED EAGLE CAST HIS EYES TOWARD THE NORTHERN horizon. Snow had fallen during the night and into the morning, but it hadn't been a hard snow. Instead it reminded him of the sprinkle sugar his father had often brought home as a special surprise for his mother. A trail would still be visible if the people had come this way; if only he could find some sign.

Letting his horse rest, Red Eagle discovered some grassy stubble half-hidden under the shaggy limbs of several conifers. That meant he could save more of the oats Riplinger had given him.

His mind on the journey ahead, he pulled out a chunk of pemmican and took a bite. He rolled it around on his tongue to soften it, then swallowed the salty juices slowly.

Stands Down and his daughter had been generous. No doubt their generosity would save his life. They had given him not only pemmican but dried fruit and tobacco from their own sparse share.

Thinking of Blue Feather reminded Red Eagle of Liza. It had been so long since he'd seen her, he feared she might have grown embittered by his long absence. *Would she know that he had spent every waking moment in search of her? And when he finally told her, would she forgive him for allowing Many Words to slip into death?*

He fingered the small leather packet where he kept the dainty cross. It was all Many Words had left to give her. *Would it be enough to ease her suffering?*

Turning the horse to the north, Red Eagle pressed his heels against its flanks. He had to make better time than this if he was to overtake Liza or any of the people.

✠   ✠   ✠

It was time she turned back.

She approached Fat Dog. "I must return to the village," she said. "I must go back."

"No," cried Fat Dog, shaking her head sternly. "You will die in the cold and snow."

"I will take my portion of meat and perhaps a small bit of meal. I will follow the river."

"But the soldiers. They will hunt you down."

"I do not fear the soldiers. I despise them," Liza said, "but they will not hurt me. I am a missionary's daughter, and a white woman."

"You are Pikuni—"

"Yes, more than a little, in here," she said, touching her heart, "but I am also one of them and they will not hurt me. Do not fear. I will reveal nothing of who travels north. But I must find my father and Red Eagle. We are moving further and further from them."

Fat Dog shook her pretty head again, frowning. "We must speak with Skunk Cap and Sharp Hand. They will not like it," she added.

But Skunk Cap listened without interruption. Frowning, he looked at the children seated around the small fire.

"It is the best choice," Liza said. "I can return and convince the soldiers that those who were with me are dead. Mad Horse is still there, beside the river. I can tell them about Rides-a-Horse who drowned, even Yellow Grass and Walks-with-the-Moon. But I will not tell them about you or the children. And I will not tell them about Cut Finger," she added softly.

Skunk Cap turned his dark eyes on Liza. She had never noticed how handsome and strong the young warrior was. Someday, he would make a fine leader.

"I think you speak wisely," he said at last. "The horses will overtake us before a day or two and we have no weapons."

Fat Dog shook her head and mumbled something to her-

274

self, but Sharp Hand nodded her agreement. "It will give us time to move the children," she said quickly. "If we cross the Medicine Line, the soldiers will not follow us."

"You see, Fat Dog, I am right," said Liza.

"I do not like it," responded her friend, clenching her teeth, "and I know that Cut Finger would not like it."

"But our situation has changed," said Liza. "The children must cross the mountain pass safely, before more storms come, and we are all too weak to stand much more. I don't believe the soldiers will hurt me."

After several more protests, everyone finally agreed that Liza would return to the other side of the river and wait for the approaching soldiers. She would take meat and meal, one buffalo robe and Bull Child's knife, but insisted that she could find the blankets and other essentials left behind on the far shore. The soldiers would rescue her and take her back to the fort, from where she would locate her father and Red Eagle. *Surely, she could find them if she tried!*

It was a good plan. And it would give Skunk Cap and the others more time to escape.

"I will be fine," said Liza, hoping she sounded braver than she felt. "God will travel with me," she added, hoping it would prove true.

But Bull Child refused to leave Liza. Shaking her head and stamping her feet, she ran away and hid, emerging only after Liza promised to take her.

"It is just as well," said Liza. "I don't think I could say good-bye to her! She is like the little sister I never had. I will take good care of her."

It was time to leave. Liza and Bull Child, carrying only what they could, left the tiny encampment just after sunrise. Several times they stopped to look back but soon it was impossible to see anything except the rugged range of mountains covered in sleek carpets of snow. Skunk Cap and the others had been swallowed up by the gray flannel wilderness.

Liza shivered but kept her fear to herself. Wrapped in their robes, heads hooded, hands gloved, Liza and Bull Child followed the winding trail that would lead them back the way they had come.

What other choice did they have?

✠ ✠ ✠

Private Schluter repacked the camp gear, then adjusted the cinch on his saddle. It was a poor cinch, nearly worn through, and he cursed himself for not paying closer attention to such details before leaving the fort. Of course, they still had Potter and Edelstein's mounts but knowing Cole's perverse sense of humor, Schluter wondered if the lieutenant would punish him for being so foolish.

He should have sensed Simon Cole's cruelty. The man had never shown mercy to anyone or anything. Just this morning, after trapping a small snowbird, he plucked nearly every feather from its body before putting the creature out of its misery. Afterwards, he smiled. Smiled!

"I killed it too soon," Cole said later, tossing the bird into the fire. Spying Schluter's shaded look of anger, the lieutenant threw his head back and laughed wickedly. "I should have skinned it alive!"

Even now, the memory made Schluter shiver.

As they took up the trail again, following the tracks of several mocassined feet, Cole talked incessantly. "The tracks are fresh," he said. "And they can't have much with them, which means they'll be anxious to trade. Bet there'll even be one or two squaws willing to take you under their robes," he said to Schluter after they'd travelled another mile or so. "I'll give you the fat ones. I'll take the pretty ones. And the young ones," he added caustically.

Schluter grunted. He'd never coveted Indian women. He'd rarely coveted women at all. He'd left a wife in Kentucky and, for the first time, he wondered why he'd left her. Though not much to look at, she'd never made a fuss when he came home drunk or late. She'd even kept quiet when he insisted on joining the army. Of course, he had promised he'd send for her, but never had, even though she'd been with child when he left.

He wondered: had she bore him a boy or girl?

Perhaps he would write to the poor woman.

✠ ✠ ✠

Red Eagle tapped his heels against the sides of his horse. He had started out early and travelled a fair distance. The sun had warmed the earth and trees dripped snow. In the wake of such hopeful signs, he felt energized. If only he had a track to follow.

He had dreamed a new dream during the night. In it he'd seen Liza Five Shots. She was smiling, her chestnut-colored hair dressed in long plaits with bits of yarn and feathers woven in. She wore a new buckskin dress, much like the one Crow Woman had made for her. The soft, yellow fringe brushed her shins and her bare feet moved through meadows he recognized as those found along the Sweet Grass Hills. Flowers bloomed everywhere and the sound of birds filled the air. She had come and held her hand out. He had taken it. Taken it, and drawn her to him, hungry to feel her under his fingers, hungry to taste her flesh and move inside her.

He hoped this dream was the window to his future. Hadn't his first dream foretold the destruction of the Pikuni?

He had to trust the vision. There was nothing else to believe in.

CHAPTER 32

SIMON COLE BELLOWED ACROSS THE SNOWY MEADOW. "Get that animal up! We should've been out of here an hour ago."

Schluter yanked on the rope. "Git up, you fool! You're ornrier'n a rat-tailed hoss, you know that?" He walked around to the rear of the mule. "Come on, don't you know your time is runnin' out? If you don't git up, I'm tellin' you, you won't like what'll be comin' your way!"

"What's slowing you up back there?" called Cole. "If she won't get up, get a gun. Only a fool argues with a mule," he added tersely.

Schluter kicked the mule's rump. "Damn it, Oh Suzannah!" he cursed. "Your life is comin' to a sure end." He unravelled the pack ropes that had become twisted when the animal dropped to the ground and rolled. Schluter yanked off the top part of the pack. "I'm tellin' you," he mumbled, "you better listen to ole Schluter. I ain't holdin' a grudge but the lieutenant will blow you to kingdom-come if you don't git up soon!" He stopped and peered into the left eye of the gray mule. "Don't ignore me," he said.

"Schluter! We've got no time to be wasting on this lazy animal!" boomed Cole, stepping around the tail of the mule. Taking his pistol out of its holster, he slipped a bullet into the chamber.

"Lieutenant! Give me a minute," said Schluter. "It's a shame to waste a good animal. Oh Susannah's a reliable packer."

"Not today! And if you take any more time, I'll strap that gear to your back," snapped Cole. "Now get her unloaded and repack the fat, white jackass, and be sure the guns are secure. I knew there'd be trouble with this one," he added. "I can tell. It's all in the eyes. Just like Edelstein and Potter." He cast a sidelong glance at Schluter.

Schluter tried to appear nonchalant. "It's true sometimes she acts like she's been raised on sour milk." He lifted a box off the pack saddle. He didn't add that any animal might crowd the fence, the way the lieutenant treated it. The man was so stingy he'd skin a flea for its hide and tallow.

Cole glared at Schluter. "You're slower than the second coming!" he growled.

"Almos' ready, boss," piped Schluter, running back to the mule. The poor animal hadn't budged since he'd packed it that morning; refusing to move, she had dropped to the snow in one giant heap. Schluter knew only too well that she was tired. The animals had been plowing through snow 'til they were as limp as wornout fiddle strings.

But he couldn't tell the lieutenant that.

"Okay, okay," said Cole, after Schluter unloaded the last, large burlap sack. The big man walked quickly around to the front of the animal. He said something Schluter couldn't hear, then turned his hard blue eyes on the exhausted beast. Taking careful aim, he pulled the hammer back and fired.

Schluter jumped as the single shot echoed across the landscape.

He couldn't look. But he heard the mule thrash about in the snow, moaning and huffing. Cole fired again and there was terrible silence.

"Now get the ropes and bridle," Cole ordered, slipping his gun back in its holster. "Don't be slow. I got plenty of ammunition," he added sadistically.

Schluter said nothing but moved through the next few minutes dumbly. He had always felt a fondness for animals. In fact, he preferred animals to people. They didn't mess with your brains.

When the two men finally pulled out, Schluter allowed himself a final glance. "Sorry ole gal," he said.

Cole laughed aloud. "Forget the jackass! She was worthless as a pail of hot spit." He laughed to himself. It was he who was surrounded by real jackasses. *Crying over a mule?*

He gave his horse a good kick. They still had quite a distance to go before reaching their destination—the British territory. But Cole knew the venture would pay off. With the outbreak of smallpox and the recent attack on the Pikuni, Blackfeet everywhere were running scared. They would trade dearly for medicine and whiskey, and especially guns. Of course, DeTrobriand was a fool, thinking Cole and his men would return. But DeTrobriand had come to trust his first lieutenant; after all, he had had more experience with Indians than almost anyone else at the fort.

The general would discover his mistake soon enough. But that didn't matter, grinned Cole. The army had never given a tinker's damn about him. He had been passed over and made a fool of too many times. Now he had an opportunity to make a new start and nobody was going to stop him. Nobody.

Perhaps he ought to feel remorse for killing two white men but he didn't. He had already killed enough Indians to make pulling the trigger second nature. Of course, killing a red man was different than killing a white man. An Indian was a varmint; Potter and Edelstein had been too stupid to fret over. He'd had enough of this poor army's existence; if he was to survive, he had to take a few risks.

Then he smiled. The troopers' deaths would actually help ensure his escape. By scalping them and leaving them humped in the snow, the army would suspect Mountain Chief and his bucks.

It really was a good plan.

Too bad the army brass had never appreciated his intelligence.

✠ ✠ ✠

Red Eagle spotted the two bodies easily.

Having intercepted several horse and mule tracks early

281

in the morning, he had followed them for some distance. The obvious question played in his mind: had these men been on the trail of the Pikuni? If so, was he getting closer to Liza?

It was now late afternoon and the sunshine waned as gray clouds rolled across the sky. The air was heavy with frost and Red Eagle suspected it would be a bitterly cold night. Shivering, he stopped to unwrap his cape, which was tied behind his saddle, then threw it over his shoulders.

His attention was drawn to the meadow.

Readjusting the heavy robe, he kicked his horse and rode across the open space. The yellow dun sniffed the air nervously and Red Eagle, too, smelled death.

They stopped only a few feet from the blue-clad bodies. Stripped of their coats and boots, Red Eagle remembered the times his father had tramped about the cabin in long underwear and red stockings. His mother used to giggle at such odd behavior.

The dead men were clearly soldiers and they had been scalped. He grimaced. *Was this the work of Owl Child or Mountain Chief? Had the Pikuni leaders sought vengeance already?*

Red Eagle dismounted and approached the men slowly. One had been killed close to the trees, the other a little further out in the meadow. An ambush?

He examined the tracks. Several animals had milled around here for quite awhile. The snow was also well-trampled by men. Red Eagle squatted and examined the prints more carefully.

He scratched his head, curiousity piqued. The prints were soldiers' boot prints. There wasn't a moccasined foot among them. That meant there had been no Indians here, only white men. But why would white men scalp these men, unless they wanted to blame the Blackfeet for something they had done?

Red Eagle turned the first man over. Frowning, he studied what remained of the young man's bloody face. It was still recognizable—the soldier he had ridden with back to the fort. The quiet, yellow-haired boy.

Red Eagle studied the bullet hole in his chest before standing up to glance around. A strange sense of dread wafted across the landscape, swirling and curling around him, as if the place was haunted.

Straightening his shoulders, he quickly crossed the trampled snow to where the second soldier lay. Red Eagle didn't recognize this one. Just another soldier, but he, too, had a bullet hole in his chest; both men had been killed by the same gun and the same man.

Red Eagle's hand went instinctively to his knife. He still felt as if someone was watching him. The killer himself? Or, perhaps, the spirit of these men?

Sighing audibly, Red Eagle looked down at the nameless soldier. *What had he witnessed? Who were the other men and where were they headed?* The young man's eyes were wide with horror yet mysteriously all-knowing. *Was he trying to give voice to his murder?*

Red Eagle frowned as he thought of Liza.

Would these other men soon cross her path?

He couldn't waste another minute.

※ ※ ※

"We can't stop yet," said Liza, though Bull Child protested. "I know it's been a long day, little one, but we need to find a good place to camp, where we have water and shelter."

Liza pulled the little girl into her arms. "Here," she coaxed. "We'll treat ourselves to a piece of pemmican." She knew they didn't have much to spare but Liza did not want to stop here. There was no stream and few trees. They would be battered by the wind and cold. If only they could get closer to a waterway. Then they could camp for more than a day, if necessary.

Liza sighed. She almost wished the army had found them already, praying that not all troopers were as ruthless as Private Scott and those who had attacked the Pikuni villages.

Bull Child watched her movements closely. "Here's a piece of meat," said Liza reaching into the parfleche Fat Dog had packed and pulling out a flat, thin cake. There was meat enough for two or three more days, but fewer if she gave it to Bull Child too freely. "Eat slowly," she ordered, then chided herself when the little girl raised her round, worried eyes.

"I'm sorry," said Liza, pulling the child close. "I'm just fretting," she added in English, for she didn't want to frighten her. God only knew how glad she was that Bull Child was with her. She might have lost her will to go on had she stayed with the others.

Liza looked around once more. The land was deceptive and intimidating, with deep ravines and rugged bluffs that dipped into the far horizons. Only the rugged rim of mountains gave her a sense of security. The majestic rampart was like a fortress and she began to wish there were a way to escape into its protective boundaries.

Frowning, she whispered, "I must be getting addlebrained." There was no way they could even reach the mountains or tramp up those rugged ridges. The soldiers following would overtake them sooner than later. "Well, we might as well keep walking," she said to Bull Child, stamping the cold from her feet.

Her next thought struck like a bolt of lightning.

What if her father had sent the soldiers? Perhaps Red Eagle and Father had gone to Fort Shaw and demanded the army's assistance in locating her. Perhaps they had insisted on Lieutenant Cole's leading a patrol.

Liza exhaled slowly. *Had she been running away from the wrong enemy? Had she been so frightened that she'd forgotten that, as a white woman and daughter of a missionary, she was entitled to help from the soldiers?*

Liza squeezed Bull Child's hand. Perhaps Red Eagle himself led the troopers.

Turning to the little girl, she cried, "Bull Child, we're going to be all right. I feel it, here." She placed her gloved hand over her heart. At the same time, she scanned the crystal white expanse and her heart beat faster. "I see someone coming!"

CHAPTER 33

*T*HE MOMENT LIZA SAW THE TWO SOLDIERS, SHE frowned. Red Eagle and her father were nowhere in sight.

But she recognized the first man. It was Lieutenant Cole. How fortunate! She flapped her arms wildly. "Here!" she yelled. "Over here!"

"Hell's bells," piped the second man, a wide grin crossing his narrow face as he spotted Liza. He kicked his horse up and clucked to the two mules in tow. "So much for the tracks we been followin'. Ain't she a white woman?"

"Or a breed," growled Lieutenant Cole as he swung his horse down the steep slope of the ravine.

Liza frowned. Obviously the lieutenant hadn't recognized her. She coaxed Bull Child forward. "It's all right," she whispered. "I know this man!"

Bull Child frowned and shook her head.

"Please, trust me?" whispered Liza. "I will not let anyone hurt you."

Tearfully, Bull Child followed her, and the two walked out to meet the string of animals and riders.

"Heavens," sighed Liza, a smile on her face, "I thought we'd be wandering forever. Like the Israelites," she added. She looked up at the lieutenant and shaded her eyes with her hand. "Don't you recognize me, Lieutenant?"

"Why should I?" muttered Cole, his ice blue eyes pinched nearly shut.

"Well," said Liza, "you escorted me all over the fort while my father and I were there, last August. I'm Elizabeth Ralston, sir."

"Hell!" snapped Cole. He drew his horse up and leaned

over. "So how come you're dressed like an Injun? You look more like a half-breed. And where's your pa?"

Liza flushed. "You remember, my father is a missionary. We've been living with the Pikuni." She swallowed her next words as she suddenly remembered that Simon Cole might well have been on the January death march. "I–I haven't seen my father in almost two months."

The lieutenant's eyes blazed as he broke in, "Miss Ralston, were you camped along the Marias River, near Heavy Runner's band?"

"Oh, no," lied Liza, wrapping her hand over Bull Child's shoulder. "We were camped further north. But we heard about the attack. We heard that there were some terrible renegades camped there. You were lucky enough, I hope, Lieutenant, to catch the rebels?" She sighed elaborately, then turned away.

Lieutenant Cole smiled and nodded, his eyes on Bull Child. "We took care of some of them. But don't worry, the rest have scattered to the four winds."

"Well," quipped Liza, "I suppose they had it coming?"

"'Scuse me for saying so, Miss Ralston, but the Blackfeet are notorious villains. We'll be better off when they're all killed off or run out of the territory. Most of them are nothing more than lazy drunks and cheating bastards."

Liza squeezed Bull Child's shoulder a second time, then raised her chin. "Don't forget, Lieutenant," she said carefully, "they are God's children."

"More like varmints," said Cole, "but let's not fret over our differences." His gaze took in her outfit. "Tell me, how did you end up out here, in the wilderness, my dear Miss Ralston?" His voice was unnaturally deep but Liza feigned ignorance.

Bull Child tugged on the middle finger of Liza's free hand. The poor child was trembling.

Liza responded thickly, "Oh, Lieutenant Cole, my father sent me away. But when I heard about the attack, why, I just had to return. Then our horses collapsed and we lost the other members of our party. I'm afraid we've been wandering around and around."

The lieutenant frowned. Unexpectedly, he turned to his partner. "We'll make camp here, Private," he said, indicating a spot near the bottom of the ravine. "You ride over to the river and fill the canteens."

Private Schluter's eyes narrowed as he dropped the mule ropes. Liza could tell he didn't seem pleased. *Was it because she and Bull Child would be an extra burden?*

Lieutenant Cole quickly dismounted, picking up the lead ropes as he approached Liza. He handed them to Liza. "Make yourself useful," he said, eyes bright, lips twitching.

He cast another glance at Bull Child.

Liza pulled the little girl closer. An uneasiness filled her as she recognized the disgust in the lieutenant's eyes. *Had she made another disastrous mistake by joining up with this man?*

As the lieutenant led the way and Liza and Bull Child followed, Liza tried to keep her growing fear hidden. She took several deep breaths. Unfortunately, she had never been very good at pretending, but she knew she had to rely on her instincts. Right now, those instincts told her that Bull Child's safety depended on Liza's ability to play a fool before these men.

Her heart ached with disappointment. She had so hoped the soldiers had been sent by Father and Red Eagle, that Red Eagle would be with them.

Where are you? Her heart cried out to the wilderness.

The two men set up camp in the flat of the ravine where a handful of bare trees formed a half-circle. Once the horses were hobbled, the private tied the pack mules together in a string. He pulled out some cooking gear and headed back to where Lieutenant Cole had started a small fire. Liza asked if she could help.

"Ain't much 'cept beans and coffee and a little hardtack."

"Sounds good to me," said Liza. She studied the man out of the corners of her eyes. Something about him eased her anxiety. He didn't have the same hardness the lieutenant displayed.

"You just rest," said the private. "You an' that little one look like you walked halfway to hell and back."

The lieutenant scoffed. "Miss Ralston have a seat, next to

me. It's been what? Six months since we last visited? I must say, I never thought I'd see you dressed as a squaw."

Liza's skin tingled under the lieutenant's scrutiny. *How had she so misjudged the man?* At the fort he had dazzled her with courtesy and good manners. Now she could see it had been a facade.

Supper was a meager affair. Bull Child ate very little while Liza nibbled at the hardtack and a few beans. Lieutenant Cole and the private ate everything else. All the while, the lieutenant watched her, keenly aware of her apprehension. Liza tried to ignore him.

She turned to the private. "We haven't introduced ourselves. I'm Elizabeth Ralston and my father is the Reverend Robert Ralston. We were originally from St. Louis."

The private kept his eyes on the fire but turned for a moment as he mumbled, "I'm Schluter, Private, originally from Kentucky."

Liza cast a quick glance at Cole then turned back to Schluter. "No first name?" she asked, her tone challenging and curt. *How dare Lieutenant Cole try to intimidate her with his hard looks and sharp tongue.*

"Uh, nobody calls me by my first name, but it's Henry."

Liza nodded and extended her right hand. "Hello, Henry Schluter."

Schluter stared at Liza's bared hand. Wiping his own across his winter coat, he extended it slowly. "Howdy," he said. He flashed a tiny smile, then turned away abruptly.

"Why don't you keep your gate shut awhile, Schluter?" growled Cole from across the fire. "And go to sleep! We've got a good distance to travel come morning." He glared at Liza, as if accusing her of interrupting something. "I haven't decided what to do with you yet, Miss Ralston, so you better button it, too."

Liza's eyes flashed. "Who do you think you are, to speak to me like that? You're an officer in the United States Army. You have an obligation to help me. Us," she added quickly, pulling Bull Child to her side.

"You may be as prim as a preacher's wife," quipped Cole, "but don't count me as a fool. You're pawning yourself off as white, but I can see the Injun in you. And Injun squaws are pretty much worthless."

Liza turned away, mortified.

"Wasn't no call to be rude," said Schluter softly.

"Shut it," snapped Cole with a hard edge. He slid his hat to the back of his head and scratched his forehead. He stood up and rolled a cigarette.

The silence was heavy as Liza led Bull Child back to their robes. Holding the child close, she rocked her until she fell asleep. Then Liza snuggled down next to her, closing her eyes. She had to forget where she was. She had to focus on where she was headed. If nothing else, she had to get back to her father and Red Eagle.

But it was clear: Lieutenant Cole was almost as terrifying as Mad Horse; indeed, the same wild look burned in his cold, blue eyes.

She reached for the small knife tucked inside her moccasin. It gave her comfort, but God forbid she would ever have to use it—again.

In the morning, she awoke to the smell of coffee. It was a memory of another life and Liza got to her feet eagerly.

"Smells good," she whispered to Private Schluter across the empty space between them. She wandered over to the fire where Henry was squatting, a long knife in one hand, a slab of bacon in the other. "My, that looks good, too." She indicated the salted pork. "Can't recall the last time I had bacon."

Schluter shifted uncomfortably.

"Where's the lieutenant?" Liza asked, her voice shrill in the crisp morning air. She didn't want the private to know how much the big, blue-eyed man had frightened her. Even now she could feel his piercing eyes. She looked around.

"Don't know," he mumbled, shrugging noncommitally.

Liza returned to the bed site and shook Bull Child. "Time to get up, little one," she whispered in her ear.

Bull Child sat up automatically, her eyes on Liza's face.

Liza stroked the soft skin of her cheek. Her fingers lingered as they rested on the child's quivering chin. "Everything will be all right," she assured her. "I promise."

"What the hell's going on?" The booming voice of Lieutenant Cole came out of nowhere like a fog horn. Liza and Bull Child both jumped. Even Schluter seemed to tremble.

"Just makin' breakfast, Lieutenant."

"If you were thinking of eating," snapped Cole, "you should have been up hours ago! The animals are saddled and we're ready to head out. Put out that fire." He picked up the pot of coffee and poured it slowly over the glowing coals. Sparks flew and embers sizzled.

Liza's face fell. *Were they to get nothing at all?*

"Hell, Lieutenant," said Schluter, "I ain't even had my coffee. A man cain't do much on a empty stomach!"

"No?" said Cole.

Schluter dropped his eyes to the ground. Liza hugged Bull Child closer to her. "Let's get our things together," she whispered.

Schluter was still grumbling as Liza and Bull Child picked up their packs.

"Excuse me, Private Schluter," said Liza. "Where shall we put our things?"

Schluter mumbled something indiscernible, so Liza turned to the lieutenant. With the coffee pot still in one hand, he was watching her closely.

"If you've got a problem you take it up with me," he said coldly. He threw the pot down and Schluter scrambled to retrieve it.

Liza bit her lip. "Uh, well, I wasn't sure where—"

He took several steps toward her.

"Uh, where I, we, should put our things," she finished lamely.

Cole reached out and grabbed one of Liza's braids in his big, square hand. He tugged on it and she stumbled towards him. He laughed wickedly.

"These are better than reins," he snorted, swinging his gaze over to Schluter. "Get the gear on that white mule. And take the girl with you!"

Liza's hands shook and she fought to keep from calling out as Schluter half-dragged, half-pushed Bull Child into the trees. The little girl's moon face was filled with terror.

"She's mute," said Liza softly.

Cole's next statement brought Liza back to the moment. She straightened her shoulders, resisting him as he yanked on her other braid, this time jerking her to her feet.

"I don't countenance anyone's defiance," snapped the lieutenant. "Ask Schluter. He'll tell you."

Liza held her breath as Cole slid his hands from her braids to her shoulders. "I don't tolerate any sort of disrespect," he added. His breath was foul and she closed her eyes to shield herself from his leering eyes.

"You know," he said, tracing one finger along her chin, "I could have you one way or the other. We both know that. I could force you, which wouldn't be half-bad. Or I could coax you. And I'm sure you wouldn't want anything bad to happen to that papoose of yours." He leaned closer to her ear. "I wouldn't mind having a piece of her, either."

Liza's heart skipped a beat, but she held herself stiffly. And then she remembered the massacre. She knew he had been there, one of those who enjoyed the killing and torturing.

"Anyway," he said, pulling back, "I guess I'll let you decide how it's going to be." He rolled his tongue across his pudgy lips and shoved her away.

But his words burned as Liza stumbled over to the trees and mounted the horse Private Schluter was holding. Bull Child reached for her and Schluter quickly lifted her up to Liza. Her small legs were hardly visible as she huddled down inside the enormous buffalo robe Schluter threw up to them.

Then Liza spied two scalps hanging from one of Lieutenant Cole's pack saddles. Except one was blonde and one was a mousy brown. They were both white men's scalps!

CHAPTER 34

*I*T WAS MIDDAY BEFORE COLE CALLED A HALT. LIZA, HER bladder so full she could barely sit up, slid off her horse. She started for a bush nearby.

"Where do you think you're headed?" snapped Cole.

"Please," was all she said.

He leaned close to her and whispered, "Don't forget I have the child."

She didn't respond. It didn't matter; she wouldn't leave Bull Child and he knew it.

When she returned, she was surprised to see Schluter busy building a fire. Morosely quiet, he lay a handful of dry fir needles and a thin bough across the gasping flames. Bull Child squatted nearby, eyes wider and face paler than Liza had seen it since the day she rescued her.

She dropped to the wet snow and moved closer to the little girl. Wrapping her robe around her, she spoke softly. "Don't worry," she said in Blackfoot, "Red Eagle will come soon. I know it."

Bull Child looked up at her as if to be sure she had understood. Then she snuggled closer.

Liza hadn't realized Cole was near enough to hear her until she heard him chuckle. "A real Indian lover," he said. He raised one eyebrow and squinted down at the two of them.

She squeezed Bull Child's fingers, as much to reassure herself as the child.

"I figured as much," he continued. "You look too Indian to be anything else. You know, the papoose looks like you. Makes me wonder if you might really be her ma?"

Liza squared her jaw and narrowed her eyes. She wasn't

293

going to reveal her fear or back down, even if it meant letting him make false assumptions.

"I thought so," Cole said. Unexpectedly, he grabbed her arm and pulled her to her feet. She had to scramble to keep from falling.

Bull Child reached for her other arm.

"Tell her to let go," growled Lieutenant Cole, his blue eyes raking her face, "or I'll start with her!"

Liza pleaded with Bull Child until the child reluctantly let go. At the same time, Cole's hard fingers tightened around her arm and he led her away from the camp.

"Don't let the child out of your sight!" he hollered back to Schluter. "And don't come bothering me, you hear?"

Liza couldn't see his face but she heard Henry Schluter mumble a reply. *Dear God,* she wanted to scream, *wouldn't he help her? What kind of man was he?*

There was a small, narrow gulley half hidden by an outcropping of rocks a short distance from camp. Looking around, Cole grunted and led her to the edge where he pushed her ahead, his eyes reflecting bitter desire. Liza slid down the embankment, then slipped on the icy slope. She landed on her back, but instantly rolled over and got to her knees. She tried to jump to her feet.

Before she could regain her footing, Cole had one hand wrapped around her wrist. "I already gave you the odds," he said. "I figure you're smarter than to try anything stupid. Who knows? You might like it better than you think."

Liza struggled to keep still. Her heart pounded like a drum in her head and her stomach rolled as she saw the determination in his eyes. "You'll have to drive that blade through me first," she heard herself saying. Her voice sounded oddly calm.

Shoving her forward into the snow, Cole kicked her in the back of her legs and she dropped. He slid one boot along her backside, laughing as she tried to push it away. "Turn over. I want to watch you—"

"You're an animal!" she cried, but Cole only laughed

harder as he reached down and flipped her over. His hands were like vises and she realized he was even stronger than she'd imagined.

His steady, cold gaze terrified her and suddenly she felt her body shrink as he tilted his head to one side, tongue sliding over his lips slowly, deliberately. He raised his eyebrows and with great care, knelt beside her, curling the fingers of his left hand around her throat. She closed her eyes.

Then he was on her. His heavy body pinned her to the snow and his weight was unbearable. She gasped and twisted under him, grappling to get her arms free. As he pushed his hands down to the edges of her tunic, she screamed. This made him laugh again, a blood-curdling howl.

If only she could get one hand down to her moccasin.

She still had Bull Child's knife.

Under his terrible weight, she fought to breathe. All the while, her stomach rebelled at the stale, putrid smell of his open mouth and filthy body.

But time stood still as she lay there, pinned, and it wasn't until she felt Cole harden against her and push her knees apart that she managed to free her fists, drawing them up to his chest. "No! Get off!"

"You can't win," he chuckled in her ear, his tongue touching her earlobe. One hand slid across her belly, the other against her breast. "But go ahead. I like a good cat fight."

Liza cried out again. He was hurting her now, his fingers squeezing the soft flesh of her bosom. But as he tried to thrust his hand under her tunic, she brought her knees together with a jerk.

Stunned, he roared in pain and she was able to move at last, but the slick snow kept her from getting away.

It was then she heard a man's voice. "Get off her!"

"Help!" she screamed.

Instantly, Cole covered her mouth with his left hand, his enraged expression sending a wave of fear through her. "What the —?" he snarled.

It was Schluter's voice. "Get off her."

Liza strained to see him but he was behind her. When Cole leaned forward she caught a glimpse of the trooper.

He stood on the edge of the gulley, looking down. His dark hair had fallen across his narrow face. His gaze was cold and hard, and he held a rifle. "I said, get off her."

"Didn't I tell you to keep away?" snapped Cole, his fingers encircling her throat once more. "I ain't done with her yet."

Schluter, extending his rifle, shook his head. "You get off her, Lieutenant. I cain't stomach no more. It's been eatin' me an' eatin' me. You shouldn'ta kilt Edelstein n' Potter. They was good 'nough men. An' you ain't gonna hurt her."

Cole frowned as he looked away, but his movements were swift and sure. Releasing her suddenly, he pulled out his knife and it sailed through the air before Schluter or Liza realized what had happened.

The private instantly fell, the blade lodged in his thigh. Blood rushed down his faded blue pants and across the snow.

"You bas—," he moaned. "You kilt Edelstein and now, I'm gonna kill you—" Crying out with pain, he jerked the knife out of his leg.

Cole scrambled over Liza, hoping to grab Schluter's gun before he did. Liza got to her knees. She grabbed for Bull Child's knife just as she heard the sound of a rifle being cocked.

She turned, the small knife in her hand.

With eyes blazing, Bull Child was standing at the top of the ravine, Schluter's long gun in her hands. Shaking, almost unable to hold the gun still, she stared down at Cole.

"I will kill you," she said in Blackfoot.

Liza's voice cracked as she circled Cole. "Bull Child," she whispered. "Let me have the gun." She reached the child's side and placed her left hand around the barrel of the rifle.

But Bull Child shook her head defiantly. Her lips quivered as tears ran down her cheeks. She raised the gun.

Lieutenant Cole laughed. He seemed to enjoy this new twist. Chest heaving, he glared at the small Indian girl. "You're going to pay for this," he said, taking a cautious step forward.

"Don't try it," whispered Liza, raising her blade.

The sound of an approaching horse startled Liza. Turning, she spotted a man on a pale yellow horse. He seemed familiar. *"Red Eagle?"*

Cole turned at the sound of the name, his blue eyes bright with rage. Jumping forward, he knocked the gun out of Bull Child's hands. But before he could retrieve it, Liza rushed at him, driving the knife into his side.

He screamed as he fell back and in the next instant, Red Eagle was off his horse and lunging for him. The two men rolled down the slope, a trail of blood following them to the bottom of the ravine.

Liza's heart pounded mercilessly, her eyes never leaving Red Eagle. The two men began to grapple over Red Eagle's knife, which he drew while struggling out of Cole's grasp.

"I should have finished you when I had the chance," Cole growled to Red Eagle, getting back to his feet. "I should have killed you the first time I saw you." He staggered as blood continued to run down his leg.

"Yes, you should have," returned Red Eagle coldly, his hard gaze never leaving Cole's face.

Tears sprung to Liza's eyes. She could hardly believe Red Eagle had found them.

"The gun!" Schluter hollered as he got to his feet.

Liza spun around to grab it, but Schluter took it from her. "He's mine," he said, the look of pain on his face replaced by a look of hatred.

She nodded and stepped back, pulling Bull Child to her.

"Now I'm gonna finish what you started," whispered Schluter, sliding down the snowy bank. He pointed the gun at Cole. "Step aside, Injun," he said to Red Eagle. "I got no call to fire on you."

Red Eagle did not move; circling Cole, he kept his knife poised. "The lieutenant is mine," he snapped back.

"Not this time," Schluter said and taking aim, he fired.

Cole, stunned that he'd been shot, fell backwards. His eyes had remained pinned on Red Eagle, but as blood flowed from his belly, he turned to Schluter. "Damn," he said, then collapsed in a heap.

Red Eagle drew back as Schluter limped over to where Cole lay. The trooper leaned over the lieutenant's body. "He weren't no good. I just wish't I had kill't him sooner."

Liza was crying as she stumbled toward Red Eagle. Too numb to speak, she felt his arms about her, drawing her close, the familiar smell like a heady perfume. She shook all over, her legs growing weak as he whispered her name.

"Liza." Her name was like silk on his lips.

"Oh, Red Eagle," she said.

His lips moved across her cheeks eagerly, tracing the trail of her tears until he found her mouth. He tasted like leather and sweat, and his heart pounded as loudly as her own.

"How did you find us?" she whispered at last, pulling away slowly. She started to wipe away tears, but Red Eagle's fingers were there first. The rough skin of his fingertips sent spasms through her belly. She laughed, her hands reaching out for him. "I knew you'd come," she said. She pressed her face against his chest and breathed deeply, relaxing for the first time in months.

His voice trembled as he slid one hand along her back and shoulders, and she tingled at his touch. "I would have never stopped searching," he said, his words hardly audible. "I had to find you. You know that, Liza Five Shots?"

She nodded at the sound of her name. "And I would have never stopped waiting," she replied. She leaned back to look up at him, her words tumbling out. "All I could do was think about you, dream of you, pray for you. I should have told you before you left."

Hushing her with a touch of his fingers, Red Eagle said, "It was as it should be. But we will talk later."

Liza rushed on. "I even told Bull Child you would find us. Bull Child?"

The girl was still standing on the edge of the ravine, her wide dark eyes bright.

"Come here," Liza said, beckoning her gently. "This is Red Eagle, the man I told you about-" She glanced up, catching

Red Eagle's bemused expression.

"You have learned the language well," he said softly. Then he, too, spoke to Bull Child. "Do not be afraid." He held his hand out.

Bull Child, hesitating only for a moment, ran to Liza and Red Eagle. With her chin held high, she pointed to the dead lieutenant. "He was one of the yellow-dog soldiers who came to our village. I saw him. I saw his eyes," she said. Then she spat in his direction. "I am glad he is dead."

Tears threatening anew, Liza dropped to one knee and pulled the child closer. She had never heard Bull Child's voice until today. "So am I, little one, so am I. But everything will be all right now. Red Eagle is here and we can go home."

"Yes," Red Eagle said. "We will go home, together." He touched Liza's cheek gently, smiling.

Liza looked up at him, hungry to draw him close again, hungry to be alone with him. "Home is wherever you are," she said. "Nothing except you, my father, and Bull Child matters."

Red Eagle pulled her close and his voice cracked. "Liza."

She looked up. His eyes were clouded. "What is it? Father? He's dead, isn't he? Dead—? Oh, Red Eagle—"

He didn't respond except to rub her shoulders. "We will travel across the Sweet Grass Hills, Liza. There we will start over. Your father wanted it for you. A new start. And I promised him."

Fighting the tears that threatened her moment of happiness, she took a slow, deep breath. She had known, she realized now, someplace deep inside.

Yes, for Father's sake, she would think about what he had dreamed for her. And across the Sweet Grass Hills was the place to begin.

✠   ✠   ✠

"Damn, ain't anybody gonna help me?"

The sound of Henry Schluter's voice startled them all.

Leaning on one elbow, the trooper was trying to sit up, but with his hands wrapped around his bloody leg, he couldn't stay upright. "I'm bleedin' like a stuck pig," he whispered. "Can you help me?" He raised worried eyes to Liza. "I cain't move the damn thing."

Liza rushed to his side, kneeling. She squeezed his shoulder. "Red Eagle is the best doctor I know."

"Well, I'd let Satan hisself cut on me if I thought he could save me," groaned Schluter. "I don't wanna die in this place. Please."

"The army shoots deserters, does it not?" Red Eagle asked as he joined Liza. "Maybe I shouldn't waste my time."

Schluter moved nervously under his gaze, sweat lining his brow and lip.

Without saying more, Red Eagle removed his knife and cut away the bloody fabric of Schluter's pant. "The cut is not deep," he said, glancing up at Liza.

"Thank heaven," mumbled Schluter, then looking from Liza to Red Eagle, he said, "I swear, I didn't know what kinda bastard Cole was. If I'd aknown, I'd never have gone along. I ain't a killer. A fool, mebbe, but no killer."

Red Eagle took a slow, deep breath and his eyes narrowed.

Liza knew the question that burned in his heart.

Schluter squirmed. "Please don't kill me. I ain't worth the pot you'd piss in," he moaned.

"DeTrobriand can have you," said Red Eagle at last, with bitter finality. He wiped the bloody edge of his knife along Schluter's leg. "If it would bring my people back, I would strip the hide off every dog-faced soldier from here to the Missouri. But nothing can return them to the land of their grandfathers and nothing can heal the scars cut across this land. The army, the miners, the settlers, you are all thieves." He spoke the last words softly.

Then, as easily as he might lift a child, Red Eagle pulled Henry Schluter to his feet. Slipping the soldier's left arm over his shoulder, he half-carried, half-dragged him back to camp.

Liza and Bull Child followed.

REFERENCE BIBLIOGRAPHY

Andrist, Ralph K. THE LONG DEATH: THE LAST DAYS OF THE PLAINS INDIANS. New York: Macmillan Publishing Co., 1964.

Bowden, Henry Warner. AMERICAN INDIANS AND CHRISTIAN MISSIONS: STUDIES IN CULTURAL CONFLICTS. Chicago: University of Chicago Press, 1981.

Catlin, George. LETTERS AND NOTES ON THE MANNERS, CUSTOMS, AND CONDITIONS OF NORTH AMERICAN INDIANS. Vol. 1. New York: Dover Publications, 1973.

Comes at Night, George. ROAMING DAYS: WARRIOR STORIES. Browning, MT: Blackfeet Heritage Program, 1978.

Crow, Joseph Medicine. FROM THE HEART OF THE CROW COUNTRY. New York: Orion Books, 1992.

Ege, Robert J. TELL BAKER TO STRIKE THEM HARD: INCIDENT ON THE MARIAS, 23 JANUARY 1870. Nebraska: The Old Army Press, 1970.

EXPLORING THE AMERICAN WEST HANDBOOK: 1803-1879. Washington, DC: Library of Congress National Parks Handbooks, 1982.

Farnham, Thomas J. AN 1839 WAGON TRAIN JOURNAL: TRAVELS IN THE GREAT WESTERN PRAIRIES, THE ANAHUAC AND ROCKY MOUNTAINS AND IN THE OREGON TERRITORY. Northwest Interpretive Association, 1983.

Frantz, D.G. And N.J. Russell. BLACKFOOT DICTIONARY OF STEMS, ROOTS AND AFFIXES. Toronto, Canada: University of Toronto Press, 1989.

Grinnell, George Bird. PAWNEE HERO STORIES AND FOLK-TALES. Lincoln, NE: University of Nebraska Press, 1961.

Diekhans, Anne M. A HISTORY OF FORT SHAW, MONTANA, FROM 1867-1892. Helena, MT: Historical Society Museum, 1959.

Hungry Wolf, Beverly. THE WAYS OF MY GRANDMOTHERS. New York: William Morrow & Co., 1980.

Lavender, David. THE ROCKIES. New York: Harper and Row, 1968.

Longstreet, Stephen. WAR CRIES ON HORSEBACK: STORY OF INDIAN WARS OF THE GREAT PLAINS. New York: Doubleday & Co., 1970.

Mails, Thomas E. THE MYSTIC WARRIORS OF THE PLAINS. New York: Mallard Press, 1991.

McClintock, Walter. OLD INDIAN TRAILS. New York: Houghton-Mifflin Co., 1923.

McLuhan, T.C. TOUCH THE EARTH: A SELF-PORTRAIT OF INDIAN EXISTENCE. New York: Promontory Press, 1971.

"Missionary Endeavors of the Presbyterian Church Among the Blackfeet Indians in the 1850's." JOURNAL OF THE DEPARTMENT OF HISTORY (December 1941). Presbyterian Historical Society.

NATIVE AMERICAN WISDOM. Philadelphia, PA: Running Press, 1993.

Rickey, Jr., Don. FORTY MILES A DAY ON BEANS AND HAY: THE ENLISTED SOLDIER FIGHTING THE INDIAN WARS. Norman: University of Oklahoma Press, 1963.

Rosenstiel, Annette. RED AND WHITE: INDIAN VIEWS OF THE WHITE MAN 1492-1982. New York: Universe Books, 1983.

Saum, Lewis O. THE FUR TRADER AND THE INDIAN. Seattle, WA: University of Washington Press, 1965.

Schultz, James Willard. RECENTLY DISCOVERED TALES OF LIFE AMONG THE INDIANS. Missoula, MT: Mountain Press Publishing Co., 1988.

Stark, Raymond. GUIDE TO INDIAN HERBS. Blaine, WA: Hancock House Publishers, 1981.

Stein, Bennett H. TOUGH TRIP THROUGH PARADISE: ANDREW GARCIA 1878-1879. Boston: Houghton-Mifflin Co., 1967.

Stocken, Canon H.W.G. AMONG THE BLACKFOOT AND SARCEE. Calgary, Canada: Glenbow, 1976.

THE OLD WEST: THE TRAILBLAZERS. Alexandria, VA: Time-Life Books, 1973.

THE OLD WEST: THE GREAT CHIEFS. Alexandria, VA: Time-Life Books, 1973.

Turner, Frederick. BEYOND GEOGRAPHY: THE WESTERN SPIRIT AGAINST THE WILDERNESS. New York: Viking Press, 1980.

Unruh, Jr., John D. THE PLAINS ACROSS. Chicago, IL: University of Illinois Press, 1982.

Welch, James. FOOLS CROW. New York: Viking Penguin, Inc., 1986.

Werner, Herman. ON THE WESTERN FRONTIER WITH THE U.S. CAVALRY: 50 YEARS AGO. U.S.A.: Historical Society of Montana, 1934.

GAIL L. JENNER, a teacher and wife of a fourth gen-
eration cattle rancher, has published numerous
articles and short stories. This is her first book with
Creative Arts.